Special thanks to my mother, Jo-Ann H., and Chevonne M. for test reading and proofreading. I appreciate your support. To my oldest daughter, Ja'Nair W., thanks for being as quiet as a church mouse (let the noise begin). To Julee W., thank you for asking me every day for six years when I would get back to writing. Last but not least, to Valerie K., thank you for listening to me ... Listening is priceless. I love you all so much.

To new, very funny, and thought-provoking friends, I love working with you all. To old friends, I miss you all, and knowing each of you has enhanced me as a person.

Joan Vassar is back, and I am putting the pen to the paper.

BLACK

BLACK

A NOVEL BY

Joan Vassar

BLACK

PROLOGUE

Jerusalem, Virginia
November 11, 1831

The sun was shining down on the makeshift platform for the occasion of a hanging. People gathered to see the slave Nat Turner, who had caused the death of so many whites, hanged by the neck until death. The slaves were allowed to attend; it was a message meant to deter like-mindedness among them. They stood for hours, the people of Jerusalem—the whites to see him punished, and the blacks to catch a glimpse of the slave who changed their thinking.

Close to the front, two colored female slaves from the Turner plantation stood together. Ellen wrapped her arm around Sophie, who was heavy with child. It was against Ellen's better judgment, but she had come because she understood Sophie's feelings. Although his fate was known, Ellen remembered Sophie passing out when word spread among the slaves that he would be hanged this day. Ellen felt sorry for her and went against her first mind trying to help. Now here they stood to watch the hanging firsthand.

A buzz started at her right, and as the crowd parted, a large black man accompanied by two white officers began climbing the steps. At the top of the steps, one could see Nat Turner himself, in worn and tattered pants, wearing no shirt or shoes. Ellen watched with a smile on her face, because although he was unkempt, he did not look broken, and it gave her hope. He walked across the platform with his back ramrod straight and hands tied behind him. Reaching the center of the platform, he turned, facing the crowd. The whites in the crowd began yelling hate-filled slurs, their anger and fear apparent. The slaves in the crowd were quiet and afraid yet secretly pleased.

Ellen saw his eyes scanning the crowd and knew he was looking for them. Sophie's body trembled, yet she stared forward as she watched the father of her unborn child face his death. Ellen gestured with a white handkerchief to catch his attention, and he focused in on them. He nodded to convey a message of thanks to her before he fixated on Sophie and his unborn child. Nat smiled to reassure her, and the crowd erupted at his insolence. He showed no reaction to the crowd as he pulled himself up to his full height and accepted the noose about his neck, and all the while he stared at *her*.

The mob became hushed as the lever was pulled and the floor fell away. A cheer went up as his body began the dance and his life drained from him. Yet, unbeknownst to the world, standing right before him was his woman, his seed ripe within her. As his life leaked slowly from him, he hoped his child would prosper and accomplish what he had not.

Although Nat Turner's life ended this day, for his seed, it was the beginning.

Later that evening, three midwives stood around the small slave cabin in preparation of the child trying to make its way into the world. It was a cool November evening, and on the bed, Sophie attempted to stifle her cries for relief. The cabin was well lit, still the setting was rudimentary; there was a bed and a stand all roughly made with many candles to assist in delivery of a child. One of the women began pacing the chamber with fear in her eyes, and she was correct in being afraid. If anyone found out what they were doing, they would all be beaten to death.

There was a knock at the cabin door; it was the slave Paul. He brought fresh water and exited almost as quickly as he had arrived.

"Thank ya, Paul," Ellen said as he was closing the door.

He nodded. "Be outside."

Minnie began pouring the water as the woman lying on the bed began panting and moaning loudly. Ellen leaned in and began speaking soft, encouraging words to Sophie.

"Ellen, she have to be quiet," Mae hissed.

"Mae, she 'bout ready. What ya wants me to do?" Ellen said calmly.

"What we gon do wit' her and a baby? They's gon find out who she is, Ellen," Mae continued.

Before Ellen could answer, she saw what she feared most—one tiny foot sticking out. Sophie began to moan and scream, and finally there was a second foot. The sounds she made became weaker as the time pressed on, and soon the hips came forward, and Ellen tried to gently dislodge him. It was a boy.

"Ya doin' real good, Sophie. Push," Ellen said, trying to help her stay focused.

And though Sophie was weak, she gave a final push, bringing the baby forth into the world.

Ellen stared down at the beautiful baby boy she was holding, whispering, "Sophie, look at him. He's healthy and wonderfully made. He must be 'bout nine pounds." She breathed in wonderment.

When she stood to take the child to his mother, reality set in. Sophie had passed on … her lifeless eyes staring at the ceiling. "Fetch Paul to come and take her away, and tell the boys to dig the hole deep enough so's nothing cain't dig her up," Ellen said thoughtfully.

"You ought ta throw him in the hole wit' her and forget the whole matter. What you gon do wit' Nat Turner's child? They gon hang you too," Mae sneered.

Ellen didn't respond. She would not snuff out his light. She set to work separating the child from his mama. Behind her, she could hear Minnie telling Mae to calm down, that they could not kill a baby. Mae left, slamming the cabin door, letting them know she wanted no part of it. They cleaned the baby and wrapped poor Sophie in coarse sheets, then Paul appeared, removing the body.

"Ellen, much as I hates to say, Mae right. What ya gon do wit' him?" Minnie asked.

"We cain't harm him, Minnie … I cain't. Folks talkin' badly 'bout Nat Turner and 'fraid to admit they wanted him to succeed. The child innocent, Minnie, and after all Nat attempted to do … I must do this.

You go on now, and speak to no one 'bout it. Let Mae know if she speaks 'bout this night, it will be the last thang she ever speaks 'bout," Ellen said calmly, looking up from the robust baby to make eye contact.

Seeing her facial expression, Minnie knew they were being threatened. "I ain't gon speak 'bout it, Ellen, but I wants ya ta know that even though Turner is fond of ya, he won't give ya this."

Wrapping the baby in a towel, they put out the candles and faded into the darkness. Ellen would raise him as her own child, and when the time came, she would tell him the truth. She would allow herself this small act of freedom. Back in her own small cabin, she put him to her breasts, her own child having died only weeks before. She fed many of the babies that came through the plantation, but this was different; he was hers now. Looking into his little face, she made a promise to keep him safe.

Nat Hope Turner was born feetfirst on November 11, 1831, the day his father, Nat Turner, was hanged, beheaded, and quartered in the square for his part in a revolt. As the years passed, young Nat came to be known as Hope until that fateful day in August 1849, when he took his first stand against the cruelty of slavery, causing him to be known from that day forward as Black.

1

Upper Canada, December 1858

The two men stood facing each other, respect showing in their eyes, an abyss growing between them. The contrast in their appearance was notable—one man older, white, roughly five foot ten with unkempt gray and brown hair. John Brown appeared to be about sixty summers, his skin weather roughened, with brown eyes set too closely in his head, just above a hook nose.

The other man was well over six feet and very black with dark brown eyes and a bald head. He was twenty-eight summers, but his eyes spoke of years of experience, making him look older. Between them existed a divide on a subject, on which they actually saw eye to eye. Black would leave the emotion out of it and think nothing of how far this man traveled to ask for his help. Although John was part of the struggle, to Black, John did not understand the full ramifications of what a revolt would mean. He, Black, had other responsibilities to consider, and the weight of the Underground Railroad was paramount.

What John was proposing would cause everything to tighten up in the South, something Black did not need. While things were heating up politically, there were those who could not wait on freedom, and he was sworn to deliver.

"I thought you, Black, of all people ..." John said, his voice trailing off in disgust.

"My patience has grown thin in the face of your attempts to school me on being a slave. I will not justify or authenticate my intentions to you."

Paling, John stated with less sting, "Disrespect is not intended here,

1

Black. I have groomed my sons in the struggle for equality. I am not afraid to sacrifice and die if necessary to abolish slavery. What I want you to understand is I am here in defense of those who cannot defend themselves. I feel you discount me because I am white."

"Your being white is not my issue, John; your being a *zealot* is. You do understand that the slaves will not rise with you." Black raised his hand to stop John from cutting him off. "It is fear and distrust of the white man that will stop them from rising with you. As for me, John, I have the weight of over four hundred families on my shoulders along with countless men and women waiting in the shadows for freedom. A revolt will not help; it will only hurt."

John backed away and turned to look out the window of Black's study; it was dark, and with the candles in the background, he could see only his reflection, the books lining the shelves and that of the very large black man standing behind him, arms crossed … tensed. He regarded and assessed him before speaking; his next words would be a low blow, but he would say what he felt after traveling all this way. The cause could only benefit from Black's presence. "Your father was a visionary," he stated calmly.

Black snorted aloud, causing John to turn and look at him. Black was smiling, although he didn't appear amiable. His father was off limits; there were those that knew who his father was, but it was not spoken of. When he was a child, it wasn't spoken of to save his life, and as an adult, it wasn't spoken of because this was the boundary that you did not cross with him.

"Reaching into the grave won't change my mind. You are welcome to stay and rest before you move on your way. I will have someone show you and your men where to bed down."

"Black, with your help, we could take back freedom and remove the stain of slavery from the fabric of the South. How can you turn your back on a chance like this? Your father would have seen the significance and the opportunities being offered here. Please reexamine your decision."

"This meeting is over, John." It was a warning.

"Thank you for your time. We will leave at first light," John stated as he moved past Black, giving him wide berth and heading for the door, exiting the study.

When the door closed, Black could feel the rage coursing through him. Everyone wanted something from him without understanding all that came along with being him. John had gone there, to an intimidating place; with subtle words he had spoken of his father. While John was a good man, Black did not work well with being threatened. As for his father, the information of who he was didn't make him uneasy or concerned. He would stand and defend all that was his.

Extinguishing the candles in his study, Black moved to stand at the window, staring into the night. Seeing the little cabins that dotted the hillside, he knew that he had made the right decision, and there was no turning back. He had trips planned that would be affected by a revolt, but he wouldn't try to deter John; he had more pressing issues, and he understood that every man had a role to play. Since his guests would leave at first light, he would lag for a few hours and then start his journey.

His mind turned to the task ahead and what would be needed to get moving. The hour was still early, and he could use some sleep. A bath and rest would not be part of his existence in the coming weeks. The time had come to focus on staying alive ... and *her*. She had asked very little of him over the years, yet she knew he would do anything for her without hesitation. He understood that between them, it was she who held the power. While he would not falter to do her bidding, she refused everything that he asked of her. He smiled to himself; she was always three moves ahead. The time had come—he was being summoned.

~ ~ ~

Southampton, Virginia, 1858

Standing in the shadows, Black stared out into the clearing at her cabin. The weather was mild in Virginia for a December evening. The night was clear, the trees standing like skeletons about him, hiding his mission from the drunken overseer who slept against the tree with a shotgun across his lap. The moon was full, lighting his way to her door. Off in the distance, a dog howled, and still he did not move. Black had learned to become one with his surroundings, and his patience ... long. He would wait.

As the hour grew late, the temperature began to drop slowly, becoming gradually uncomfortable.

Motionlessly he stood when something caught his eye; a man rounding the turn stepped off the path and stared straight at him, yet he saw nothing but darkness. Black watched as the other man stepped closer, attempting to adjust his sight to better assess his surroundings. In plain view Black stood as the man backed away and turned his focus on the watchman who had fallen asleep in a drunken stupor.

"Hard to get good help!" he yelled, kicking the sleeping man awake.

Black continued to stare as the man groggily began to stir. Realizing where he was, he scrambled to his feet, mumbling something that sounded apologetic. He swayed and stumbled forward to stand face-to-face with the man who was clearly in charge. This was a man with whom Black considered himself to be familiar. Youngblood was an overseer who had been with the Turner plantation for decades, and he was bred for his profession.

"I oughta send you packing. How you keeping watch drunk and asleep?" Youngblood snarled. He turned back to look into the darkness. Again scanning the night, he looked for a sign … nothing. "Get moving, and be alert."

"Yes, sir," the other man replied, stumbling down the path to begin his patrol.

Black saw Youngblood's stance visibly relax after staring right in his direction. It would not be this night, but he would be back to deal with Youngblood. *There is a time and place for everything*, Black thought as Youngblood turned, following the other man between two slave cabins in the opposite direction down the path. Stepping farther into the night, Black looked about at the leafless trees and the full moon and smiled; each time he came back, he felt stronger, armed with the weapon of comparison.

Unmoving silence enveloped him as he stood for what seemed an eternity, and then out of the darkness, a voice stated simply, "It's time to move."

Moving toward the clearing, Black began taking the steps that would bring him to the door of her cabin. Just as he moved out into the open, he issued the one order that mattered to Otis, his next in command.

"Should anything happen while I am with her, do whatever it takes to maintain freedom."

Otis smiled into the night before stating simply, "I will."

"Youngblood is mine," Black said as he walked leisurely away from Otis.

Reaching the cabin, he pushed on the heavy wood door and entered; firelight danced about the walls, bathing the room in orange and blue hues. Bending low, he stepped into the small room, adjusting his eyes and looking about for her. Against the far wall and to the left was a small feather bed on the dirt floor with the blankets neatly rolled into a makeshift pillow; closer to the fire was a larger feather bed, also neatly made and on the floor. To the right of the fireplace was a wooden table roughly made, and in the center lay the Holy Bible, opened randomly. Turning to the far right of the cabin where the firelight did not reach, he could see her sitting, staring into the night, keeping watch as she always did.

A soft Southern drawl sailed out of the darkness. "Much as I hates to send for ya, I's happy ya here."

"You coming home with me?" Black asked, closing the door quietly behind him.

She cackled at his question before responding, "No." The word hung there before she continued. "Ya don't needs me; I would only slow ya down. You's needed; that should always come first. Get a chair from the table, and come sit at the window wit' me so's we might track any disturbances as we catches up."

Doing as she asked, he brought the chair from the table, placing it where his back was against the wall and his eyes trained on the door. Watching as he moved about the cabin made her proud; he had grown into a fine man. Removing the shotgun that was slung haphazardly across his chest and hanging from his back, he leaned it against the wall before taking off his cowhide coat and hat. Seating himself next to her, he pulled the gun across his lap, and while she watched the window, he watched the door.

"I's happy that ya look so well," she said, never turning her attention from the window.

At her words, he turned and assessed his mama; her skin was like

5

worn leather that had been overexposed to the elements, extra creases about her eyes and mouth. The mixture of firelight and her complexion showed her coloring to be that of a deep caramel, her gray hair plaited in two braids that hung to her shoulders. She must have felt his scrutiny, because she began rocking back and forth in her chair. As he watched her, he could see that she had gotten older and a little frailer than she had been at their last encounter, yet here she sat watching the window to protect him. She was beautiful, and he loved her; she had cultivated and grown him to the man he was, and for that, he would forever be thankful.

"I'm glad that you sent for me, although enough time had gone by that I would have come, anyway. You have my attention. You sent for me because ..." His voice was low and hopeful.

"My sending for ya ain't as interesting as ya wants it to be. I wants ya to take Sunday and settle her to a free life."

"So you are sending her with me and staying behind?"

Turning her eyes on him, he could see the sharpness with which her brain was moving. "Time she moved on."

"I thought we agreed that when I took the child, you would come too. I can get you to my home."

"When ya leaves, they gon chase ya something fierce. Ya don't need no deadweight travelin' wit' ya."

Desperation laced her words, causing him to turn and stare at her. She seemed anxious, and in an attempt to help her feel better, he said, "You know that I will let nothing happen to you. I would raze this place to the ground. You need never fear again."

"I don't want war for ya; I wants happiness. When I closes my eyes to this world, I wants to do it knowing that you's free and any children that ya might has is free ... I knows that you still angry, and I knows that ya want a battle. I's asking ya not to. I's asking that ya hold the peace."

"I want the reason you sent for me."

"It's Sunday. She been workin' in the big house 'tween both the Turner children, and Turner's son has taken a shine to her. Turner done up and decided to sell her to the Hunter plantation in South Carolina. He come down here ranting that she done bewitched his son the same way ..." The words trailed off.

6

The thought of Turner yelling at his mama made his blood run cold. Sunday was a child that Big Mama had taken in when her mother collapsed in the fields and died from exhaustion. She was a mere child. *Turner's son must be practicing*, Black thought in disgust. He had no time for a child, but he couldn't leave her in this situation. Although it was common practice, such actions made him angry. The Hunter plantation was known to be unusually cruel. Turner was definitely threatening her, and the thought caused Black to smile, a smile that did not reach his eyes.

"I will take the child with me. He has threatened you, and I can no longer take chances with you. You will come too," he said as he stood and began pacing the cabin. "You say that you'd rather have peace than war. If this is true, then you need to understand that I will kill even the livestock should you say no."

She noted a second gun strapped to his left side as he began pacing. The thought of him waging a war that he could not win terrified her. He could not end up like his father all those years before. It was clear that she could not contain him any longer; she would leave to keep harmony. Turner would not come for her; they were old now … but his son would come for Sunday. She knew the look.

His pacing brought him to stand in front of her chair. "Mama?" The word was a question, and she understood. He was dropping the gauntlet right at her feet.

"I's old and tired now. I don't wants to hinder ya ever."

He did not respond to her concern, because every time he came, he made provisions for her, and this trip was no different other than he would not move any other slaves during this journey. He would move only the child and Big Mama. This would be the one selfish act that he would allow himself. She felt handled by him, he knew, but he would never be bold enough to speak what he really believed. His mama did not want to leave Turner, because she loved him. Big Mama and Turner had a history that may have started off against her will, but it changed, becoming mutual. One thought rang true: when she was forced to make a decision between Turner and his safety, she chose him. He could do no less. She could no longer stay on at the plantation. From what he could see, Turner was starting to deny her wants, and that could be dangerous. In the past, Turner would have never taken a child from her care.

"Where is Sunday?" he asked, his mind now on the move.

"She in the next cabin down the path. I'll fetch her."

"You will get ready to leave, and I will get the child," he stated, heading for the door.

She stood as Black was about to exit the cabin, and stretching her stiff body, she moved toward the table. Black watched as she picked up her Holy Bible, and she appeared delicate to him. Still, he knew she understood that to keep the peace, this day had to come. This was not part of her plan, but it was part of his. She had forgone freedom long enough for Turner.

Stepping from the cabin, Black assessed the night, and antagonistically, he moved onto the path without regard for the fact that Turner had men watching for him. In the clearing, Otis moved from the trees and met him. Black broke the silence, saying, "Big Mama has finally given in. Go to her. She is to wear my coat. And take care with her; she is frail. I am going just up the path to fetch the child, and we will move out tonight."

Otis never responded. Instead, he faded into the night, and Black continued up the path to get Sunday. When he reached the cabin, he looked about before entering. He pushed on the heavy wooden door, and it creaked on its hinges. A warm fire met him, and as he stepped forward, his eyes scanned the small room; he was taken aback at the vision before him. Sunday stood naked, clothed in nothing but firelight, and she appeared the frightened doe. Her hair was pulled back off her face, her skin a cocoa brown. She had huge eyes and a well-formed mouth that pulled him in. Black could see the rapid beat of her pulse at the base of her throat. Lower still, she had full, beautiful breasts, a tiny waist, hips that flared out, and very shapely legs. *When did she become a woman?* he asked himself, and then it hit him: it was not him that she was expecting.

Hearing the door swing open, Sunday knew the time had come. Will, the master's son, had been kind above what a slave could expect, but this was still more than she could bear. He had attempted not to order her, but in the end he did so by telling her that he was ready to come to her. She was to wash herself and be naked and waiting for him. When she heard the door, she spun around, and taking in a sharp breath, she was surprised. It was not Will. Adjusting her eyes, she evaluated him; his skin was black as midnight, and he stood well over six feet. He wore a coarse white shirt slightly opened at the throat, and over the shirt was a leather harness that held a gun on his left side. He wore dark britches and boots that looked issued from the cavalry. Lingering at his feet, she almost did not have the nerve to look back into his eyes. This, she thought, was the most embarrassing of ways to encounter anyone, let alone Black. When she found the strength to meet his eyes again, they were shaped like almonds, and his skin … smooth. He was almost beautiful if he didn't appear so dangerous.

"Am I too late, or am I on time?" he asked, trying to gauge the kind of time they had and something more.

"He ain't come yet," she answered, wanting to sink into the dirt floor under her feet.

"Get dressed. I'll be out front."

Scrambling, she found her clothes, dressed, and timidly came out of the cabin to face Black. He was standing with another man, and together they turned when she approached. Black said something to the shorter man, and he slid past her into the cabin, closing the door behind him. Turning back to Black, she asked, "He ain't gon kill him, is he?"

Staring at her, he could sense her uneasiness under his scrutiny, and he intended for her to feel this way. His being in charge was paramount to everyone's safety. She would not question him. Understanding his position would make life easier on her, and if he dug deeper, he would have to admit that he did not like the concern in her voice for the master's damned son.

Setting his emotions aside, he stated without preamble, "We leave tonight, and this situation must be addressed; we can leave no loose ends. Don't ever question me again."

"I cain't go wit' you. I cain't just leave."

"Are you unsure about where you stand with him as a slave? Perhaps you think love has blinded him. You realize that Turner plans on selling you to the Hunter plantation?"

"Will promised me that he ain't gon let them take me." His words stung, and the humiliation of him seeing her naked almost made her scream.

"So you are going to give up being free at the promise of a slaver?" He had no patience, and suddenly he wanted to shake her until she came to her senses. Every second that he spent talking with her was life or death.

"No, it ain't 'cause of him that I wants to stay. I won't leave Mama. She's all I has. I has to trust that he will help me stay on wit' her," she whispered.

It was something he could relate to, because he felt the same about Mama. He took mercy on Sunday and gave her something. "We will not kill him, but your being gone will only make him come looking for you. Time is important, because Mama is coming with us, and we will move at a much slower pace. I have to keep them off us, because, like you, I want her safe. There are some warmer clothes in the other cabin. Go change; we leave soon." When she would have spoken again, he cut her off. "Go now." Turning, she moved down the path and disappeared into the cabin with Big Mama.

One by one, the men began stepping out from behind the leafless trees. There was no talking except Black's low, velvety voice issuing orders, and whomever he spoke to just faded off into the night to do his bidding.

"We have very few night hours left, and they need to be spent wisely; take care of the dogs, and get the cabin where she lived handled," he said to no one in particular, yet the men moved off into the darkness.

One of the men came forward with a wheelbarrow, and he directed Big Mama to get in. Starting toward his goal, Black began pulling her, while the men fell in front and behind them to protect them. Big Mama smiled to herself, though she had freed herself mentally long ago. Physically, this was her first step toward freedom, and she was moved.

All hell broke loose just after midday when a knock came at the study door. Seated behind a large mahogany desk, Jacob Turner looked up to see Youngblood enter his study. He encroached to the middle of the room and stood, taking his faded brown hat from his head. Turner looked him up and down before addressing him. Youngblood had oily hair and a patch that covered his left eye, courtesy of the slave Hope, now called the legendary Black. He was scowling and showing blackened teeth due to tobacco chewing, which added to his pasty complexion. Youngblood smelled, and Turner was offended to be in his company, but he had to admit that Youngblood was the best at what he did. The problem was he enjoyed it way too much.

"Youngblood." Irritation laced Jacob Turner's voice when he finally addressed him.

"We found Will tied up, and the slave Sunday is gone." Stating the facts, Youngblood's voice was tight, his embarrassment evident at having to report being bested yet again.

Turner contemplated the ramifications before speaking. The girl was gone, and now his son could move on. The money he would have received for her sale would have been worthless in the face of his son's anger for selling her. Still, he would have sold her just the same to stop Will from the same fate he'd experienced years earlier with Ellen. Love with a slave—his own father had been ashamed, and it kept him, Jacob, from dealing effectively with the business of running a plantation. What hurt and what he would never admit was she had never given him credit for the sacrifices he made in the name of loving her. There were matters out of his control, social protocols that had to be followed in his life as a white man. He was a victim too, loving her and being unable to show it. Ellen never saw matters from his view, and it pained him.

He was old now and still loved her, and she knew it. She withheld herself from him to punish and to force him to force her; yet he did nothing. There were things he wanted from her, and at the top of that list was her willingness. He had allowed her to keep the boy, and he had kept the secret of the boy's true identity. Now that secret had cost him much, and the boy was belligerent in his stance against the very institution of the South. Ellen had acknowledged nothing. He would talk with her today; enough was enough. He didn't want the girl back, but it was time she recognized all that he had done.

"Sir." Youngblood's voice had pulled him from his thoughts.

"Will—is he all right?"

"Yes, but he's spitting mad. He wants the slave Sunday back."

"I will speak with the old woman and question her; you are to leave that to me. I will see this matter through. We will not waste time chasing one slave."

Youngblood knew that would be his position, and it gave him great pleasure to deliver the next blow. "The old woman—the one they call Big Mama—is gone too."

Jacob's world tilted. He must have misheard. Had she chosen the boy over him again? Calmly, he responded, "Had you attempted to track them before coming to me?"

Youngblood's expression was blank when he answered, "Yes, we attempted to track them with the dogs. When we went to let the hounds out of their cages, they were asleep, and the ones that were awake were sneezing profusely. The old woman's cabin is covered in black pepper, and the horses appear drugged, as well."

Turner paused for a moment before saying, "That will be all. I will send for you when I need you. In the meantime, get things back in order."

"I will, sir." Turning on his heels, Youngblood left without a backward glance. Inside he was gloating. The old bitch had bested Turner now, and he didn't like it, either. He would wait patiently. The son and father were one in the same—nigger lovers. Old man Turner would call upon him, and he knew it.

Jacob Turner watched him, reading Youngblood's thoughts as he left his study. His mind turned to Ellen; she understood the silent deal struck between them, the deal that simply stated she was his and she would die here with him. She had finally forced him, and now he would force her.

They stopped at three empty safe houses along the way, more so for Mama than for the group. Black pulled her, allowing no one else the privilege, and when it seemed he had reached exhaustion, he pressed on. Sunday watched him from behind as his muscles strained against his shirt. The men walked about them, keeping them surrounded and not easily seen. It grew colder the farther north they traveled, and while she was more than uncomfortable, the colder it got, the more liberated she felt. Big Mama, Sunday noticed, appeared to have moments when she seemed mindless with exhaustion. Still, she was quiet, never complaining, the pain only visible in her expressions.

As they trekked through the trees, it felt like they made no progress. Everything looked the same. They walked for what seemed an eternity, and still there were more trees and the occasional stream. The days seemed gloomy and overcast, always with the threat of bad weather; at night, when they traveled the most, it was freezing. They journeyed with ten men who never spoke. Oftentimes they would disappear into the night and hours later reappear, falling right back into step, and to Sunday, they seemed unaffected by the weather.

Their pace was modified to fit her and Big Mama, and there was no doubt she could barely keep up. It was when she thought she would fold like her mother had in the fields that she decided it would be acceptable if she died advancing toward freedom. At least this circumstance had merit. The days were running together, and since no one spoke to her, she was silently becoming hysterical. Sunday was about to give up and sit down, telling them to leave her, when they came to a little cabin nestled in the trees. The sun had just gone down, and she felt cold to the bone. The men fanned out, moving toward the cabin first to assure that it was safe.

Coming to a stop and still holding the wheelbarrow that supported Big Mama's weight, Black said, "You did well. We are closer than you think."

He knew what she was thinking. Shame laced her voice when she said, "I cain't go no further."

"Come," he said, moving toward the cabin. They would not speak of defeat.

Big Mama said nothing, her exhaustion so great that she could form no thoughts or words, so she groaned in acknowledgment that they were coming to a stop. Before he could knock, the door swung open, and a stout older white man with deep blue eyes and gray hair greeted them. "Black," he said, the smile reaching his eyes.

"Herschel," Black responded, showing beautiful white teeth.

The sudden intake of breath caused both men to focus on Sunday.

Involuntarily, she backed away from the older man, moving closer to Black; pressing against his side, she attempted to hide. Herschel must have realized Black's situation and rushed forward to help him with Big Mama. When they got her to her feet, Black scooped her up, moving into the cabin. She groaned again, and he whispered something that only she could hear, causing her to look at him feebly, nodding her head.

Turning toward Sunday, Black said, "Come with me. She will need you to attend to her."

Focusing on Big Mama rather than fear, Sunday followed him behind a screen that separated a small sleeping area from the rest of the room. A large bed in a wooden frame stood in the corner. There was a white woman with blonde hair, younger than the man Herschel, adjusting a colorful quilt on the bed; she looked up and smiled reassuringly.

"Place her on the bed. I'll fetch something to eat and drink for her," she said in a soft tone.

"Thank you, Mary," Black said, never looking at her. "Help me get her shoes off," he said to Sunday, who ran to do as he asked.

Sunday began rubbing Big Mama's legs, and Big Mama tried to swat her off. The white woman he called Mary returned with a bowl of stew and a cup of whiskey.

"Eat something, even if it's just a little. Drink this; it will numb you," Black said.

Big Mama did as she was told and faded into a deep sleep shortly after.

Sunday, on the other hand, was frightened of the white folks, and tired as she was, she was beyond sleep. She needed to stay alert. There was a lantern on the chest next to the bed lighting the small space. The quilt that covered Big Mama was splashed in yellow, red, orange, and blue. On the screen that divided the room, there were flowers painted in a scene representing springtime. Big Mama snored lightly in the background while Sunday took in their surroundings.

Seated on the floor in front of the bed, she looked up when Black appeared in the makeshift doorway. The very presence of him seemed to steal the air from the cabin. She took in the sight of him; his eyebrows were pressed together over his tired, almond-shaped eyes as if he were contemplating something major, his mouth set in a lazy smile. Stepping behind the screen, he folded his arms across his massive chest and stared at her. She noted his thick neck and the way the corded muscles in his shoulders traveled to his large arms. He wore a clean brown shirt opened at the throat, his suspenders hanging down around his hips. She wanted him to go away. She needed space. He wanted to talk, but she didn't think she could. Sunday welcomed freedom, and being her own person was appreciated, yet she felt overstimulated. She had thought herself stronger, and she was finding that she wasn't. Big Mama was asleep, and Sunday just wanted to fall apart as quietly as possible. He would have to break the silence, because she could not; all her strength was being used to maintain her composure.

"Do you trust me?" he asked in a low soft voice.

"Yes. I has been told to trust only you. Mama pressed the understanding of that."

"You are afraid. Why, if you trust me? Mary and Herschel are good people. They are here to help."

"I need air. I feel like I's gon be sick." Her words were barely audible.

"Come," he said, reaching out his hand and pulling her to her feet.

Herschel and Mary sat at the table as he shuffled her past them. Black grabbed a shawl hanging by the door and then draped it about her shoulders. Once out in the cold air, Sunday began breathing deeply, filling her lungs. They walked through the cold to the outhouse, and she hesitated. Embarrassed, she looked up at him, and he curtly nodded toward the door. Stepping inside, she attempted to handle her business quietly. When she came out, she could see that he was paying her no attention. He was standing watch.

He began walking deeper into the woods where two small buildings stood. As they drew closer, she could see that one building housed the livestock and his men, as well. They seemed to be tireless in their effort to maintain safety. Reaching the second building, Black pulled the door open, and they stepped inside. From the outside it appeared run down, but on the inside, it was warm and clean. He moved toward a pot of boiling water sitting over a fire. Grabbing the ladle, he began to spoon the steaming water into a basin for her. "I will be right outside should you need me," he said, walking backward to the door. He shoved it with his back and disappeared into the night.

15

He waited for a time, and when she didn't come out of the bathhouse, he knocked before pushing the door open. He scanned the room for her and found her seated on the bench in front of the fireplace. She looked up when he came through the door, and he could see she was crying. He remembered feeling like that when he became free, unsure and happy at the same time. She was smart, because she understood there was more to being free than just leaving the plantation.

"You are upset? Tell me what you need."

"I's happy. I's just 'fraid to close my eyes that all this might go away. I heard stories that white folks helped. Don't thank I believed it."

"Herschel and Mary have been doing this longer than me. You have nothing to fear, and I will let nothing happen to you," he said, and she nodded.

"Where is we?" she asked.

"We are in Pennsylvania. This is a free state. We will continue moving, because freed men and women have been known to end up back in the South, stolen from free states and sent back to plantation life as slaves. It's harder when that happens, because freedom has been tasted."

"Where does ya plan on leavin' me?" she asked, holding her breath.

She had huge brown eyes that were red from crying, her pouty full lips trembling with emotion. He had dressed her like a boy because it was warmer; still, the memory of her standing naked before the fire was in his head. She would come home with him, no doubt about it. Still, Black asked the question to see where her mind was. "Is there somewhere you want me to take you?"

She shook her head before finally saying, "I thanks its why I ain't leave—'cause I would be on my own. I knowed he would come for me, and then there was Big Mama."

"You will come home with me."

A combination of relief and fatigue had taken over, and she broke down and wept. It was the release she needed from all the pent-up energy she had within her. It was a shoulder-shaking cry that, once started, she could not stop. Bending, she covered her face with her hands and continued this way until she felt his hand on her shoulder. His touch quieted her; still, she trembled uncontrollably. No one other than Big Mama had ever touched her to comfort her. No one ever cared.

He did not speak. Instead, he reached down, scooping her up. Seating himself on the bench, he brought her to rest in his lap. Pulling her close against him, he felt her body relax. "You are exhausted. You need sleep. I am here watching over you and Mama; take a minute to compose yourself. I will take you back to Mama after you calm down."

There, pressed up against him as she was, he could feel her trembling from the exertion of crying. She didn't speak, and soon he felt her body go limp. He sat looking at the fire and the steam as it rose from the pot, and he held her. At some point, he attempted to stand and carry her back to the cabin, but she frowned in protest. Leaning back against the wall, he allowed her to rest against his chest and gave himself permission to admit that he needed this contact. He too had not been comforted by anyone other than Mama. There was the occasional woman he would submerge himself in sexually, but he was careful not to let them in. They understood what he wanted and pushed for nothing beyond the physical contact; often they were older and unable to have children. Offspring was something he didn't want—not living where the very basics of humanity could be so corrupt.

This small amount of contact made his mind wander back in the past to the events that made him the man he was. Youngblood had taken an interest in him, telling him that he knew who he was. There were moments when Youngblood had called him a high-handed nigger, letting him know when the magic wore off that he would beat him like he deserved. Being young, Black did not understand that the magic was between Big Mama and Turner. She had warned him to stay away from Youngblood, but there were days when it seemed interaction with him could not be avoided. It always seemed personal with Youngblood, and he could not understand why.

In his mind's eye, Black could see Youngblood as he approached him and the older slave, Mack, while they cleaned the stables.

"Mack, take my horse, wipe him down, and feed him," Youngblood ordered.

"Yes, sir, Mista Youngblood, right away," Mack responded, but he was old and unsteady on his feet, causing him to bump into Youngblood as he tried to take the horse.

Mack was a brown-skinned, much-older man with cotton-white

17

hair and stooped shoulders, Black remembered. "You pushing me, boy!" Youngblood growled.

"No, sir, I wouldn't dare," Mack responded.

"You talking back, boy," Youngblood responded, backhanding Mack across the face, causing him to fall to the ground.

Youngblood began kicking him, and Mack moaned, covering his face. When Youngblood went to hit him again, Black stepped in, grabbing his hand.

"I been waiting for you, boy. This here is a special damn day," Youngblood said, showing blacked teeth.

Turning his attention to Black, he came at him, and Black sidestepped. When Youngblood turned and charged him again, Black grabbed him by the collar and began beating him. He couldn't stop himself, and his actions caused a crowd to gather. He could hear his mama screaming, and when he tried to back off, Youngblood had picked up a pitchfork, coming at him. Black had picked up a hoe, and he swung with all his might at Youngblood, hitting him at a long angle, splitting his face. Blood spilled from Youngblood's left eye where it became stuck to the gardening tool, and Youngblood hollered from the pain.

In the background, the male slaves on the plantation became riled, and the overseers couldn't get them in check. James, Otis, and Elbert, other slaves that Mama had cared for, started dragging him away.

Elbert said, "We have to move now."

"I can't leave Mama," Black was saying.

Otis stepped forward, saying, "They finna kill you, there ain't no mistaking. One way or the other, you won't be wit' Mama."

He remembered turning to his mama and taking her by the hand. He tried to drag her along, but she wouldn't move. Frantically, she whispered to him, "Go, boy, and don't look back."

James grabbed him by the collar, yelling, "Let's go! If we don't leave now, we ain't never gonna get the chance again."

He kissed his mama, telling her how sorry he was that he had broken her heart. It hurt that she had refused to run with them, instead staying to deal with the aftermath of his actions. He suspected that she pleaded with Turner for his life, giving him, Otis, Elbert, and James time to run. When he reached a free state, he remembered throwing up for days because he was worried about her and didn't know if he would ever see her again. It seemed to him at the time that freedom had come at a high price, and, feeling defeated, it was more than he wanted to pay.

The four of them had moved on to Upper Canada, working odd jobs until they could purchase some land. Elbert and James ran with a rough bunch, becoming outlaws of sorts, disappearing for months at a time and then reappearing with lots of money. Black wanted that life, but his concern for Mama led him down a different path. Sending Herschel in his place, he purchased the land on behalf of his boss. Once his life was stable, he ventured back into the South to find out what had become of his mama.

When the time came to go back to the plantation, Otis decided he would not let him go alone, and before Black knew what was happening, all four of them were standing in the trees looking at her cabin. He remembered stepping into her cabin after two years and her weeping at the very sight of him. Maintaining his composure, he showed no emotion; he had expected to find her dead, and he almost fainted at the sight of her. Reaching out, she drew him near, hugging him, and his eyes watered up, so happy was he that his mama was well.

Bringing him back from his thoughts, Sunday stirred in his arms and looked up at him, raw emotion in her eyes. He said, and his voice was low and deep, "You ready to go back to the cabin?"

Sunday shook her head. Snuggling closer, she reveled in the protection he represented. While it was inappropriate to sit like this with a man she barely knew, it was the first time in her life she ever felt truly safe. *Just a few moments longer.* She thought about the unsettling plantation life that she had endured, the humiliations she witnessed, and the fear of wondering when it would happen to her. More than being a slave physically, she hated her mental bondage and the fear that ruled her. Fear was her constant companion, and never did it leave her side.

"May I know ya real name?" she asked.

"Black," he said curtly.

Feeling him tense up, she said in a low whisper, "I ain't never felt safe before till now. I just wants to know ya. I's sorry."

Moments passed in silence, and then she felt his body relaxing again, so she snuggled closer. Then, into the quiet of the room, he said, "Nat."

2

January 1859

They traveled for weeks more at a grueling pace and for what seemed an eternity. The farther north they traveled, the colder the weather became. It began snowing, but the journey was made easier by horse and carriage; his men rode horses, keeping the carriage surrounded. Mary had come with them, and to the naked eye, they all appeared to belong to her. As they pushed on to their destination, there was very little conversation. Mary was, of course, warm and kind, but as slaves, they had learned not to speak with white folks freely. Big Mama, while kind, was closed off to Mary, not even making eye contact with her and answering only the questions she asked. Sunday felt sorry for Mary, because at times, Big Mama made her feel that same way. Sitting as they were in the carriage, not speaking, gave Sunday time to reflect on the past.

Living with Big Mama, there was one rule: they did not speak of Black. Sunday remembered coming home one evening from working in the big house and finding Black standing at the window of the small cabin she shared with Mama. She had been a child still and newly come to stay with Mama, and when she stepped through the door, she could see he was angry. He barely noticed her, and she was thankful, because Black was large and very scary.

Turning to Big Mama, he said, "I want you to leave with me."

"You has business to be 'bout. You ain't got time to chase wit' me," she responded.

"You avoid and put me off. I have time to move you and make certain you are safe. What holds you here?" he asked, and his voice shook.

"He promised not to look for ya if'n I stays," she whispered. "It's better this way. I's old. You got better thangs to think of. Stop worryin' yoself 'bout me."

He folded his arms over his chest, and to Sunday, it looked as if he would explode. Instead, he said calmly, "The day will come when you will not be able to put me off. You will be left with no choice but to come with me or I will kill him."

He did not give Big Mama a chance to answer. Turning, he moved past Sunday, never really seeing her, and slammed the cabin door. When he was gone, Mama sighed, and she looked visibly shaken. Still, she managed to say, "What goes on here ain't for nobody else. You understand me, child?"

"Yes, Mama, I understands," she said, and Black was never mentioned again.

Now, as a woman, Sunday began to see it all differently as she turned her mind away from the past and focused on the present. She thought of Black telling her his real name, and it became clear why Mama seemed shrouded in mystery. If she knew that Black had told her his name, Mama would fade away where she stood. It all began to make sense now. Big Mama had the power. It also explained why Turner always seemed angry and frustrated to Sunday, with Mama always seeming calm and collected. The other slaves seemed to think of her as their mother too, Sunday noticed, and when they had a problem, they came to her. Mama spoke on their behalf with Turner, often getting what was needed from him.

Though she and Mama did not speak of him, the slave grapevine was a ball of energy, and they all knew about the legendary Black. Yet when the slaves spoke of him, he seemed to be that of a children's story and not at all real. Black was seen as the gateway to freedom by way of Big Mama, though never did Mama flaunt her power; Mama was quiet and reserved, getting what she wanted while not appearing to want anything. She was shrewd, and during this journey, she did not speak, keeping her own counsel. She only observed. Mama seemed closed off even to her, and Sunday began to worry about it. When they stopped to rest and stretch, if Black approached, Mama only spoke to him, and when he responded, she seemed genuinely interested in what he had to say. She would cause him to smile by her responses audible only to him. Mama didn't seem sick, and Sunday was happy with that.

Sunday also noticed that he had seemed restrained with her since he told her his real name. She was bothered by the way he avoided her, and so she waited for the opportunity to speak with him again.

Then one evening, as the carriage slowed, she heard one of the men yelling. Mary smiled, but not knowing what to expect, Sunday became nervous. Reaching out, Mary touched her hand, saying, "It's all right."

Pulling back the curtain, they rode through a large gate with men standing watch and at the ready. The carriage rolled down into a valley where cabins dotted the hillside. She could hear the large gates close behind the carriage as it moved into what looked like a little city. Although it was cold, she noticed that people began stepping from their cabins. At first they seemed to stare. She then realized that they stepped out and began working, taking the horses and relieving the men of their heavy loads.

Otis stepped forward and began speaking. "We traveled light this time—only two. Thank y'all for always being willin' to help. You may go and find your beds. If you have a problem, I will be around a while longer. Please come find me."

The crowd began to disperse, and the carriage continued rolling for a time until it came to a stop in front of a large, country-style house with shutters and a porch that seemed to wrap all the way around. Swinging down from his horse, Black moved toward the carriage, opening the door to help the women step stiffly from the cab. As the carriage rolled away, the house came into better view, even though nighttime was well under way. Black scooped Mama up and climbed the steps, issuing orders to an older black man standing by the door.

"Hot water, Paul, please. Have the boys bring the water—no lifting for you," Black said.

"Paul?" Big Mama turned and looked at him.

"Hush now, Ellen. I'll see you later, I ain't gon nowhere," he crooned.

Nodding her head in response, she gave herself over to exhaustion, and Black continued down the hall with her in tow. Over his shoulder, he called to Sunday, "Follow me; she will need attending."

They walked down a long hall that was well lit by candles. As Sunday followed Black, she observed the pictures hanging on the walls. One canvas depicted a Southern scene that she herself had lived of slaves working the fields, picking cotton. They were faceless, but still the scene was detailed and bursting with color. In another painting, there were stallions running free with their manes blowing in the wind, and in comparison, there was another painting of a man shackled at the foot, his eyes alive and engaging. The paintings were brimming with vitality, and the mood of the painter was visible. She got sidetracked staring at the shackled man, and Black had to call after her, causing her to have to run in order to catch up.

Coming to a closed door, she moved out in front of him. Opening it and stepping aside, she allowed him to enter first. As he moved past her to let Mama down in a chair, Sunday's eyes swept the room. There was a fire burning in the fireplace, making the room cozy. In the center of the chamber sat a canopy bed with a powder-blue lace covering, and to the left were two large, black sitting chairs that faced the window. In the far corner stood a black screen with a blue design that divided the chamber pot from the rest of the room, and to the right sat a large matching black porcelain tub. When she turned to ask whose room this was, she saw it—a large painting of Mama just above the fireplace. She was sitting in her rocking chair in the cabin, staring out the window at a full moon. It was only a side view of her face, but there was no mistaking it was her. It was a scene that Sunday had witnessed herself many times, and looking at the painting, she realized it made her feel safe, as well. And then it dawned on her. *He painted it.*

There was a knock at the door, and in walked three young colored men, carrying steaming buckets of water, followed by an older black woman with gray hair, carrying food.

"Black," she said with a strange accent.

"Iris, good to see you," he responded with a smile.

"I will help them get settled," she said, smiling back.

"Thank you, Iris," he said.

"Where would you like me to settle the young miss?"

"Bring her to me when you are finished here."

Helping to pour the water in the tub, Black left with the three young men carrying the buckets, all of them talking to him at the same time.

When the door shut behind her, Iris turned to Sunday, saying, "Shall we undress her and help her in the bath? The water will take the cold from her bones and relieve the stiffness. Tell me your name, child."

"Sunday, and yes, I'll help."

It was a struggle undressing her. Big Mama was always so aware of her surroundings, but fatigue made her limp and unfocused. She seemed to appreciate the water's warmth as they helped her into the tub. Sunday scrubbed her while Iris readied the bed. When they removed her from the tub and dressed her for bed, she could barely keep her eyes open. She had bread and butter with warm milk, and when she reached the bed, she was asleep instantly.

While Sunday was wondering how they would empty the tub, Iris pulled the string hanging on the side of it, and the water began to drain. Sunday looked at her amazed, and Iris smiled, saying, "Drains out to the bottom of the house—no scratching the beautiful tub."

"Oh," Sunday said. "Iris, can I know who house this is?"

"Black's," she said, and when Sunday was forming her next question, Iris said, "Come, he wants to show you to your room. I will bring your food after you have spoken to him."

Dismissed, Sunday thought as she followed Iris back through the hall to a closed door. Iris knocked and then continued down the hall, leaving Sunday standing there staring after her. The door swung open, and Black smiled, saying, "Come in."

The walls were lined with books that sat on polished black wood shelves. The large desk and chair that matched the shelves sat in the corner facing the door with the window to the left, deliberately placed to watch the entrance. A sofa of gold velvet material rested against the wall; it was the only splash of color in the study. Turning to look at Black, Sunday noticed that he appeared to have cleaned up, wearing a white shirt unbuttoned at the throat, brown trousers, boots ... and a gun strapped at his side.

It seemed that her first acts of freedom were just to ask questions. "Can ya read?"

"I can," he said, saying no more.

She was not deterred. "Do you reads for fun?" she asked, fascinated.

He grinned before responding, "I do not read for amusement. I am so far behind what white men know that I read to educate myself and those around me."

"Why you wants to know what white folks know?" she asked, confused.

"I want to know what they know, because you can't argue with success. I will teach you to read."

When she smiled, he could see the fatigue on her face. "You will stay here with Mama," he said as if not saying *Mama and me* changed the reality of the situation.

Relief flowed through her, and it was visible to him.

"You will take my chamber, and I will move to another room."

She did not need a room as pretty as Mama's. She just needed to feel safe. "Any room will do; it don't matter—"

He cut her off, saying, "My things will be moved later. For now, use what you want. Come. I will take you."

She did not argue with him. Instead, she followed him to the door, and when he was about to open it, she asked, "Where is Mary?" She was so overwhelmed that she had just noticed that Mary was gone.

"She's gone home. You'll have time to see Mary; she will be around."

Sunday followed him back past Mama's room to a door on the opposite side of the hall. He turned the knob and allowed her to enter first. There was a fire burning in the fireplace. The room was more masculine with a large bed in the middle, a tub, a chamber pot, and no privacy screen. A black chair sat facing the window like the ones in Mama's room. The tub was filled with steaming water, and there was food on a small table by the chair.

"Get some rest," he said to her as he turned to leave.

"Wait!" she almost screamed as he was just about to exit the chamber.

He turned, looking at her. He could see the anxiety that filled her, and he hated that she was afraid. "Take a bath. Iris has laid out a shirt of mine and a robe. I will come back."

She nodded, so filled with emotion was she that she could not speak. This was more than she could have ever expected and certainly more than she could handle.

"I will give you some privacy; then I will return."

She bathed in the large tub that was obviously built for his size. The water was perfect, and the soap smelled of roses. Stepping from the tub, she dried, dressed, and ate. As she sat waiting for him to return, it occurred to her that she was worried about Will, his father, and the problems their running would cause. She understood why Mama kept arguing to stay. It wasn't because she didn't want freedom; it was because it kept Turner in check. The more time she had to mull over the issue, the more she began to see clearly all that took place living with Mama.

The realization that Will, who owned her, would come for her made her stomach roll. What choice did she have other than to leave? She would not have survived the Hunter plantation. The fact that Black was there meant that Mama didn't think that Turner was going to change his mind. She never sent for him lightly, so the fact that she, Sunday, was here made it evident that Mama had thought this through. Clearly, no one counted on Mama leaving, and judging by her behavior, she didn't either. Sunday wondered if Mama had worries. As she thought through all the happenings, she saw even more clearly now all that Mama had endured.

She was leaning her hip against the bed when he entered the room. It was as if she didn't want to touch anything, as if she didn't feel as though she belonged.

He was standing with his hand still on the knob when he asked, attempting to get her permission before entering her room, "May I come in?"

"Yes, please," she responded in a whisper.

Closing the door quietly behind him, he moved toward the chair and relocated it to face the bed. He sat facing her, and, leaning back in the plush chair, he just observed her, and she allowed his scrutiny. She was dressed in one of his robes with the belt tied about her waist, confirming just how small she was. The only flesh showing was that of her toes, which peeked from just under the robe. Her huge eyes seemed to draw him in. They were a deep chestnut brown and filled with emotion. This was intimate, not sexual, and he would not examine it too closely right now. He needed sleep, and he learned that one's mind must be refreshed in order to dissect even oneself.

"I can stay wit' Mama; then you ain't gotta be put out."

"I'm not put out, and I would think for once Mama should have her own space, don't you?" he asked.

"I ain't thought of that."

"What's wrong with this room? Is it because my things are here?"

"Oh no. Just don't need this much space."

"What is it that you truly fear? I would like to know."

His query seemed to shock her, and when she recovered, he could see that she was contemplating what should be said, causing him to make his next statement. "When I ask you a question, I always want the truth. Never lie to me. I have given you my name, and I will always be truthful with you. Let us keep on the path on which we started."

"Will. I's 'fraid of Will and his father," she said, looking him in the eye.

"You have feelings for Will?" he asked, his eyes intense.

"He ain't been mean to me," she said, never looking away.

"You have not answered the question."

"I guess I has some feelin' for him. He ain't been mean to me. I took care of him and his sister. I was they personal slave."

His expression was closed when he asked, "Are you saying that you took care of his physical needs?"

"He ain't force himself, but I think that's why I was gave to him and not Miss Rose," she answered.

"And when I came to get you from the cabin?" he continued, questioning her.

"He asked me to be there, and I ain't think I could say no. You come 'fore he did." She held his gaze, not breaking eye contact, and she did not squirm from his questions. "I knew the time was coming. I got away longer than most. I ain't special. It was 'cause of Mama that I got away as long as I did."

His eyes narrowed before he asked, "Are you untouched?"

Finally, she lowered her eyes, but not out of shame; the question just seemed so forward. Raising her eyes back to meet his, she said, "Yes, 'cause you happened along. I don't know which was worst—waitin' or prayin' that it won't happen. I have tended some of the women taken against they will ..." Her voice trailed off.

He thought of her shame for not being raped, while feeling empathy for the other women that had endured. "If Will has been so kind, why do you fear him?"

"I fears he will come to drag me off, and he will be changed 'cause I ran. I fears he and his father will come for me and Mama. If'n you don't let them take us, they will destroy what you has built."

"Do you think I would turn you and Mama over to them?" he asked with a smile on his face.

"Not Mama," she whispered.

"So Will is a kind man, and I am a brute." His eyes sparkled with amusement.

"I don't wants ya hurt," she said with all seriousness. "You the one person who has made me feel safe. I rather be a slave again than to see ya hurt. I thought I wouldn't ever be safe, and I's thankful to ya. It's more than most will know."

His expression went blank, and his world tilted as he realized that she was attempting to watch over him. He had not felt a connection with anyone other than Mama, and the intensity of this association was tangible and charged.

"Come sit with me and feel safe. I will hold you until you sleep. I am done talking."

She stared at him, longing for what he offered and still afraid that if she allowed herself to get used to this, she would not be able to endure when it was taken from her. Sunday was frozen where she stood, unable to move.

"Come," he said, and the word was low and gravelly.

It was the push she needed to step forward and climb into his lap. Snuggling against him, she exhaled. "Thank you. I needs this," she said against his chest, and he could feel the warmth of her mouth as she spoke, but he did not respond.

They became quiet, taking comfort from one another. He thought of the words between them and the way this connection left him feeling. The realization that he needed this probably more than she finally set in; he had the weight of so much on him. Big Mama had taught him to keep his own counsel, and he felt weak for needing more. If he were being honest with himself, he felt engulfed by all that had transpired in the last ten years. Freedom had taught him that slavery came in many forms, and oftentimes a man could be in bondage and not recognize it. Attempting to stay ahead of the game was harder than he made it look.

Being free and being responsible for the freedom of others made him feel as though he were drowning. She was a lifeline for him.

They sat that way for a time, silent, and he thought she had fallen asleep. "Nat, is you ever 'fraid?" she murmured, using his real name.

"Yes."

Yes, Sunday, I'm afraid of you.

Will Turner was rolling with rage; Sunday had gone and left him, or had she been forced to run? He could focus on nothing else but her. His father had invited his longtime friend Robert Myers, who had come with his daughter. He was sure that it was to match them, and he had no adversity to the match, but to his father's disappointment, he could not forget Sunday. She was his, and he planned to have her back. Turner, as Will called his father, had been careful not to push him. It had been clear for all to see when his mother was alive that his father did not love her, instead choosing the dark woman over her. Turner treated his mother civil, and in exchange, his mother turned a blind eye. When she was put to rest, the dark woman became their nanny, and his father made no effort to remarry. Will had not judged, and like his mother, he looked the other way.

In the weeks after Sunday left, Will had begun dealing with Youngblood himself. He instructed Youngblood to ferret out any and all information pertaining to Sunday's whereabouts. Youngblood was coming up empty, and Will was feeling unable to cope in the face of finding nothing. Sunday was his slave, and had Turner not posed his threat, all this wouldn't have happened. Big Mama would not have allowed her to be sold, but what they didn't know was he would not have allowed it either. Now, as if to add insult to injury, Black had taken her. Will avoided his father at all costs because he blamed him. Will's only solace was that the old woman left too, and he was sure his father, the old bastard, felt worse.

Will had known him when he wasn't Black and was just a slave. They had been playmates of sorts, never really friends. It was more for his entertainment—not the same as having a friend. This was the reasoning he used when dealing with Sunday. He wanted her sexually, but he also wanted her willing. It was all he could think about. He decided he wouldn't take, he wouldn't be rough, and when he thought she was ready, he would give a gentle push. In reality, he also knew that even the gentlest of pushes would have seemed like an order because of his status.

He would be stepping into Turner's shoes, and the plantation would fall to him. His first order of business was to get Sunday back ... intact. The very thought of Black breaching her made him sick with jealousy, yet he knew Black would see her beauty. There was no mistaking her worth, slave or not. Youngblood, he knew, would be the key, and he would use it to bring this situation to rights. He understood the weakness of men by facing his own. He would marry the Myers girl and do his duty as his father had, and he would love his children, but he would have Sunday. Strangely, he felt a kind of calm run through him because, knowing Sunday, she knew he was coming.

Although social protocol dictated, it was improper to have anything with her more than sport; he was taken with her ... it was just the truth. Unlike Turner, he was real with himself, and he stopped wrestling that demon some time ago. He would not flaunt it; he would be respectful to his future wife and children, but he was his own man, and he would do what he wanted, when he wanted ... and with her.

He would send for Youngblood, give him more instructions, and lay down the rules as to how she should be handled when found. As for Black, they would have to meet man to man. He could not have her.

The day was very cold and overcast as she stepped out onto the porch, but to Sunday, it was beautiful just the same. Out in front of her, cabins dotted the hills, with smoke coming from the chimneys; the trees were leafless as they stood along the dirt paths. The cabins were a dark brown, and while they all were the same in color, they were all different in size. At the bottom of the stairs, Mary sat bundled up on the back of a wagon, waiting to show her around. She would move about freely and enjoy the tour of her new home, she thought, as Mary yelled up the steps, "Come on, Sunday!"

As Sunday and Mary rode along the pathways, the people approached, causing the wagon to slow and then stop so that they might introduce themselves. Some of the people Sunday knew from the Turner plantation, and she was surprised to see them. They were slaves who had disappeared in the night, never to be heard from again, and she, Sunday, thought they had been caught and killed for running. Instead, here they were, happy and doing well. The people of Fort Independence were warm, welcoming, and a hardworking bunch. Mary helped with the introductions, and for Sunday, the names and faces were all a blur. Still, she was happy to make their acquaintances.

Mary pointed out the side of the land where the crop grew, and she confirmed what Black had already explained. The crop produced by the fort was wheat, which was a change from what they all knew—and that was cotton. Wheat, according to Black, did better than cotton because everyone needed to eat. When harvested, the wheat was transported far and wide, and the proceeds were used to fund freedom and maintain it. Sunday had never seen the likes, and she realized that if she had not seen it for herself, she would have never dreamed it ... not on her own.

As the wagon moved on slowly, Mary continued her grand tour, and Sunday could hear the pride in her voice. "In the center of our little town is Black's pride and joy."

"Oh?" Sunday responded before asking, "What is it?"

When the wagon came to a stop, Mary smiled, saying, "Come see our school. Every child of age living here can read, write, and figure. The adults are also required to learn to read and write. The elderly people have the option to learn if they would like, but for everyone else, it's a requirement."

Sunday just listened speechlessly as she climbed from the wagon with Mary and headed inside the school. As they entered the cabin, it appeared like any other cabin from the outside, weather beaten with the wood a little faded on the side on which the sun shone the most. In front of the school was a bell that hung at the top of the three stairs leading to the front door. Once inside, there were lots of little desks that dotted the room, and to the right at the front of the room was a larger desk and chalkboard. Against the far wall was a second chalkboard, with letters that were painstakingly written, along with numbers too.

"You teaches the children?" Sunday asked.

"I teach along with other adults that have learned to read and write. It is a joint effort, and again, one that Black requires. We make it work, and like him, we are all proud of it."

Sunday noticed that the smaller desks had chalkboards along with inkwells, and she thought it all magical. *Slaves learning,* Sunday thought. *Life is different.* Turning to Mary, she asked, "Learning cain't be easy, can it?"

"You'll be fine; Black tells me he will teach you. If you need me, come find me."

At the back of the room, all kinds of books lined a large bookshelf; the one room had no color other than brown, and the only splashes of color came from the many books that lined the back shelf. Sunday knew she would have to come back when the children were here to see how it all worked. It was so interesting that she felt learned from just standing in such a place. The thought of standing in a school made her smile; there was a day when such a thing would have never been possible for her.

Leaving the school, they continued on with their tour of the fort, and Sunday was impressed.

Moving along, Sunday realized they couldn't see everything in one day. Still, Mary pointed out the highlights. As the tour came to a close, Sunday noticed that the land was walled in, and there were men whose sole job was to patrol and keep mayhem out. There was a building that housed the men working the patrol, and though some had families and their own cabins, they lived and trained together while on patrol. She was also shocked to learn that Black worked with them, living in the barracks when his shift came.

In the coming weeks, Sunday realized the fort had one goal— *independence*—and there seemed to be a harmony among the people as they worked to achieve it. This didn't mean that problems didn't arise—they did—and when they did, the people made appointments to see Black to work through the issue. Otis and Mary helped Black tackle the problems that arose, and after a while, Sunday came to understand that they were husband and wife. Mary was about five foot eleven with long blonde hair and a thin frame. Being unusually tall for a woman,

Mary was unforgettable upon introduction, and Sunday found her to be honest and refreshing. Mary was slightly taller than Otis, who was about five foot nine with a muscular build. He had black hair that he kept cut short and brown skin that was flawless. Otis was funny and warm, which, to Sunday, added to how handsome he was.

Sunday and Mama had a routine of helping Paul and Iris keep the house in order. Paul was an elderly man with a tan complexion and blue eyes that seemed discolored from age rather than a natural coloring. He had gray and black hair on the sides of his head, and he was bald on top. She found that Paul and Big Mama had been friends for many years. Iris had been free for a time and became a slave later in life. She had gray hair that she wore braided or pulled back in a bun. She was beautiful and thin with a musical accent. Iris was from a small island she said was called Barbados. When the chores were done, Iris sometimes told Sunday about her home. Sunday learned something important from speaking with Iris, and that was the colored experience was way bigger than the plantation.

As for Black, he was a little more relaxed since Mama and Sunday had arrived. He began work in his study very early in the morning and often never left until well after dark. He would get up to stretch and see Sunday exploring from the window. Mama came every day at noon, bringing lunch for him, and though he didn't have the time, he made time for her. They would talk about his business and the people she saw coming and going. When she could advise him, she did, but these days, he was teaching her, and he could see her pride.

She was shrewd, and he sometimes hated it, but there was nothing for it. She made him smile. "You know ..." she said one day three weeks after their arrival, letting the words hang in the air before continuing. "Sunday is twenty-one summers, there 'bouts, and it's time that she was introduced to a nice young man so that she could start a family."

She had his attention with that statement. He looked up from the papers he was reading and assessed the triumphant look on her face. Putting his pen down, he stared at her. There was no need to match wits with her; he never won, and he knew for sure if there was a chance of winning, this wouldn't be the conversation. He offered no response.

"I's sure ya know plenty of hardworking menfolk that we could has here for supper." She almost gloated with no shame.

"You mad at me today?" he asked, his tone slow and easy.

"Maaad?" she responded, dragging the word.

Leaning back in his chair, he said no more.

"Why would ya thank I's mad at ya 'cause I's tryin' to help Sunday?"

Ignoring her question, he said, "I thought you wanted to discuss farming today."

"Nope. Sunday was what I's thankin' 'bout, but farming sounds good. It's just I noticed some of the young men's studying her. What 'bout the two young mens what brangs the water and the firewood? Both them seem nice and hardworking."

He didn't bite, and changing the subject, he said, "I plan on traveling back into South Carolina in about a month. I have been staying around to give you and Sunday time to become better acquainted with Fort Independence."

Switching her hat from mischief to business, she asked, "The Turner plantation?"

"I plan on stopping there just for information. They do not plan on letting the matter drop, and I need to stay on top."

"I agrees," she said without flinching. "I still has my concerns. What you plannin' for Youngblood?"

"Youngblood, I'm afraid, believes in an eye for an eye, and I can't say that I disagree." His smile was lazy and carefree.

"Turner?" She was anxious, and he could see it.

"Turner is an old man. I think Will is the problem," he said, looking back at the stack of papers.

"I don't want Jacob hurt, but he ain't to be misjudged, neither. You be careful. He can be more treacherous than he looks. Don't take no more slaves from his plantation, neither. Ya never knows who can be trusted."

"I thought of that, but you realize that the slaves that came from that plantation were vetted by you. There is always the possibility of a traitor in the group from any plantation. There is also the chance of a slave being sold to another plantation to bring about my destruction."

"Maybe if'n ya silence Youngblood, it will set thangs to right," she said as she leaned back in her chair and held his gaze steadily. "Make it a mystery; the mind works against ya when ya has to wonder. Do it, and never let him be found; this will kill two birds with one stone. The slaves will rest better that he gone, and the unknown will increase fear. When all else fails, I too believes in an eye for an eye."

He nodded.

"Youngblood needs to go missin' as soon as possible; they will involve him, 'cause for him it's personal, and it ain't no need to push him; he already fixated. Kill him and they's forced to has to pay for relief against ya. And peoples what can be paid, well ... they goes to the highest bidder. Kill him and cripple them," she said calmly, ever thinking.

As he leaned back in his chair, he stared at her with a newfound respect. Still he did not speak; he just listened.

Mama wasn't finished either, and then she continued, "You ain't to be fixated on Youngblood, Turner, or Will. Yo prize is obtainin' and maintainin' freedom. Don't look back at Mack or the young men what died 'cause of what happened 'tween you and Youngblood. You has bigger enemies—this ain't a black-and-white issue; this is 'bout money. The South is dying. We hears the talk as slaves; they talks like we ain't even there. You must stay the course, killin' any man that attempts to separate you from freedom. Yo capture means the fall of many. Settle this, and as I said, I don't want Jacob hurt, but if'n ya has to cross that bridge, don't hesitate, and leave nothing for them to find."

"I agree, and I will take care of it," he said. He had never heard her talk so much and be so clear about what she thought. During his growing up, they whispered a lot and used sign language. She was always concerned that the white folks would hear.

Black's quiet way allowed her mind to wander back to the week after his birth. She invited Mae to her cabin to discuss her silence and the baby. Mae let her know in no uncertain terms she wasn't getting her ass beat for Nat Turner's baby. She offered Mae some homemade biscuits and buttermilk, and one hour after Mae entered the cabin, Paul was throwing her in an unmarked grave. It was as though Mae had run off. The goal was to protect him as a child and keep him alive;

Mae had been a threat, plain and simple. The goal even today had not changed.

She stood, and so he stood. "We does what we has to," she said, moving toward the door.

Again, he offered, "I will handle it."

She nodded, leaving the study with him staring after her.

The hour was late when Black went to his studio in an attempt to release some energy. He'd begun a painting of the auction block. The canvas depicted a line of slaves shackled together, waiting to be bid on. There was a woman center stage in a white dress contrasting her brown skin, and the dress was pulled down about her waist, exposing her breasts. Her eyes were sad, and the canvas was filled with earth tones, and to the right of her, the auctioneer was dressed in blue trousers and a white ruffled shirt, his hand at his mouth as he called for the bid. She stood proud, not bending in the face of such disgrace.

Black had not gone to Sunday's room; he was trying to make her independent. The problem was he could no longer tell if she needed him or if he needed her. It was now becoming hard for him to sleep without first holding her until she slept. As he was making all kinds of excuses and thinking about the discussion with Big Mama, there came a knock at the door. Walking to the door, he opened it, and there Sunday stood in his shirt and robe after her bath, toes peeking out.

"I waited, and you ain't come," she said. "Can I come in?"

Stepping back, he allowed her in. "Why are you still up?" he asked.

She entered the sparsely furnished chamber, noticing a cot on the floor, a chair by the window, and then the canvas. Stepping closer, she observed the woman's pain and her effort not to be broken. She turned to tell him how beautiful the painting was when she noticed him for the first time; he was wearing black trousers and no shirt. As he wiped his hands free of the paint, his muscles rippled effortlessly, and he was beautiful standing there with the candlelight dancing on his midnight skin.

"I cain't sleep witout you," she whispered.

"I'm not a damn nanny, Sunday."

Whatever she had thought he would say, it wasn't that. "I thought ya like setting wit' me in the evenings," she responded, reassessing him and his mood. He looked aggravated, and for the first time since she was a child, she regretted being in his presence.

"What will you do when I'm not here, gone on one of my trips? I will probably be gone for weeks. What will you do then?" he said, and he was snide—and worse yet, he couldn't stop himself.

"Wait for ya to come back to me," she said, looking away, not wanting the rejection she saw in his eyes. "I shouldna come bother you. I can see you's busy."

The air between them was alive, but she felt as though she were dying.

"Wait for me to come back … with who?" he asked. "Who will sit with you at night when I'm not here?" he continued, his eyes narrowing.

She didn't understand this conversation. "Ain't I allowed to need you no more, Nat? Do you sees me as weak 'cause … I needs you?" she asked, her voice catching. The game was changing. There were new rules, and she would learn to play by them. She needed to breathe and headed for the door.

Stepping up behind her, he placed his palm flat against the door, preventing her from opening it, and in an effort to hide from him, she placed her forehead against the cool door and closed her eyes. She could feel that he was in a foul mood, and she was unsure what she had done to make him so angry with her. *What is happening?* she thought. All she wanted was to leave so that she could cry alone. But against her ear, he whispered, "I'm sorry. Please don't go."

She did not move, and the truth was she couldn't; why was this so intense? Before she knew what he was about, he picked her up and carried her to the chair. And to her shame, she balled up on his lap, leaning against his naked chest, and his skin was hot to the touch. The comfort he offered was made potent followed by a hurt, and still she was not clear, because the hurt was coming from him.

Although she was in his lap, she was not with him, and he deserved it. He couldn't even feel her breathe. Speaking into the quietness, he said, "Please forgive me, Sunday."

"I wants to go back to my room, please," she said with no emotion, struggling to pull away. Being this close to him made her feel like she was drowning. It was dangerous to need him; she had been worried that the bond she felt with him would be taken away from her. Yet, thinking only as a slave, she thought it would be forced from her grasp. Never did she think he would snatch it back. The concept was new, and it occurred to her that she was weak.

Using the momentum of her trying to pull away, he lifted her to straddle him in the chair. "You never answered me. Who will sit with you at night when I'm gone?"

"I understands now," she said, holding eye contact with him when really she wanted to disappear. In order to balance herself, she had to place her hands on his shoulders, making her aware of him like she had never been aware of any man. She had been a slave, so her sensibilities weren't spared. Still, this was new. His eyes were filled with emotions that she could not read, and she felt exposed. *Nowhere to hide*, she thought.

"Answer me," he said, his voice grave, the words more like a plea than a demand.

"I understands," she said again, not flinching. "You ain't a nanny, and I don't need to bother you when you so busy." Her voice was steady, not allowing her hurt to show—at least she hoped not.

Pressing down on his shoulders, she tried to get up again, and when she raised herself up on her knees, he pulled her close. Wrapping his arms around her waist, he buried his face between her breasts, and she was so startled by the contact that she started shaking. She wanted to back away, but she needed him so badly. It was clear she could no longer come to him, and she would have to accept that.

As she struggled with her feelings for him, he admitted, "I need you too."

"Why you treatin' me this way if'n you needs me?"

"I'm jealous." It was all he would say, but damn Mama for making him overthink things.

"What you jealous 'bout?" she asked, and her voice was a little softer. "I loves ya, Nat." Completing the hug that he started, she wrapped her arms about him and kissed him repeatedly on his bald head.

As she kissed him softly, she felt him relax, and still he offered no response. He leaned his head back to give her better access, and she kissed his eyelids and then his nose and then … she pressed her lips to his, and she was engulfed by his masculinity and the emotion she felt coming from him. Abruptly, he stood, and walking her over to the cot, he laid her down. Pressing her legs apart with his knees, he lay between them, and while he still leaned up on his hands, he gazed down at her.

She could see the uncertainty in his eyes, and wanting him to feel loved, she repeated reassuringly, "I loves ya, Nat."

At her words, he leaned down and kissed her, pushing his tongue roughly into her mouth, and she whimpered. She allowed him control and gave over to him. He continued kissing her, making her want more. And then she felt him abruptly backing away from her, trying to scale down the intensity. Breaking the kiss, he lay down next to her and pulled her up against him. She snuggled close, trying to offer him the well-being he consistently offered her; she realized that he needed her tonight. He carried troubles that she couldn't understand, so she offered him her love and silence as he worked through his feelings.

3

February 1859, Virginia

The weeks turned into months since Sunday left, and new issues arose. Will was a man who thought through his problems, and new to the list was his getting married. He would marry the Myers girl to get his father and her father off his back. Robert Myers was about business, and to move forward, he needed to get the marriage out of the way. The two families were having dinner, and it seemed as though his father was pressing for the marriage now. He would give the old man this win mostly because it was in his best interest. Rose, his younger sister, would eventually marry, and all this would be his.

Amber Myers was plump, and Will was sure that he was not fascinated with heavy women. Still, she had an appeal. She had fiery auburn hair and a heart-shaped face. She was not unpleasant, but her figure was a little too full. He decided that he would conduct this marriage like a business and in doing so carve out a deal that would leave him free to do as he pleased. They had money, the Myers clan, and lots of it. Plus, she was Robert Myers's only child. He could do worse ... lots worse.

Stepping into the sitting room, he observed the women engaged in polite conversation. Rose was discussing the furniture with Amber. They sat on the couch with their dresses spread just so, and he could not help but notice that his soon-to-be wife had wonderful and full breasts.

Entering the salon, he made his way over and spoke. "Ladies," he said. "You both look lovely this evening."

"Thank you, dear brother," Rose answered, smiling.

"Thank you, Will," Amber replied.

As Will spoke to the women, he thought on the fact that he and his sister were never really close, yet they were not enemies, either. They had really just existed in the same space since their mother died. He traveled and went to school, returning to help run the plantation. Learning the family business was a requirement, and the political climate in the country threatened his very way of life. Turner, thinking ahead, made the connections to secure him and his sister a better way of life, and he could respect that. Smiling, he was about to engage Amber when he noticed his father and Robert Myers off in the corner having a drink.

"Will," his father said, waving him over. "Tell us some stories about your time away."

Before turning away, Will excused himself, and Amber nodded. Watching as he walked away, she assessed him. He was tall and thin yet not what one would call skinny. Will had short blond hair and the bluest eyes; his nose was sharp, and his jawline strong, his face free of hair. His style of dress was plain yet elegant; he wore dark blue trousers and a white shirt with a matching vest and bowtie. Will was more than she had expected; at twenty-five summers, she was considered an old maid. Amber was pleased, and with the way things were going, they would be married soon.

The butler announced dinner, and they made their way into the formal dining room. They sat at one end of the long table for conversational purposes, the men speaking of politics and the women fashion, each skirting the real issue, the Turner-Myers merger.

Jacob Turner, tired of pleasantries, steered the conversation toward the subject everyone wanted to discuss. "Have you young people taken the time to become acquainted?"

"I was hoping that we could sit on the porch this evening and enjoy each other's company," Will said, staring at Amber.

Smiling shyly, she answered, "Why, yes, of course."

"I was hoping for a short engagement," Jacob Turner said, eyeing his son.

"I agree," Robert Myers chimed in. "I want grandchildren—and soon."

Will watched as Amber blushed, and to his surprise, he thought her striking. Backing away from thoughts of Amber, Will focused in on her father and considered him. Robert Myers had unruly gray hair and pitted skin; he was a rough-looking fellow with eyebrows that needed to be combed. Myers was skeptical about the match, Will knew, but Amber was no spring chicken, and she was fat. They were all winning, and the key was not to act as though the Myerses were doing the Turners a favor.

"A short engagement and a timely marriage allows me room to travel with your sister," Jacob Turner said, and Rose smiled at her father's comment.

Just then, Tilly approached with the plates on a rolling cart and began serving a fine Southern meal of garlic green beans, scalloped potatoes, and fried chicken … mile-high biscuits to boot. They laughed and talked through dinner, and Will could see that his father was pleased when he excused himself, asking the young women to retire to the porch for some fresh air. Rose, of course, declined as Amber stood in her beautiful green dress that matched her eyes. When Will held his arm out to her, Amber placed her hand on the crook of his elbow and allowed him to lead her away. As they moved toward the front of the house, Will decided he would settle it right away. He would have them married in the next two weeks, if he could help it.

The weather was mild for February, and Will was surprised; it had been very cold just days before. He opened with the weather, trying to break the silence. "Nice weather we're having. Feels like springtime."

Seated on the swing, Amber swayed back and forth. She smiled prettily before offering a nod.

"You like living in Boston?"

"It's nice, and I have my friends," she responded.

"Are you opposed to living in Virginia?" he queried.

"I'll miss everyone, but no, moving here is fine. We will be able to visit, won't we?"

"Yes, of course."

Just then, Youngblood appeared on his horse as he made his nightly rounds patrolling. Seeing them seated on the porch, he moved from the path and offered, "Good evening."

Will stepped down from the porch and excused himself before

speaking with Youngblood in hushed tones. "Have you found anything yet?"

"I think I have a lead, but it's still too soon. If this pans out, you will be pleased," Youngblood responded.

"Get me a report and not promises."

Just as Will was about to walk away, Youngblood asked, "What about your father?"

"What about him? Right now he's driving me crazy, so I think we are safe, but once I'm married, he might get in the way." Turning, he walked away from Youngblood and back up the stairs where Amber waited patiently.

Nudging his horse forward, Youngblood tipped his hat and moved along.

"When would you like to get married?" Will asked her, trying to gauge what he needed to expect.

"Whatever date you set is fine with me," she said, staring out into the darkness.

"It's settled, then—the second Saturday in March. We'll marry here in the parlor." *So much for getting acquainted*, he thought. She really had nothing to say, and if he gave it thought, it was probably for the better.

Reaching out his hand, he said, "Come. I will walk you up to your chamber."

Amber stood and preceded him into the foyer of what would soon be her new home. Stepping through the front door, she weighed her surroundings. The elegant spiral staircase was to the right of the door. The wooden banister was polished to perfection, and paintings of the Turners' angry-looking ancestors lined the walls. Across from the stairs was a sitting room done in yellow with splashes of brown. In the parlor was a black piano with a large burgundy sofa and matching chairs that looked like thrones in the middle of the room. She hated the furniture and hoped Rose wanted it when she married.

She thought of the formal dining room and its beauty in contrast to the other rooms. The table was polished so that the candlelight reflected off of it and it gave the room personality. On the second floor were six bedrooms, all with four-poster beds, and each had themes, such as the sunroom or the Victorian room. Each had large gaudy furniture with splashes of purple that made the rooms look too busy. Rose's room was pink and white with a canopy bed, an ivory vanity, and matching drapes. Amber couldn't wait to add her own touch; she would whip this place into shape.

As they climbed the stairs coming to her chamber, she heard him say, "You can plan the wedding, and I will go along with your wishes. I would like you to be happy."

She eyed him, checking for sincerity, and found that he was not readable. Smiling, she said, "Thank you, Will. I appreciate that." She wanted him to really see her. Sadly, she knew he was just going through the motions, so she would turn her mind to the wedding and enjoy that.

Leaning down, he kissed her cheek and pushed on down the hall to his room, bidding her good night.

Canada

Sunday and Black fell into a routine. She came to his office every day just after lunch, spending one hour behind closed doors learning the alphabet and eventually to read. He could have sent her to the school or to Mary, who was really the resident teacher, but he wanted to teach her. Black wanted to see her growth, and he wanted to be part of her progress. They read books about anything and everything, and she was a fast learner once she got beyond the embarrassment of sounding out the word.

She had begun writing her name, and he found that she had a terrible hand, so they practiced and practiced some more. When they spoke, he used bigger words, and she would say, "Slow down; what do that word mean?" Black would very patiently explain the meaning of the word and then spell it. He found that he loved the time he spent with her; still, his troubles were back with a vengeance as time approached for him to leave.

In the evenings when she had fallen asleep, he was still up contemplating life and his responsibilities. And he realized that he had great fears where Sunday was concerned. Although they cuddled and sometimes he stayed all night, he did not move beyond holding her. He was a man, and he wanted her like he had never wanted anyone, but he was held back by the life that had chosen him. There were issues that haunted his very existence, like being the legendary Black. He understood that death would find him sooner rather than later, and he didn't want to leave her without protection. If he were killed, she would be associated with having been his woman. He understood the association, because being Nat Turner's son left its mark on his life.

Children were his next issue. He did not want them—it was simple. Until the first generation of free black people happened, he could not see himself having children. Try as he might, he could not grasp having offspring while he himself was considered stolen property. The idea of his offspring being whipped was incomprehensible. Lastly, while he feared dying and leaving Sunday unprotected, he feared her dying on him in childbirth—like his mother—even more. The very notion kept sex off the table, and selfishly he wallowed in these thoughts, telling her nothing, doing the very thing he asked her not to do—deal in dishonesty with him. The worst of it was that he justified his behavior by saying it was best for her.

They had arrived at the fort in early January, and now in late February, Black had a new problem. Sadly and to his shame, he was starting to look forward to leaving, hoping that it might clear his head and give him his control back. He was in love and felt weighted by his emotions and doubts. In his studio he painted, trying to alleviate stress, and all the paintings were of her … Sunday staring at him as she took a bath, only visible from her shoulders up; Sunday lying on the carpet, reading, her eyebrows drawn slightly together as though she were deep in thought; Sunday in his shirt and bathrobe, looking out the window … she was killing him. Silently, he partook in what she offered, paralyzed in fear and hiding, yet unwilling to give it up. *Mine*, he thought, and he had the grace to feel embarrassed.

Big Mama sat with him at lunch and after her chores. They spoke about many things—his plans, business, and what was needed to maintain Fort Independence. Sunday would sometimes join them for lunch, staying for her lessons after Mama left. Mama found that she was able to speak with him about many things, but Sunday was not one of them. He kept her to himself, and though she tried to broach the subject of Sunday, he never bit.

If Sunday was present, he was engaging to both of them, but to discuss her was off limits. Mama could see that he was in love with her and unable to find a happy medium between worry and contentment even after all that he accomplished. It was clear that he was spending the evenings with Sunday, but Mama just knew that they had not yet been intimate, because his frustration was still too evident. Smiling, she was happy that they were finding love.

"You and Sunday thanking 'bout marryin'?" Mama asked one afternoon, taking him by surprise.

"We have not discussed marriage," he responded carefully.

"Do ya wants her for a wife?" she asked, not deterred.

He smiled, but he was angry. She was prying, and he didn't want to talk about it. Unsure how to end the conversation and move on to something more appropriate, he leaned back in his chair and stared at her.

Unflinchingly, she held his gaze and waited.

"I do not wish to discuss marrying Sunday with you."

Just then, there came a knock at the door, and Sunday entered. Stepping into the study, she felt the tension. "I can come back for my lesson," she said as a way to offer them more time.

"Come in. I have been waiting for you," he said, changing the mood.

"Mama, you want to stay and take a lesson wit' me?" Sunday continued, trying to gauge the mood in the room.

"Naw, baby, you two go on 'head and start work. I has thangs that need tending," Mama said, standing.

He stared at Mama, smiling, before saying, "Mama doesn't need a lesson; she can read already."

Whipping her head up and making eye contact with Mama, Sunday was shocked. "Mama, you can read?" she asked, incredulous.

"I can. You two get on to work. I'm gon to get on out the way," Mama said, giving him a final look that said, *When you are ready to talk, I'm here,* and then she was gone.

Standing, he began pacing the study. He had pent-up energy, and walking over to the window, he spoke to Sunday while looking out. "Would you like to go into town?"

He smiled at the way her face lit up.

"I would love that," she responded with the excitement of a child.

"I will meet you out front within the hour." Needing to get some air, he opened the door and told her, "Go get ready."

Making her way back to her bedroom, Sunday brushed her hair and her teeth. She put on her warmest overcoat and headed back to the front of the house. Passing through the kitchen, she found Mama and Iris sitting at the table talking and giggling. When she walked into the kitchen, they stopped talking, looking at her.

"What's the matter? Why y'all staring at me?"

"Where are you going?" Iris asked, answering her question with a question.

"You goin' out wit' Black?" Mama continued in the same fashion.

"Yes." Sunday was just about to ask what was going on when Paul appeared.

"Black is out front waitin' on ya, Sunday," he said.

"Mama, see ya after a while, all right?"

"Go and have a good time, child," Mama said, nodding her head. Sunday turned just as Paul sat down and Iris poured him some coffee. They began to whisper again, this time including Paul.

Stepping out the front door, Sunday saw him standing in the noon sun. He wore black trousers and a black shirt, his gun strapped at his side, peeking out from under a black jacket. He was standing in front of a black carriage with four matching black horses, and she realized that she was not going on a trip into town with Nat. He was all business, and then she saw them—about eight men on horseback just ahead, waiting patiently.

When he stepped aside, she noticed that the carriage had gold lettering painted on the side ... FBFG. She descended the stairs, and Black helped her into the carriage. As the carriage started rolling, she asked him, "What does the letters mean?"

He smiled before saying, "FBFG—it stands for *first black free generation*. We are a generation that had to take back our freedom, but we are not the FBFG."

"Do you thank we will see such a day? I hears the talk, but I never really figured on it," she said, truly interested.

He decided upon the truth. "I think it's coming sooner rather than later, and you will see it in your young lifetime."

She noticed that he spoke as though he wouldn't see it, but she did not acknowledge it; she couldn't. The carriage rolled toward the gate and began to slow, eventually stopping before reaching the gate. Black's eyebrows drew together as he pulled back the curtain to look out and assess the situation. There were people all standing in the paths, smiling and waving. When he turned back to her, puzzled, she had already opened the door and hopped down.

The women piled around her, wanting to know where they were going, and children were hiding in her skirts as she spoke energetically with their mothers. The men stood off to the side, smiling, and seeing him, they approached, shaking his hand, offering how good it was to see him.

"She comes every day to help with the children and be with the women. They love her," Joe the blacksmith was explaining. Black nodded, leaning against the carriage and waiting. It was his turn to assess her. She wore a serviceable brown dress with a jacket of cream and matching gloves; her hair was in five large cornrows hanging about her shoulders. In the noon sun, her cheeks glowed with health, and when she laughed, he was moved by her beauty, both inside and out. He thought about what Mama had said about the young men that brought the water and wood. They *were* taken with her, and he smiled, shaking his head.

Once they were back in the carriage and rolling out the gate, he commented, "I see that you have made friends."

"Yes, they's wonderful and welcoming. They works hard during the day to keep thangs running, and they's teachin me what it takes." She laughed.

Their conversation turned to the countryside and where they lived. As Black watched her stare out the window, he asked, "Do you understand where we live?"

"I understands some," she answered.

"We live in Upper Canada, separate from America. Slavery here has been abolished for twenty-five years. It's why I chose to come here."

"Oh, so some black peoples is free?"

"Yes, but as long as all colored people are not free, then neither are we," he said in all seriousness.

She nodded, thinking on what he had said.

"Have you even been to town while at the plantation?" he asked.

"No. Only Tilly was allowed to go."

"You are in for a real treat then."

At his words, she was excited, and he found that he loved making her happy. He wanted her to enjoy herself. Yet, outside the carriage, the men rode with the instructions to let no one approach as they rode.

When they reached town, they stepped from the carriage and began making their way from shop to shop. They bought candy for the children, a book for Mama, and a beautiful brush and comb set for Iris. They went to a dress shop, where she picked out the material for five dresses, and she couldn't wait to tell Mama. Black picked fancier materials with the request that the dresses be dropped off at the fort. Sally, the dressmaker, took her measurements and told him it would be about three weeks.

They were leaving the dressmaker and stepping out into the fading sunlight when Sunday noticed a man approaching them. It was the overseer, called Mr. Tim, from the Turner plantation. He was a tall man, with jet-black hair and coal-black eyes, standing well over six feet. Mr. Tim had sharp cheekbones and unreadable eyes, and seeing him made her feel faint. Fear gripped her, and she stopped talking abruptly, causing Black to take notice of her sudden mood change. Looking around, Black saw him too. Sunday stepped closer, placing her hand in his. She was trembling, and he gave her hand a squeeze to reassure her.

"Evening, Black … Miss Sunday," he said.

"Tim," Black responded, and Sunday moved closer to Black, saying nothing.

"I stopped here to rest before making it to the fort."

"I will see you at the fort," Black said, dismissing him.

Nodding his head, Tim turned and walked away, and just then, the carriage pulled up.

They did not speak in the carriage on the way back to the fort, but Sunday sat next to Black, feeling protected by his presence. The mood changed, and seeing Tim, she didn't know what to expect. Strangely, he seemed to be taking orders from Black. As they rolled through the gate, they headed straight for the house. Climbing out of the carriage, she was tired and trying to ready herself for what was coming.

Before entering the house, he turned to her. "I have a meeting. I will come to you when I'm done."

She couldn't speak, so she nodded her acknowledgment. They entered the foyer, and Tim was waiting patiently in the sitting room for their return. She kept on to her room, passing them as Black stepped into the sitting room. Hearing their footsteps moving toward the study, she turned back in time to see the study door close. In her room, she paced, waiting for Black to come to her.

In the study, Black spoke to Tim. "You came sooner than I thought."

"Youngblood and Will have teamed up. Will wants Sunday back, and Youngblood ... well, you know," Tim said, trying not to overstate. "They sent me to find the girl. Will wants her back."

Sitting in the chair behind the desk, Black watched Tim pace back and forth. He felt like pacing, but he would not show weakness to any man. Instead, he sat and spoke calmly. "What are you not telling me?"

Unrolling a paper from his satchel, Tim handed it to Black. Reading it, Black placed it on his desk, saying, "The likenesses are getting better, and we are up to $2,000."

"I wish you would take this seriously, Black."

Changing the subject, Black said, "Sunday is afraid of you. Why?"

Confused, Tim said, "What?"

"She was trembling when you walked up. Why?"

When it dawned on Tim what Black was asking, he said, "You know that I would never hurt a woman; she is afraid because she knows me as an overseer. She doesn't know I work for the cause."

"I'm not accusing you, Tim. I'm trying to find out if you may have had to do something to be convincing—and if it was to her."

"It wasn't," he answered, and he was angry.

"When do you have to be back to the plantation?" Black asked.

"I leave at first light," he snapped, and Black ignored him. Tim was a good man, and the role he played was a tough one. Black had asked because he needed to know, yet he was unclear how he would have responded if the answer had been anything other than a no. "I will give you time and follow."

Turning on his heels, Tim was heading for the door when Black said, "I apologize. I do not mean to offend you."

Taking a deep breath, Tim said, "I am not angry or offended. I saw that she was afraid, and if I loved her like you do, I would have questioned me too. We are friends as always. Take the bounty on your head seriously for her sake as well as your own. I will be back at the plantation before you so that I'm there to back you up. Will is marrying the Myers girl the second Saturday of March. That is the best time for anything you have planned. People will come from far and wide to attend the wedding. Give me three days so that I can see my family before you start out."

"Three days," Black said with understanding, and he watched him leave. Sighing, he made his way to Sunday's room, and she was not there.

Walking down the hall to Mama's room, he knocked, and when she bid him to enter, he asked, "Have you seen Sunday?"

Looking up from her sewing, she said, "No. Somethin' the matter?"

"No. I was just looking for her," he said.

Closing the door behind him, he started to search the kitchen, the upstairs, and the sitting room in earnest, but she was missing. Opening the front door, he looked about and didn't see her, and just as he was about to make his way down the steps, he saw something move out the corner of his eye. She was standing in the shadows, unmoving and staring out into the night. Walking over to her, he stood in front of her and leaned against the railing, crossing his legs at the ankle and his arms across his chest.

"Why are you out here?"

"I needed some air. You leavin', ain't ya?" she asked, wanting to get to the basics. It was selfish, she knew, wanting to keep him all to herself, but she couldn't help the way she felt.

"I'm leaving in three days," he answered.

She was silent for a moment before saying, "I won't see you till after you gets back?"

His silence was the answer.

The next three days were a bevy of activities. Black was held up in his office with people coming and going. Try as she might, Sunday didn't even catch one glimpse of him, and her heart hurt. She didn't go to his office because she wanted him to focus on staying alive. She saw that Mama went into the office and didn't come out for hours. The men from the last trip seemed to be readying themselves, and she wanted to scream from anxiety. When day one came to a close with no sight of him, she gave up and tried to keep herself busy.

On day two, she found Mama reading in her room by the sunlight. "How you feeling?" Mama asked her.

"I's well," Sunday answered.

"He's important, and he don't belong to just us," Mama said, trying to help. "Lovin' someone like him is difficult, but you can do it."

Sunday's eyes watered up, but she didn't cry. "I feels ..."

"He feels the like. You's wonderin' why he ain't been intimate wit' ya yet."

Sunday didn't know how to respond, so she decided upon the truth. "I wants him, but it don't seem right me telling him," she whispered.

Mama smiled before saying, "He loves you, and he wants you. I sees that. He is 'fraid of gettin' you wit' child."

Sunday's eyes rounded in shock, and then her eyebrows creased together. "Why would he think 'bout that? He's a man."

"Men has fears too, child."

She was shocked and couldn't find the words, so Mama continued, "Iris and me can help ya not get in a family way. We'll mix a drank that ya take every morning till you wants to get in a family way."

Staring at Mama incredulously, she nodded. "When can I start?"

"In the mornin', and ya cain't miss a day," Mama said.

"Why ain't he talked to me?"

"You cain't rush thangs. He will."

Walking over to the chair, Sunday gave Mama a hug and a kiss and left the room.

When Mama was alone again, she thought, *Now let's hope he don't do something foolish.*

She loved them both, but she could only do so much.

At the close of day two, Sunday headed back to her room to get ready for bed and possibly a good cry. She was emotional and just wanted sleep, welcoming oblivion. Entering her room, she saw the fireplace had been tended and was burning. Black stood with his hands jammed in his pockets, staring at the flames. He was a sight to behold for her aching heart.

He wore black trousers, work boots, and a black shirt, and his gun was strapped at his side. Looking up as the door opened, he smiled. "I've been waiting for you."

"You come to tell me good-bye?" she asked, holding her breath.

His eyes serious, he shook his head, saying at the same time, "I'm here to hold you."

She moved toward him slowly, and he opened his arms, stepping into his embrace. They just held each other for a time in silence. Breaking the magic, he said, "Get ready for bed. I'll be back."

"Don't leave me," she whispered. "Please."

Walking over to the chair, he sat and watched her get ready for bed. He was playing with fire, and he knew it. Still, she was safe; he didn't want to make love to her and then leave. He wanted to spend time with her, fanning the flames of passion, provided he could bring himself to touch her. His fear was just too great. Sitting in the plush chair, he watched her unlace her dress and push it down over her hips. She wore a shift that was thin, and with the help of the firelight, he could see her breasts through the cloth. Her underpants were made of the same material, and he had to swallow hard to keep himself in check. He saw no embarrassment or shame in her eyes as she walked over to him and climbed onto his lap. Taking his face in her hands, she pressed her lips to his, and then, with a boldness that allowed him to feel her desperation, she pushed her tongue into his mouth. And though the contact was intense, he attempted to commit her taste and smell to memory.

He was drowning in the love he felt for her, and in this moment, it was the most intimate experience he had ever shared with another human being. Black had tasted first his own freedom, and then he helped others experience freedom. Yet in this very instant, he understood that slavery was the backdrop, a situation that was happening; it wasn't life in its entirety. In his pursuit of freedom, he realized that he never contemplated happiness, and now that he had liberty he needed to chase life. This moment of clarity almost humbled him … if he wasn't so damned afraid.

She snuggled against him and went to sleep, and when she woke, he was gone.

Black and Otis rode out on horseback ten men deep headed for South Carolina first. He planned on moving an entire family—a husband, wife, and two young daughters—to Pennsylvania. They were experiencing brutal beatings that left one child with a permanent limp. The fact that Will Turner was marrying caused a lot of the plantation owners from the surrounding cities and states to be in attendance, leaving the path clear for Black and his men.

The opportunity of such an uninterrupted trip made Black call a change to the plan, adding more time to the trip. In South Carolina, they moved the family; in North Carolina, they moved a boy of seven whose mother died and whose father was sold to the Wilson plantation in Virginia. At the Wilson plantation, he found the father of the boy, reuniting them; he accepted the request of a woman with a baby about five months old. Although moving the slaves off the plantations was easy, traveling presented its own set of problems because the owners were traveling the roads, as well. They employed Herschel, who drove them in a covered wagon with three of his men strapped and ready to do business with whoever dared to try to stop them.

The weather was mild in the south, and Black continued to press on, trying to make up days. He and his men had come across some of the wanted posters, and in some of the posters, the drawings were a cross between him and Moses (also known as Harriet Tubman). Black couldn't tell if they were searching for a woman dressed as a man or an actual man. He replaced the posters with drawings of his own and lowered the bounty on his head. The wanted posters he drew always depicted Mack, the slave that died that fateful day when he and Youngblood locked ass. The captions from his posters read:

REWARD $100.00
WANTED DEAD OR ALIVE
BLACK
RUNAWAY SLAVE
APPROACH WITH CAUTION—VIOLENT AND DEADLY

The posters he left told nothing and left nothing for people to go on. The message was clear in one aspect, though—he was violent and without a doubt deadly. He wanted that point driven home, and as he changed the posters, Otis would shake his head, saying, "Sometimes I think you just plain crazy ... still, it's crafty, very crafty."

Black smiled before saying, "I figure since they are looking, then I should give them something to look for."

"Moses is like you; she don't care either," Otis said.

"Speaking of Moses, we need to stay ahead of schedule so that we can meet her in Pennsylvania. She will take the family along with the woman and the child and help them get settled in New York. The father and the boy will come to Canada."

"We will divide the men and take two back with us through Virginia," Otis confirmed.

"Let us ride so that we can bring this trip to a close. We still have the convention coming up, and I need to be there for that so that I can see what John is about."

"You know what he's figuring; he is attempting to overthrow the gobment to 'bolish slavery. He looking for followers, and he angry that you won't join forces wit' him."

His expression grim, Black said, "Harriet sent word that he

approached her, and she declined. He is now blaming me for her refusal, as well."

Shaking his head, Otis said, "If it ain't one thang, it's another."

"Agreed. Let's move out."

~ ~ ~

They rode hard, sticking to the shadows, watching Herschel's back until they crossed the line into Pennsylvania. As they approached the safe house, a small-framed man holding a shotgun stepped from the cabin. When he finally recognized them, he lowered his gun and came forward to greet them. Black swung down from his horse and greeted *her*. She wore a rag tied about her head and a brimmed hat to hide her eyes. Moses had small eyes, a large nose, and thick lips. She was an older woman, and the hard life she led showed. Dressed in a brown suit, she was no-nonsense as she stared up at him.

"You going to shoot me, Moses?" he asked with amusement in his eyes.

Smiling, she responded, "As long as I knows who ya are, ya safe … otherwise, you ain't long for this here world. I don't like visitors."

He smiled, and then they were down to business. They got the slaves settled, feeding them and giving them a place to sleep. She went over with them what would happen next and what they could expect. She asked if anyone wanted to go back to the plantation, and Black smiled at her question, because he knew she would shoot them if they opted to return to slavery.

When she and Black had a moment to talk, she signaled him to step outside so they could speak privately. "John is angry with you 'cause of my refusing to join him," she said, concerned.

"I am aware, and you do not need to worry about him. He was angry with me before he spoke with you," Black replied.

"Does he not see that matters in the country is changing, and war is coming?" she stated incredulously.

"Civil war is coming. It's why I chose Canada," he said matter-of-factly. "John's problem is impatience; it will still be years before they call a halt to slavery and even longer before they address the backlash from it. I am not interested in war. As a black soldier, you will fight and die like them, but you will not gain the respect due a soldier."

She agreed and knew that the supplies and weapons given to colored soldiers would be subpar. The war would be a nasty bit of business, but she wanted to talk about other issues. "Your mama left with you, and since then, Youngblood has sent overseers as far as New York trying to track you. What will you do 'bout him?"

Harriet was a kind woman, risking her life in service to others, carrying the name Moses as he carried the name Black. Being legendary while still alive was a weight that he carried about his neck at times, and he was sure it was the same for her. She worried for his well-being, and he for hers. In the end, he didn't want to tell her anything that would make that weight any more cumbersome.

Keeping his own counsel on the Youngblood issue, he said, "No worries. All will be well."

She smiled and did not press that issue, but she asked, "Have you seen the wanted posters?"

Black actually laughed out loud, throwing his head back. "I did," he said, showing all his white teeth. "The drawings look like a cross between me and you. I replaced the ones I encountered with posters I drew."

Moses chuckled too. "You got wit. Watch yoself, and don't underestimate."

"I promise to keep my eyes peeled," he said, his tone more serious.

"I will move out in the morning with the peoples," she informed him.

"I'm moving out tonight. I'll send word when I'm back in Canada. Will you come to the antislavery convention being held in Canada?"

"Yes, I'll be there."

"You will stay with me, then. I will not be back this way for a while. I have to address the issue with John. He is making political waves with his rants."

"John Brown is troublesomeness, but you will endure. You just hates being the legendary Black at times, and you hates that what you do is needed."

He nodded. She was right about how he felt, and though he didn't show it, hearing Youngblood's name made him angry. If she was hearing about Will and Youngblood, the matter was serious. He would out Youngblood's light and think no more about it. Black was ready to make his stance known.

The Turner house was well lit and open to guests coming and going. Great care was taken to make the house as lovely as possible. In the parlor, the large black piano reflected the elegant candlelight as the fire danced on the many wicks. The furniture was moved out and replaced by beautiful cream-colored, straight-backed chairs that were divided into two groups on either side of the room. Against the wall were tables that overflowed with refreshments in preparation for the festivities. The slaves stood around the porch at dusk watching through the windows as the younger Turner took his vows.

Black and Otis stood among them, and though they were recognized by the slaves, they gave no reaction to seeing them. When Will kissed his bride, everyone cheered, and the celebration moved to the ballroom. Otis gave Black the nod, and they separated to handle business. Youngblood patrolled the outer perimeter of the plantation, keeping watch and discouraging the notion to run.

Breaking from the party and all the distraction it caused, Black moved silently in the shadows, following his prey back to the stables. He listened as Youngblood gave orders to another overseer to keep patrolling. "Anyone found making a run for it will be whipped for his trouble. I'll be at the main house; the younger Turner is requesting to speak with me. You can find me there should you need me."

Black watched from the shadows as Youngblood stepped onto the path, whistling a tune. As Youngblood made his way between the cabins back to the main house, he turned, looking about cautiously. Seeing nothing, he resumed his step. As Black continued to observe his victim, his blood raced with the anticipation of resolution. He smiled into the darkness as he watched Youngblood's steps falter for a second time; the overseer looked about again, still seeing nothing.

When he turned back to continue up the path, he was blindsided by a punch square to the jaw. He staggered, trying to get his bearings, but Black, who had been tortured both physically and emotionally, had no mercy for him. Spinning Youngblood quickly, Black locked his arm about Youngblood's neck, effectively closing off his airway. The more Youngblood struggled, the weaker he became until he faded. Tightening his forearm about Youngblood's throat, Black pulled him into the trees, and once in the shelter of total darkness, he yanked upward, twisting Youngblood's neck until it cracked.

Letting Youngblood's body drop where he stood, Black stared out toward the main house. He wanted to go and shake Will's ass down and leave no loose ends. Black would leave this warning, the disappearance of Youngblood, but should he have to come back again, he would burn this bitch to the ground. Mama was safe with him now; her presence on this plantation had kept the peace, and that peace was now broken. Sunday was his, and he would never let her go. All bets were off, and he would make certain they understood that.

Turning his attention back to Youngblood, he reached down and slung him over his shoulder. Lifting his leather-brimmed hat from the tree branch, he placed it on his head, walking deeper into the woods. Reaching the horses, he found that Otis was there with the man Youngblood had spoken to in the stables, also dead. Black and Otis slung both bodies over one horse, and they moved out and headed home.

At the safe house in Pennsylvania, Moses had moved on, and both bodies were thrown into an unmarked grave and buried. As he mounted his horse, pointing it toward Canada, Black realized that he couldn't just go home. He had too much pent-up energy. Turning to Otis, he said, "I'll be along later, maybe a few days behind you."

Otis looked at him like he'd lost his damned mind. "You know Sunday is waiting for ya. Why are you gon send me to explain why you ain't there? She is going to know. Don't."

"I have not asked for your help," he said quietly. He knew Otis was right, but he just wasn't ready to see her. Turning his horse, he broke from the group and rode off.

"Shit," Otis hissed.

4

MARCH 1859

The weeks dragged by for Sunday, and she found that at night she did more thinking than sleeping. The time she spent talking with Mama and Iris was invaluable. They explained a lot about men and women, things she didn't know. Mama began speaking about Turner and Black, for that matter. She found that while Big Mama had been good to her, she didn't really know her. They were sitting at the kitchen table one morning discussing not getting pregnant when Mama said, "The drinks ain't foolproof, but they's better than nothing. I used them when Turner came at night."

"How long did he visit before you got pregnant?" Iris asked, trying to estimate for Sunday's sake.

"'Bout two years," Mama confided.

Sunday was shocked at the conversation and afraid that Mama would stop talking, so she made no comment. She left the questions to Iris, who said, "I didn't know you had children, Ellen."

The sun was shining through the kitchen window on Mama, her skin radiant and healthy, her gray hair platted in two braids. She played with her napkin as she sat to the table folding and refolding it. Sunday stared at the yellow tablecloth with red flowers, almost counting the splashes of red, trying to go unnoticed.

Mama took so long to answer that Sunday looked up just as she said, "Yes, I had a child wit' Jacob, a girl. She died 'fore Black was born. Between the breast-feedin' and the drink, I never got wit' child again. It was for the better I had Black and the other boys and then Sunday. As far as children go, I's content."

Sunday could hear the sadness in her voice. Unable to ignore her pain, she reached out and squeezed her hand. Mama reciprocated.

"I was not lucky enough to get pregnant, but as a slave, I think it was for the better too. I didn't meet Paul until later, and he had a daughter that was sold to another plantation," Iris said.

"I know. I was there when it happened. Black ain't been able to find her. She probably dead by now," Mama said with no emotion.

"I love Paul, and it hurts to know that he can't find his child," Iris said.

"I understands," Mama said, shaking her head.

The three of them were silent for a moment, and then Iris said, "You need to drink the mix daily and ready yourself for when he comes back. He's cranky because he wants you."

Embarrassed, Sunday stared back at the tablecloth, and then Mama chimed in, "This is gon to be interesting; he's in love. He needs to accept it. Oh, he knows he loves ya, but he don't know what to do 'bout it yet."

Sunday just listened without comment, mostly because she was in shock. She didn't know Mama talked that much and could be so clear about her thoughts; it would take some getting used to.

As she did her chores, she found that they helped to pass the time. In the dining room, she polished the beautiful mahogany table with matching chairs and china cabinet until she could see her reflection in the wood. On the wall to the left of the table was a large mirror framed with intricately carved wood painted gold to add to the beauty of the mirror and the room. The sofa in the sitting room was a burnt orange that rolled out around the top like a scrolled piece of paper trimmed in brown. It stood on small wooden legs that she got down on her knees to polish. Pulling the drapes back and allowing the sun into the room added to the atmosphere.

Sunday polished the banister and even the steps, making them gleam. On the second floor, which she only ventured to once, she opened the windows, airing the rooms and adding flowers. All the rooms had large beds in the center; the first room had a black wrought iron bed with a cherrywood dresser that held a large mirror. In the corner was a matching stand for the water basin. The second room had a cloth headboard and footboard of cream with a matching wood dresser painted white and polished well. The drapes were a light blue, adding color to an otherwise white room. In the corner was a matching stand and basin. Lastly, in the third bedroom, the bed was like the ones downstairs with the four posters that reached the ceiling; the covering on the bed seemed to be animal fur. Diagonally from the bed and off to the right of the fireplace sat a black tub. She noticed there were no pictures to dust like downstairs, and she thought to ask him if she could hang some of the paintings.

The dressmaker had come early one morning with the dresses, and Sunday had a fitting in her room. The dresses were casual and serviceable. She had a yellow, blue, green, brown, and cream dress for a total of five, and it was the most clothing that she ever owned. Sally, the dressmaker, was a young, beautiful white woman with lots of gold hair piled high on her head. She kept her hair pinned so she could work, and it added to the beauty of her face. She tucked and pinned, and then tucked and pinned some more until Sunday was sore from standing so completely still. Just when she was about to call an end to the fitting, Sally pulled two more dresses from the box.

Sally handed a dress to Sunday and stood back as Sunday tried to make sense of the dress; it was a finer material and felt good to the touch. Sally stepped forward and showed Sunday how to get the dress on. Two layers of lush fabric fell to her feet and clung ever so slightly to her thin figure. The dress was midnight black and cut to leave her shoulders and back bare. A fancy shawl completed the outfit. When Paul pushed a stand-alone mirror into the room, Sunday didn't recognize herself. Never had she owned anything as beautiful as this dress.

"I made undergarments for you to go with this dress," Sally clucked as she grabbed at Sunday's waist, pinning the excess material. "Do you like silk? It looks great on you."

Moving around her, Sally kept working, and Sunday was admiring the woman in the mirror until she heard Sally gasp, and then it hit home. She couldn't wear the dress because of a beating that she had sustained when she was a child that left her with serious and angry-looking scars. Wearing a dress with the back out was not something she could do. She had allowed herself to forget, and she had promised herself that she would not fail to recall her past. She tried to turn and hide, but Sally grabbed her arm, saying, "Don't hide. Stand tall; you have nothing to be ashamed of. Wear the dress. You look beautiful, and don't forget it."

Sunday tried on an olive-green dress, and Sally adjusted it. She worked tirelessly right in Sunday's room, getting her clothing ready. They were silent, and as Sunday watched her work, she didn't know if she could wear the fancier dresses because of the scars. She couldn't help it; she worried that she was wasting Sally's time. Life had been so good that she had not really given the past much thought; now she felt bombarded with thoughts of plantation life.

As the days pressed on, the clothing situation had her down, and she was concerned that she had wasted Black's money on dresses she could not wear. She didn't even know how to broach the subject with him. Spending time with him and feeling safe had pushed some bad memories into the shadows, and she found they were there waiting to spring out at a moment's notice. She wanted his touch, and she felt empowered that she had chosen him. Now she was faced with the shame and the scars; she feared him seeing them, plain and simple. She wanted to be beautiful for him, and her apprehension was not born out of fear of rejection—it was born out of fear of pity. She did not want Black's pity; she wanted his protection, his passion, his masculinity, his loyalty, and his love. In exchange she would give him her honesty, her passion, her femininity, her loyalty, and her love.

His life was about the struggle of obtaining and maintaining freedom, and while she appreciated the value of what he did, she wanted to be a woman experiencing the man she loved. Sunday wanted a moment just to be.

Sunday had gone down into the little city that made up Fort Independence to be with the women and help with the children. She was just trying to be of service and feel useful. They laughed and talked while chasing the little ones around, and she realized she loved visiting. The families were hardworking, and there always seemed to be something to do—sewing, cooking, cleaning, or starting gardens—and Sunday was in the thick of it. Work took her mind off the things she worried about, but mostly keeping busy helped her manage missing him. She missed him so badly that it hurt, and she was worried because she knew he lived a dangerous life.

Late one afternoon, Sunday decided to go and help Bea, one of the women who lived near the gate within the fort. Bea was a short, dark-skinned, plump woman, and she was very jovial. Sunday liked being in her company because Bea made her laugh. Bea had two small boys, and she was married to Joe the blacksmith. During her visit with Bea, Sunday heard a commotion on the pathways, and Bea stepped to the door, opening it. Because the little cabin was so close to the fort gate, Sunday could hear the pounding hooves of the horses and the slamming of the gate after the men entered.

Elated, Sunday excused herself to Bea and rushed back to the house to wait for him. She figured that Black had work to do before he could come see her, and she would just wait. She was pleased he was home, and she couldn't wait to tell him so. Once at the house, she began pacing the porch, because she was too excited to sit. She almost screamed from the sheer pleasure of having him home. He was home, and that was all that mattered.

The sun was beginning to set when Sunday finally gave in and sat on the porch. She patiently waited to catch her first glimpse of him. The weather was very chilly. With her coat and scarf pulled tightly about her, Sunday sat staring in the distance. The sky turned purple as day blended with night, and just when she thought she would burst from the excitement, Otis rode up, his horse sidestepping and slightly agitated.

"Hello, Otis."

"Miss Sunday, good to see you," he said, trying for small talk.

"Everythang go all right? Everyone safe? Where is Black?" she said, asking one question after another.

"Everyone is fine, and we has two new additions to our family at Fort Independence."

"Black," she said. She could sense that something wasn't right. Watching Otis a little closer made her realize that he was uncomfortable talking to her. He had something to tell her, and he was sidestepping like his horse. The thought that Black might be hurt dawned on her, and she grabbed the banister to steady herself.

Otis, seeing where her mind was going, quickly said, "Oh, he ain't hurt. He had to take care of some business, and he will be along in a few days."

Sunday looked at Otis, trying to get eye contact, and he lowered his eyes to the ground. She could see him pleading for her to let it rest there, but she didn't. "I's sorry you was tasked wit' havin' to tell me Black ain't here."

"He will be along shortly," he said again reassuringly, stepping over her statement.

"I's sure he will be along after a while. I don't know if I feels sorry for you for havin' to tell me or me for havin' to hear the lie," Sunday whispered as she turned to go back up the steps.

"Sunday," Otis said, swinging down from his horse.

"Go to Mary. She misses ya. Black is grown and *free* to do what he wants."

Black lay in front of the fireplace naked and totally in his glory, the flickering light dancing off his beautifully carved body. Camille loved him and was aware that he was looking for comfort and was not in love. He seemed distracted and mentally not with her. She didn't press him, glad to be in his presence and waiting patiently for him to take her again. He did not disappoint.

Pulling her up on all fours, he entered her slowly from behind. Unhurriedly, he began a rhythm of stroking her in and out. When he approached the edge, he backed away, changing positions and placed Camille on her back. Leaning down, he kissed her mouth, lingering on her breasts, and then entered her again. She was tight and offered the oblivion he needed.

"Oh, Black … ohhhh," she moaned.

Hearing her find satisfaction, he let himself go, unable to find the same pleasure he had achieved in previous encounters with her. Grunting his completion, he fell on top of her, and she held him. When he steadied his breathing, he moved to lie next to her on his stomach.

"What could have you so troubled?" Camille asked.

"The same old stuff," he said, never truly answering her.

She was older than he was by twelve summers, and she knew the day would come when this would end. Rubbing his back, she said, "I want you to be content. You deserve happiness, but you have to allow yourself to be happy. It's a choice."

He did not respond. Instead, he turned over and allowed her to lay her head on his chest. At dawn on the third day, he dressed to head home. Kissing Camille in the doorway and never looking back, he rode out.

It was time to face his life and Sunday.

5

UPPER CANADA, APRIL 1859

In the days that followed, Sunday didn't come out of her room, leaving Iris and Mama to debate about which of them would go and talk to her. Mama won the honor of having to deal with her broken heart. Walking back through the hall from the kitchen to Sunday's room, she knocked on the door and waited. When Sunday didn't answer, Mama opened the door and peeked in.

Sunday sat in front of the window looking at the trees that were starting to show signs of life. She was trying to focus on the flowers and the colors that had come together, loudly announcing that spring had arrived. And although spring had begun, the weather had a chill that matched the way she was feeling. Adding to the chill was Mama wanting to talk about the very issue that highlighted her stupidity. If Mama had come to talk, the burden of this conversation would be on her because Sunday didn't want to talk.

"We missed ya at breakfast. I come to see 'bout ya and make sure ya well," Mama said and then waited. Sunday didn't respond, and so she continued. "They say Black had a good trip and should be home directly."

She could hear Mama's voice getting closer after the door clicked shut, and when she placed her hand on her shoulder, Sunday looked up, acknowledging her presence in the room. "I's well."

Mama smiled down at Sunday and could see that Sunday had been crying. "May I ask why ya been cryin'?"

Sunday stood, giving Mama the chair, and she unceremoniously plopped down to sit in front of the chair. Mama reached out and rubbed her back until Sunday finally gave in and laid her head on Mama's lap.

"He is confused and has made a mess of thangs. It ain't a excuse—it just what's happening," Mama whispered.

Sunday began to cry softly, and when she could finally speak, she responded, "I don't want his touch now."

"I understands. Be thankful that you can say, 'Don't touch me.' I has felt like you feel right now and many a day had to accept his touch. You has the power."

"I cain't face him. How can I face him? I knows he is wit' another woman. I could tell from the look in Otis's eyes."

Trying to remain neutral in the face of Black's actions was difficult, and Mama didn't want Sunday to think she loved him more than her. Mama understood that she was the tie that would bind them even if they couldn't move pass this. When she spoke to Sunday, she attempted to offer her food for thought. "Decide what you angry 'bout so you can be clear when you talks wit' him. Is you angry 'cause you thought you had an understandin'? Did he make an agreement wit' you and you wit' him? Is you angry 'cause he went to another woman and ain't see you as woman enough? Is you woman enough? Do you wants to talk 'bout his actions, and can you handle the truth? Can you deal wit' the truth as he figures it? How will you carry on from here? Can you forgive him? Is there somethin' to forgive? Is you woman enough to set the rules for what you will and won't take? Do you knows what you should and shouldn't take?"

She looked up at Mama, saying, "He sees me as weak and not woman enough."

"How you see yoself?"

"I sees me as weak. It hurts so bad," Sunday whispered.

"This don't excuse him. It just makes clear the matter and divides it so's you can figure on it. Example, you hurt, yet you ain't made no commitments to one another. You angry 'cause you *thought* you had an understandin' … not the same as having one. First, deal wit' yoself, then deal wit' his actions gon forward after settin' the rules. And most impotant—once you set your limits, you must be prepared to live by them."

"So just forget this happened."

"Hell, naw … setting limits can be sore business for both of ya. Make sure he don't forget this won't be accepted. Make his ass figure on it long and hard," Mama said, smiling.

Sunday couldn't help it—she laughed aloud.

Black rode hard, making it to Fort Independence by nightfall, the men greeting him as he came through the gate. They lined up to give their reports, and Black listened, interested in them and what they had to say. Admittedly he lingered, unable to face her, and where he had attempted to get comfort, he had now added guilt. Anthony had taken his horse to the stables. Grabbing his saddlebag and hanging it over his shoulder, Black made his way to the barracks.

Stepping into the barracks, he saw a long line of beds all neatly made on either side of the room. It was well lit, and he could see the door leading to the stables on the opposite end of the aisle. As he was thinking about the shift and who was on duty, he saw Otis come through the door. He was relieved to see him because he didn't want to have to go get him from his home. Facing Mary wasn't at the top of his list. He was sure Otis told her. *Big mouth.*

Upon seeing Black, he whistled and said, "Coward. You here 'cause you cain't face her."

Black grinned sheepishly before saying, "Even though she may not know, I just …" Black trailed off. He and Otis were like brothers in the struggle. As far as a personal life, he had nothing to discuss, so this was different.

"Oh, she knows and gave me a set down to boot. You have a problem on your hands," Otis said, happy to deliver the message.

Black became silent, and Otis put his hand up, saying, "Before you blame me, I told you to come on home wit' us. You said you ain't asking for my help."

Staring at him, Black wanted to punch him, but he knew this was his fault. He sighed before changing the subject. "How are the new additions, the boy and his father?"

"The father is called Smitty. He is a blacksmith, and his skill is needed here at Fort Independence. The boy is Curtis and is well behaved. They will be a fine addition."

Otis noticed that Black had changed the subject; it was his way when he couldn't cope. Still, he offered, "When I came to love Mary, it was difficult, and I made the same mistakes. Mary being a white woman and my being colored and a slave added to the hurt. She trusted me to stand against the world with her, and I came up short, embarrassing her. I have not failed her since."

Black listened, not commenting, and, to Otis's surprise, he said, "Thank you." Turning on his heels, he left the barracks, heading for the house.

Once in the foyer, he could hear voices, so he walked toward them. Stepping into the kitchen, he saw Iris and Mama giggling, and standing at the double sink washing dishes was Sunday. Mama was the first to notice him, and she stood, coming to hug him. Iris became no-nonsense, asking him, "Where will you take your bath?"

He had his arm around Mama, and while Iris spoke, he stared at Sunday. She wore a yellow dress that complemented her skin tone with her hair pulled from her face by a ribbon, leaving it tamed and riotous at the same time. He was attacked by his own senses. He missed her, and this was the first time he allowed himself to admit it. Somehow she looked older and more aware, and he was sure he was the reason.

Before he could answer Iris, Sunday responded, "He can take his bath in his own room. I has moved to the bedroom upstairs on the end of the hall."

Iris, being the traitor that she was, turned and began taking her orders from Sunday, and Black sighed. *And so it begins …*

Assessing him, Sunday saw that he was tired and covered in dust from his travels, and she steeled herself against the emotion she felt when he stepped into view. He wore brown pants with black boots and a short black cowhide overcoat, his saddlebags thrown over his shoulder. He was a sight to behold, and she had to stop herself from thinking of him with another woman. The thought suffocated her, making her forget to breathe. She began working through Mama's questions right where she stood, backing away from the sensation of being hurt.

Iris and Mama left to tend him, and when they were alone, he asked, "You left my room?"

"Is there an issue wit' me and the room upstairs? If'n it is, I can move into one of the cabins," she said, never breaking eye contact.

"Are you threatening me?" he asked, his voice low and menacing.

Although she wanted to faint from his tone alone, she responded and did not flinch. "Why would you feel threatened by me of all peoples?"

His eyes narrowed as he collected his thoughts, and then he said, "Why would you move into one of the cabins?"

"Is that what I said? Or did I say if'n you has issue wit' the choice I made - if'n you has a question, ask it. Don't try to bully me."

Folding his arms over his chest, he stood there, unclear on what to say next. He hadn't expected this, and he didn't know whether he was pissed off or aroused.

Drying her hands, she placed the towel on the sink, and stepping past him, she said, "I hopes ya sleep well. Ya looks tired." And then she was gone.

In the coming weeks, Black noticed that Sunday made herself so busy that he barely saw her. After doing her chores, she left the house, and from the study window, he could see her with the children or heading to the school. He sighed, rubbing his forehead. As he stood in his usual place at the window watching her, his pain from missing her was acute. When she encountered the people of the fort, he noticed that the interactions appeared warm and welcoming. She came to him for nothing, not even her reading lessons, and this only made him feel more left out.

Mama still came to eat lunch with him. As she entered the study one afternoon, placing a tray of cold chicken, warm bread and butter, and hot coffee before him, she asked as she was seating herself, "You gettin' much done?"

Placing his pen down on the desk, Black leaned back in his chair and smiled. Mama was a welcome distraction. "Yes. I'm trying to prepare for the conference coming in a few weeks. I received a letter from

Frederick Douglass stating he would like to attend the conference, and he wondered if he could stay on with us. I sent a message back saying that he is welcome and that it would be an honor to have him."

Mama offered, "Iris, Sunday, Paul, and me will make the house ready."

"Moses will come too, and I suspect John will want to stay to see if I have a personal issue with him. Frederick will travel with William Garrison. If nothing else, this should be interesting."

"Judging from the look on yo face, this is comin' soon. What was the date on the letter?"

"April 5, 1859," he answered.

"Hmm … 'bout a week ago, when the gatherin' happenin'?"

"The conference is May 2 and will last for two days."

"Iris and me will plan the supper and ready the rooms. Sunday can sleep on wit' me so's we has an extra room."

"Leave Sunday in her room. I will sleep in my studio."

Mama stared at him; she could see his pain and his attempt to hide it. She knew he would not talk to her about Sunday, and so she did not comment. Nodding her acknowledgment, she stood and headed toward the door. Just before leaving his study, she said, "I needs to get wit' Iris so's we can get started."

After Mama left, he stood and walked over to the window to stretch and to look for Sunday. She was standing by a tree speaking with the blacksmith and smiling up at him. Black was jealous as he watched them engage each other. The little boy was holding her hand, trying to pull her along, and she was giggling. The scene was more than he could stomach, so he headed outside to see what they were laughing about.

Sunday saw Black step out onto the porch and into the sunlight. He stood there for a moment, dripping with masculinity, and she was unsettled. She loved him, but she felt enslaved to her love for him and not freed by it as she had in the beginning. This caused her to back away from him and admit that she was not strong enough to partner him, and she hurt with the realization. He wore black pants and boots with a white shirt opened at the throat, his gun strapped at his side, and as he moved toward them, she could see that his mood was anything but amiable.

Curtis saw him coming and tried to hide in Sunday's skirts; he must have sensed Black's mood, as well. The blacksmith was a light-skinned man with light-brown eyes and high cheekbones. He was handsome by any standard, and he stood the same height as Black, although his frame was smaller. Sunday trembled inside, but on the outside, she behaved as though she didn't notice his mood, and if Smitty noticed, he never gave it away.

When Black reached them, Smitty reached out his hand, saying, "Good to see you this fine day. My son and I are grateful for all you have done for us. This here is Curtis, and I am Smith, but folks just call me Smitty."

Curtis looked up at Black, and stepping forward, he shook his hand, never letting go of Sunday's hand. She could feel him shaking, and she smiled, thinking, *Me too, Curtis.*

"Nice to finally meet the two of you, as well." Black smiled, the smile never really reaching his eyes. "I see you have met Sunday."

"Yes. Miss Sunday has been keeping Curtis busy while I work."

Unsure of what Black would say next, she spoke up. "Curtis and me been enjoyin' each other's company. I thank he is my friend 'cause I has cookies."

Curtis was brown skinned like his father, with short black hair, brown eyes, and a sweet smile.

Black smiled down at him, a real smile, before saying, "Cookies are important. I could understand that."

Before taking his leave, Smitty said, "Thank you again for me and my son. If ever I could be of service—"

"I will," Black said, shaking his hand again.

As little Curtis and his daddy walked off, Sunday, trying not to be alone with Black, made her move to leave when his words stopped her. "How long are you going to avoid me?"

"You's a busy man, and I's tryin not to be bothersome."

"Have I said that you are in the way?" he answered, trying to control his attitude.

"What difference do it make if'n we talks? Do you really tell me anythang?"

He stepped toward her, and she stepped back against the tree. Black leaned in, appreciating the sun on her skin and the beauty that radiated from her, even in anger.

"It troubles me that you avoid me." His voice was low and filled with emotion.

He was so close that she swallowed before saying, "I understands it bothered me that you dodged me too."

Stepping back from her, he shoved his hands in his pockets to keep from touching her, and in her eyes, he saw the pain he caused. He wanted to say sorry, but the word stuck in his throat. "Try to get to know me again. I won't fail you twice," he pleaded.

They stood there staring at each other, and she was angry with herself because her eyes watered up, and the tears spilled over. Mentally, she scolded herself for being weak and wanting to run to him. He reached out, and she sidestepped, whispering, "Don't."

"Please don't give up on me." He turned and walked away.

Sunday was shaken as she watched him head back toward the house. He was intense, and all the emotions that she had surrounding him were raw. She wanted to run off toward the fields, but the men were there readying the soil. She retreated to her room, where she actually broke down and cried. Mama must have seen the exchange because she appeared and offered her support. Sunday hadn't even heard her enter the room.

"You doin' way better than you thank," Mama said soothingly.

"But I cried in front of him," Sunday whispered.

"The goal here ain't to hide yo hurt; it's to make him see the pain he caused. He needs you, and he sees how much now. Keep doin' what you doin'."

Smitty finally had the opportunity to get away for a few hours and go into town. He had two goals; one was to send a telegram, the other was to visit the local whorehouse. Stepping into the dry-goods store, he was greeted by the clerk, a tall, middle-aged white man with bad posture and pasty skin. When he spoke, his voice was soft and patient.

"How can I help you today?" he asked.

"I would like to send a message, please," Smitty answered, looking around the store.

"Certainly," the clerk said. "What will it read?"

I HAVE ARRIVED AND WHAT I HAVE FOUND WILL MAKE
YOU HAPPY FOR A MONTH OF SUNDAYS

"That will be thirty cents," the clerk said.

Smitty paid the thirty cents to complete his transaction and left. He was on a mission. Stepping into the afternoon sun, he headed for the saloon for a stiff drink and a willing woman.

Gazing out the window, Black watched night fall. He had not come out of his study for hours, waiting for the hour to grow late so that he didn't have to encounter anyone. Iris and Paul, he was sure, had gone home, and Mama would be asleep. As he walked back to his room, he switched directions, heading for his studio. The studio was his tension reliever, and he was looking forward to drawing her.

Sitting in the chair, he sketched her eyes and the pain he had seen. Once he completed the drawing, he was unsure why he had sketched her, hurting himself with every stroke of the charcoal. Leaning back, he tried to relax, and still those eyes came to him, haunting him. Standing, he began pacing the studio, trying to get comfortable in his own skin. He decided to go to bed, and as he made his way down the hall, he heard a noise in the kitchen.

Sunday sat at the kitchen table alone, sipping a cup of warm milk. She too was having trouble sleeping. When she looked up, it was directly into his eyes, and because it was so unexpected, she felt it physically. She wanted to hold his gaze, but it was too heavy, and so she put it down, unable to bear the weight. She thought if she said nothing, perhaps he would continue on to his room and make it easy on both of them. The pain she felt was born of wanting his touch and realizing there was a faceless woman who welcomed his touch, as well.

"Can't sleep?" he asked.

Clearing her throat, she whispered, "No."

"May I join you?" he asked, waiting for her permission.

It was his home. "Course ya can."

He took the seat across from her, and he was so thankful she didn't run away that he decided he would try for her friendship. "We are having a dinner party in about a week. Has Mama or Iris told you?"

"I saw Mama today. She ain't mentioned it."

"We will have four guests—John Brown, Frederick Douglass, William Garrison, and Moses. They will be staying here at the house."

She had not heard of the men, but she had heard of Moses. Sunday was actually interested. "I can move in wit' Mama. How long is they stayin'?"

"You don't have to move in with Mama. I'm giving Moses my room, and Garrison and Douglass will take the rooms upstairs. They will probably stay here for two days, as they are attending an antislavery conference in Chatham." He sighed.

"Ya don't wants them to stay?" she asked, not expecting him to answer.

"I have no problem with them staying," he answered, gauging what to say, and then deciding just to speak freely as he had asked her. "The problem is John. He is a friend, and he is fierce in his stance against slavery. He wants me to join forces with him in a revolt that will probably see us both dead by the end of this year."

As he spoke, she showed no reaction to his words on the outside; on the inside, she was screaming. She realized he dealt with rough issues, but this was a serious dose of reality.

"You has decided on joinin' him?" she asked, holding her breath.

"I can't join him. The people here depend on me, and the people that can't wait on the law to change depend on my helping them take their freedom. I don't fear dying young; I have come to terms with that. I fear dying and not having made a difference. I fear dying now leaving you and Mama unprotected. Otherwise, I have accepted the inevitable."

She needed to change her focus. It seemed she had no idea what he dealt with. "I takes it you told John that and he ain't acceptin' no for an answer?"

"I declined. The rest is not his business. He has become sour and has attempted to use my father as leverage."

"What you willin' to do for him?" she asked. "Is you willin' to help him at a distance?"

"I see no reason to send men to their deaths on something I know will not work. He is attempting to overthrow the government. I can respect his cause but not his method, and I am not opposed to killing a man who stands between me and freedom. I am opposed to recklessness."

"We needs to figure on handling him, and you needs to figure on some 'tween that will calm the waters."

Black's eyes narrowed as he watched her, and she looked deep in thought. He was about to comment when she said, "If'n ya don't gives men, can you gives the guns? If'n you don't gives the guns, can you gives coins?"

She stood up and began pacing between the table and the sink, deep in thought. Then she turned to him, saying, "If'n you gives coins, it won't be tracked back to you, and if'n this revolt works, you will have more strength."

Smiling, he said, "The revolt won't work. The country will have to go to civil war, and every man will have to choose a side. Not just forty men—*all* will have to choose."

"What is you willing to give in coins? What you gives needs to say I'm supporting you, but I's forgoing to do it. The amount also needs to say you believes in him."

He just stared at her, and she said, "I ain't telling you nothing new, is I? You already thunk all this."

"Yes, but hearing the plan spoken and so well thought out has helped me." What he didn't say was how intelligent he thought she was and that he was praying she gave him another chance.

Over the next week, Black was gone from the house doing his turn in the barracks like the rest. Sunday, Mama, and Iris planned the meal for the dinner and readied the house for guests. The dressmaker was back to help Mama and Iris with their dress choices for the evening. The residents of Fort Independence came forward to help, making it a real affair. The men cleaned the outside of the house and gardens leading to the back of the house. The flowers were a riotous collage of color, making the setting magical. The women baked pies, cakes, and a variety of breads and biscuits.

It was understood by the inhabitants of the fort that while they were fortunate enough to obtain freedom, there were those who were not. The weather had become warmer, and it looked as though the people planned to party in the streets. Sunday was humbled and began to think maybe her past thoughts were selfish. She had not seen Black until the day the guests were to arrive.

It was early morning when the coach pulled up to the gate of the fort carrying three guests, Moses, Frederick, and William. Sunday and Mama welcomed them, and Iris directed the staff with getting the luggage. Black came from his study to greet them and make introductions.

"Moses," Black greeted her. "I hope your trip went well."

"Traveling was good. I's honored to be here."

"Gentlemen," he said to Frederick and William.

In unison, they replied, "Black." And they all shook hands.

Just then, the people who had gathered around parted, and a white man on a black horse came forward, followed by about twenty men. Some were white and some black, all with guns. Without an introduction, Sunday knew who he was. He swung down from his horse and climbed the steps, greeting Black, the other men, and Moses.

"John, I am glad you are here," Black said.

"Black," he responded, shaking his hand. John's expression was closed.

Turning, Black made the introductions. "Lady and gentlemen, allow me to introduce to you my family—my mother, Ellen, my aunt Iris, my uncle Paul, and my queen, Sunday."

Moses stepped forward, first taking Sunday's hand and giving it a squeeze. She wore a brown dress with black boots. On her head she wore a white, flowery piece of cloth pinned to cover her bun. She had small eyes that were sharp with wisdom and dark brown skin that showed the rough life she led. Smiling at Sunday, she said, "Nice to meet Black's queen."

Sunday didn't flinch at the introduction, and Black was yet again impressed. They were having problems, he and Sunday, but Black wanted to be clear that she was his.

Frederick stepped forward with a head full of curls that were black and gray, his skin smooth like leather, his complexion dark. He had a large nose with brown eyes and a mouth that made him appear angry. When he spoke, he was eloquent and sounded educated, his voice like velvet. "Sunday, the pleasure is all mine."

"Mr. Douglass," she said.

"Call me Frederick, please."

William was next, and Sunday thought him kind. He had a slim face, blue eyes, sharply angled cheekbones and nose, and very small lips. He was balding with a small amount of hair combed over the bald spot. Like Frederick, he was educated, and when he spoke, his voice shook slightly. "Sunday, it's nice to meet you."

"Good to meet you; we's so glad to have you," Sunday replied.

John stepped forward with wild gray and brown hair; his skin was weather roughened, his brown eyes set too closely in his head just above a hook nose. Standing closely, Sunday could see that he wasn't angry; he was hurt. "May I call you John?" she asked, and he smiled.

"Of course, and it is a pleasure to meet you, Sunday," he said, and she smiled.

After all the introductions were made, Black turned to the crowd that had gathered and said in a loud, strong voice, "I give you Frederick Douglass, William Garrison, Harriet Tubman, and last but not least, John Brown. These people standing before you remain true to the struggle. Their very presence ensures that the loved ones you left behind to forge a new life will one day be free. We will not give up the fight for liberty. Our goal is to witness the first black free generation. We are fugitives. Let us hope the next generation is not."

The people began to cheer. Black held up his hand, and the crowd grew hushed. "Let us celebrate and enjoy the accomplishments we have made. May we never grow tired of defending freedom, yet let us actively pursue life."

As his guests followed Black into the house, Sunday could hear the fiddlers start with their upbeat tunes, and when she looked over her shoulder, she could see the people dancing in the pathways. They were setting up tables and weighing them down with food and drink. She smiled. The festivities had begun.

They planned a great meal of trout and a vegetable medley along with white wine. Black requested that dinner be light so that he would be sharp while discussing business. Out in the back of the house was a large bricked pit with large flames, and standing around the flames were the men working with the meat. It was like an assembly line of men and women making the meal happen, yet so much more was being cooked for the following days. There were collards, mile-high biscuits, yams, and chicken, and even a goat was slaughtered.

They were doing it big, and as twilight started, lanterns were lit to keep the activities going. As Sunday stood on the porch, she noticed the barracks was empty; all the men who watched over the fort were on duty. Three men were stationed on the porch, and three men were in back of the house. All along the pathways, men stood and just watched, speaking with no one. As she observed the setting before her, the gravity of the situation seemed to hit home. He was always on duty.

Leaving the porch, she headed to her bedroom, and she found Iris waiting, wearing a peach dress that went well with her complexion, her hair pulled back in a bun. Except for the gray hair, Iris was ageless, and Sunday thought her beautiful.

"Come sit," Iris said. "I will comb your hair."

Sunday sat as Iris braided her hair into cornrows, starting at the front of her head and bringing it all the way around until it stopped at her crown. Placing a small pin at the end of the braid to hold it in place, Sunday actually felt like Black's queen. Iris helped her shape her eyebrows, and Sunday fidgeted from the pain. Handing Sunday some lavender bath salts and a light-colored gloss to roll over her lips, Iris turned to leave. Before exiting the room, she said, "Wear the black dress. You have come too far to stop now."

Sunday stared after her, and then Iris was gone. Sunday took her bath, and the lavender was just right and not overpowering. When she began to dress, her hands shook from her nerves. Picking up the black dress and walking over to the mirror, she stood there holding it up to look at herself. She could hear him saying, "My queen, Sunday." With strength she didn't understand, she began to dress. Standing in front of the mirror, she stared at herself, examining her appeal as a woman. The first time she tried the dress on, she had backed away from the image of herself dressed in fine clothing. But tonight, she felt beautiful, and she decided to enjoy the feeling. As she smiled to herself, she heard a knock at the door.

Iris was back, handing her a case and saying that Sally had left something for her. Opening the case, there was a pair of earrings along with a matching necklace of black pearls.

"They belonged to Sally's mother, and she says she will be honored if you wear them," said Iris.

Iris helped her, and when she finished, Sunday stepped back, admiring her handiwork.

"Say your ABCs three times before you come downstairs," Iris said.

Sunday smiled, nodding her head as she watched Iris leave the room.

Black leaned against the wall in the sitting room just off the dining room. He waited to catch sight of her. He wore black trousers, black boots, a black shirt, and the harness for his gun. Everyone appeared to be enjoying themselves as the music from the fiddler floated in from the porch. Otis, Mary, and Herschel had come out to mingle. Black's guests talked and debated with Mama and Iris. At times there would be bouts of laughter coming from one group or another. Patiently he waited, and still no Sunday. He was just about to go to her room when she appeared in the doorway of the sitting room.

He was floored by her beauty. She wore an off-the-shoulders black dress, along with matching earrings and necklace. The dress belled slightly at her tiny waist, making it flow as she walked, and he could see that the slippers were laced up her legs with every step she took. She was looking for him, and when she spotted him, she walked toward him, noticing no one else.

When she reached him, he smiled down at her, saying, "Hello, my beauty."

She was going to respond when Frederick walked over, wanting her attention. "Sunday, you look exquisite."

Turning to face him, she smiled. "Yo handsome yoself, sir."

When she turned her back, Black saw the scars from an obviously vicious beating. Placing his hand on the small of her back, he stepped up and whispered in her ear, "You are so beautiful."

Turning from Frederick back to Black, she smiled and placed her hand in his. She was thankful for his approval. Frederick, seeing three was a crowd, wandered off to speak with Big Mama.

Sunday mingled with the guests, and she was glad to see Mary.

Black stood off to the side watching her, never speaking unless spoken to. He really was guarding the house. Several times the men came to speak with him, and he gave directions but never moved. Sunday worked the room and then ended up back at his side. When she touched his arm or held his hand, he ached from wanting her.

At dinner, she was seated to Black's right side, and he resided at the head with Otis at the opposite end, Mary to his right. They ate and had polite dinner conversation, realizing that a compromise must be met, and it needed to be one that everyone could live with.

When the dinner came to a close, the guests stepped out on the back porch to enjoy the weather and the music. Black leaned up against the wall, and Sunday stood with him. They both saw John approach with a look of determination, but Black had other plans.

"Might we have a word in your study?" John asked.

"John, your word will keep until morning. I am trying to enjoy the company of a beautiful woman. Have mercy, man."

John looked between Sunday and Black and then nodded. Sunday reached out and touched John's sleeve, saying, "Rest, John. We believes in you."

She saw him visibly relax, saying, "In the morning, Black."

Inside the house, the evening was winding down, but in the pathways and at the front and the back of the house, the party carried on. As the guests thinned out inside, Sunday saw Mama in a plum-colored dress, her hair braided in two plaits that were pinned at the top of her head. She was beautiful. When Sunday approached, Mama did not waste time in saying, "I's proud a both a ya."

"We all did good," Sunday answered.

Black had moved off, speaking with Otis. They looked deep in thought, and then Otis was gone. Black leaned against the door again, staring at Sunday. Feeling a pull, she went to him, and standing in front of him, she looked up with those huge, soulful eyes. It was his undoing, and leaning down, he asked, for her ears only, "May I kiss you all over your body?"

She thought of him coming to terms with dying young and found that she would never be able to come to terms with his early demise. Thinking of the troubles that plagued him, she realized that she feared never knowing his touch. The faceless woman had faded, and she wanted to move forward with him. "Yes," she whispered.

Everyone in the room receded into obscurity, and there was only her. Swallowing hard, he could hear his own heartbeat, and when he was stronger, he asked, "I want to feel you inside and out." His voice was strangled.

She did not try to hide or shy away. Instead, still looking up at him, she said, "I wants you to teach me tonight how to be yo' woman in every sense of the word."

6

MAY 1859

Leaning back against the door, he closed his eyes and attempted to breathe. He was trying to steady himself, and when he opened his eyes, he stared down at her, drinking in this moment—the moment when she accepted him as her man, the moment he was free to touch her, the moment when he knew that he needed her more, the very moment when he knew she made him stronger. He dabbled in the fear of being happy; now he just feared never experiencing her. There were no words that he could speak that would accurately say what he was feeling. Grabbing her hand as though it were a lifeline, they walked toward the stairs, and they climbed them slowly with her in front of him. He watched as her hips swayed, and he was hypnotized. At the top of the steps, she stopped, and he gave her a moment before they moved on down the hall to her room.

Once at the door, he opened it, allowing her to enter the room first. A fire was burning, bathing the room in hues of orange and blue. When Sunday attempted to walk toward the chair, Black grabbed her arm, whirling her around until her back was against the door. Leaning down, he kissed her—and not like the gentle kisses that she had shared with him in the past. His touch was possessive, turbulent, and rough, and she had not expected the intensity he offered.

Breaking the kiss, he whispered in her ear, "Are you sure?"

"Yes," she answered between breaths.

Effortlessly, he lifted her into his arms, carrying her to the bed and laying her down. First he unlaced her slippers, and sliding them from her feet, he caressed her calves. Leaning over her, he kissed her again roughly, and she shuddered. Flipping them until she lay on top of him, he pushed her to straddle him, causing her to have to bunch her dress up to free her legs. Allowing his hands to roam under her dress, he palmed her rear end in his large hands, and he felt the weight of wanting to be inside her. He slid his hands upward, pushing the dress over her head, and she sat on top of him, naked, save for her pantaloons. He couldn't get enough of looking at her and touching her. Permitting his hands to wander to her back, he stroked the scars, and he was amazed at her beauty and inner strength. He stood abruptly, picking her up with him. She slid down his body, causing him to groan from the contact.

Black stepped back and removed his gun and then his shirt, his muscles rippling with the slightest effort. He removed his boots, pants, and then his long underwear, and when he was naked before her, he reached out, taking her hands and placing them on his chest. There was no question he needed her touch, and she followed suit, doing as he requested. He had never felt this kind of intensity before and did not know if he would be able to hold himself in check.

As Black stood before her naked, Sunday wished that she could draw. Black was a true work of art. He had broad shoulders, large arms, and a massive chest. Continuing her assessment of him, she saw that his stomach was trim and carved into bricks of muscle, and down between his legs, his maleness jutted forward, and she felt no embarrassment. He had large thighs corded with muscle, and she swallowed hard at the very thought of his touch. When she looked back into his face, she knew this was one of the most intimate moments in her life, and she was thankful to share it with *him*.

He didn't speak because he couldn't, and reaching out, he pushed her against the large post of the bed. When he stood in front of her, he pushed her pantaloons down over her hips until they were in a pool at her feet. Turning her to face the post, he pressed his body against hers from behind, and he moaned out loud from the contact, and she trembled. Stepping away from her, he kissed the back of her neck and then her shoulders. He trailed kisses down her back, almost kissing each scar individually. He loved her so much he hurt.

He moved her to lie on the bed, and leaning over her, he kissed hard, causing her to pant. Breaking the kiss, he began kissing her neck and shoulders. When he got to her breasts, he took her nipple into his mouth, sucking and then biting her lightly. He heard her breathing become ragged, and in response he did it again to her other nipple. Continuing his exploration, he trailed kisses down her stomach until he reached her womanhood, and she attempted to push him away. He was not deterred, and sticking out his tongue, he tasted her, and she cried out, trying to close her legs. Pressing her legs farther apart, he began stroking her with his tongue, and when she shook and wept her satisfaction, he eased his finger into her, feeling her tighten and release with each wave of sensation. It was his downfall.

He picked her up while she was in the throes of an orgasm, and snatching the fur from the bed, he threw it on the floor in front of the fire. Black wanted to take her on the floor because he didn't want her to get away from him, and the firmness of the floor ensured she would take everything he had to give. Laying her down and pressing her legs apart, he whispered, "Bend your knees." His voice was laced with emotion.

She did as he asked, and he moved between her legs, kissing her. He shared the taste of her sweet nectar on his lips with her and he did not know he could feel this way. He reached down between them and placed his shaft at the mouth of her and pressed. He felt her stretching to accommodate him as he entered her. For better leverage, he backed out and pressed forward, swiftly impaling her.

She tried getting away from him, and when she couldn't, she sobbed his name. "Nat."

Sunday, shoving at his chest and crying his name, brought him back to awareness. He gritted his teeth, and as she squirmed beneath him, he attempted not to slip and fall before time. She was so hot and tight he was dying, and looking down at her, he whispered in a strangled voice, "Please, baby … don't move." When she stilled, he continued, "I love you, Sunday. Please, baby, give me a chance to show you." His voice was hoarse.

At his words, she stilled, and reaching up, she caressed his face. He leaned down, closing his eyes and kissing her. She moved slightly beneath him, trying to adjust, and when he thought he could take no more, he sank deeper. Groaning, he shoved his tongue into her mouth and began moving, and she whimpered. She was turning him on, and he was trying to control himself. Slowly he began to stroke in and out, and when she started moaning, he drank the sounds of pleasure. She opened her legs a little farther, and to his surprise, she reached around, grabbing his ass to push him deeper into her, and he was lost. Picking up momentum, he began thrusting into her, and the sensation was so intense he groaned and clenched his teeth to make it last.

"Oh, Nat!" she cried out. "Nat ... Nat ... Nat ..." she moaned mindlessly, enveloped in the pleasure she was feeling.

Hearing his name over and over was like falling from a cliff into a sea of sensation. The tingling started in his feet and traveled up his body until he was sure that he would die. Throwing his head back, he groaned as he was hit with wave after wave of pleasure. He had not known that an orgasm could be so violent, and there in the throes of such mindless passion, he spoke the truth. "Sunday ... I love you ... I love you ... I love you ... only you." And he collapsed on top of her, still convulsing and tingling.

She hugged him in the aftermath of their lovemaking, and she cried. Turning to lie flat on his back, he pulled her on top of him and whispered, "I promise, only you ... only you." And he held her while she cried.

When her crying subsided, she just rested on top of him, facing the fire, and he could feel her tears as they rolled off his chest. She had not questioned him, and he was thankful. Whatever he thought his reasons for going to Camille were, they seemed insignificant now. He caressed her back, feeling her scars and wanting her again.

"I was afraid ..." Correcting himself, he continued, "I am afraid of getting you with child when we are not a free people. I do not want our children to be fugitives." Hesitating, he said, "I should not have gone to her, and I understand now the pain I have caused you. I am asking for your forgiveness ... *please*. I am committed to you, Sunday."

When she didn't answer, he turned them over, and looking down at her, he asked, "Can you forgive me, baby?"

Breaking eye contact, she returned, "I forgives you, Nat."

He did not like the way she lowered her eyes, and he said, "Don't look away. The shame is mine to bear, not yours."

Bringing her eyes back to his, she could see that he was hurting too. "I forgives you."

He groaned when she said the words again, and it was her sincerity that moved him. Leaning down, he kissed her. Pushing her legs apart with his knees, he entered her, planting himself within her to the hilt. Slowly he pulled all the way out of her and plunged forward, wringing low, soft cries from her. He stroked her over and over, and his breathing was labored and strange in his own ears. When she began meeting him thrust for thrust, he became unglued. She felt so good.

Picking up speed, he began pounding into her, and still she stayed with him. "You are mine," he said, wanting to make sure she understood.

"Yes. Yes. Yes," she responded as she wrapped her legs around his waist, trying to lock him to her as she began to shudder.

Black became frenzied in his strokes, and as she acknowledged being his woman, a satisfaction washed over him so complete that he could not fight it. The sensation started in his feet, engulfing him within seconds, and he moaned, "My queen," before he stiffened, finally letting go.

They remained in each other's arms before the fire, quietly enjoying the bond they had built. In the background, they could hear the people celebrating and the music of the fiddlers as they continued to entertain. It was their last thoughts before they had fallen asleep, arms and legs wrapped about each other.

They were awakened by a knock at the door. Black stood, dressing, and going to the door, he stepped out into the hall. He found Mama standing at the door with a concerned look on her face. The real world was intruding, and he wasn't ready.

"Mama, what is it?"

"John is downstairs waitin' and pacin' the porch. He's angry and feelin' overlooked that he ain't seen you this morning."

"Have water brought up, and have him seated in my study. Tell Paul to send for Otis so that I can resolve the John issue. Do not fret; I need to tend to Sunday before I meet with John."

As she turned, heading to do as he requested, Black stared after her, and he was roiling with anger. The weight of his obligations was encroaching on his quiet time with Sunday. And seeing Mama stressed upset him even more. He sighed. The day had begun.

When he returned to the room, Sunday was clothed in his shirt and sitting on the bed. The fire had died, and although it was spring, the room still had a chill. Taking his robe from the chair, he handed it to her, and as she was slipping her arm into the sleeve, there was another knock at the door. Black opened the door, and stepping aside, he allowed the boys in to fill the tub. They were followed by Mama, who brought food, and Iris, who brought his razor and clothes.

No one spoke, and Sunday suspected it was because he looked so angry. Mama reached for his hand as she was leaving and gave it a squeeze; Black reciprocated. When the door closed, he locked it, and walking over to the mirror, he began shaving. Sunday waited patiently, saying nothing. She understood he was working through the annoyance he was feeling. She busied herself drawing back the drapes, allowing the sunlight into the room as she looked for something to wear.

When he was finished shaving, he began undressing, and it was different in the light of day. Black was beautiful, and though he thought her beautiful, as a man, she doubted he would understand why she used such a word to describe him. It wasn't just physical; it was his strength, his intellect, and his masculinity that called to her. She watched him step in the water and lie back in the tub, and she admitted that she had never seen anything so magnificent.

"Come. Get in with me," he said holding out his hand.

Removing his shirt and robe, she walked over to the tub and climbed in. Black could see the dried blood smeared on her thighs. When she was leaned back against him, he asked, "Are you aching?"

"I's sore, but fine," she replied. "What happened this morning that got ya riled?"

Evading the question, he said, "I want you to move your things down to my room."

"Why cain't I stay up here?" she asked, "What would Mama and Iris say?"

"No one would dare say a word," he answered, his words forceful.

"Why cain't we stay upstairs?" she asked.

"I have myself set up downstairs in case of trouble. My bedroom is set to watch the back of the fort."

She thought of him always wearing his gun, watching the window and the door, and it all made sense now. "I will move my thangs today," she said. "Now what got you so riled?"

"John is downstairs angry because I have not yet met with him."

Turning in the tub to face him, she asked, "Then why is we bathing?"

"We are bathing leisurely because I am enjoying you and because John is not my boss. Trying to bully me will not work, and I am also trying to calm down to keep from wringing his damn neck," he said, and his eyebrows were drawn together.

Sunday smiled before laying her head on his shoulder and feeling his arms around her. "I want thangs to go well so's you can move on from this matter wit' John. Will you find me when you done talkin' wit' him?"

"Why would I come find you? I expect you to be there during the meeting. He likes you and not me," Black said, smiling.

She popped her head up and looked at him. He continued, "I know this is a heavy burden, but I want you as my partner in all things. I will understand if you don't want the weight."

"I want you, Black ... all of you," she said in a soft voice.

He was moved.

Black opened the door to his study and found Otis standing at the window and John seated on the sofa. Chairs were brought in for William, Frederick, and Moses so they could join the meeting. Black could see that John was aggravated because he thought this would be a private meeting. Ignoring John, Black ushered Sunday over to his desk, seating her in one of the extra chairs behind his desk. They were just about to get started when John's son Owen entered the study, sitting next to his father.

"Good morning," Black said.

The room at large responded, and Frederick spoke up first, asking, "Black, do you plan on joining the conference in Chatham?"

"I did, but I am unable to make it. The conference will last several days, and based on my schedule, I will not have time," Black said, having just come to the conclusion that he should sit this one out.

Moses joined in, changing the subject. "Folks is callin' for war. They feels it's the only way to realize freedom, and I agrees."

"I believe Lincoln will be elected, and it will be the catalyst for a civil war," Garrison said. "I, at one time, believed that we could abolish slavery without war; now I see no other way."

"I am to travel to meet with Lincoln after the conference. Freedom is upon us, and we need to think of how we will live as a people after we are free. There will be thousands of black people displaced once freed. When I came to the North, I discovered while I am not a slave, racism is now the issue," Douglass stated.

"We can only address one thang at a time," Moses replied.

"I'm afraid violence is the only way; until we go to war, we are at a standstill as a nation," Garrison said.

John took his cue and chimed in. "I am planning a revolt to take back the South. I agree with Garrison; violence is the only way. I plan to take Harpers Ferry and seize the armory. I will provide every slave for miles around with a weapon. We will take the South; no more appealing with reason to the unreasonable."

Black and Otis did not speak; they just listened, and Sunday sat quietly observing. These were debates that Black had heard before, and he understood that saying very little was important.

It was Garrison who asked, "How many men do you have, John?"

"I have sixty, and if Black will join forces, I would have more. The people in this room could make a difference in an uprising. Slaves will follow you, and together, think of what we could accomplish."

Moses laughed out loud, causing everyone to turn and look at her. "I'm sorry," she said, trying to collect herself. "You speaks of overthrowin' the gobment as though there ain't no cavalry. What you speaks is death, plain and simple. You will be hanged, and if you cain't see it, the grave is calling you, John."

"My father is attempting to help. How dare you damn laugh?" Owen said, staring at Moses.

Unmoved, she stared at Owen, asking, "How will yo family fair? How will yo women get along after this?"

"Black," John hissed as he stood, pushing his disheveled hair back from his face. He eyed Black, and blowing his breath, he began pacing.

Leaning back in his chair, Black stared at John while considering his own words carefully. "John, you know that I don't agree with a revolt. It's reckless, and nothing good will come from it. I believe in you and your cause; it is my cause. I did not support you for two reasons—one, my family, and two, I do not wish to see you hanged."

"How could you, Black, not understand? You, the son of Nat Turner himself, sidestepping the cause," John mocked. "They are looking to you for answers, and because you will not join, they will not join."

Sunday jumped from the vehemence in John's voice, and Black calmly said, "I am the son of Nat Turner, who died in a revolt thirty years ago. Yet here I sit, a fugitive from Virginia thirty years later. He made a decision based on his life as a slave, and that I can respect. Still, he was hanged, as you will be, John. I am my own man, and when I address you, it is with respect. Lower your tone when speaking to me … lower your damn tone."

Owen stood, so Black stood, and John, seeing where it was going, raised his hand to his son, saying, "He is right. I am out of line."

Frederick stood, making for the door. "I fear I need air. I will be on the porch."

Garrison wandered over to the window. Standing next to Otis, he whispered, "We almost had a ruckus."

Otis smiled but didn't comment.

Moses left, following Douglass out of the study. John began pacing, and his son stood and left the study. Otis followed Owen out, leaving William, John, Sunday, and Black.

"Don't be a martyr, John," Garrison said. "The country is going to war. You are needed for bigger things."

"I appreciate your kind words. I need to speak with Black. Can you excuse us?" John responded.

Garrison nodded and exited the study. Turning to Sunday, John said, "I apologize to you, miss."

She nodded but kept quiet.

"I need your help, Black," he said.

Black was annoyed, and he tried to rein in his temper before speaking. "I will not go back down this path with you, John. We're done."

Sunday noticed that he had not offered the money because he was livid, and she suspected that would mean more grief. When Black stood, she stood as if to dismiss him, but John would not be discouraged.

"I understand that I may not live, but this is my calling," John said, holding Black's gaze.

Sunday knew the exact moment when Black softened. "I don't want to see you hanged, John," he said gruffly.

"If I am hanged, I can live and die with that," John replied.

"I cannot live with being hanged," Black said, looking him in the eye.

"I understand," he answered.

"I will give money to your campaign silently. It is all I have, but I want you to have it. I want you to know, John, that by giving you money, I feel I am helping you to an early grave."

"My decision is made, Black. Like you, I am my own man."

They settled on an amount of $300, and Sunday did not know he meant that much. Seeing the exchange, she realized Black was rich. He still looked annoyed when John left. She asked if he was all right, and he said, "It was a waste of money, but more importantly, it is a waste of a good man."

The guests stayed for another day, and the original plan was that Black and Sunday would ride into Chatham to attend the conference. But Black was tired after dealing with John; the last thing he wanted was to have two more days of debates and discussions about his father. As the people of Fort Independence continued to have a good time, Black backed away from anything that looked serious. He needed a break, and he understood that he needed not to overthink.

Black stood on the front porch watching everyone enjoy themselves when, out the corner of his eye, he caught a movement. He turned, trying to focus, and Tim came into view. And though they hadn't spoken yet, Black knew Tim brought news of the Turner plantation. As the celebration continued, both he and Tim acknowledged they would speak later.

When Otis stepped onto the porch, he also noticed Tim. Looking in Black's direction, he shook his head as if to say, "Here comes the bullshit."

Virginia
May 1859

Jacob Turner moved out of the master suites he shared with Will's mother, giving those rooms to Will and Amber. Will was thankful because he still needed his privacy; being married was more than he had bargained for. It had been a month and a half of compromising with Amber on issues of furniture, time spent together, and when they would travel. The furniture issue he couldn't care less about, but he couldn't plot with her on his ass all the time. Matters had come to a grinding halt where Sunday was concerned, and Will had no choice but to seek Turner out for help.

After the wedding, Will sought Youngblood out to crack the whip, and he couldn't find him. It was as if he had vanished from the face of the earth. Checking among the overseers, he found that Richards was missing too. Youngblood's belongings were still in his cabin, and his horse was still in the stables. At first Will thought wishfully that Youngblood was with a woman. But more than a month passed when Will decided it was time to go through his belongings looking for clues.

Will dreaded going through Youngblood's cabin because he'd known that Youngblood wasn't clean. He looked as though he never bathed, and his teeth were black from tobacco chewing. But when Will entered the cabin, he found it to be more organized than expected. Youngblood kept journals filled with information about other plantations and their slaves. There was an accounting of every slave who had lived on the Turner plantation going back as far as 1800.

It appeared the Youngbloods had been overseeing for the Turner plantation for more than half a century. He found a series of journal entries from the year Nat Turner revolted. Paying close attention, he found that Nat Turner had slaughtered Youngblood's brother, his elderly father, and his brother's children that fateful night when he went on the rampage. According to the documents, Youngblood himself was sixteen at the time. Staying on with the Turner plantation, Youngblood discovered that one of the slaves was pregnant with Nat's child. There were notes about a slave—Sophie—who disappeared the day Nat was hanged, November 11, 1831. It seemed that when Youngblood realized who Sophie was, she was gone. He had been following closely the slave Hope and his mother, Ellen, the one called Big Mama. In one of his last entries, he found there was a slave on the Turner plantation that knew where Black was holed up, and he was following that lead. He seemed to trust an overseer by the name of Tim, and the slave was a blacksmith that went by Smitty. Will removed all journals from Youngblood's cabin.

Before Will could make an appointment with his father, he was summoned by Turner, and so, armed with a list of his father's mistakes, he took the meeting. Stepping into his father's study, he shut the door quietly behind him, and Turner looked up, bidding him to come forward.

"Your sister and I are going to Boston, as I am considering a match with Anderson Wilkerson. This will be a good match, as he has ties in Mississippi and is a lawyer in Boston."

Will impatiently went to the business of the day. "Youngblood is missing." He noticed that his father wasn't the least bit surprised.

While Jacob Turner had made his fair share of mistakes, he wouldn't be disrespected. "Youngblood is dead. I don't see him walking away without a word."

"If you thought him dead, why wouldn't you notify me?"

"What would I be notifying you about? He's missing; you can see that," Turner responded.

Will narrowed his eyes and assessed his father, and he was ready for him. "I think the slave Black killed Youngblood. I think you have left this family open and vulnerable in your pursuit of that nigger bitch Ellen."

Turner was roiling with anger but chose his words carefully. "So you have it all figured out, do you? I must admit I had shame about loving her, and at this very moment, my heart aches that she is not here." He paused for effect and then continued, "I have nothing to be ashamed of in your company. You are traveling the same road, yet at a faster pace. No matter my mistakes, Black is a worthy opponent, and Ellen, nigger or not, is the smartest woman I know."

Will hadn't expected his father to admit he was wrong, and it took the wind out of his sails. "I want Sunday back, and if you hadn't threatened to sell her, this wouldn't have happened."

"I was attempting to stop you from the same sorry fate I have experienced."

"I had not asked for your damned help!" Will yelled, and he was ashamed that he was so emotional. A small curl fell to his forehead, and he nervously pushed it back.

Turner put down his pen and leaned back, looking at Will. "I am willing to forgo Ellen if you will forget this nonsense."

"'Willing to forgo' … You ignored our mother and us for her, and you have been the cause of financial hardship on other plantation owners so you can have her. How many do you think he has helped run? Now, after you have had what you want, you are willing to forgo as an old man. I think Ellen is the one who has forgone here, not you. So don't you make a deal with me with collateral you don't have." He was purple from emotion.

"I have loved you—" Turner tried to say, but Will cut him off.

Lowering his voice and shaking with the effort, he said to his father, "How damned many has he helped run? That is the question I have asked."

"You will go up against Black, and you will not win; he has nothing to lose and everything to gain. If I know his mother, Ellen, she has groomed him to win. Let this go, and enjoy the wife you have and the children to come," Turner pleaded.

"It would seem, Father, you have groomed him to win, and I expect your help getting Sunday back. I don't care what you do with the old woman, but I want her back, and I want her back unharmed," he qualified before turning and leaving the study. He went to his room and paced, his breathing labored, his hands shaking from his anger.

It was the middle of the day, and Amber sat in her room reading when she heard her husband in his chamber. She wanted to speak to him about traveling, so she knocked on the door. When Will opened the door and saw Amber, he grabbed her by the arm, snatching her into his room. He kissed her hard, bruising her lips, and without preamble, he bent her over the side of the bed, lifting her skirts, and entered her.

She moaned as he stroked her roughly, slamming into her until she began to shudder. Unexpectedly, he was seized by pleasure, and he grunted until his satisfaction was complete. Stepping back from her, he straightened her skirts and turned his back, allowing her privacy. He was ashamed of how he had manhandled her, and when he turned to tell her so, she was just staring at him.

Clearing his throat, he said, "I am sorry. I don't know what came over me."

Amber did not respond. What was there to say? This was the most passion he had shown her in the weeks since they married. The painful part was he was more than reserved about everything with her. If she was going to be in a marriage, she wanted it all. She could be married, she thought, spending most of her time in Boston visiting, and if this continued, that is how it would be. She would not wither in this godforsaken place and be ignored. Robert Myers had spoiled her, and she would not step down.

Sensing that he needed to make it right, he stepped forward and kissed her again. Against her lips, he whispered, "I am truly sorry."

She allowed him to kiss her, offering nothing; he had to work for it. Will undressed her slowly and himself quickly. Amber stood before him, totally naked, bathed in sunlight, and to his surprise, she was breathtaking and lovely. She was plump around the middle, yet she had the most beautiful complexion of cream. Her long red hair flowed about her, and she had full and firm breasts, her nipples like strawberries and erect. Laying her on the bed, he tasted her nipples, and she moaned. Kissing her down her stomach, he stuck his tongue in her navel, and she quivered. Leaning back over her, he kissed her gently and entered her, and Amber cried out. Their pace was slow yet deliberate, with Will attempting to control his pleasure. When Amber began to orgasm and spasm, Will was pulled into her web of ecstasy, and together they could be heard reaching their destination by the slaves passing in the hall.

They lay covered in a light sheen from the exertion of their lovemaking. She didn't attempt to dress. Instead, she snuggled against him, and in response, he reached down, pushing his fingers into her womanhood. And just before sleep took him, he thought, *I can have them both.*

They slept that way for hours with his fingers inside her, and though he did not think *mine* ... actions spoke louder than words.

Jacob Turner sat in his study staring after his son, Will; he understood the boy's plight. He felt intense about Ellen, and it had gotten him in the hole with his children and Ellen herself. Deep down, Ellen, slave or not, wanted what he supposed all women wanted. He had to admit he allowed the situation to get out of control. Will was right. When he first heard of Ellen's leaving, he was angry until he realized the only way to save his son would be to let her go. He would not pursue the fight to drag her back, yet the fact that she walked off and gave no notice meant she was done. Jacob realized that he had pushed too hard taking the stand about Sunday and Will, and now he was paying the price.

Over the years, he had not feared the slave Black because he didn't think he had to. Now that Ellen was gone and Youngblood was missing, he knew he had been warned, plain and simple. Will, being new to the situation, didn't understand, and it appeared he would not see reason. He needed to speak with Ellen, and he didn't know how he would accomplish seeing her. He knew that damned rabid-ass slave Black would blow his head off as he approached. Jacob sighed. He just wanted Ellen back, and more importantly, he just wanted life back as he understood it.

Placing his head in his hands, he allowed himself to weep silently for the blurred lines that marked his world with Ellen and for the walls that had been built keeping his children out. And when he was empty, Jacob decided he had to help his son.

7

MAY 1859

Black stood in his study contemplating the information being given to him and Otis by Tim. It would seem the older Turner took the warning at face value. Will, on the other hand, could not understand that he needed to back off. They drew several conclusions from the information gathered by Tim. Will was picking up where Youngblood left off, and lastly, one of the runaways at the fort had been feeding Youngblood information. Black had an idea of whom but had to be sure.

Tim continued, leaving nothing out. "He approached me, asking if I would take an assignment and come to Canada to search for the slave Sunday. My orders were to confirm her whereabouts, not to take action at this time."

In an effort to conceal his concern, Black sat at his desk and leaned back in the chair to keep from pacing.

Otis whistled, saying, "It's gon to be an all-out war."

Black didn't speak; he just listened as Otis asked Tim, "Did Will mention who it was sending Youngblood information?"

"He is feeding me with a long-handled spoon. If I need to know, then he will tell me. I was careful in my coming and waiting in the wings to speak with you. Whoever is forwarding information must not think we are working together," Tim responded.

"You are an overseer, and they recognize you, so whoever is working with him just got here," Black replied, finally adding to the conversation.

"Maybe," Otis responded. "We moved many in the last year. Maybe Youngblood's patience is startin' to yield fruit."

Black nodded in acknowledgment.

"What would you like me to tell him?" Tim asked.

"It doesn't matter what you tell him; someone here will inform him as to her whereabouts. All you can offer is the truth so that we might keep our enemy close," Black answered.

"I can just not go back," Tim replied.

"True, but if you don't go back, we will not know what is going on. If you don't go back, they will think we killed you, and they will just send someone else. Killing Youngblood was a calculated risk, and still here we are. I will need to think about my next move. This is not a game I wish to continue playing," Black said, and his voice had an edge.

"I think we should go back and just kill Will," Tim said.

"Remember, if I kill Will, as the plantation owner, he is more prominent. The fallout will be greater, and more than likely, other slaves will pay for his death or disappearance. It is the reason we went the Youngblood route. I will think on it, " Black answered, remaining nonchalant.

Tim cleared his throat before saying, "I think he wants to break you—and in front of her."

Black's smile was carefree and easy when he said, "I am sure he does."

He would go back to the Turner plantation, there was no doubt. First and foremost, he would ensure the safety of Sunday and Mama before he made any decisions. And he would start by getting an understanding with the people of Fort Independence that traitorous behavior would not be tolerated. The people here came and went as they pleased; they were not prisoners. He required loyalty in exchange for his protection, and he would leave no stone unturned in his quest for the truth. When he was finished, the newfound snake of Fort Independence would know what a dog knew: don't bite the hand that feeds you.

As Tim and Otis stepped off into the corner, they debated the best course of action. Black was deep in thought and engaged no further, his mind turning to the past. It *was* personal with Youngblood for him, and though he would never admit it, he had been afraid of him as a child. Mama had told him not to be afraid, and he had lied, telling her he wasn't. Youngblood even knew his identity, calling him the son of that savage nigger Nat Turner. In his youth, Black heard stories about Nat Turner, but he had not known the truth until Youngblood told him. Black remembered crying to Mama, not wanting to be his son. She told him, "Never hate yoself; you has to embrace all of you to win."

He remembered Mama told him about Sophie dying in childbirth trying to bring him safely into the world. She told him about their love, Sophie getting pregnant, and Nat wanting freedom for his family. Mama spoke about the kind of courage it took to rise up against your oppressor and be called a savage for wanting to be free. She told him she was proud to raise Nat Turner's son, and it was then she told him his full name, Nat Hope Turner. Mama made it clear that while what his father had done was unsuccessful, it was the beginning of a new thought among slaves. "Even slow movement forward is still progress," she told him.

Black remembered when his fear of Youngblood had changed to anger, and along with his emotions, so had his thought process. He was about twelve at the time and walking to the stables when Youngblood rode him down on his horse. The day started the same as it always had back then, with Mama giving him direction. She had secured a new position for him among the slaves to keep him away from Youngblood. He remembered clearly …

"Hope, I made it so you will work in the stables caring for the horses," Big Mama said as they sat down to breakfast in their little cabin with the dirt floor.

"I want to be with Elbert, James, and Otis in the fields," he answered, disappointed.

"Hush now. I don't want them in the fields, but they's big now, and I cain't change it. Do as I say—finish up eatin', and go to Mack. I will see ya at supper," Mama said as she stood, heading for the door, and then she was gone.

He finished eating, and wandering out the door after Mama, he headed to the dreaded stables. As he walked slowly between the cabins, he was angry that she was treating him like a baby. When he stepped out onto the open path, he could see Big Mama standing at the cabin of an elderly slave. She looked up, smiling at him, and then her smile was gone. Seeing the change in her expression, he began to move toward her.

But she began running toward him, and then he heard it—the pounding hooves just behind him.

"Hope, watch out! Baby, watch out!" Mama yelled, and her voice was frantic as she moved swiftly toward him.

He could see that she was looking just past him, and when he turned, all he could see were the legs of the stallion. He was surely about to be run down when he felt himself being yanked by the collar. And when she dragged him from the path of the stallion, she pulled him to her bosom, weeping with relief. He hugged her, and he was shaking.

"Is ya all right? Is ya hurt, child?" Mama asked while squeezing him close.

He was about to answer when he was knocked out of the way by Youngblood, who grabbed her by the throat with both hands, yelling, "You bitch, you almost caused an accident!"

He tried pulling away to defend his mama, but she stayed him. Gripping his arm tightly as she pulled him behind her, trying to protect him, she said, "I's sorry, Mr. Youngblood, sir."

"I almost broke my damn neck because of you. You trying to save that rotten egg of Nat Turner's; you think I don't know your secret?" Youngblood growled as he began shaking her, trying to choke the life out of her.

A crowd of slaves had gathered, and one of them went and got the master. Black could hear his mama gasping for air when old man Turner showed up, ordering, "Youngblood, unhand her now, damn it."

But Youngblood's grip tightened, judging from the sound coming from Mama. He was cutting off her airway, and when her grip lessened because she was becoming weak, Turner ordered two other overseers to intervene. And when Mama was finally released from Youngblood's hold, she did not look back. She dragged Black away to their cabin where she checked him out, though she was the one with the bruised throat and busted lip.

It was at that moment that he realized his new role where Mama was concerned. He would be her protector, and to do so, he could not remain a slave. In hindsight—and he could see this because he was a man now—while Turner called for her release, he never lifted a finger to stop Youngblood. It all came down to social protocol; she was the slave, and he was the master. Jacob Turner was angry that she would risk life and limb to save Nat Turner's child. Turner wanted him gone, but he feared losing Mama. To put it plain and simple, he was tired of sharing her.

When Black grew into a man, Youngblood had moved into his peripheral vision, and being free had become the center of his attention. Black was bigger, more physically fit, and younger, and the threat had been reprioritized in order of importance. He had not run because Mama's health was failing, and he would not leave without her. Then came that fateful day of the confrontation between Youngblood and himself, and he had no choice but to run. She told him to go, that it was time; she told him that she could manage old man Turner better with him gone. He left carrying the shame of leaving Mama behind, and his focus became Youngblood once again.

Two years passed, and he just wanted closure about Mama, and finding her alive had saved them all. He continued moving through the South, helping runaways and fighting with her to come with him. She refused, saying that it was best that way. When he got older, he realized that his mama loved old man Turner and wouldn't leave him. He understood for the first time what it meant to be jealous. Mama held the power, and with her presence on the Turner plantation, a type of peace was forged. Still, it was fragile at best. And as he got older, he knew that she was safe because they realized he was out there and that he was formidable—and they did not hunt him, because Turner wanted only her.

As Otis and Tim continued to debate, he realized he was emotional. He stood abruptly, causing them to stare after him as he headed for the door. Black needed some air because he was suffocating, so he walked off to gather himself. He would speak with Mama and then Sunday about security. As for Turner, both the young and the old, he would bring the fight to them. They would not have to look for it, and it would be personal.

During the festivities, Smitty worked hard in the stables. When the time came, he went in search of a willing woman. As always, business first, and once in town, he went to the dry-goods store to handle matters. His telegram read:

> I AM HAPPY HERE LIFE IS LIKE A LAZY **SUNDAY** AFTERNOON AT **FORT INDEPENDENCE HOPE** TO SEE YOU SOON

Headed toward a good drink and an amiable woman, Smitty was looking forward to the bright future the reward on Black's head would bring. As for Sunday, he couldn't decide whether to keep her or turn her over to Youngblood for the money he promised. He had options, and they kept getting better.

Black and Sunday rode silently in the carriage into town. It was a beautiful day, and he just wanted to be with her. Sunday stared out the window drinking in the sun and the scenery, and Black took in her beauty, thankful for their time together. Outside the carriage, four men rode horseback, keeping watch. The ride was a little farther than their first visit to town. He could see that she was excited, and it was moments like this that mattered for him.

They stopped at a warehouse called Everything. The store sold all types of goods, and Sunday was like a child in her exploration. As they stepped through the door, to the right was a large, black wood-burning stove with an intricately carved design. The stove stood about six feet high on fancy legs, with the trim and handles painted silver. It was the fanciest stove she had ever seen, and to Sunday it was too beautiful to cook on. She wandered over to get a closer look and touch it; she couldn't wait to tell Iris and Mama about the fine-looking stove.

While she moved about, Black went to the back looking for Virgil, the manager and bookkeeper. Upon seeing him, Black smiled. Virgil was a man for whom Black had a lot of respect.

"Virgil. Good to see you," Black said.

"If I'm seeing you, the matter is business," Virgil replied, getting straight to it.

Sunday, looking for Black, walked up, and he introduced them. "Sunday, this is my very good friend Virgil Silver. Virgil, this is my Sunday."

Standing closely to Black, she smiled, saying, "Fine to meet ya."

Virgil was a white gentleman of about thirty summers. He stood about six feet with brown hair, and his blue eyes were spaced evenly in his face. His nose was small or rather proportional to his mouth, making him handsome. Virgil wore a blue suit with a blue tie and white shirt.

"Nice to meet you as well, Miss Sunday," he responded, smiling at her. "Feel free to pick something nice for yourself. The women's section is in the back to the left."

Looking in the direction, he pointed. She turned back and looked at Black. He smiled reassuringly, and taking the hint, she said, "Thank you," before moving on down the aisle.

She was assaulted by the smells of spice, wood, and newness. There was a reason the store was called Everything. The inventory had no theme, and it had anything a person could think of. In the women's section, it had lotions, soaps, and perfumes that were pleasing to the senses. Sunday was familiar with these types of wonderful items, but they were nothing that she had ever owned. If she ever had to choose, it would be the soap. She found a soap that smelled of gardenias and a matching lotion. In her excitement, she almost missed a fancy bottle of perfume called Melody, and while the smell was average, she picked it because she could read the bottle. She was pleased on so many levels, and she smiled.

As she moved along, her excitement grew as she came upon the clothing for women. Dresses in all colors with ruffles, layers, and decorative buttons were hung neatly on hooks for easy access. Behind the dress display were yards of fabric in all colors for the choosing. In a large bin were parasols in all colors to match the dresses and fabrics. Sunday was in heaven as she strolled about, allowing her senses to be stimulated. *This place is like magic,* she thought.

She turned looking for Black, but he and Virgil seemed to have walked through a door in the far back of the warehouse. As she thought about Black, she noticed he seemed agitated lately, and after the guests left, he spoke very little and always appeared deep in thought. She didn't press him, but she wanted him to talk to her. Mama noticed the change in his demeanor, and she advised waiting. "He will talk soon enough. He workin' through thangs," she had said reassuringly.

In the back room where the real business was handled, Virgil asked, "What exactly are you looking for?"

Black did not hesitate when he said, "Fifty Smith & Wessons and thirty Sharps rifles."

Virgil whistled. "What did you do with the other merchandise I moved to your place?"

"Nothing," Black responded.

"Is that all you are going to say?" Virgil smiled.

Black stared at him seriously, and Virgil lifted his hands, saying, "I thought I would ask. We will deliver at night, same as before, and as always, should you need me … well, you already know I am at the ready."

Black nodded, and when they concluded their business, they stepped back into the warehouse with the understanding that the guns would be delivered in five days.

Sunday was admiring a large cream-colored porcelain tub when they walked up. The tub could fit three large people easily. She was just about to walk away from the tub when Black said to Virgil, "I would like the tub delivered, as well."

When she looked up at him, his eyes twinkled with mischief, and she breathed in sharply. Virgil had the grace to nod and act as though he had no idea what he was talking about.

Black ushered Sunday from the warehouse after purchasing some soaps and perfumes for her, and she was thrilled. They rode back through town to the dressmaker. Sunday returned Sally's necklace and earrings, thanking her for her kindness. Black stood outside with his men waiting while Sunday and Sally pored over material.

When they were back in the carriage, she noticed he remained as silent as he had when they had left for town that morning. It was as if she imagined the teasing about the tub. Night had fallen when they reached the gates. Black sat opposite her in the compartment, a small slice of moonlight showing through the curtain. She was reminded of when she was little and how foreboding he appeared when he came to see her and Mama. The horses pulled the carriage through the gates, and as they were approaching the house, he finally spoke. "I will talk with Mama in her room. I will see you later."

"I will be in the kitchen if'n you needs me," she replied, and rushing up the front steps, she was gone.

Black stood with his hands in his pockets, watching the carriage rattle down the path. He knew she was confused by his behavior, and still she did not question him. He needed to speak with Mama and Sunday to prepare them. As for the blacksmith, he needed to be dealt with, and so did his child, who was innocent in all this. Little Curtis's presence was what delayed Black from stretching Smitty's neck, but it would not stop it. It could be no other than the blacksmith because up until now, Turner—young or old—showed no interest in tracking him. If they had, Tim would have been aware before now. The only new additions were Sunday, Mama, the blacksmith, and his child. It was the blacksmith. He could feel it.

Following Sunday up the steps, he walked along the hall until he came to Mama's room. He hesitated at the door before knocking.

"Come in," she invited.

Entering, he smiled by way of greeting, and walking over to the chair, he sat. "How you feeling, Mama?"

She smiled, saying, "Betta than you."

He chuckled, deciding that she looked good and had put on weight. Her complexion showed good health, and he was happy. She wore a blue dress with a white collar and matching shoes. She deserved more, but it was a start.

"What's worryin' you? Talk to yo mama," she said, turning serious.

"It seems Will sent Tim looking for Sunday," he said with no emotion, his face closed.

"I see," came her answer.

"It appears the blacksmith was working with Youngblood," he said.

"How you knows this?" she replied, her interest piqued. "Where you get this blacksmith from?"

"He came from the Wilson plantation. Curtis was still in South Carolina, and we backtracked to get him. Timing points to him, and I am sure that he is not aware Youngblood is dead. I will not investigate here; I am waiting for word. Tim will have it soon, I am sure."

"What will you do when word comes? There is a child to figure 'bout."

"There is only so much considering I can do for the next man," he said, his voice tight.

"I agree, but you's Nat Turner's child, and the same will be true for little Curtis," she said, holding his gaze.

"Do you have a plan for the child? Because I will kill the blacksmith no matter what, and I will kill him publicly to ensure there is no miscalculation of me as a man … ever."

Slowly, she nodded her agreement before saying, "The child cain't remain. You has to find him somewhere safe to go."

"Sunday will want him, you know that," he said. "We cannot keep him."

"You needs me to speak with her?"

Staring at Mama, he stated the truth. "I have done myself a disservice by speaking with you before her. I cannot hang a man and fear speaking to my woman. I will speak with Sunday."

Even with the gravity of their discussion, she chuckled before saying, "Will?"

"Let us take this journey one leg at a time," he said, standing.

And she knew the answer. Again, she nodded her acknowledgment.

As he entered his room, he sighed, so exasperated was he with this debacle. He knew he could put Sunday off no longer. There were several candles lit in the corners of the chamber, creating a magical atmosphere. She stood next to the tub as steam rose from the water. Next to the tub stood a food tray with sliced chicken and fruit with bread and butter.

"Bathe wit' me, and talk to me," she said shyly, and his love deepened.

When he was naked, she handed him a glass of whiskey that he did not sip. Throwing the drink back, he said, "After you."

She untied his robe, and standing before him naked, she did not break eye contact. Stepping into the tub, she reached out for him. When Black stepped in and eased down into the tub, she followed suit, and water sloshed over the side. Leaning back in the tub, he closed his eyes, and she settled between his legs.

108

They passed some time in silence before he said, "Will has figured out where you are."

Turning in the tub, she straddled him and asked, "And this has ya riled?"

Opening his eyes, he offered honesty when he said, "I do not like it … at all."

She heard the hard edge to his voice. "What ain't ya tellin' me?" she asked.

"It appears the blacksmith is at the bottom of it all."

She stiffened, water sloshing about them, her mouth shaped like an O, her surprise evident. "Curtis," she said, her surprised expression turning to concern.

"He cannot remain." It was said softly, but she knew it was the final decision.

She wanted to debate with him but knew he would be insulted. He was not the type to make decisions lightly. Sunday suspected his concern for Curtis was why the blacksmith was still alive. "I understands."

"You have no argument?" he asked, surprised.

"I has plenty of arguments, but none sound good to my own ears. If'n you kill Smitty, I don't want Curtis to be here."

"That was my way of thinking," he answered.

"Curtis is already 'fraid of ya. I understands 'cause when I was younger and you came to see Mama, I was 'fraid of ya too. When you would speak wit' Mama, you always seemed riled and vexed. Yo' being 'round made my stomach hurt."

He almost laughed out loud until a thought took hold in his head, and he asked, "And do you fear me now?"

"I'm merely statin' my figurin' of Curtis's feelins being seven and you being so … so large of a man," she said.

"You have not answered me."

"No, I ain't 'fraid of ya. A little unsettled at times, but I trust that ya let nothin' harm me. I believes in ya," she whispered.

Leaning back in the tub, he closed his eyes again and did not respond. Sunday moved forward, placing her head on his shoulder, and for a time they were still. When the water grew cool, they stepped from the tub, drying each other off.

Once in the bed, he lay on his back, and Sunday lay with her head on his chest and snuggled close. Into the quietness, he said, "I never want you to fear me."

"I was a child, Black."

He smiled, because she never called him Black when they were alone. She leaned up on her elbow and kissed his cheek, and he pulled her to straddle him. His manhood was pressed against her bottom, and she squirmed, getting comfortable. Leaning over, she licked at his lips and then kissed him, and he hissed. She kissed his chest, and he was moved by the innocence with which she seduced him. She gave him pause, and he realized he could not wait to be a part of her.

Grabbing her bottom, he guided her onto his hard member, and he groaned as she slid down him. "Shit, Sunday, easy," he said, his voice strained.

When she began to move, he was so mesmerized by her sexuality that he had to struggle to calm down. She found a rhythm and began rocking up and down. Her soft cries filled the room, and still he could not look away. Her breasts bounced with her movements, and, gentleman that he was, he grabbed her bottom, helping her in her efforts. At times, she threw her head back, moaning her pleasure, and it was the most erotic experience he had ever had. She smoothed her hands over his chest, touching him and then touching herself. Her breath caught, and he could feel her begin to shudder, but she never broke her stride. In the throes of sheer ecstasy, she threw her head back as the sensation took her. Seeing her so enthralled broke him down, and he approached satisfaction in complete surrender.

"So good. Oh, Black," she sobbed.

Even in his desperate search for fulfillment, he did not attempt to overtake her. Instead, he allowed her to pull his seed from him with slow and deliberate strokes. And only when he was empty and he could feel his testicles tighten did he call out his pleasure. Black's deep, ecstasy-stained voice filled the room as he groaned her name mindlessly over and over again. Sunday collapsed onto his chest, still quivering. They drifted into a deep sleep, still connected to each other and their passion.

110

In the coming days, Black spent a lot of his time in the studio rather than his study. He was brooding—and not about killing Smitty. In his mind, that was a done deal; because of the child, he would confirm the truth before acting. He had so many issues to separate, and the main one was the well-being of Sunday in the event of his untimely demise. He was filled with this energy that could not be squelched.

He worked two easels, so intense were his emotions. One canvas was of a black stallion reared up on his hind legs, three men standing around him with ropes about his neck. The stallion's coat glowed with health, and with his nostrils flared and mane blowing about him in his anger, his strength was tangible. The colors vibrated off the canvas—the wooden gate, the men dressed like cowboys, the light cloud of dust unsettled in the scuffle. They were attempting to break him, and the stallion was resisting vehemently. The second canvas was of a black man being brought down the gangplank of a large ship. Around his neck was a gray metal collar, his hands cuffed before him. Two long chains were connected to the cuffs and the collar, and he was being pulled by two overseers trying to drag him down the plank. The men stood on either side of the plank dressed as colonials. The slave was dressed poorly in torn brown short pants; he wore no shirt and was barefoot. Eyebrows pushed together over angry eyes and flared nostrils, he was attempting to pull backward, and there was a third man with a whip poised. They were endeavoring to break him, and he was refusing to be subdued.

There was a knock at the door, and putting the brush down, he answered, "Come in."

"You wanted to see me?" Otis asked as he shut the door behind him.

"I will deal with Smitty. I would like for you to take the child to Camille with the message that I will pay for them."

Otis nodded, hating to see Curtis go yet knowing it was for the best. "When?"

"When Tim confirms," he answered.

Staring at the paintings, Otis said nothing of them, understanding that they were Black's private things. "I'll take care of it," he said. Turning to leave, Black stopped him.

"Sunday—" his voice faltered. "Any children that we might ..." Black didn't look at Otis.

"I will look after Mary, Mama, and Sunday in the event of … it will not come to that. We will watch each other's backs," Otis said.

"Thank you, brother." Black's voice was heavy with reality.

In the wee hours of the morning, Black was still painting and pacing when she knocked on the door. "Enter," he commanded.

Sunday walked in, still looking foggy from sleep. "You hasn't come to bed."

He smiled at her irritation. "Why are you up?"

She stopped yawning and stared at him. "I missed you." She was cranky.

Walking over, she stared at the paintings, and she was struck by the comparison. Every stroke showed the heaviness under which he lived. "I love the paintings," she said and nothing more.

He wore no shirt or shoes, and as he put the brush down, she noticed that he was splotched in paint on his chest, arms, and hands. Just over his left ear he had gray paint, as though he thoughtlessly scratched his head while deep in thought. Everything he did was sexual to her, even when he wasn't trying.

He did not respond about the paintings. Instead, he crossed his arms and assessed her. Narrowing his eyes, he asked, "How are you not with child?"

She found that when he asked random questions, they were not random at all. He just spoke as though she was part of the original thought. At any rate, he blindsided her, and she answered, "Iris and Mama gave me a drink. I drinks it daily to keep from gettin' heavy with child. Mama warns it ain't perfect, though."

"Do you want children, Sunday?" he inquired.

"I wants yo child, but I don't wants to add to yo burden. I cain't promise I won't get wit' child, but I will try not to."

"I don't want to leave you with a child and alone. Most important, I don't want you to die in childbirth. I am terrified of that." His voice was laced with emotion.

"I's 'fraid of losing you too, but I's most 'fraid of you dying and me not having yo child. I fears ya slippin' through my fingers like all this ain't happened." She moved forward, and snaking her arms about his waist, she kissed his chest, whispering, "You's my king."

Pushing her against the wall, he took her mouth in a violent kiss, and she returned his fire. She unbuttoned his trousers, and with his help, she pushed them to the floor until she was on her knees in front of him. Leaning over, she kissed his feet one at a time, paying homage to him. She placed butterfly kisses up his leg, when she reached his balls, she kissed them. Moving farther up his body, she came to his stiff maleness, and without hesitation, she took him in her mouth, sucking him. Black closed his eyes, leaning his forehead against the wall. When he thought he would spill his seed, he pushed her back from him, and he could feel the suction of her resisting. "No more," he groaned.

Lifting her, he took her against the wall, the sounds of lovemaking, their ragged breathing, their cries of pleasure and soft pleas for more filling the studio. When they approached paradise, they moaned incoherently until spent. Finding her mouth, he kissed her, and against her lips, he said, "Marry me, Sunday."

Still breathless from their passion, she whispered, "Yes, my king."

8

JUNE 1859

Jacob Turner sat opposite his daughter on the train bound for Boston. Rose stared out the window watching the countryside roll by. Rose's features were the complete opposite of Will's. She had long black hair curled to perfection, and she had blue eyes, a heart-shaped mouth, and a tiny nose. Rose was trained properly to be a good wife; she would be safe with Anderson, and he would be good for her. In the first leg of the trip, Jacob would secure her a lady companion and then set out for Canada.

The railcar was stuffy but not unpleasant, and in the background, there was a low buzz of polite conversation. A black porter approached, asking, "Would you like to take your refreshments here or in the dining car?"

"Here is fine," Jacob responded, never looking at the man.

Nodding, he turned and left. He was back within moments with sandwiches cut small and coffee with all the trimmings. After he served them, he disappeared, and Jacob said, "I have business to attend in New York. I will come back for you in a few weeks. You will have a companion while you are with Anderson. I hope the two of you will enjoy each other's company. I want you to be happy."

"Yes, Father, I hope so, as well. I will await your return," Rose answered with a small smile.

Rose ate a small amount and went back to staring out the window. She loved her father, but she was saddened by his treatment of her mother. The truth was that she did not want a match, but it was really the only way to leave the plantation. She would be obedient as her mother had been, but a match in which she tolerated her husband's touch was not what she had in mind. Out of the corner of her eye, she watched her father push back from the tray, wiping his mouth with a white napkin.

Leaning back, he began staring out the window, and she considered him. In his youth, her father was tall yet trim; unlike Will, he had dark hair, blue eyes, and a strong jawline. Now in his advanced years, he appeared defeated rather than old. Seated across from her, he sat on the red velvet bench trimmed in black wood that shone from regular upkeep. He wore a gray suit with a white shirt and black bowtie; his gray hair had a yellowish tint and was a little longer than he usually kept it. On his face was the constant look of a man in pain. Strangely, and though she loved him, she was not taken with the need to comfort him. To hell with her brother and her father; Rose wanted control of her own person, and she would take it from there.

As the train rocked and swayed, she smiled at the thought of leaving Southampton. She would be fair with Anderson, allowing him to pick his own poison. Rose would be honest about who she was, and if he didn't like it, he could join her list of people headed for hell.

"Next stop, Boston!" the porter yelled.

Southampton Virginia

Will sat in his father's study, ordering supplies for the plantation. Turner was organized, and it was easy to follow his lead. In handling certain business, he found easier ways to get matters resolved. He offered Youngblood's position to Tim, but Tim had turned it down, saying he preferred working for him behind the scenes. After giving his request some thought, Will realized that he would need Tim for other issues.

There was a knock at the study door. The slave Tilly stepped in, saying, "There is a man from town here to see you, Masta Will."

"Show him in, Tilly."

When Will looked, there was the clerk from the dry-goods store standing in his study. "Mr. Johnson, was there an error in my record keeping?" he asked, figuring he owed him more money on the credit account.

"No, not at all, Mr. Turner." He hesitated before saying, "I am here for Mr. Youngblood, sir. I have two telegrams for him. I have sent my errand boys to bring the messages, but they seem to think he has left your employ."

Mr. Johnson was a young, dumpy fellow, easily intimidated, working for his father—like Will—until he would take over one day. Will stood, coming to stand toe-to-toe before saying, "I will take the messages, Mr. Johnson. Thank you for being so dedicated."

He handed Will the messages and made his departure, thanking Will for his time. Once alone, Will read the telegrams.

I HAVE ARRIVED AND WHAT I HAVE FOUND WILL MAKE YOU HAPPY FOR A MONTH OF SUNDAYS

I AM HAPPY HERE LIFE IS LIKE A LAZY **SUNDAY** AFTERNOON AT **FORT INDEPENDENCE HOPE** TO SEE YOU SOON

Life was coming together. Youngblood had placed a spy at the fort before he disappeared, and he had been right; Will was happy. He called for Tim, and pacing the study, he waited. When Tim appeared, Will said without preamble, "The blacksmith has sent word that Sunday is indeed holed up with him, confirming what you have said."

Tim's expression was closed as he heard Will confirm what Black had been saying all along. The blacksmith was the leak. He was careful when he asked, "What next? He's offering nothing new."

Handing Tim the messages, Will said, "He has offered where he is holed up."

It was clear that Will was matching what Tim said to what the blacksmith was saying. Tim smiled before saying, "When do we leave?"

Wandering over to the window, Will pushed his hands in his pockets, staring off into the distance. He needed time to devise a plan. Turner was in Boston with Rose, and the plantation couldn't be left unattended—and he had Amber to consider. Will would not rush; he could see his goal in sight, and he would approach it cautiously. He needed a win and badly, but he would delay satisfaction, controlling himself first so that he could break Black. Sunday needed to see him broken first for Will to get his status back with her.

Tim cleared his throat, snatching Will from his thoughts. Once he had Will's attention, Tim restated, "When?"

Turning from the window, Will responded, "I don't know yet."

Tim, thinking that Will didn't trust him, said, "I see," as if insulted that his loyalty wasn't appreciated.

Will responded, "You can't approach him without a plan; I need time to think this through. He will stop at nothing; we cannot be hasty."

Tim smiled, noticing that Will refused to say Black's name. "I will be ready when you call."

~ ~ ~

It was Tim's turn to send a telegram, and the message was short and simple.

~ ~ ~

It was midnight, and in the sky hung a quarter moon. The weather was still, and a breeze periodically blew, allowing some relief. Trees were in full bloom, some with flowers, others with large leaves concealing the activity happening at the fort. Black stood dressed for his name with legs spread apart, arms crossed and gun at his side, watching as the gates opened to admit a large wagon being pulled by a team. When the gates closed behind the wagon, Black stepped forward to greet Virgil.

"I brought the tub, as well, my friend," Virgil said by way of greeting.

Black threw back his head and laughed, shaking his hand. "Nosy bastard."

"Did you think I wouldn't mention it?"

Shaking his head, Black responded, "I hoped you wouldn't."

The men moved the merchandise to the barracks, breaking off into teams and lifting the tub, taking it into the foyer. When Black and Otis had inspected the guns, Black paid Virgil, concluding their business.

Otis escorted Virgil and his men back to the gate. Black walked up the path, slowly making his way back to the house. When he reached the steps, Mama stood at the top, her expression closed.

"What is it?" he asked.

"Jacob is at the local inn," she answered.

Climbing the steps, he stood looking down at her, saying, "Hmm."

"He's lookin' to see me," she replied.

It was slight, but he heard it: the small catch in her throat that said she still loved him. He would not examine how he felt, so he asked, "And do you wish to see him, Mama? Is he here to rescue you from your savage son?"

"You green wit' envy," she commented.

Black offered no response. He was angry.

Mama continued, "When I was a young girl, yo daddy, Nat, took a shinin' to me. I believed I could have loved him, but Jacob separated us. He was the authority in our lives. I's angry 'bout it, and when I came to know why he separated us, I hated him for it. Nat and I stayed friends, and when he met yo mama, I felt a stab of jealousy."

Still Black offered nothing, and his irritation was tangible.

She smiled before saying, "Yo' mama was beautiful inside and out. She 'came my friend, and I realized that she was brought to stop yo' daddy's interest in me. In time, I accepted that I loved Jacob wit' all of my heart and soul. He was weak, and I knew he wouldn't never free me. When you was born, I loved you wit' all of my heart. You, Black, was my freedom. I chose to love you. You's my son. Jacob is just as jealous of you. It is a different love, and I knows ya understands as a grown man 'cause of Sunday. We cain't help the way we feels. I loves him, and I needs to see him. We's old now, and it may be the last time."

"He must come here," he said as he began moving to the door.

"Will ya harm him?" she asked, her expression closed.

"You will not leave with him." He stopped, staring at her, making no promises. "If he chooses not to come here, you will not see him."

"I ain't yo prisoner," she said calmly.

"You are my mama, but Turner can be a prisoner with no problem," he said just as calmly.

When he walked away, she stared after him, speechless.

As Black walked down the hall, he decided to spare Turner … for now. Will and Smitty were his real issues. He would address the rest when the smoke cleared.

~ ~ ~

The next afternoon Jacob sat in the restaurant by the storefront looking out through the words O'Reilly's Inn. He stirred and poked at his soup, never really tasting it as he watched the window. Picking up the glass of whiskey, he was about to take a sip when into his line of vision rode three of the largest colored men he had ever seen. Stopping in front of the inn, one of the men swung down from his horse and walked in. He stood with his back to the door, assessing the room at large, when his eyes settled on him.

"We here to carry you to see Mama," Otis ground out.

Jacob was afraid; in the social settings he was accustomed to, he had never been addressed with such venom by anyone, let alone a slave. And Otis was one of his own, yet at the very mention of Ellen, he stood, placing his hat on his head and walking out the front door. The day was overcast but still warm. Jacob stepped down from the wooden boardwalk, and one of the other slaves came forward with a horse. Before he could get his wits about him, Otis came forward, searching him roughly. Once Jacob was patted down, he mounted.

Although he was old and his body hurt as he rode toward her, he kept up the pace. When they passed through the gates of Fort Independence, Jacob knew Will did not stand a chance. He rode through the paths of the little city, still being escorted, and the people stepped out curiously to stare at the spectacle he made. The master was on display, and he didn't like it one bit. Still, he held his superior attitude.

When they arrived at the front of the house, Ellen stood at the top of the steps in a plum dress, as beautiful as ever. She was the very picture of health, and he felt shame at his treatment of her. Climbing down from his horse, he started for the stairs, only having eyes for her, when he saw Black standing to the left of her. He was older, bigger, and angry. Dressed in all black and carrying a weapon, he leaned against the wall. One of his legs was bent at the knee, and his foot was braced against the wall as he leisurely watched the scene before him.

Jacob faltered at the sight of him, but he loved her, so he climbed the stairs, and once at the top, he said, "Ellen."

She stepped back and looked up at him when he reached the top of the landing. "Jacob," she replied.

"I need to speak with you privately."

She looked at Black as if to ask his permission. His expression was closed, and she was unclear how to proceed. Black slowly unfolded himself from the wall and nodded for them to follow him. Stepping through the front door, he gestured toward the sitting room. Mama led the way, and Jacob followed. Once in the sitting room, they both turned and looked at Black.

Turner spoke up, saying, "I would like to speak with her alone."

Black leveled his eyes on Turner, his body tensing, and taking a menacing step forward, he was about to …

"Black, come wit' me, and give them time to speak."

Sunday's voice broke the silence from where she stood behind him. He stood there eyeing Turner before finally retreating back to the door. Once in the doorway, he said in a tight voice, "I'm just outside the door."

Jacob had stood his ground, and though he was afraid, he did not step back when Black stepped up. Only when the door closed and they were alone did he show signs of stress. He grabbed at his collar, loosening his tie and mopping his forehead with a handkerchief. As she watched him, she saw that his hair was too long. He wore a blue suit with a white shirt. The color had faded from his eyes, and his mouth was set in a straight line. Her heart squeezed for him, and he was still the most attractive man she had ever known. She hurt for herself and for him.

In an effort to control the situation, she said, maybe too harshly, "What you want, Jacob?"

"Ellie, please, let's not speak angrily. We both know this will probably be the last time we see each other."

She sighed but was not deterred. "Jacob."

"You look beautiful," he whispered.

She rolled her eyes, and to her old-ass shame, she wanted to run to him. When she offered no response, he continued, "I am here hoping you can talk to … to *him* so that this matter between him and Will can be stopped."

"Black is his own man. If'n you needs to speak with him, please do so. If'n ya came to talk 'bout matters 'tween Black and Will, it ain't in my control. You's squandered yo time, Jacob."

"He will listen to you." He sounded desperate.

"I cain't get him not to kill you. Let me make one thang clear to ya, Jacob. I wouldn't ever direct him, even if'n I could, not to defend all that is his; this is yo doin'. Why would ya take a child from my care to sell to the Hunter plantation? Ya forced my hand, Jacob. And I ain't no dummy—ya did it for spite and to save yo son the shame of loving a colored woman. Ya thanks I cain't see." She was emotional, and her voice had climbed a couple of octaves.

"Ellen," he groaned. "You have not acknowledged all that I have done for you, all that I have risked to turn a blind eye while you raised that damned militant out there. I don't want him to kill my son, Ellie; surely you can understand that."

"What would you has us do, Jacob? Give him Sunday 'cause he is entitled?"

She had him there; he had tried to get Will to stop this matter. Sinking down on the couch, he placed his head in his hands. "I love you, Ellie. What could I have done to change things between us?"

"Ya could of accepted loving a slave, like I accepted loving my masta. You, Jacob, could a brought yo high-and-mighty ass to my cabin when our child took her last breath, 'stead bein' relieved that you ain't had to deal wit' it. Ya cain't fix this, and if'n ya came to me for my help, ya ain't gon get it." She was shaking and breathless from speaking. When she got herself together, she quit the sitting room, leaving him to stare after her.

Seated on the couch, Jacob could feel his chest constrict. Black appeared in the doorway, and with no empathy, he said, "You will be escorted directly to the train."

"Ask her to come back. I still need to speak with her," Turner responded.

"If you come back, I will kill you. This was a courtesy for *her*. I will not extend kindness to you again," he said, standing in the doorway, never addressing Turner's statements.

Stepping out into the hallway, Jacob caught sight of Sunday; his anger was visible as he opened his mouth to blame her. He felt hurt and wanted to lash out. When he was about to speak, Black cut him off, saying, "You can go back to Virginia dead or alive. The choice is yours. I can accommodate whatever you choose."

Snapping his mouth shut, Jacob turned on his heels and walked out onto the porch, making his way back to the horse provided. As he was escorted back to the gate, it was like a long walk of shame, and he now felt worse than he had when he arrived. He hurt from loving her. It was all he could think about.

Sunday did not speak right away, holding her peace. Black leaned back against the wall, shaking with anger. It was time, he thought, to bring all matters to a close.

9

July 1859

Will watched from the window as a carriage rolled up the drive and pulled in front of the steps leading into the house. Out of the carriage stepped his father without Rose. Even from such a distance, Will could see that he did not look well. Meeting his father in the foyer, he found Amber helping to get him seated. Turner looked ashen, causing Will to call for a doctor.

When the doctor arrived, he was shown to his father's chamber. Will waited patiently in the hall, pacing while his father was examined. Although he had feelings of indifference toward his father, he did not want him to die. When the doctor came from the room, Will came to him, dreading what he would hear.

"He is plumb tuckered out is all; see to it that he gets rest," the doctor told him.

Will nodded and showed the doctor out. He went back to Turner's room to check on him. His father was propped up in his bed napping when Will returned, and just as Will was about to back out of the room, Turner spoke.

"Will, I am asking you to see reason and let this girl go. You are a wealthy man; you will inherit the Myers's fortune as well my own with the exception of what I set aside for Rose. You have a wife who loves you, and you seem to have some small affection for her. You have already done better than I have. Stop this while you still can. Your wife is from the North, and she will not turn a blind eye to this."

Although Will was happy that his father was all right, he was tired of hearing him speak already. "Amber is my concern, not yours. Get some sleep."

Will was already headed to the door when his father's weak voice followed him. "I have seen him and Sunday. I have been to his home. He is no easy win."

Spinning to look at his father, he said, "You saw Sunday? How is she?"

"Will, are you listening to me? He loves her, and he will kill anyone who tries to take her. Let this go, son," Turner pleaded.

Narrowing his eyes, Will asked, "Why did you go to Canada? I thought you went to Boston for Rose."

"I did go to Boston. I attempted to get Ellen's help to stop this fight," Turner said as he began to doze.

"Get some rest," Will said again to his father, and turning, he left the room. He was roiling with anger. Turner had gone to a slave that he owned, for God's sake, to get help with another slave that he owned. What the hell was this world coming to?

He would give Turner a few days to recuperate, and then he would put his plan in action. Turner was part of the problem, not the solution. Will underestimated how old and beat down his father truly was.

Turner saw Sunday, he mused. It was time to move forward.

Black stood at the window, tracking the dark clouds in the sky rolling their way. Watching the fields, he could see the men dancing at the first sign of rain. The weather depicted his mood since Turner's departure from the fort. He had not seen his mama in days, and he suspected she needed time. When she spoke about the death of their child, he could feel her pain. Black heard her speaking to Turner, and her anguish was evident. Turner may have missed it, but he had not. She rarely got emotional, and when her voice rose, he thought she would break down, but she didn't. The thought of being irrevocably broken from Sunday would kill him, and he was sad for his mama.

Several issues plagued him. One was marrying Sunday and her last name becoming Turner. Also on the list was that he really wouldn't have time to spend in celebration of their marriage. A gathering would have to come later; he had serious issues to address. What he wanted was to leave everything to Sunday, knowing that she and Mama would always be taken care of. It was a subject that needed discussing.

He looked around when she knocked on the door and then entered. She wore the cream-colored dress, and her hair was braided in one french braid with a brown ribbon tied on the end of the braid. Seeing him at the window, she joined him, happy to be near him.

"I haven't seen you all day," she said, looking up at him.

He smiled back, happy to see her; still, he stayed on task. "We need to talk."

"All right, love, what ya wants to talk 'bout?"

"We need to marry as soon as possible." *Damn, that came out wrong,* he thought.

"Why?"

"I am leaving soon, and I want to make sure you are taken care of before I leave."

"I fathom yo concern, Nat, but I wants this to be 'bout our love. I don't want it to be 'bout bidness." Her tone was sharp. "I was a slave, so's I ain't expecting much. I just wants ya to live in the moment wit' me," she said, trying to reel in her attitude.

"You come first, Sunday. I am riding out for your safety; that is my main focus. Don't fight with me."

They stared at each other, but before they could speak, there was a knock at the door. Otis entered, and seeing Sunday, he hesitated before saying, "I have a telegram from Tim."

Walking over to where they stood, Otis handed him the message:

MY CONDOLENCES AT THE DEATH OF YOUR FRIEND
SMITH

Black looked up at Otis, saying, "Move the child to Camille."

Otis never responded; he just turned and left, leaving them as they were.

Life was intruding on them with large doses of reality. Sunday kept the tremble from her voice when she asked him, "Who is Camille?"

Black paused before saying, "She is who will keep Curtis and care for him, and she is a kind woman." It was all he was willing to give.

"I's sho you has agreed to continue carin' for them. So you is plannin' to stay in touch wit' her." It was really a statement.

He offered no response.

Sunday did not expect an answer, and turning, she left him to his reality. When she stepped out into the hall, she was assaulted with feelings of jealousy and pettiness. *Damn him.*

Stepping out onto the porch, Black saw that the rain had stopped. The smell of damp earth and summer assailed him. It was late afternoon, and the overcast sky made it appear later than it was. Off in the distance, he could see men walking toward him, and he vibrated with expectation. There was a scuffle, but the blacksmith was subdued as they brought him to the bottom of the stairs. Paul appeared at his side, an angry look on his face. Black stood silent for effect and to give the crowd time to assemble out of curiosity.

When Black spoke, he addressed Smitty. "I think we have a problem. You have traded information about Fort Independence for personal gain." It was not a question.

Snatching his arms free from the men, Smitty stood staring up at Black. There was no fear, no shame, and it occurred to Black that Smitty thought Youngblood was coming to help him. He thought about Sunday and Curtis and the hurt this was causing. There was a calm that washed over him as he looked about at the crowd that had gathered.

When he spoke, the message was clear, his voice strong and steady. "I have risked my freedom and my life for what we have built. I offer protection to your families in exchange for your loyalty. I will accept nothing less than your loyalty for me and my family." He paused, and then, unstrapping his gun and handing it to Paul, he slowly descended the stairs. He wore a white shirt open at the throat, brown trousers, and black boots.

When he came face-to-face with Smitty, he said nothing, and they stood quietly eyeing each other. Smitty wore a sweat-stained white shirt that was ripped from the scuffle and black trousers. The intense eye contact with Black made his eyes begin to bounce from Black to the crowd searching for a sympathetic face … and he found none. Black could tell when it registered to him that he would die.

Smitty said, trying to save himself, "I have done nothing wrong." He managed to maintain eye contact.

Dismissing his lie, Black responded, "You have traded information about a woman from the fort to a slaver. The women and children of Fort Independence need never fear the men they live with. They should always feel safe in our presence. We stand guard in protection of them. What we have built affords us to be men, having a say in how our women and children are treated. You have negotiated with the safety of my woman … these women." And he raised his hands to indicate the women standing about. "And you will pay." An angry buzz broke out among the crowd.

Black jerked his knee up, connecting with Smitty's testicles; the man doubled over, and Black leaned down, grabbing the blacksmith by the face, head butting him. Blood spewed down Smitty's white shirt from where his forehead split open, and he moaned and fell to the ground in a fetal position. The crowd parted, and Paul came forward on a horse, handing Black the rope. Placing the noose about Smitty's neck, Black allowed the men from the crowd to step forward and grab Smitty. They tied his hands behind his back and then walked him to the nearest tree. Black patiently waited as they placed Smitty on the horse and strung him up.

The crowd parted as Black made his way to stand next to the horse. Facing the crowd, he spoke, and his rage was apparent. "I will not compromise your safety or the safety of my family. More importantly, I will not be tested. I am a man who will not tolerate being crossed. I have boundaries, and this man has crossed the line. I will defend my boundaries at whatever the cost."

And with a loud, guttural sound, Black slapped the horse swiftly on the hindquarters, and it bolted forward, causing the blacksmith's body to lurch upward, yanked by the rope. Black leaned back, bending one leg at the knee, and braced his booted foot against the tree. Along with the crowd, he watched as Smitty's body violently jerked and danced in the air as his life was sapped from him. And when he was reduced to tremors with no real signs of life, Philip, one of the fort's men, came forward to cut him down.

His voice cold and hard, Black said, "Leave him to hang."

Off in the distance, the sun broke through the clouds in a burst of orange-and-purple blends and then began to settle as the night approached. Still, Black remained leaned against the tree long after the crowd had dispersed. And when darkness had completely fallen, Black pushed off the tree, heading to the house. It was then that he saw Sunday standing on the porch almost at attention. They did not speak as he reached the landing and continued on into the house. Once he cleared the doorway, she stepped in line behind him. Turning to close the door, she looked out into the night, seeing Smitty's body still swinging.

In the following days, Black did his time in the barracks, and Sunday did not catch even a glimpse of him. She knew he was angry with her for being upset about the Camille woman, and as childish as it was, she was jealous. Adding to the issue was his intense mood of late, if the blacksmith still swinging from the tree was any indication. The people of Fort Independence went about their business. When she stepped from the house, she could smell Smitty's rotting body, and she understood why Black had sent Curtis away. She suspected they were all numb to violence after being slaves since it had been part of their everyday lives. Still, she wanted him cut down, but she wouldn't ask because she understood the message.

Sunday went about her chores with Iris, and eventually Mama came out of her room. Mama had been missing from daily life since Turner left, and Sunday knew it was to deal with her feelings privately. She was happy to see her, and though she wasn't her old self, she was still Mama.

Sunday stood cleaning the kitchen when Mama asked, "What is we cookin' for supper?"

Iris stared at her in utter disbelief when she said, "You are joking, right? How can you eat with that man's ass swinging from the tree like that?"

"I could eat," Mama said.

Sunday listened to their exchange, but her mind was on Black. She wanted to see and talk with him. She missed him. Excusing herself, she went about the rest of her chores and decided not to seek him out. As she headed for the dining room to dust, she could hear the women debating, and she knew Iris was happy that Mama was feeling better.

While she worked, Black appeared with Otis, telling her they would exchange the tub in their room for the new one he had bought. The sight of him made her heart squeeze, but she did not try to engage him in front of Otis. Other than that very small conversation, he offered nothing else and walked away. He worked with Otis until completing the move, placing the old tub in one of the upstairs bedrooms. She thought he would come back and talk to her, but he didn't.

The day wore on that way, and at dinner, Sunday sat with Paul, Iris, and Mama, everyone eating and no one talking. Iris fried a chicken that Paul killed, and they had biscuits, mashed potatoes, and lemonade. After dinner, she helped clean the kitchen and headed toward her room. She saw a light under his study door, but she wasn't brave enough to knock. Try as she might, she couldn't shake the jealousy, and between Mama, Turner, and the faceless woman who now had a name, she thought it better if she just went to bed.

When she stepped into the room she shared with him, she saw the beautiful cream-colored tub. Closing the door, she leaned against it and cried. Undressing herself completely naked, she lay in the bed, leaving two candles to burn. The weather was warm, and sleeping naked helped with the heat, and when she finally dozed, her eyes were swollen from crying.

Black paced in his study. He had been working through some figures, but all he could think about was her. He understood his mistake, but he would not give into childishness. Understanding his own moodiness, he knew one could not help the way one felt. While he was angry with himself for hurting her, he was angry with her for not understanding that she was his world. He steered clear of saying hurtful words to her; his life was heavy enough without ringing bells that could not be unrung. He went to his studio, and he did not paint.

In the morning when she woke and dressed, she saw that he had never come to bed. It was official: his time in the barracks was over, and he was avoiding her. While the realization hurt, it was better this way, because she was saturated with emotion and needed time to think. Again, she was back to feeling like all she wanted was something of him that was just hers. Every once in a great while, she just wanted to be selfish. She headed down to the school to be with Mary and the children.

Black was standing in the window of the study and saw her head down to the school. Trying to get focused once again, he went back to working the books when there came a knock at the door. "Come in," he called to the door.

Otis stepped through the door and just stared at him before speaking. "Do you want me to cut him down?"

Nothing … no response.

Otis acknowledged his lack of a reply to mean "Go away."

When Otis left, Black leaned back in his chair before standing. Removing his gun and pulling his shirt over his head, he restrapped the gun back to his shirtless side and headed for the door. Stepping out into the sunlight, Black was every bit the alpha male radiating power and authority. He stood on the porch assessing the task at hand before walking to the stables. There he retrieved a shovel and some rope.

The people of Fort Independence saw him and continued working, many saying nothing because he looked so serious. Others brave enough stepped forward asking if he needed help, respect showing in their eyes. Graciously, he declined, offering a small smile meant to reassure. Walking back to the tree where Smitty was still swinging, he began to dig, offering no reaction to the stench or the flies. Black worked the ground, digging a hole big and deep enough to stuff the blacksmith in. He worked tirelessly, his dark skin glowing with perspiration and his muscles rippling from his exertion. Sunday, wandering back to the house, saw the scene before her, and involuntarily, she thought, *Black is beautiful.*

When the sun was high in the sky, he completed the hole. Cutting Smitty down, Black tossed him unceremoniously into the grave. It was noticed by the people of the fort that instead of taking Smitty to the cemetery, Black buried him on the beaten path, his message unforgettable. And when his task was complete, he commenced digging a second hole. Upon finishing with the second hole, he stepped back, and turning to the tree, he began stringing a new noose. When he was done, the message became even clearer.

He offered lessons about the borders of man and what lines not to cross. And leaving the second grave open, he walked away with the shovel thrown over his powerful shoulder. Never did he utter a word.

$\sim$ $\sim$ $\sim$

Down at the barracks, he bathed and changed his clothes before heading back to the house. Once back at the house, he went to the study and continued working. Mama knocked at the door, bringing him a cool drink and something to eat. She was followed by Iris and Paul—but not Sunday. They came in, sat down, and began talking to each other—from what he could tell, about nothing.

Leaning back in his chair, he just stared at them, allowing them to basically talk to each other, figuring they would get to him.

Finally, Mama asked him, "Ain't ya gon to eat? Iris makes good chicken."

Iris chimed in, saying, "I told you he couldn't eat after burying that man."

"The man can eat," Paul said to Iris.

They all turned and looked at him, and he realized they were trying to be supportive. Shaking his head, he gave them a real smile before saying, "So you all think I have gone crazy?"

It was Paul who responded by saying, "Naw, son, we love ya, and we know the load ya carry."

He didn't expect that, and he slowly stared from one face to another, seeing they were all serious. Then he answered, his voice gruff, "The three of you have taken great care of me and often at the expense of your own lives. I can do no less. Everything we have started with the bravery of you, Mama, and you, Paul. Go about your day. I am fine, I promise."

He thought he had gotten away, but Paul came forward, causing him to stand and shake his hand. This action opened the door for Iris and Mama; they came forward, hugging and kissing him. He frowned at them, but they were not dissuaded. When they left, he thought about Sunday, and he sighed. He went back to work, and he did eat.

Later that night as Sunday finished up the kitchen, Mama took Black his dinner. She returned some time later with an empty plate, placing it in the sink as Sunday washed. Mama noticed Sunday staring out into the darkness of the yard from the kitchen window as she washed the same spoon over and over again. She smiled before saying to Sunday, "He is in the study. Ya can just go see him; ya ain't got to be miserable."

Sunday's head snapped around, and she gave a weak smile. Still, she offered nothing. She focused on the last few dishes, and drying her hands, she yawned. Mama didn't back away.

"Why ya so upset, child?"

"I ain't upset, just tired. I's gone to bed early."

"So ya ain't gon talk?"

"No, Mama, I needs to figure it out on my own."

Mama nodded. "I's here."

Sunday hugged her, saying, "I know. I just needs a minute."

"I understands," Mama replied, and her sad eyes said more.

"We'll talk in the morning; I has something to tell you."

Mama's interest was heightened. "Oh?" she said.

Stopping in the doorway, Sunday whispered, "He asked for my hand."

"And you said …?"

"I said yes," Sunday responded her voice flat.

"Ya don't want to marry him?" Mama asked.

"Let's talk in the morning," Sunday said, and turning on her heels, she left the kitchen.

Mama wouldn't even bother to ask him. She knew he wouldn't talk to her about this.

The hour had grown late, and instead of going to bed, Sunday headed outside. There was a light breeze blowing as Sunday sat on the steps in front of the house. She could still smell a slight sour odor in the air, but it was faint. Though she was tired, the porch was better than the lonely bedroom with the new tub. She was working through some of what she felt, but one issue remained. Was his sexual contact with the faceless Camille as intense? An insanity to know riddled her, but she would never ask.

Off in the distance, she could hear the crickets and all the sounds that made up summer. In her life, she never got to sit leisurely thinking, and now that she could, she found that it was dangerous; she thought too much. Sunday was overcome with insecurity, and just hearing him say *Camille* was hard. She would move past it on her own; she didn't want to talk about it. Sighing, she stood, and as she turned for the door, he was standing there quietly observing her.

Startled, she breathed in sharply at the sight of him. He stood leaning on the door frame, legs crossed at the ankles and his arms folded across his chest. Although it was dark, she could still see he was angry. He was blocking the door, and she knew it was on purpose.

Finally, he said, "I was looking for you."

"I's settin' on the porch gettin' some air. I's headed to bed. Excuse me, please."

He did not move. Instead, he asked, "How long?"

And to his surprise, she responded with an honest answer. "I's jealous, so you tell me—how long does jealousy last? I ain't clear. You has mo' experience wit' women than I has wit' men." Her voice carried bite.

He stepped back without response, allowing her to pass. When she was out of sight, he smiled.

About an hour passed before he headed back to their room. He entered the chamber and found her asleep wearing a thin shift. Undressing himself, he stood naked on the side of the bed, and leaning down he kissed her face, causing her to wake.

When she opened her eyes and looked up at him, he was hypnotized. Leaning down, he picked her up to position her the long way across the bed, and then he removed her shift. Sticking out his tongue, he traced her lips with the tip until she finally accepted his kiss. Black felt her shaking at his touch. Still he did not relent; he kissed her neck and then, moving between her breasts, he trailed kisses leading up to her deep, chocolate nipples. He licked around each nipple, teasing her before taking it into his mouth and pulling on it, causing her to moan.

Leaving each nipple wet and shining in the candlelight, he continued down her stomach, licking and kissing. When he reached between her thighs, he pushed her legs apart, tasting her. He saw her back arch from the intensity of his mouth against her flesh, and he was more than aroused. She was beautiful in the throes of passion, and he felt privileged to witness her rapture. He backed away, just staring at her womanhood, committing it to memory that he might paint her flower, and then leaning forward again, he licked at her lightly, causing her to plead for more.

He was not engaging in foreplay; he *wanted* her to orgasm so that he could make her come again. Her breathing was ragged, the sound filling the chamber. Black listened as she offered low and soft whimpers as if trying to communicate her pleasure. And when finally her back arched, she attempted to push him away, trying to fight the overstimulation, but Black subdued her, staying with her until she was spent. Standing, he leaned down, kissing her so that she could taste her passion on his tongue, and while she focused on the sensation and her flavor, he yanked her down to meet him at the side of the bed. Lifting her bottom to him, he plunged forward, entering her to the hilt. Roughly, he began slamming into her, repeatedly, taking her, making her his. Gritting his teeth, he groaned with each stroke, and when the sensation to orgasm started to chase him, he pulled out of her and flipped her, pulling her onto her knees. He slammed into her again, riding her, his movements frenzied. Sunday cried out as she began to spasm. Squeezing her bottom, he yanked her by the hips to meet his every thrust. Completion hunted him down, and when he could no longer elude the inevitable, Black threw back his head, his Adam's apple dancing as he brutally came.

"Ah, ah, sssssss, oh," he groaned, the feeling so powerful that he was shaken to his very core.

He separated from her, and climbing into the bed, he pulled her along with him until he settled in the middle. They lay speechless, looking at the ceiling, trying to catch their breath, with Black deep in thought. He understood that her jealousy was based on how they felt about each other; it was clear she thought it was this way for everyone.

It was not this way for everyone, and he never felt this damned extreme about anyone. He thought of seeing her as a woman for the first time, undressed for Will … and he backed away from the thought because it was not the road to peace. Oh, he understood her jealousy; he was plagued by it himself.

The idea that Will was willing to lose everything to have her made him crazy. His voice was deep and sounded strange to his own ears when he asked her, "Why do you suppose Will wants you back?"

"Will wants me back 'cause he sees me as his slave."

Black laughed a low rumble from deep in his chest. "Surely you see he wants you because he wants to be a man to you, not an owner. The owner part is a formality meant to control."

"Why is we talkin' 'bout this, Black?" she asked, leaning up on one elbow.

He was *Black* when she was annoyed. "I am attempting to instruct you about jealousy," he said, smirking.

"This ain't a good example," she responded dryly.

Becoming serious again, he said, "I have never experienced what we have before emotionally or sexually. It is not this way for everyone, Sunday."

She stared at him, and he did not back away from her scrutiny. He continued when she didn't speak.

"I know you hurt, and I know that it is my doing. You have nothing to be jealous of. There is truly no one for me but you. Curtis is with her because that is the best choice for him. Otis will handle the issue from here on out."

She did not speak, but she snuggled closer, placing her head back on his chest. He was offering to understand her pain, no matter how childish, and it was more than she hoped for. It was reassuring and in the end what she needed. Instead, when she spoke, it was to address their upcoming marriage. "I understands that you has much on yo plate, but I don't wants a hasty marriage."

"Is it that you don't wish to marry me, Sunday?" His voice faltered.

She reached up, caressing his face, and looking him in the eye, she said, "Oh, baby, no, I would die if I cain't be yo wife. I just wants ya to plan to live wit' me rather than die on me. I feels like ya's given up, and all ya thanks ya has left is to marry me to save me. I needs you."

"Is this too much for you?" he asked, and she could feel him tense.

She was honest when she said, "Yes, it's too much for me at times, and it's too much for *you* at times. I wants all of ya, even that part that is too much. This is my life too now, and I wouldn't trade it. I cain't be witout ya."

He sounded afraid when he said, "I can't just turn it on and off, Sunday. This is me; this is who I am."

Leaning back, she smiled at his look of concern before saying, "You thanks I would ask ya not to be yoself?"

He was silent, attempting to control his insecurity.

"I's askin' ya to please make time for me … make time for you … make time for yo family. You ain't got to stop being mean and moody."

He chuckled, but still he did not speak; he just listened. They settled, and finally he could feel her even breathing, signifying that she had fallen asleep. Black lay awake thinking of what she was asking, and he was troubled.

Black was in his study when the house came alive and everyone finally started to wake. He was still thinking about all that Sunday was asking of him, and he worried that he could not produce. She was right—there was a lot on his plate, but most important was to back Will off of them. The blacksmith had been taken care of, and Black would ride out soon. He needed to try to meet her halfway, and while he had anxiety, he knew there was nothing he wouldn't do for her.

He could smell the food and hear the clink of dishes. Standing, he headed to the door. Black made it down the hall to the kitchen and stood in the doorway. The table was laden with scrambled eggs, bacon, and biscuits, and the smell of coffee in the background made his stomach growl. He felt awkward as he stood watching them seat themselves. Iris, Mama, Paul, and Sunday spoke about the weather, the wheat, and the young man who helped Paul at the stables, and they laughed. Black stood watching, and just when he was about to lose courage and back out of the kitchen, Paul noticed him.

"Did you need something?" Iris asked, and they all stood ready to handle his request.

Sunday did not move, and she smiled, which made him frown at her.

"I was going to bring your food later," Iris continued.

He jammed his hands in his pockets and then took them out of his pockets before saying, "I came to have breakfast with you all."

They all just stared at him like he had a chicken growing out of his head.

It was Sunday who took mercy on him, saying, "Sit next to me, Nat."

Once seated, Paul continued with his stories, and Black just listened. Sunday threw back her head, laughing at something he said, and Black couldn't take his eyes off her. Seeing her smile and hearing her laughter moved him. When finally he looked back at Paul, his eyes connected with Mama's. He frowned at her, causing Mama to smile, and he smiled too.

They ate and talked with Black spectating, and when breakfast came to a close, Paul headed to the stables, and the women began clearing the dishes. Sunday went to the sink, and Iris waved her away, saying, "We'll clean the kitchen. Go."

Black took her by the hand, and they followed Paul out of the house, going left when Paul went right. They walked along the side of the cabins and into the trees.

Finally, Sunday said, "Where is we goin'?"

He stopped, and throwing his hands up, he said, "I am spending time with you."

They were through the trees with the sunlight peeking through the leaves when she stopped and looked at him. His facial expression was confused. Sunday couldn't help it; she burst out laughing, and he frowned at her while walking toward her. She turned and began running to get away from him, but her laughter made her weak. He ran after her, and when he caught her, he picked her up, swinging her around. She giggled, and she couldn't stop.

"Exactly what is so funny, Sunday?" he asked, enjoying everything about her. "You're laughing at me."

Breathlessly, she lied, "No, I ain't."

They lingered in the shade where it was cooler, talking about everything and nothing at all. She asked him when he wanted to get married. Black responded by telling her that he couldn't marry someone that laughed at him, and it was his turn to run. She chased him, but he was too fast.

Placing her hands on her hips, she yelled after him, "Get back here, Nat Turner!"

She stared at him dressed in blue trousers, black boots, and a white shirt that he had unbuttoned because of the heat. He was stunning in his masculinity, and she couldn't take her eyes off him. Seeing him laugh made him look so young and carefree, and she was happy. She was so pleased that she walked toward him, and when she reached him, she hugged him, burying her face against his bare chest.

Sunday wore a yellow short-sleeved day dress with hard-bottom black shoes. Iris had been experimenting with new braiding styles, and her hair was braided in lots of little plaits that hung and curled on the end. The hairstyle made her eyes even more expressive, and he was lost when she stared up at him. He considered her small stature, and he was struck by his concern for her safety.

She could feel when he tensed, but she continued to hug him. Feeling his arms close around her, she sighed. Leaning her head back, she looked up at him, smiling. She had beautiful teeth, and her front left tooth was chipped. He had never noticed before, and he decided not to ask how it got chipped because it would probably make him mad. Taking her by the hand, they walked at their leisure back to the house.

She chatted about the children and the fact that she had been reading with them when she went down to the school. She told him she was getting better, but she still had a ways to go on the writing. He reassured her that it would improve; he wished she would come back and let him finish teaching her, but he said nothing. As they came out of the trees and walked beside the cabins, he noticed that the people of Fort Independence watched them as they worked at whatever chore they performed. They called to Sunday, and she called back, asking after their families. At him, they just waved.

When they reached the front of the house, she stared at the tree, the open grave, and the noose that hung from the branch. Black noticed her reaction, and he commented, "I am serious about your safety."

She squeezed his hand and whispered, "I ain't wantin' ya to change."

10

August 1859

It was finally coming together, the makings of a plan that would bring Black to his knees and return Sunday. Will would begin by calling a meeting of the surrounding plantation owners, bringing to everyone's attention the number of runaways that had escaped in the last year alone. Turner was no longer the boss, and unlike his father, he would address the issue by tracking him.

When he ventured from the study, he saw his father heading toward him. Turner was slower and still weak, but he was out of bed. His father wore a white shirt and gray trousers with a black belt and shoes. Tilly must have cut his hair, because it wasn't unruly.

Upon seeing him leaving the office, Turner called to him. "Will, I would like to have a word with you."

Holding the door to the study, Will waved his father in, and shutting the door behind them, he turned, asking, "What is the problem? Are you not well?"

"I'm fine … I'm fine. I received a word of thanks from Ben Matthews on finally addressing the runaway causing them all grief. What did you tell them, and why are they coming here?"

"I have narrowed down that runaways are getting help from a slave called Black. I have not said he came from here; what I have said is if we catch him, we can make an example of him."

"I have been to his home, William. A few plantation owners and some overseers that have the upper hand when dealing with submissive slaves will not work with him. The law is different in Canada. Let this slave go."

"How many times can you tell me that he is a better man?" Will asked calmly, attempting to mask the hurt he was feeling.

"Listen to me, son. I am right about this. I have been wrong so many times in my life. I promise my words are not because I think he is a better man," Turner responded, seeing for the first time that his son's actions were not all about Sunday.

"My decision is made," Will said, dismissing his father and reaching for the doorknob to let him out.

"I forbid you to continue in this foolishness," Turner hissed as his complexion became purple from his anger. "I have pleaded with you ... no more, Will. I am putting my damn foot down. I will remove you from being in charge until you come to your senses!" He was yelling loudly now.

Calmly, Will stared at him before saying, "You are not in charge, old man. I will not be undermined, and you will not get in my way."

"This is my house, and you are the guest!" Turner yelled, loosening his tie. His face was sweaty.

Will slammed open the study door and strode away with Turner yelling behind him. His booted feet striking the wooden floor, as he stalked from the study. Turner ran behind him, yelling his name, and then suddenly he grabbed at his chest, crumpling to the floor. Will had his foot on the first step when he saw Turner clutch his chest with an expression of sheer pain. Amber was at the top of the steps asking what all the yelling was about. Swiftly Will turned, running back to his father. Down on his knees, Will loosened his father's already loose tie and further unbuttoned his shirt, trying to give him relief. Turner was gasping for air, and his skin had a purple tint. It seemed that the blood vessels in his eyes burst, because his eyes were red and bulging.

As Tilly came running toward them, Will yelled, "Fetch Doc Peters now!"

Turner, his father, was dying; Will began shaking him to keep him responsive, but it was clear the doctor would not make it in time.

"Hold on, damn you." He pulled his father close, cradling his head in his lap. "Hold on ... please," he whispered.

Jacob Turner took his last breath in his son's arms, an expression of pain-filled shock frozen on his face. Will did not acknowledge that he died. Instead, he examined himself. All these years, he *had* been jealous of his father's feelings for the dark woman. He had also been embarrassed for himself, his mother, and his sister. When Sunday came along, it seemed the perfect revenge until he fell in love with her. The game had backfired on him, but he didn't realize he felt this way until Turner tried to stop it.

In his grief-induced fog, he heard Amber talking to the doctor. Focusing in on Amber, he could see the concern in her eyes. Releasing his father, he stood and walked slowly back to the study, issuing orders in a low and calm voice. "Have the slave Toby come and ready the body. I will send a telegram to notify Rose. Thank you, Doctor—looks like your services will not be needed."

Amber followed him, and once in the study, she asked, "Dear, is there anything I can do?"

He stared at her for a long moment. He was slightly dazed, but eventually he found the words. "Yes. Direct the slaves to get the house together. I want my father in the front parlor ready to receive guests by noon tomorrow."

"I'll take care of it, dear," she said, and she stepped toward him.

He put his hand up, stopping her. "That will be all for now, Amber."

She stopped, and though she wanted to run to him, she respected his wishes. When she was gone, he realized he cared for his wife, but he loved Sunday. The death of his father made him feel lonely, and for some reason, his mother popped in his head. He felt like an orphan. It was a feeling he didn't understand; he was almost thirty summers. And when he was sure that he would not be interrupted, he cried. It was a good shoulder-shaking cry, and when he was empty, his mind turned to Black.

Black was not the better man.

Boston
August 1859

Anderson was about to sit down to the breakfast table to wait for Rose to join him. He was just about to start reading the paper when there was a knock at the door. The butler approached, and Anderson waved him on. "There is a delivery of a telegram for Miss Rose."

Rose was coming down the long hall when she heard Alfred talking. "It must be Father letting me know when he'll arrive."

Alfred was reluctant to give her the message, and he stared at Anderson for support. Shrugging, Anderson nodded his approval. She took the message, scanned the paper, and immediately began to weep. Anderson rushed to her side, taking the telegram from her hand.

FATHER HAS DIED COME HOME IMMEDIATELY

Anderson was angry that Will didn't even try to soften the blow. "Come and sit," he said as he called for Alfred to bring some water.

Alfred appeared, his face serious, with a glass of water. Anderson handed Rose the glass, and after taking a sip, she attempted to calm down. Rose finally found her voice. "I want you to marry me. I do not want Will in charge of me."

Anderson's face registered shock from her words. He wanted to marry her—he was fond of Rose—but he was the damn man. Rose read his thoughts, saying, "Maybe you'll be invited to my wedding. I don't see why my husband would mind my being friends with an old male acquaintance. I'm sure Will knows best."

It was later that afternoon when Anderson and Rose stood in his parlor facing his good friend, the Honorable Judge Joseph Milford, as he recited the words making them man and wife.

"You may now kiss the bride," Judge Milford concluded.

Rose looked up at him as he planted a chaste kiss on her lips. Anderson was tall and thin with thick glasses. He had brown hair, blue eyes, and a very big nose. His mouth in conjunction with the rest of his face was very small. There was no mistaking that he was handsome, but one had to look twice to see it. He wore a brown suit, looking as though he were heading to court. She wore a white day dress with limp flowers picked from the garden. Rose was happy and sad all at once, but now that she was married, she was ready to face and deal with Will.

With their vows said, she was now Mrs. Anderson Wilkerson. There would be no celebration. They headed for Virginia immediately.

∿ ∿ ∿

Rose stepped into the parlor just as two slaves were about to close the coffin. The room had a faint smell of death; the guests, being polite Southerners, behaved as though they didn't smell it. The house was open for the slaves to come pay their respects, but they were a superstitious lot, opting not to enter a house with a dead body. Will came forward, taking her hand, ushering her forward to view their father. Jacob Turner was stretched out in his best Sunday go-to-meeting clothes, his hair combed neatly. When Rose looked down at him, she felt nothing but sorrow. She loved him. She did not cry; her emotions were private.

After a few minutes, six slaves came forward, closing the coffin and carrying it out of the house down to the horse and buggy that waited. It was a hot August day even though it was cloudy. The guests followed on foot, and the slaves sang old hymns as they moved toward the cemetery. Off in the distance, tombstones marked the final resting place for those who had gone before. At the gravesite, they prayed for his soul again. The preacher was fire and brimstone, so by the time the mourners headed back to the house for repast, they all felt like they were going to hell.

Once in the dining room, the tables were loaded down with all the trimmings of a good Southern meal. The guests mingled, telling funny stories about Jacob Turner, some true and some made up.

∿ ∿ ∿

In his study, Will had called a meeting with ten plantation owners. He began informing them about the slave Black, who was robbing them of their property and money. Will's hope was to involve as many plantation owners as possible to make it hard for Black to venture back to the south. The men were riled up because their very way of life was being threatened. And Will Turner was smart enough to exploit it for his own gain—or so he thought.

"Since I have taken over my father's duties, I count fifteen slaves who have run. I believe they received help from the slave who calls himself Black."

Edward Hunter posed the question, "Wasn't he one of your slaves?"

"He most certainly was not a slave from this plantation. Runners are dealt with severely," Will responded.

"Youngblood thought he was from this plantation. He also maintained that the slave is the infamous Nat Turner's son and the reason his eye was missing," Hunter said in an accusatory tone.

Will had not expected Youngblood to be so free with information about their plantation, and he would make certain his successor understood that gossip would not be permitted. "Youngblood has gone crazy; he just upped and walked away. How could you take his word?"

"Youngblood struck me as a lot of things, but crazy was not one of them. I think he is dead, if you ask me," Wilson said.

Matthews chimed in, asking, "How long has Youngblood been gone?"

The men all began talking at once, and the situation was far from organized. Will realized that he would have to let them vent first before he could get the group to move forward. He also understood that if he kept trying to discredit Youngblood, it would work against his cause. Will wanted to move forward with the plan to bring about Black's demise. All he could think about was Black being the man in Sunday's life. Will shut his eyes against the thought of Black touching her. Most disturbing was the thought of her accepting his touch with anticipation.

At the very back of the study stood Tim, watching the scene as it unfolded. He listened and did not comment, thinking to himself that Will Turner had missed his mark with this bunch. They could just as easily lynch him instead of Black. The men started venting, and he noticed that Will stopped talking; clearly he understood he may have bitten off more than he could chew with this group.

He would send Black a message when the time was right, Tim decided.

The morning after Jacob Turner was laid to rest, Will slowly descended the grand staircase to find Anderson standing in the parlor staring out the window. He turned to Will.

"Morning, Will."

"Good morning. I would like to thank you for getting my sister home. I appreciate your looking after her while she was in Boston."

"No need to thank me; it's my job to look after my wife," Anderson replied, dismissing Will's shocked expression.

"You married my sister without my approval?"

"I married your sister with your father's approval. I'd like us to be friends, for Rose's sake," Anderson said, smiling and extending his hand.

Stepping back from Anderson, Will did not shake his hand. Turning on his heels, he stalked away, fuming at the nerve of Anderson Wilkerson.

Watching Will's retreating back, Anderson smiled, thinking he would rather not be friends with his new brother-in-law.

~ ~ ~

Black was seated behind his desk when Sunday walked into his study. He could see that she had something on her mind, so he waited.

"I wants to hang some of yo paintin's round the house. They's wasting in the studio."

He stared at her with no response for a time. She was not deterred. "You gon has to do better than the silent treatment."

"I'll let you take whatever paintings you want if you will let me teach you how to shoot," he said gently.

"I'm ain't interested in learnin' to shoot no gun," she responded, her eyebrows drawn together.

"That is my offer."

Sunday thought about the deal, and finally she said, "So, can I has all the paintin's?"

"Once I paint them, I have no use for them. Painting is a stress reliever for me," he said, shrugging. "The only paintings you can't have are the ones I painted of you."

"When we start shootin' lessons?"

145

"Tomorrow," he said.

"Since you don't care 'bout the paintin's, I could have taken them witout barterin', right?"

"Correct. Everything in the house is yours."

"Horseshit," she said, stomping her foot.

Black threw back his head and laughed out loud. Sunday was his breath of fresh air.

Sunday had moved on to the next subject. "I has decided on a date for the wedding."

Black's expression changed from carefree to serious. He said nothing and waited.

Sunday, recognizing the change asked, "What's wrong?"

"What day do you want to get married?" he asked, stepping over her question.

"Please, tell me," she whispered.

He stood and walked over to the window, nervously jamming his hands in his pockets and taking them out to do it again. Sunday sat waiting to hear what was to come.

"It's my name. I don't want you to be Sunday Turner."

She visibly relaxed. "I don't understand. Ain't that's who I am? Sunday Turner? Is you changin' yo name?"

"I thought of that, but I am Nat Turner's son. I wish to keep his name."

"Thank God," she whispered. "I fell in love wit' ya, Nat Turner; I wishes to be Mrs. Nat Hope Turner. I love yo name. I never gives Will Turner no thought when I thinks of being yo wife. I sees ya as yo own man. I don't want ya to change."

He was filled with emotion and tensed. He did not speak, so she said, "Come to our room in 'bout thirty minutes," and she was gone.

Black was thankful she had given him a few minutes to manage how he was feeling. He had not expected her response, and he was at a loss for words. After thirty minutes, perhaps longer, he headed to their room, and opening the door, he found Sunday in the tub.

"Close the door, and come get in," she whispered.

Black smiled, his surprise obvious, and undressing quickly, he climbed in. They had been so busy spending time out of the room that they had not used the tub together since it had arrived. It was August, so the water was room temperature. The windows were open, the curtains drawn back, letting in the sunlight and a light breeze. He was leaned back in the tub, relaxing.

"You are a bad influence," he whispered.

She laughed, climbing up to straddle him, and in all seriousness, she continued, "Now 'bout the wedding date."

"What date would you like?" he asked, the stress from earlier gone.

"Can we marry September 20?" she asked.

"We can get married any day you want. Why September 20? Is that your birthday?"

Leaning back, she gave him a small smile, and he was kicking himself before she spoke. "I do not know my birthsday."

"Pick a day, and it will be your birthday," Black responded, not missing a beat, yet deep down he was bothered. He did not ask her birthday because most slaves didn't know when they were born. It was common practice for the owners not to tell the slaves, even if they knew. He offered her no pity.

"You knows yo birthsday?" she asked.

"November 11, 1831."

"I figured ya knew," she whispered, impressed. "I wants to be Mrs. Nat Hope Turner. Can I share yo birthday?"

"You can have anything you want from me, Sunday," he said, and she leaned up and kissed him.

"So you wants to jump the broom in September?" she asked.

"No, I actually want to get married and record the marriage license at the courthouse. I want what is legally mine to pass to you should something happen to me," he snapped, his words a little more forceful than he wanted them to be.

"I ain't thought of it that way," she said, looking deep in thought.

"I'm sorry. I didn't mean to snap," he said, leaning back and closing his eyes.

She laid her head on his chest, listening to the water dance around the tub.

He closed his arms about her, holding her close, and said, "I don't want to embrace being a runaway."

She understood, and she found that he was struggling with having a family and being a runaway. Turning, she settled between his legs, and leaning back against his chest, she asked, "Will we marry here at the fort?"

"We will marry here. Herschel is a minister, and he will record the license," Black said.

"Ya seem riled up. Is September 20 too far away?" she asked.

"No."

They stood, drying each other, and they didn't rush to get dressed. Instead, they lay across the bed bathed in the sunlight, Sunday's cocoa-brown body and his midnight-dark skin. They talked in hushed tones, laughing and debating. It was a new level of intimacy being experienced by both. When Sunday finally dozed off, he continued to watch her. He loved her.

Long after she had fallen asleep, he remained in thought. Will was devising a plan, Black was sure of it, and all scenarios played in his head. He wanted to marry her now, but he understood her complaint. The truth was he was excited about marrying her and spending his life with her. He had not allowed himself to hope before her. Now it scared him that all he did was plan the future, hoping for more. He wanted Will to go away, and if he didn't go peaceably ...

Sliding from the bed, he dressed and headed through the kitchen where Mama and Iris sat. Grabbing an apple, he headed out the door, ignoring their nosy gestures. As they watched his retreating back, Iris said, "Sunday is sleep in the middle of the afternoon. What do you make of that?"

"Same thang you makes of it," Mama said.

The next afternoon Black led Sunday through the stables, walking the center aisle from what was considered the front door to the back. On either side of the aisle, the horses watched them moving along; Paul was mucking a stall when they appeared. Black held a Sharps rifle in his hand and a box of ammunition under his arm. Sunday followed him, barely able to keep up, until finally they stepped out the large back doors. There was a fence off in the distance and trees behind it. The day was hot with no breeze at all. Placing the box and the gun on a makeshift table, he turned, giving her his attention.

"Are you ready?" he asked, his face serious.

She wasn't ready, but she nodded.

Pointing to the gun, he said, "This is a single-shot Sharps rifle breechloader. The butt of the rifle is inlaid wood. This metal arm is the folding block. Here you have two triggers, one to set and the other to release. This mechanism that folds down is your sight; the barrel is thirty-four inches long and can mark from six hundred to a thousand yards." He paused, looking at her. "Are you following me?"

"I's listenin'," she said.

He handed her the rifle, giving her a moment to get used to the weight. She struggled a little, but he did not step forward to help her. Instead, he put his hands in his pockets. Paul came forward with another rifle, handed it to Black, and then stepped back. Black began to demonstrate loading the gun. Opening the top chamber, he lifted what looked like paper from the box and stuffed it in. Pulling the arm back, he cut some of the paper off. Unfolding the sight, he lifted the gun, placing the butt against his shoulder and firing. Down along the fence, a bottle shattered, and Sunday jumped from the unexpected noise.

"Now you try," he said.

She was about to refuse when he said, "I need you to be able to defend yourself and any children we might have."

It was said for her ears only, and he was pleading with her. He helped her load it. Then, standing in back of her, Black positioned the butt of the gun against her shoulder and showed her how to hold her arms. Setting the sight, he talked to her about what she saw. Then, talking her through setting the triggers, he stepped back, saying, "Ready when you are."

Sunday took the shot, and the kick knocked her back, making her stumble. She fell on her ass, and her shoulder was sore. Frustrated, she stood, saying, "One more 'gain."

When she fell, he thought this was a bad idea, and he was about to go help her when Paul stayed him. He nodded and watched her struggle with getting back on her feet and reloading the gun. When she was ready to shoot again, he handed her cotton for her ears. The men started gathering to watch. Some had pointers, some even stepping forward taking some shots to demonstrate. Black stood back and watched the first part of his plan in motion. It wasn't enough to give her tools and resources; he was showing her how to manage herself and in the process giving himself peace of mind.

Later that night while in the tub, he saw that her shoulder was bruised. He offered, "I have a Smith & Wesson pistol for you."

She lay on his chest as he leaned contentedly back in the water. "Hmm," she responded. Sunday had had a long day, but it was not lost on her that he was warming to children. He seemed more alive, and it gave her hope.

Stepping from the tub, they dried, and once in bed, he made slow love to her. When they were satisfied, he placed his head on her stomach as she caressed his neck and shoulders, and he drifted off to sleep.

In the morning, Black was seated behind his desk working when Otis came in to check on him. He looked serious, causing Black to put his pen down. "What is it?" he asked.

"We have a telegram from Tim," Otis said.

Black offered no response.

Otis handed him the message and waited.

John is making noise Turner carried by six A
Black Sunday approaches

Looking up from the telegram, Black shook his head before saying, "I cannot deviate from the plan. I have to marry her before I can ride out."

"When do you marry?"

"September 20 is the date," Black responded.

"About three weeks away," Otis replied.

Leaning back in his chair, Black sighed before saying, "Send Tim a telegram."

"I'll head into town now," Otis said as he headed for the door.

When Otis opened the door, Sunday was just about to knock. He exchanged pleasantries with Sunday, asking after Mary. As they spoke, Black was deep in thought. He would bring the fight to Virginia to keep it away from the fort.

Sunday's voice pulled him from his thoughts. "Is we going shootin'?" she asked.

He stood, heading for the door behind Otis. "Yes. We need to make a point of you coming in to read with me so I can see where you are."

"What happened?" Sunday asked.

"Not now, Sunday. We are going to spend time together."

The days passed quickly, with Sunday practicing shooting regularly. When they weren't shooting, they were in his study with him teaching her how to add and subtract. She had gotten better at reading, but to Black, she was not where she should be. They argued some about her lack of focus, as he was relentless in his need to see her self-sufficient.

They went over the books, with him showing her his system, and when she answered yet another question wrong, he blew up to his shame.

"Damn it, Sunday, pay attention."

She stood and put her hand on her hips before saying, "I's done for the day."

He responded, "We are done when I say we are done."

Staring at him, her eyes narrowed before she answered, her voice low and menacing, "You's wrong. It cain't be when you say, 'cause I's done now." She turned and walked out, slamming the door, muttering under her breath.

Black stared after her, shaking his head.

He didn't come to dinner and waited for her to go to bed before he ventured out of the study. As he approached the kitchen, Mama sat alone at the table. She looked up when he entered the kitchen.

"Sit and join me," she said.

Doing as she asked, he sat, and she stood. She moved toward the stove and brought back a plate of country-fried steak, mashed potatoes, and green beans for him. Reseating herself, she asked, "Ya pushin' her hard. Why?"

Putting down his fork, he sighed before answering. "If something happens to me, I want you two to be able to manage."

Mama smiled. "Big as you are, I thank she meaner."

He chuckled. "I think you're right."

They talked for a while, just spending time. Black never mentioned Turner's death, and he felt no guilt.

He walked Mama to her room and went to find his own bed. Sunday was sleep; she wore a pale rose shift for a nightgown. Instead of undressing, he sat on the bed, and it dipped under his weight, causing her to wake. Seeing the expression on his face, she sat up leaning back against all the pillows. The argument forgotten, she said, "Black."

He measured his words before saying, "I am not planning to die. I just want you to be able to help yourself in my absence."

Opening her arms, he leaned forward and kissed her tenderly. When he pulled away, he handed her a velvet box. He saw her eyes light up. *Thank God for Virgil*, he thought. Living like he had, he had not even thought of rings.

"Open it," he said.

Doing as he asked, she opened the box, and there on the velvet bed were three rings. The two smaller rings were hers, the band solid gold with diamonds all the way around. The second ring a solid band with a high-set diamond. The third was a plain band of solid gold, only wider and fit for a man. She cried as he took the ring with the single diamond and placed it on her finger.

"I love you," he whispered as he pushed the ring on her tiny finger.

She cried and laughed at the same time, kissing him. "I loves you more," she whispered.

Sunday stood, dancing over to the mirror to look at herself. Black undressed and came to stand behind her in the mirror. She could feel his stiff manhood pressed against her back, and she wanted him inside her. Turning, she stuck her tongue in his mouth, kissing him with passions that matched his own. Pushing her shift up, he lifted her, impaling her right where they stood. And there in front of the mirror, he palmed her bottom lifting her and dropping her repeatedly onto him. Muscles straining, sweating, and teeth gritting, he continued like that until she threw her head back, weeping his name.

Dropping to his knees, he laid her on the hard floor just under the window. Feeling the soft breeze blowing at his damp skin, he rode her until he was weak from climaxing … mindless words of love on his lips.

Bliss.

Tim received a telegram.

YOUR MESSAGE LIT A FIRE

He smiled and responded to Black in a telegram of his own.

THANK YOU FOR YOUR COMFORT DURING THIS DARK TIME
ANY LIGHT YOU CAN PROVIDE WILL BE GREATLY APPRECIATED

Black responded in yet another telegram.

WHEN YOU NEED ME I WILL COME AND SHED LIGHT

In the days approaching the wedding, Black doubled up on the security around the wall and the house. He moved into the barracks the week before the wedding, doing his time with the men. Sunday saw very little of him, but she didn't complain. Mama and Iris had her tied up with hair, dress, and shoes. They were taken with her ring, and in truth, neither they nor Sunday had ever owned anything so fine.

Sally made Sunday a white, off-the-shoulder dress, cut low enough to show off her beauty yet not low enough to scandalize. Mama and Iris sighed when they saw her in it; the matching transparent veil was embroidered with flowers, adding to her femininity. When she said that she wanted Black to see her, they all yelled, "No!" Sunday jumped, startled.

"Black cannot see your dress until the wedding," Iris said, and Mama nodded to confirm she agreed.

Iris tried different braiding styles on Sunday, and they couldn't decide what would go with the dress. They plucked her eyebrows, and the pain was great, but they did it early so the swelling would have time to go down. When the women were finished prepping her, they put the dress away so no mishaps would happen. Sally left with the promise that she would be back to stay a few days for the wedding. They walked Sally to the porch where she was picked up by the horse and buggy that escorted her back to town.

It was Iris who seemed anxious for them to be alone. They wandered back down the hall to the kitchen, each taking a seat at the table. Looking off to the opposite side of the kitchen where the hall continued, Sunday wanted to go and lie down. Mama leaned back in her chair when Iris said, "I have been counting, and you have not come around since the end of July."

Sunday's head popped up, and her eyebrows drew together as she desperately counted. Mama never moved, giving her a minute to think. *Oh no.* She had been so busy with learning to shoot, read, write, and problem solve that she never thought about it. She hadn't missed a drink. She stood and then sat and then stood and then sat.

Mama took no mercy on her when she spoke. "We told ya it ain't foolproof."

Sunday stood. "I's gon to bed, and you two ain't to speak on it."

Mama was about to speak when Sunday lifted her hands. "I cain't hear ya. I needs a minute to figure. You ain't to tell him … I will."

Once alone in her room, she paced until she was finally exhausted, and then she lay down. He would be in the barracks all week, which gave her time to get used to the idea before breaking the news to him. Standing again, she took off her clothing and stood in front of the mirror. She looked no different. Maybe she would come around and just be late. She would make certain before telling him anything.

11

September 1859

Black saw the tailor while at the barracks; Joseph made him a fine black suit cut to perfection. When he dressed completely so they could see how he would look, Otis commented, "You look like a gentleman and not the mean brute we used to."

Black laughed, saying, "I may look the gentleman, but I can assure you I am anything but."

The men wanted to go to town for women and drinks. Black declined, saying he did not need the trouble. They laughed, especially Otis, who understood the hard lesson there. When Black made up his mind that he wouldn't cheat, it was not for Sunday; it was for himself. Understanding his own emotions, he found that because he loved and needed her, to deal in infidelity was more a betrayal to himself rather than to her. He would not engage in cutting off his nose to spite his face.

In keeping with his instincts, he called a meeting in the barracks. The men who patrolled as well as the men with other duties came to get instruction about how life would be until after the wedding. The room was crowded with men spilling out the front and the back doors of the barracks. They stood between the neatly made beds with pea-green blankets neatly folded back. A breeze blew through the room, and because of the cross ventilation and the proximity to the stable, there was a faint smell of horse.

Standing in the center with Otis, Black said, "Three days before the wedding, Fort Independence will be locked down until two days after the ceremony. Though the people are free to come and go, at the three-day mark, whoever is out will stay out, and whoever is in will stay in until the ban is lifted. Should someone choose to leave, the gate keepers should take names so that we might keep track of the comings and goings." He paused and then continued. "Each man will have a partner while they patrol, and the security around the house will double. Otis will notify you if you have been chosen to watch the house. Any questions?"

Someone deciding this would be a good time to tease him said, "How did you trick a nice woman like Miss Sunday into marrying you?"

"I've been hiding the real me. When she finds out who I really am, it will be too late," Black said, chuckling, and the men laughed, as well.

The men talked with Black, as it was a rarity for him to mingle, and many were surprised that he knew all their names. After a while, the crowd thinned out, leaving Black and Otis standing behind the barracks. The sun was going down, as the men went about wrapping up their day. Harvesting wheat was hard work. Black and Otis stood watching off in the distance as the men worked.

Otis, reading Black's mind, said, "We'll bring the fight back to the plantation to spare the fort a siege."

"If we can manage to stop the women and children from going through a battle, I would prefer it."

"This ain't just your fight, Black. We all love Sunday."

"I know," Black said, looking at Otis. "I actually feel better that she can handle a gun. I just want what's best for everyone here."

"The people here want what's best for you, as well. This issue with Will ain't your burden. The people here know that. The chance of being tracked can happen to any one of us."

Black was silent for a time before confirming, "You will look after her and Mama if—"

Otis cut him off. "My job is at yo' back. You will care for them yoself."

"I just need to get through this wedding, and then we ride out. Let us hope that John doesn't bring the military down on us in his wake."

They continued watching the men work off in the distance, and both had the same concerns. Black turned, about to shake Otis's hand, saying, "I am headed back to the house."

Looking down at Black's hand, Otis knocked it aside, pulling him close in a brotherly hug and clapping him on the back. "Congrats, man. You deserve it."

"Thanks."

Later that night Black stood at the canvas in his studio, filled with emotion. The painting depicted a large black man standing naked with his hands at his sides before a mirror, his skin the darkest, his head bald, his face obscure. His reflection was shackled at the feet, with large iron cuffs at his wrists, the cuffs and shackles a gunmetal gray. The chamber, in which the man stood gazing at his likeness, had a wall of books in all sizes and colors; the furniture was of high quality with splashes of gold and brown. Yet his reflection showed him to be standing in a rudimentary cabin with a dirt floor.

He painted from an angle where his reflection and his reality were visible to the observer. Black smiled when his vision became legible; the painting represented his personal growth. There was a time that his reality was misunderstood even by him, but now he had grown enough to compare. In his newfound state of mind, he anticipated tomorrow and her, and he was humbled. He knew all the possibilities, but she was self-sufficient, and he had hope. In his absence or death, Otis was there for her and Mama, though it seemed that he only thought of death. It was peace of mind that drove him. Now, with the coming of his wedding, he had happiness. It was dawn when he put down his brush, heading down the hall to his room.

When they hit the three-day mark, the fort was locked down just as Black had ordered. The house became a beehive of activity. The women cleaned and began cooking; the brick oven in the back of the house was fired up, and a large side of beef was turning over the pit. The house was open for the activity as the women came and went, preparing for the big day. Black stayed in his study, venturing out at night to go to his studio.

He did not seek Sunday out, giving her some time to herself as she prepared to become his lawfully wedded wife. There was still work to be done, and he worried about the Will situation. Now that Turner had died, Black wondered how long he had before the situation became volatile. He understood that grief did strange things to a person; it was why he had doubled the patrol. Black wanted to give her his full attention. He would be alert, but he would attempt to enjoy the moment.

Before they locked down Fort Independence, Black and Otis went into town to buy a few things from the dry-goods store. Black really went out before the lockdown to make certain there wasn't a message from Tim, and there wasn't.

Now, just hours before the big day, he stood in the window, watching the people move about. They laughed and danced on the pathways. The fiddlers were all over, making good music that drifted to his study through the open window.

There was a knock at the door, and before he could answer, in walked Otis, followed by Elbert and James. Black had not seen them in about a year, and it was uncanny how they managed to show up at the right moment.

Elbert broke the silence. "So you have gone soft."

"I'm afraid I did," Black said, smiling.

James stepped forward, hugging Black and clapping him on the back before saying, "I am happy for you, man."

"Thanks."

Elbert was a dark-skinned man about six feet tall with lifeless eyes, a small nose, and full lips. He kept his hair cut short on the sides with a little extra on top. Wearing black trousers, a white shirt with the sleeves rolled up and cavalry-issued boots, he appeared every bit as deadly as he truly was. James, being the complete opposite, was an extremely light-skinned man and not quite six feet. His face was symmetrical, with green eyes, high cheekbones, a pointy nose, and full lips. He wore glasses, making him appear warm when in fact he might kill before Elbert did. He wore all black down to the boots.

The men sat catching up with Elbert and James. When he and Otis became part of the Underground Railroad, James and Elbert decided it wasn't for them. They had all ridden out before for the purpose of freedom, and it was always successful. For Black, it felt good that the four of them were together again. They wandered so much that Black had giving up trying to keep tabs on them. He found that they came and went when the mood struck them. They were their own men, and Black understood that.

They wandered from the study down to the barracks, talking and—as the day wore on—drinking. Even Black, who did not drink much, got drunk, and to the surprise of the men, he talked even less when drunk. Otis did not drink, and he wouldn't if Black did. Elbert and James could hold their liquor, and Black decided early on that he would not try to outdrink them. They laughed and talked about women, life, and the issues that men think about.

"Have you met Sunday?" Black asked.

"We have," Elbert responded. "And we saw Mama."

"Mama looks good. Now she expects us all to marry," James said.

"Mama is just being nice. She knows no decent woman would have either of you," Otis said.

"Thank God for that," Elbert responded.

As the hour grew late, they all grabbed beds in the barracks to sleep off the drink. When they woke the next morning, it was the day of the wedding—and the day Black's life would forever be changed. Black bathed at the barracks and started getting dressed. He couldn't find his tie or his right shoe, and his suit was at the house instead of in the barracks. Otis was tired of playing traveling companion to Black's old-lady behavior, so he called in Paul for help. Elbert and James laughed but were little to no help.

Back at the house, Sunday was being pulled in many different directions. In the bedroom, they had her seated naked in front of the open window so she wouldn't sweat. Iris took her time braiding Sunday's hair into a crown, highlighting the beauty of her face. When she began dressing, Mama, who rarely showed any emotion, broke down and cried, and they had to stop and cry with her. She was happy, and so were they. Finally, when Sunday was dressed and standing in front of the mirror, she was a sight to behold. Mama stayed with her while Iris ran to see where they were in terms of getting started.

Coming down the hall, Iris saw Black standing in the foyer across from the sitting room with Paul, Otis, Elbert, and James. They were all dressed in dark suits, but Black stood out as he smiled at something that was said, and Iris realized that he looked younger than usual. It was wonderful to see him happy. She came to stand among them, and Paul placed his hands on her back before kissing her cheek.

"We are ready when you are," Iris said.

Black nodded, and Otis waved Herschel and Mary over.

Mary smiled at Iris before asking, "Is she ready?"

"She is," Iris answered.

"Let us take our places then," Herschel said, dressed in all blue, with his gray hair combed neatly back.

Stepping out onto the porch in the morning sun, Black took in the scene before him. The people of Fort Independence stood around the house as far as the eye could see to watch him exchange vows. He turned to face Herschel with Otis and Paul at his side. The moment was hushed as though not real when one of the fiddlers stepped forward, climbing into a wagon parked in front of the house and seating himself in front of the piano he began to play …

Once the music started, Black could see movement out of the corner of his eye. Turning, he looked down the long hall as Sunday made her way toward him in a long white dress with Mama holding the train. The corridor was slightly dark, and with the sun behind him, he could not see her in detail. Black did not take his eyes from her, and when she reached the door, stepping onto the porch and into the sunlight, he was captivated. She was a vision to witness in the white dress with a splash of chocolate skin as the dress revealed her bare shoulders. She came to stand next to him, facing Herschel with Mama and Iris at her side. Her hand found his, and he could feel her trembling.

The music abruptly stopped as she came to stand next to Black.

Clearing his throat, Herschel began, "Dearly beloved, we are gathered here today to join this man, Nat Hope Turner, and this woman, Sunday Turner, in holy matrimony." Pausing for effect, he continued, "Nat, do you take this woman to be your wife, to live together in matrimony, to love, honor, and comfort her, and keep her in sickness and in health, and forsaking all others, for as long as you both shall live?"

Black responded strongly, "I do."

"Sunday Turner, do you take this man to be your husband, to live together in holy matrimony, to love, honor, and comfort him and keep him in sickness and in health, and forsaking all others, for as long as you both shall live?"

She answered in a strong voice, "I do."

"Please face each other," Herschel instructed.

Black and Sunday turned and faced each other, with Black reaching out and lifting her veil. She heard his sudden intake of air when her veil was folded back.

Herschel said, "Nat, repeat after me. I, Nat Hope Turner, take you, Sunday Turner, to be my wife, to have and to hold from this day forward, for better, for worse, for richer, for poorer, in sickness and in health, to love and to cherish, till death do us part.

"Now Sunday, you repeat after me. I, Sunday Turner, take you, Nat Hope Turner, to be my husband, to have and to hold from this day forward, for better, for worse, for richer, for poorer, in sickness and in health, to love and to cherish, till death do us part.

"Black, you may now place the ring on her finger."

"I give you this ring as a token and pledge of our constant faith and abiding love," Black stated in a strong voice. She could feel his hands shaking as he pushed the ring on to her finger.

"I give you this ring as a token and pledge of our constant faith and abiding love," she whispered before pushing the ring onto his large finger.

Herschel spoke again, his voice theatrical. "We have come together in this place and have heard the willingness of Nat and Sunday to be joined in marriage. They have come of their own *free* will and in our hearing have made a covenant of faithfulness. They have given and received rings as the seal of their promises. By virtue of the authority vested in me under the laws of Upper Canada, I now pronounce you husband and wife. The bride and groom may now kiss."

Black stepped forward, and right there in front of everyone, he pushed his tongue in her mouth, kissing her as she had never been kissed before. The women sighed, and the men cheered. Spinning her to face the crowd, he announced to the onlookers, "My queen."

The celebration had truly begun, and Sunday was jostled from person to person as each hugged her and shook Black's hand. Elbert came forward, shaking Black's hand as he stared down at Sunday, and she stepped closer to Black. She offered her hand to shake, as well. Seeing his eyes made her uneasy.

Elbert, seeing her reaction to him, smiled and leaned down, whispering, "You are right about me, but you need never fear me. I would kill a man for you if you just asked." Sunday's eyes grew round with surprise as she looked up at Black. He smiled, shrugging as if in affirmation. James came forward, as well, and she had the same feelings, but she smiled just the same.

As the people celebrated, Black took Sunday by the hand, leading her to his study and shutting the door. Once inside, she stared at him in his suit, and he was the handsomest man she had ever seen. He loosened his tie, removed his jacket and vest, and opened his shirt at the throat. Black stepped forward, kissing her again, and it wasn't sexual; he was just experiencing his wife, and she kissed him back, experiencing him in a new way, as well.

Finally, he asked, "Do you feel different?"

"Yes," she answered. "I feels like I can boss ya 'round now." Her eyes sparkled with amusement.

He stared down at her, his face serious, when he said, "Tonight, you will receive forty tongue lashes for your bad attitude."

She was breathless when she whispered, "Oh, I hopes so … I wants to be punished."

And it was his turn to shake his head. Now he was aroused, and he had to wait all day. He pressed his lips against hers, kissing her deeply before saying, "You are a very bad woman."

He kissed her shoulders, placing his lips right on a scar from where she had been beaten. Finding the nerve that he just didn't have before, he asked her, "Why would they beat you? I myself have no scars, and I am a man." It was as if he were ashamed of that fact.

She smiled at him reassuringly. "This is what you wants to talk 'bout … now?"

"Does it bother you? Would you rather I not know?" he asked.

Still smiling, she answered, "I'll tell ya whateva you wants to know."

"Then I want to know."

"When my mama was used up and collapsed in the fields, I ran to her, and they beat me for gettin' in the way. Big Mama nursed me back and kept me wit' her."

He just stared at her, and he realized she was right and that he shouldn't have asked. She watched him wrestle with what she said, caressing his face before saying, "I's safe in yo hands. Don't thank too much, baby." Pulling him down to her, she kissed him.

Taking him by the hand, she led him back to the celebration, reengaging him in the pleasure of the day. Black allowed himself to be brought back to the present … for now.

The merriment raged on through the day with Mama and the children dancing on the paths as the fiddlers kept the music going. At the bottom of the steps, there were tables loaded with food and drink. As Sunday engaged with the people, laughing and enjoying herself, Black stood back, watching. Elbert wandered over, and at his approach, Black smiled.

"You are a lucky man," he said to Black.

Black did not comment.

Elbert continued, "Even I am in love with her."

"You are too jaded to be in love," Black stated, not taking the bait.

Looking Black in the eye, Elbert said, "I am proud of you. We will wander, but we will not stay gone so long."

Black was moved.

Otis and Paul wandered up, and the conversation turned to the things that men talked about. James, being a ladies' man, descended the porch and danced in the pathways with the women, while some of the men looked annoyed. Still, they knew the real him, so they kept their thoughts to themselves. Black smiled. He loved them, but they were trouble.

Over Otis's shoulder, Black could see Sunday talking with the women and swaying to the music. Excusing himself from the men, he walked over to her, and to the surprise of everyone, he took her hand, leading her down the steps. Once at the bottom of the steps, he pulled her into the crowd and began to dance with an expertise that was enthralling.

Sunday, not being light of foot, almost forgot to dance while watching him. Black's trousers hung from his hips just right, and his movements were fluid. Sunday was stimulated.

As the music stopped and people applauded, she stared up at him, her face serious, whispering, "I thinks I's ready for my tongue lashing."

As the sun set, the party was still going strong, and Black did not announce their departure. Instead, he left everyone celebrating, and taking his bride by the hand, he led her to their room. Once inside, he stood at her back as she faced the mirror. Leaning down, he kissed her shoulder, and she reached up, caressing his face.

"I love you, Sunday. You are my world," he whispered.

Looking up at his reflection in the mirror, she answered, "I loves you, Black."

He unzipped her dress and helped her out of it. She stood wearing a shift cut off at the shoulders. Carefully, he helped her put her dress away, and she was amazed at how attentively he helped her get ready for the night. He read her thoughts, saying, "I think Mama and Iris were supposed to help you, but I don't want to wait to spend time with you."

She smiled as he hung her dress and then removed his shirt and shoes. Sunday noticed that it was the first time that he did not wear his gun. As he moved about the chamber, they talked about the wedding, laughing about her facial expression when Elbert whispered his allegiance to her. She was laughing hard when she said, "I's 'fraid of him."

Black smiled and replied, "You never need to fear him, although I can see why you would." He chuckled.

He removed his trousers, and they climbed into the bed and continued talking, and Sunday curled up next to him. While he was talking about Otis and being teased by the men, he heard Sunday's light snoring. Looking down at her while she slept, he laughed to himself, thinking that there was no place in the world he would rather be. Music was drifting through the window as he fell asleep.

Sunday woke in the wee hours, not feeling well and needing the chamber pot. Climbing out of bed, she tiptoed over to it. After using it and washing her face and hands, she realized she felt weak. Racing back to the chamber pot, she heaved, bringing up nothing, though the action helped relieve her stomach. Back at the basin, she washed her face and rinsed out her mouth. Turning to get back in bed, she found him sitting up and staring at her. This was one of those moments, she thought, when her stomach hurt, and it was his fault.

Sunday climbed back into bed, curling up next to him, her stomach settling as she stilled. Black lay on his back and pulled her on top on him. They lay like that for a time in silence until he asked, "Do you have something to tell me?"

"I don't wants to speak on it," she whispered.

Black wrapped his arms around her and his child. *All this in one day*, he thought. He was unsure of how to broach the subject, so he allowed the quietness to continue. At that moment, all he could think about was her not feeling well, and he wondered why she wouldn't come to him. How long had she known?

Finally, when he could take no more, he asked, "I thought you said you would tell me whatever I wanted to know?"

He had her there, but she still said nothing. She wanted to just get used to being married, and she didn't want to think about anything else, though she understood that the thought was childish. She hated adding to his stress, and she couldn't face the issue right now. Hoping for sleep again, she closed her eyes, wishing that he would follow suit, but he did not.

"How long have you known?" he asked.

She did not reply.

"Answer me. That will not work for this," he pleaded.

"I knows ya don't want no children. I's sorry 'bout this."

"You think that I fault you?" he asked, surprised by her words.

"I feel like I's addin' to yo worry."

"Sunday, you are adding to my worry by not telling me what is going on with you. Your being with child was a joint effort. I am a man; I understand that," he said, a little harder than he had intended to.

"So you's happy 'bout this?" she whispered.

"I am numb, and the only thing I can think of is you hiding from me."

She understood that. The problem was she couldn't even be truthful with herself. Sunday did not offer that bit of information; it seemed like an excuse. Instead, she spoke the truth. "I's numb and shocked, but I wants this child, Nat."

"Then why wouldn't you talk to me?"

"I's 'fraid to worry ya," she answered.

The conversation had gone full circle, and he was quiet for a time. When he spoke, it was also the truth. "I am not unhappy about the child; I am terrified of losing you."

Hearing the emotion in his voice, her eyes watered up, and when he felt the tears rolling off his chest, he flipped her over.

Looking down at her, he whispered, "Don't cry, please."

Pulling her onto her side, he slid down and kissed her flat stomach before snuggling against her. Sunday rubbed his neck and shoulders while holding him close. Black thought about his wife and child and was so overcome with emotion that he cried, unable to stop himself.

Sunday just continued to hold him, reassuring him through touch until finally she said, attempting to comfort him with reason, "My mama had no trouble in birthin'. I promises to take care and do what ya say."

Leaning over her, his eyes still red from crying, he kissed her, and she welcomed his touch. He was about to pull away, concern for her in his eyes, when she whispered, "Make love to me, Black."

He groaned at her invitation before asking, "Are you sure?"

"Yes."

Pushing her legs apart with his knees, he entered her, and slowly, he made her his wife. She was hot and tight, and to his shame, he could not last. Each stroke was more intense than the last, and completion dogged him. And though he could see the horizon, he wasn't ready. He tried to back away from the sensation, when she abruptly began to shudder. Black had no choice, and placing his face between her neck and shoulder, he came.

They held each other, and slowly the tension began to ebb. Into the quietness, he said, "I can only deal with me and you for now."

"I understands," she said, feeling the same way.

12

SOUTHAMPTON, VIRGINIA
OCTOBER 1859

The meeting was under way in Will's study. In attendance were the Hunters, Wilsons, Matthewses, and Robinsons. The original invite included the ten surrounding plantations, but the others were vocal about this being a Turner issue that Will was pawning off on them. Will was desperate, so he didn't argue the point, mostly because it had some merit, and he was happy to have Hunter in the group. Edward Hunter was a man of action.

They talked strategy and finally decided on bounty hunters. Edward was angry about Northern aggression; he did not want the North dictating to him. What Will Turner cared about most was that Edward wanted Black stopped. The head of the Hunter plantation had the means and the men at his disposal to help him get Sunday back.

Will took in the scene before him, and he hoped they could move forward. He focused in on Edward Hunter, who was really an elegant fellow, well dressed in a brown suit. His speech was sophisticated and his tone soft, yet without mistake, he was deadly. He was about sixty summers but looked younger. In stature, he was about five foot ten. His hair and beard were white and trimmed to perfection, and he had black eyes and a small nose and mouth. And when he spoke, his eyes seemed to convey danger. It was clear that Edward meant to send a message to the slaves about running and to the North that he was his own man. He was also a man who was never seen without his gun strapped about his waist. Yes, Will intended to be right by his side.

"We will send twenty of the best trackers into Canada to find this slave and bring him back," Edward said to the room at large.

"I want him stopped, as well, but at what cost? Before we move forward, I want to talk dollars and cents," Ben Matthews said.

Will wanted to kick the horseshit out of Ben Matthews's fat ass. Everything about him was round—his face, his stomach … even his fingers were shaped like ten sausages. It appeared that every time they moved forward, he did something or said something to derail their progress.

Hunter was shrewd in his response. "I think the bulk of the cost ought to come from Will, as this was his problem to begin with."

Will turned red, but he controlled his response because he needed them. "It appears that I cannot shake the blame for this catastrophe. Keep in mind that Nat Turner lived and died before I was born, and this Black, whoever he is, was not one of my slaves."

Edward responded, "Son, you want the help or not?"

Will buckled, asking, "When can we get started?"

"Since you say that he is armed and dangerous, we should kill him on sight. Then we can see who he travels with."

Will responded, "How long will it take to rally twenty and head to Canada?"

"About two weeks. We could gather the men and head out in that time frame," Robinson answered.

"I will be ready to travel with them," Will said.

Tim had to smile. If nothing else, Will Turner was resilient. He would send word to Black … that light was needed.

They agreed to meet back in Will's study in five days to make certain they would be ready. As for Will, he wanted to take his wife to her father in Boston so that she would be safe. Instead, he had to leave her at the plantation. Rose was gone, and Turner was dead; he needed someone to stay and manage matters while he was gone. There was nothing for it; Amber was going to have to step up.

Black sat in his study thinking. Although he had been married for two weeks, he was dazed about the situation. He had come to a point where he was happy about the child, and when Sunday entered a room, all else was forgotten. Good health showed in her face, and he watched her carefully. He reduced her target practice to one day a week, and she had gotten better, hitting three out of five targets. Still, he knew that she would have to stop. As for keeping the books, reading, and writing, he had stepped that up.

At night they talked about their day, and he made it clear that though Mama and Iris knew about the baby, he did not want her condition widely discussed. He wanted to keep it between them until he returned from dealing with Will. Her safety and that of the baby were paramount with him. He had not even discussed it with Otis, and it was not a lack of trust. It was Black just wanting to be private until he worked through it.

There was a knock at the door, and Otis stepped in before Black could answer. The look on his face told Black the time had come. "There is a telegram from Tim," Otis said, handing it to him.

THERE IS AN ISSUE THAT HAS COME TO MY ATTENTION
I AM HOPING YOU CAN COME TO SHED LIGHT ON THE
MATTER IMMEDIATELY

Looking up at Otis, Black smiled. "Ready the men."

Otis nodded and left to get things in order. Black went looking for Sunday, and he found her asleep in their bed. He sat on the side of the bed, and the movement roused her.

Seeing his expression, she asked, "What is it?"

He hesitated before saying, "I need to leave. The time has come to deal with Will."

Sunday's heart sank; she wanted to plead with him not to go, but she didn't. The child was making her weak. Finally, she asked, "When?"

"We will leave late tonight, and I will take only ten men. The rest will remain here with you. You will be safe here. Elbert and James knew I had a matter to attend to. They will wander up in a few days to make certain you and Mama are all right. Make no mistake: you are in charge in my absence. Mama is most intelligent; if you are unsure, defer to her."

She was afraid, but she kept her head. Being with child had her emotions running wild, and she wanted to tell Black to forget Will Turner. When she spoke, she gave him the truth. "I don't want ya to leave me."

"I know, baby," he whispered. "Now, with the baby coming, I can't leave this matter unresolved. I will be back before you know it."

Understanding between them was so deep. They removed all their clothes and just held each other. Black rode out the gate at midnight, and she cried.

They rode nonstop into the states, resting only once at a safe house on the edge of Pennsylvania. There they regrouped and went over the plan. Before riding out for Virginia, Black sent one of his men to Moses to let her know there would be a tidal wave of runaways coming her way. They rode out, and sticking to the back roads, they moved toward Southampton at a record-breaking pace, so eager was Black to have the matter with Will done. He resented having to come back, leaving his wife and child. Inside he was angry for being a slave and about being forced into being a fugitive.

Now with the baby on the way, he truly had some understanding of his father and of his revolt. He had to work to keep his head about him so that he could see his child grow up. This is what it had come down to—he would defend what was his and at all costs. When this matter was done, he would be a farmer and businessman ... a father and a husband. Black would leave no man alive to own his wife and child.

It was noon when Black and his men made it to the Turner plantation. Philip was sent forward to work the fields and find Tim. Tim, being on the lookout, made the connection and rode out just beyond the field. Black was leaned against a tree, waiting leisurely and without care of being seen. When he and Otis saw Tim approaching, they walked toward him.

"Black," Tim said by way of greeting.

Black responded, his expression closed, "Tim. So what have we got here?"

"Will has incorporated the help of at least four other plantation owners—Wilson, Hunter, Matthews, Robinson," he said, counting out loud.

"The plan?" Black asked.

"Bounty hunters. They feel if they catch you, they could get the rest of the matter under control. Will isn't being forthcoming with them about Sunday or that she is his goal," Tim said honestly.

Black had to fight to not show reaction, but he managed it, sticking squarely to business. "When will they all be together?"

Tim smiled at the question. "Your timing is uncanny. They will meet today here and ride out in about five days for Canada. The next few days will be spent recruiting the best to track you."

Otis just whistled.

Tim continued, "They will start arriving in about two hours. You want to get it started tonight. I'm ready to leave this place."

"If they get here in two hours, once the meeting is under way, I think we should get the fire started. No reason to wait for late night; they expect that," Black said.

"Philip is making his rounds, and the ones that want to try to run know what to do," Otis said.

"We need to get this done and get out," Tim said as he headed for his horse. "John is making noise, and I believe soon Virginia will be crawling with the military."

Sunday was now holed up in Black's office working through the books. On her first day in the study to handle the books, she had found a gun holster like Black's lying on the desk. She laughed, knowing it was for her. Now she had taken to wearing her gun daily, mostly because she knew it would please him. While she wasn't expecting trouble, she had promised to follow his instructions, and she did.

Paul was left solving the issues that Otis handled, and he was cranky. All they ever saw was Otis coming and going. She and Paul didn't know that he paid the men and dealt with the barracks and kept it running smoothly. Paul had to move among the cabins paying the men while trying to keep track of who got what. If he wasn't so annoyed, Sunday would have laughed.

Mama and Iris took over some of Sunday's chores to help out and to keep themselves busy. All in all, she felt overwhelmed, but she managed. Black handled the messages that came and went and the paying of the bills, and he also ordered all the supplies. Now those tasks fell to Sunday, and she struggled to stay on top of things. Still, she hung in there making it work. As far as the baby was concerned, there was nothing she could do; she had to nap daily, and it seemed to help. It was when she woke, for just that small amount of time before she got busy again, that she worried about her husband. She just wanted him home. She literally ached for him.

It was getting on to four o'clock, and the field hands were just starting to call a halt to the workday. Leaving the horses just beyond the fields, Black and his men began moving toward the house. Once they drew closer, they separated. The slaves recognized them and continued working as though nothing was amiss. As the slaves filed out of the cotton fields, Black and Otis walked in. Tying rags over their noses and mouths, they found the buckets of kerosene left by Philip, and they began dumping between the plants. They worked their way to the edge of the fields to make certain the fire encompassed all.

With the fields handled, they made their way to the nearest water supply to clean the kerosene from their hands and faces. Black and Otis separated as they walked away from the water pump. Stepping off between the cabins, Black could see the young overseer on horseback staring right at him. Turning his horse toward Black, he began to gallop forward, and Black moved out onto the path, presenting a clear view to the man on horseback. Tim, seeing the exchange, rode forward on his horse at the same time, and upon seeing Tim, the overseer swung down from his horse to confront Black. It was obvious that seeing Tim caused him to misjudge the situation.

Walking up to Black, he asked, "What you up to, boy?"

Black could see the man begin to assess him, and he smiled. He wore all black down to the boots, his bald head making him appear menacing. It was clear when the man pieced together that he might be Black the slave causing the ruckus, and turning to Tim, he asked, "Is he one of ours?"

Tim responded honestly, quietly, "No."

When the man attempted to pull his gun, Tim threw Black his shotgun. Bringing the butt of the gun up in a sharp movement, Black slammed the overseer in the face, dropping him where he stood, a dazed look on the overseer's face as he went down.

Dragging him off the path, Black could hear Tim saying, "He didn't even see that coming."

Black was annoyed. "I'm not here to brawl."

Otis ran up. "The overseers are tied up; about three got away. They must be new; I don't know any that we captured. It's starting to get hectic, and the slaves are beginning to get anxious."

"Light the fire so that we can force their direction," Black said as he headed for the house.

Swinging down from his horse, Tim fell in step with Black as Black handed him back his gun. Cracking the gun, Tim checked the ammunition while never breaking his stride. Otis walked off in the opposite direction. They were about to bring the matter to a close.

Will was standing in the hall looking toward the front door and trying to find out what all the yelling was about when he saw Black step through the door. Reaching for his gun, he realized he hadn't worn one since he had returned to the plantation. Turning, he ran for the study, and Black, seeing him, took off in hot pursuit. Tim called after him, but Black, seeing the cause of his trouble, did not hear. Will Turner was his total focus.

Reaching the study, Will attempted to close and lock the door while breathlessly yelling, "It's Black! Black is in the house!"

Will was having trouble holding the door.

"Help me, damn it!" he yelled to the men standing behind him, but fearing being shot through the door, the plantation owners did not come to his aid. Instead, they watched as Will struggled to hold Black off.

Hunter, being a man of action, pulled his gun, while Matthews, Robinson, and Wilson hid behind the furniture. Will, unable to hold the door against the force, turned and ran for the open window, and just as Black opened the door, he hurled himself out. Relentless in his chase, Black ran for the window, took aim, and shot. Will was hit, and it slowed him down, but he was still moving. Just as Black was about to take the next shot, Hunter let off two rounds, hitting Black twice in the back. And though he was hit, Black took the second shot anyway, bringing Will down. Tim reached the study just as Hunter was about to shoot again, and without thought, Tim aimed and shot. The force of the shotgun knocked Hunter off his feet and stained the wall red.

Black turned to Tim, and walking toward him, Black said, "Sunday is going to kill me." He passed out cold in Tim's arms.

The chaos seemed to escalate, and hearing the shots, two of Black's men came running, and Tim was thankful to see them. Together they assessed the situation, deciding that Wilson, Matthews, and Robinson were liabilities. Following past direction from Black that all loose ends should be tied up, they shot and killed the three remaining plantation owners, leaving no witnesses.

The men regrouped in the front of the house. The fields were already ablaze. Tim looked for Will and figured that he might have been hurt but not dead. Starting from the window, he worked his way out, and though it wasn't totally dark, he couldn't find him. Black was shot twice in the back and bleeding like a stuck pig. Philip cut his shirt off him, and with a hot knife, he cauterized the holes. Cutting the shirt into strips, he tied the strips around Black's chest to keep the bleeding to a minimum.

They were loading Black into a wagon when Tim noticed that Otis had not appeared. Tim and Philip went looking for him and found him shot to death on the edge of the fields. They found a blanket used for the horses and covered Otis, throwing him into the wagon with Black. They headed out, and as they hit the back roads, they found many of the Turner slaves doing the same.

When Tim looked back at the scene, he saw the strangest thing. Some of the slaves were attempting to put the fire out rather than run.

Philip was in charge with Black down and Otis dead. The wagon slowed them down, but they kept moving. They had to go deeper off the main road because they had too much company on the back roads with the number of runaways moving. When they stopped to water the horses and plan the next move, Tim noticed that Black did not look good. Black looked gray, and his breathing was labored. It appeared that every breath he took might be his last.

Tim approached Philip. "We need to stop so that we can attempt to help Black."

"I have directions from both Otis and Black that, should they die or become injured, I am to get them back to the fort. Black has Sunday, and though he may die, I want to get him back to her."

Tim understood that; he felt the same. He nodded, and they moved out again. Tim was troubled that Will had gotten away; it could make matters worse for all of them. He would have to go get his wife and child and move them to the fort until he could gauge the situation. He sighed, replaying in his head what went wrong, and Otis … there were just no words. He did not want to face Mary. They sent three men ahead for help. They would have to move slowly until they made it to Canada.

The days began to run together, and Black's breathing became shallow, and he was fevered. It was clear to all that he would die. The goal was just to get them home.

Sunday was standing in the window of the study when she saw a commotion from the window and thought her king was finally home. Swinging the door open, she headed down the hall. The day was overcast, and a slight breeze blew as she stepped on to the porch. She could see a wagon moving toward her, and she could hear a woman screaming. It looked like Mary. Elbert rode up and swung down from his horse, and her heart sank.

Mama stepped up behind her and asked the question that Sunday was afraid to ask. "What happened?"

Elbert said, "Black has been shot, and it don't look like he'll make it."

As Sunday stared at him, he appeared to be getting farther and farther away. She was fainting. He reached out, grabbing her and shaking her to get her to focus.

Mama just stood there stone-faced before asking, "What else?"

"Otis is dead," he continued.

The wagon pulled up, and the men began removing Otis from the wagon. He was wrapped in a blanket. They had to fight Mary off as she screamed incoherently. Sunday, watching the scene, sprang from her dazed state to action. Moving off the porch, she helped grab Mary so they could move him. Mary buckled where she stood, weeping.

"No," she sobbed. "This can't be … Otis. Please, Otis, no … baby, get up."

Sunday wrapped her arms around Mary, pushing her blonde hair from her face. She could feel Mary's thin frame shaking as sorrow enveloped them, and Sunday's heart squeezed as she listened to her pleas. Mary went limp, and Sunday just rocked her as she cried.

Mama and Iris came forward, taking Mary from her with Mama saying, "Let's try to save him."

Sunday turned to the wagon and saw Black's still body. When she attempted to climb up, her knees gave out, and Elbert helped her up. She scrambled to his side and heard his shallow breaths. If she was going to save him, she had to get moving. The men came forward with a board and moved him gently, taking him to the chamber they shared.

Turning to the men, she yelled, "I needs a doctor! Send him to me now!"

Philip stepped forward, saying, "I'm as close as we got. I know the basics, but he needs a real doctor. The doctor in town don't treat colored folks. Black didn't trust him, anyway."

Following the men to the room, Sunday worked with Mama to get him settled. Once in the bed, they cut the clothes from his body, trying to determine all his injuries. They bathed his skin, and he was burning hot. Sunday knew they needed a doctor to tell them the best course of action. Mama stayed at his side when Sunday stepped into the hall, issuing orders. Upon her return, she sat with Mama, watching over Black until the sun went down. They bathed him again, but his breathing had not improved, and they were both beside themselves.

There was a knock at the door, and Sunday stood, calling, "Come in."

Philip, James, and Elbert entered, along with the boy who brought water to the house. Philip spoke first. "You called for us, Miss Sunday?"

The water boy stepped forward, handing her the items she had requested, and he took his leave. When she spoke, her voice was calm and sure. "Can you men step into the hall just a few minutes? I'll call ya back directly."

When they left the room, she began to undress, and Mama, being dazed, didn't even appear to notice. Sunday put on the black shirt, trousers, and cavalry-issued boots that the water boy brought for her. When she opened the door to invite them back in, she was strapping her gun back at her side. Elbert looked at her dressed like that and smiled. It was official: he *was* in love with her.

Sunday got straight to the point. "He needs the doctor, and I means to go get him."

"He don't treat coloreds," Philip said, confused.

"The three of you will ride out wit' me to brang him back."

Elbert, following her, said, "So you want to steal the white doctor and bring him here?"

Now that she was hearing the plan out loud, it sounded perfect. "Yes, and I wants to leave *now*."

James smiled, but he had no response.

Philip said, "Miss Sunday, this ain't a good idea."

Turning to Philip, she asked, "Do ya know what's happenin'?"

Philip stared at her, his confusion unmistakable.

She continued, "I's givin' orders. I ain't askin' you."

Elbert couldn't take his eyes off her.

Opening the door, she called for Paul, and he came rushing down the hall. Breathlessly, he asked, "Sunday, what is it?"

"I's ridin' out wit' the men, and I want this house locked down till I return. You's to remain in front of this door, letting no one in but Iris to help Mama." Stepping into the room, she returned, handing him Black's gun. "If'n anyone disobeys my order, shoot to kill." She then said to Philip and James, "Have the carriage brung 'round. When we get to the gate, I needs to stop to instruct the men. I'll be out in a moment."

Philip and James left to do her bidding. Elbert and Paul stood in the hall in front of the bedroom door. When the door was shut, Elbert shook his head, and Paul smiled. Still, with the situation as it was, Paul felt obligated to say, "She carries Black's child. They's in yo care."

Elbert nodded, afraid to examine the depth of his emotions. That damn Black was a lucky bastard.

Inside the bedroom, Sunday leaned over, kissing him before whispering, "Goin' for help. Don't leave us, baby ... please."

When she stood, Mama said, "Don't take no for an answer."

She nodded, and striding past Mama, she squeezed her shoulder. Stepping out into the hallway where the men stood, she made eye contact with Elbert. His lifeless eyes holding hers, she could feel him assessing her pain, and she hated it. She could see that for him, people fell into two categories—prey or predator—and he was good at evaluating. He wore brown trousers, a black shirt open at the throat, black boots, and his gun strapped at his side. Gauging him as a man, she found him formidable.

Elbert looked for any sign that Sunday might be with child and found none. Dressed in all black down to the boots, with her hair back into five thick cornrows, he found her determined. Her huge eyes conveyed the pain she felt, and he knew he would do anything for her. Shaking his head, he willed Black to get better so he could leave.

"Ready, Elbert," she said before turning and heading toward the carriage.

Elbert and Paul followed in her wake. Once at the door, Paul locked up behind them after the two stepped onto the porch. Sunday waited to hear the door being locked and then turned, moving down the steps. At the bottom, Philip, James, and the carriage waited, the driver stepping down to open the door for her. As she went to step up, Elbert lifted her, and when she was seated, he climbed in.

She hadn't thought he would ride in the carriage; she was hoping for a private moment of weakness. As the carriage raced toward the gate, he must have read her thoughts. "You cannot be in the carriage alone with him."

Sunday nodded. She had no energy to talk. The carriage began to slow and then stop when they reached the gate. Before passing through, Elbert opened the door and stepped down. Turning back for her, he lifted her down, and the men, seeing her out late, came walking toward her.

They circled around her, and she gave them a moment to quiet. Then, with Elbert standing at her back, she said, "Fort Independence is now locked down till I says different. Should someone leave, they will not be allowed back. I has an errand, and it is the onlyist time the gate will open." Her voice was loud and clear, and no one asked a question.

Back in the carriage, they rode in silence toward their goal. It was a full moon, and that was the only light for miles. She could feel Elbert in the shadows, but she kept her eyes to the window, watching the trees roll by. Her mind turned to her powerful husband lying helpless, and she wanted to die. And Otis … she could still hear Mary's sobbing.

He offered her some privacy, as much as he could. Sticking with the task at hand, he stayed away from his grief, pushing it off in the corner of his mind. Black, Otis, and James were his family, and even though he and James were misfits, Black had accepted that. Now he would delay grieving for Otis in an attempt to help her save Black. The whole situation had him feeling helpless, and to add insult to injury, his delayed grief was causing him sexual tension.

The carriage came to a stop on the edge of town in front of a small house that appeared less than modest. There was a lamp in the window, and when the carriage stopped, the light disappeared from the window.

Opening the carriage door, Elbert swung down and said, "Give us a minute."

Philip and James swung down from their horses and separated, both with their guns drawn. Jack, the driver, stood in the carriage, holding a shotgun trained on the front door of the house. Sunday watched as the doctor came out with his shotgun aimed at Elbert.

"What do you boys want?" he asked, and his fear was evident.

"Put your gun down. You have no wins," Elbert said, and his voice was flat like his eyes. Giving the doctor no time to think, he stepped forward and up the few steps of the porch. Reaching for the barrel of the gun, he pushed it straight up in the air and then took it. "Stay," he said, and he walked into the house.

Confident that the other men had the situation under control, Elbert went through the house. After some time he reappeared on the porch, continuing past the man to the carriage, opening the door. "Ready?"

Sunday's voice was stronger than she felt when she said, "Yes."

Helping her down from the carriage, she stepped forward, and before reaching the doctor, Elbert said, "Inside."

The doctor turned, leading the way. James, Philip, and Jack turned, watching the night. Once inside the house, Sunday could see it consisted of two rooms. The front room was where he saw patients, and the back room was where he obviously lived. The two rooms were so small that they were well lit from the one lamp, and she could see the place was spotless. Everything was in its place, and everything had a place.

The doctor had brown hair, thick glasses, a bulbous nose, and large brown eyes. He was lean and just shorter than Elbert. Sunday saw his shock when, adjusting his glasses, he realized that she was a woman. He was leery of Elbert, so he just stood waiting.

Elbert stood to her right holding the shotgun, and to her left was a desk, chair, and examining table. Moving toward the desk, she leaned one hip against it and then said, "My husband is needin' medical care. We came to ask yo help."

"Is there not a black doctor you could get help from?" he asked.

Elbert stepped forward, and Sunday held her hand up, stopping him, and she continued, "I suggest, Doctor, that you get yo thangs and come wit' me."

The doctor didn't move. He and Sunday just stared at each other. "So you are taking me against my will?"

"Sometimes, Doctor, life offers situations where choices is slim. Let me give you an example. I needs a doctor, and my onlyist choice is you. You, on the other hand, wants to live, and yo onlyist choice is to do what I say. Just as you don't want to treat niggers, niggers don't want to be treated by you. Again, slim choices and desperation—they makes for a strange blend," she said, staring him right in the eye.

"I can't work under this kind of pressure," he said, and he was clearly shaken.

"You be amazed what ya can get used to, and make no mistake—if'n my husband draws his last breath, so will you," she said, her voice low and sure. Dismissing the doctor, she turned to Elbert, saying, "Five minutes—I wants him in the carriage. I'll be waitin'."

They both watched as she headed for the door, and the doctor regretted her leaving. The last thing he wanted was to be left with this man, facing those eyes. He was just about to start packing when Elbert grabbed him by the collar of his unbuttoned shirt and undershirt all at once. "We ride back in silence. You will speak when spoken to, and you will keep the rest of your thoughts to yourself."

The doctor gave him a nod, and an agreement was struck, amiable or not. Moving about his examining room, he began packing. "May I ask why medical attention is needed?"

"Gunshot wounds in the back."

"How big is this man?" the doctor asked.

"He is 'bout six foot three, and he weighs 'bout 220 pounds."

The doctor began packing, and though this was not his choice, he would do his best. He moved about gathering his supplies. One of the other men stepped in when asked and helped him move the supplies to the carriage. After locking up his house, he climbed into the carriage, sitting next to the woman. The large black man with the threatening eyes sat opposite them, staring him down, never taking his eyes from him.

Seeing the doctor climb into the carriage, she was so relieved that her eyes watered. All she wanted was her husband; nothing else mattered. She would deal with the fallout later. As the carriage started moving, she almost broke down and cried, but she held herself together. Now was not the time. Across from her, Elbert watched the doctor, and the doctor's fear was real. She needed him until Black got back on his feet. Turning to look out the window into the darkness, she braced herself as they moved swiftly back toward the rest of her life.

The carriage pulled to a complete stop with the two men still staring at each other. Once inside the gate, Sunday could see Philip and James break from them to manage the men at the gate. The three inside the carriage continued on to the house. When they came to a stop in front of the house, Elbert climbed out first, allowing the doctor to do so after him. They both turned to help her down, and Elbert growled, causing the doctor to step back.

They fell in line going up the steps, Sunday, the doctor, and her muscle. She banged on the door, and Paul came running. "How is he?" she asked, afraid to know.

"The same," he responded.

"Follow me," she said to the doctor.

They walked the long hall through the kitchen and back to the hall, where it continued on the opposite side. She opened the last door on the left, seeing Mama and Iris sitting at Black's side.

The doctor moved into the chamber, laying his bag down on the small table. He opened the window and started issuing orders. "I need hot water and more light."

Sunday turned, saying, "Get the stove goin', Paul, and has one of the boys brang us some water. Mama, brang me a lamp and mo' candles. Iris and me will help you," she said.

Elbert moved off into the corner, silent, intimidating, enforcing peace of mind.

"I can't work from this bed," the doctor said to Sunday.

Turning to Iris, she said, "Go has the men brang a cot up from the barracks. Me and Mama can manage."

Iris hurried off just as Paul and Mama came in with the supplies, followed by two young men carrying water. The doctor moved to the table and began unpacking his bag; there were scissors, clamps, and little bottles of liquids. The more he unpacked, the more she feared what he would do to her husband. Two men moved into the room, setting the cot up as the doctor requested. They had to lift the tub and move it over to make room; the table and his tools were moved closer to the cot. Another table was brought in to get his setup right, and Sunday was getting frustrated, because it seemed like they were just moving furniture.

The doctor said, "I need the young men to help lift him and place him facedown on the cot."

The men moved forward to lift Black, and the doctor yelled, "Don't touch him yet!"

They all stopped, just staring at the doctor, whose face was red. Trying to calm himself, he began to explain, "The first part of healing is cleanliness. We must be as clean as we can. It is essential to life and death. I want everyone in this room to wash their hands every time you leave and come back. Once we get him settled, there will be no visitors except those that must be here."

Everyone filed out into the kitchen, washing their hands up to the elbow, as instructed. Elbert never moved, and everyone acted as though he was not there. Finally, the doctor allowed the men near the bed, and as gently as they could, they placed Black facedown on the cot. Covering him from the waist down, the doctor ordered the light moved closer. Once the light was moved, Sunday could see the wounds, and they were angry. The smell was bad like rot, and she had to concentrate to keep her stomach under control.

"Everyone out now. We will call you when we need you," the doctor said.

When everyone filed out of the chamber, there was just the doctor, Paul, and Sunday. Washing his hands again, the doctor picked up a knife and began opening one of the wounds. As the knife made contact with his flesh, the wound started bleeding. Before Sunday could think, he picked up the large tweezers and began digging around inside the wound. After what seemed forever, he pulled a metal ball from Black's back, dropping it into the water. He repeated the process on the second wound, finding no metal ball. Instead, he found a third wound thought to be an exit.

"Clean the blood," he ordered Sunday. He asked Paul to dump and replace the water.

"Don't worry; he is unconscious. Clean his whole back," he said, and Sunday did as instructed.

Once the water was replenished, the doctor cut away all the skin that looked dead and then asked for whiskey and a bowl. Paul hurried off, and when he came back, the doctor placed thick white thread in the whiskey. Threading a big needle, he began sewing all three wounds shut with the whiskey-drenched thread. Once he was finished, he ordered Sunday to clean Black's back again, and then he sprinkled some powder over each wound. After everything was said and done, he found the chair, easing into it. Turning the whiskey bottle up to his mouth, he drank deeply.

The doctor ordered Mama and Iris to change the bed dressings on the bed that Black and Sunday shared. After they had changed all the sheets, he asked that the dirty sheets be burned. Sunday asked whether they were moving him back to the bigger bed, but the doctor said no and that he wanted Black to stay where he was for now.

"What now?" Sunday asked.

The doctor responded, "We wait."

Looking at her now changed bed, she couldn't sleep in it, and walking over to the cot, she kneeled down beside the head of the bed. The activity in the chamber was still as they waited for a sign. Sunday leaned her forehead against the top of his head, and she noticed the strangest thing—he had not shaved in weeks, and his hair was growing back, and it was curly. It was her undoing, and rubbing his curls, she broke down.

There in front of the doctor and Elbert, she kissed his forehead and cried. "Please don't leave me, Nat," she sobbed. "I needs ya, baby. I loves you. I cain't live witout you. How am I 'posed to go on?"

Elbert stood in the corner, shotgun in his hands, feeling like an intruder. He listened to her words, watching as she kissed him, pleading with him to come back to her. Her shoulders shook from her grief, and he knew he should look away, but he couldn't. He wanted to go to her and comfort her, but he was frozen. Elbert had never witnessed love like this, and he was moved by her. She had the ability to appear strong even at this weak moment, and to his shame, he was jealous. When finally he tore his gaze away, his eyes clashed with the doctor's.

Dr. Shultz held his gaze; being a doctor, he expected her grief. He had not expected to see emotion in those eyes. They sat in the same room dealing with the same issue, experiencing something totally different—the doctor, fear; Elbert, jealousy; Sunday, grief; and Black, oblivion.

By morning the fever had broken, and his breathing was better, but he did not wake. Elbert went to take care of his personal needs, and

James stood in his place, eyeing the doctor. The doctor was fed and allowed to bathe upstairs, and he slept. Sunday stayed by Black's side. Mama came, forcing Sunday to eat, and she agreed, but she would not leave him. She wanted everyone to go away, but she needed them—the doctor for Black and Elbert for the doctor.

Paul came to discuss Otis. "We needs to bury Otis."

"You wants to has the service in the dining room?" Sunday asked.

The doctor said with authority, "We cannot have a service in this house. He is healing; we are fighting infection."

"Have him set up at the barracks," she said, following the doctor's orders.

Otis was placed in a pine box that was nailed shut; it would not be an open-casket service. The beds were moved and the coffin placed in the back of the room. Chairs were placed before it, and Mary sat in the front row. Herschel preached about what a good man Otis was, and Mary sat dignified, staring off into space. James escorted Sunday, and she sat next to Mary. She didn't speak and just stared at the box, sorry for Mary, Otis, and Black. Mama had been right; if they had stayed, this wouldn't have happened.

Mary, sensing her despair, reached out. Touching her hand, she whispered, "I love you, and I want you to save Black." Sunday cried, and it was Mary who did the comforting.

Elbert left to be with Mary, while Sunday and James stayed with Black. Mama, Iris, and Paul were at the funeral. Leaving James with the doctor and Black, Sunday wandered up to the front porch and watched as the carriage came by to carry Otis to the cemetery. When she could take no more, she walked back in the house and shut the door.

As she wandered back down the hall, she wondered if she would be in Mary's shoes soon enough.

13

OCTOBER 1859

It had been four days since Otis was buried, and Black was still unresponsive. There was a routine that fell into place with the doctor, Elbert, and Sunday. They learned to coexist in the chamber. Sunday and the doctor spoke when needed; Elbert did not speak at all. A second chair was placed in the corner for Elbert; the doctor used the other chair, and Sunday slept on the floor next to the cot and Black.

Sunday asked, "Why ain't he woke up? His back looks betta, and his fever is gone."

Dr. Shultz answered, "To be honest, I'm not sure. Things just happen in their own time."

They kept him clean and turned him, which was an ordeal. His hair grew and grew, and Sunday didn't even recognize him. They continued to care for him and wait. In keeping with fighting infection, he had no visitors except those who helped in his care in some way. The silence was easy for Elbert, but Sunday and the doctor just wrestled with their thoughts.

Shultz did not know niggers lived like this. He had heard of this place, but he still had not expected all that he was seeing. Even if this man lived, Shultz was sure that the man in the corner that never spoke would kill him; it was a type of damage control. Strangely, he wanted to help her, and he wanted her husband to live. She appeared tired and unable to deal with the smell. He thought she was with child, but he dared not ask. He spoke when spoken to unless it was necessary. He would follow the rules.

Although he was aggravated, Elbert did not speak. Sunday looked worn out, and he was afraid she would make herself sick, but he did not press her. He didn't think he could watch her sleep on the floor another night. Making up his mind, he decided that if she fell asleep on the floor again, he would pick her up and put her to bed himself. He wanted the doctor to stop assessing him. Penned up in the room with the three of them was making him crazy ... still for her ...

Night had fallen, and they had all been given a chance to move around and take care of their personal needs before they were back in the room. Mama, Paul, and Iris had come, staying for three minutes and then leaving. It was October but still warm, and the doctor kept the window cracked to promote fresh air. And once again when the house settled, Sunday fell asleep on the floor by the cot. Elbert stood and walked over to her, scooping her up. He could see that his sudden movement caused the doctor alarm. Moving back toward the bed, he was about to lay her down when she opened her eyes.

"I cain't sleep in this bed witout him," she whispered.

Sighing, Elbert changed directions and walked over to the chair, sitting. Sunday curled up against his chest and slept. As he held her, he knew he was making matters worse on himself. Making eye contact with the doctor, Elbert growled at him, and the doctor looked to the window.

Black had been in a dream state, yet he could feel her touch and her love. It had grown cold as though she left, and he was forced to have to push through the pain and fogginess to find her. Slowly he opened his eyes, unsure of what had happened or where he was. Staring at the ceiling, he recognized his room. He felt weak, and he needed her. His mouth was dry. The words he needed escaped him, but finally when he could muster the strength, he turned his head trying to understand. It was then that he saw Sunday on Elbert's lap curled up against his chest, and the eye contact between them was violent.

Holding Black's gaze, Elbert knew there would be hell to pay. Still, unflinchingly, he held her. The doctor stood because he thought he saw movement, which woke Sunday. Elbert did not move; he only stared. *Shit*, he thought.

A white man stepped into Black's view, and because of the scene with Sunday, Elbert, and now this man, Black thought he had gone to hell. She came running forward, crying, and the white man was handing her water to give to him. He tried to drink but could only muster a small amount; he was weak. Sunday was talking and crying at the same time.

"Nat, ooh, baby. How ya feelin'? Baby, can ya hear me?" Sunday whispered between breaths and tears. "Oh, Nat." She continued to cry.

The white man was smiling as Sunday was hugging and kissing Black. Black tried to fight it, but he couldn't. He fell back to sleep, but not before grabbing her hand.

In the coming days, Black stayed up a little longer each time, but not enough for anyone to talk to him. He didn't speak; he just watched the movement around the room. They moved him back to his own bed, making him eat and drink on a schedule. Philip and James helped him with the chamber pot, and Elbert never moved; he just sat in the corner eyeing the white man. And though he tried, Black could not piece together what had brought him here.

Mama spent time with him, sitting in a chair near the bed. She held his hand, and he gave her a squeeze every now and then to let her know it would be all right. Paul and Iris came forward, and Iris cried like Sunday. When Sunday stepped into view, his eyes followed her. He could talk; he just didn't. Sleep seemed to claim him against his will, and it took all his energy to stay awake.

Even though he didn't talk, Sunday spoke to him, telling him that she loved him, and he hated that she cried all the time. Finally, when he felt stronger and not like he would fall asleep at a moment's notice, he asked, "The baby?"

"I's fine, my love. The baby is fine," she whispered, kissing his face.

In the corner, Elbert saw the exchange and turned his eyes away.

There was pain associated with her, and when he attempted to focus elsewhere, the doctor was watching.

~ ~ ~

After a few days, the doctor began pushing him to talk. "I'm Dr. Shultz. How are you feeling today?"

Black just stared at him, and it almost seemed like he wouldn't answer when he said, "I want a bath."

"Absolutely." Turning to Sunday, he said, "Tell them to bring water."

Sunday stood, about to head for the door. Black grabbed her hand, stopping her. His voice was soft but strong when he said, "I want to bathe with you."

Sunday turned, and without the slightest bit of embarrassment, she answered, "Anythang ya wants."

The doctor was about to give them instructions until he saw Black's expression. The boys came, moving the tub back to the center of the room and filling it. While they were readying him for a bath, Paul came, offering to shave him. Helping him to a chair, Paul removed all hair. Black looked weak. His eyes were sunken into his head, and his cheekbones were sharper, announcing his weight lost, but he was still Black.

The boys that poured the water left. After wiping Black's head free of the shaving cream, Paul left. Black, still sitting in the chair, wore his robe to cover himself, and staring from one corner of the room to other, he watched Elbert and the white Dr. Shultz. He had limited energy, so he had to pick what was worth expending it on, and right now, there was only her. The three remained in silence until Sunday came back. The strangest thing was that she only spoke to him. Why wouldn't anyone tell him what was going on? He wasn't sure, but he thought they were going to have to bathe in front of these two.

"Look at you," she said, smiling at Black. "Paul shaved you."

Turning to the doctor, she said, "Elbert will show ya to one of the rooms upstairs. I'll send for ya if'n I needs ya. If'n he continues to heal, I'll let ya go in 'bout two days."

The doctor looked at Elbert before saying to Sunday, "I wondered if we could talk later, privately."

She smiled at the doctor before saying, "This here *is* private, Dr. Shultz. Please, express yoself."

She had used his name for the first time, and it made him fidgety. He wanted to tell her that he would cause her no grief, but he couldn't talk in front of Elbert. "Later. I'll give you two some privacy."

Black sat quietly watching the exchange, and she was gorgeous. At first he thought it was him, but when he started experiencing longer periods of consciousness, he saw that she was different. She wore all black down to the boots, her gun at her side; the trousers outlined her shape, and she was sexy as hell. Her hair was braided back, making her eyes bright, and her skin had a glow. She was different.

Crossing the room, the doctor left, followed by Elbert. When she heard the door shut behind them, she turned her attention to Black. He stood, removing his robe, and she helped him into the tub. The water was warm and welcoming, and when he leaned back, he felt a stinging. There was a knock at the door; it was Paul bringing a tray of food, and he left immediately. Locking the door behind him, Sunday began taking off her clothes.

Waving his hand, Black got her attention, and pointing to the front of the tub, he said, "Come and stand in front of me."

Moving out in front of him, she removed her clothes slowly. She unhooked her gun and removed her boots, and then she unbuttoned her shirt, letting it fall to the floor. She unbuttoned her trousers, and, pushing them over her hips, she was left with a white undershirt. Pulling the undershirt over her head, she stood before him naked, and he could see that she was with child. She was exquisite in motherhood, and he had not expected to feel so moved. Her breasts were larger, her nipples an even deeper chocolate, and her belly, though small, was visible. This was not sexual; it was familiarity, and he needed it. She came forward, climbing in, and when she was settled between his legs, he wrapped his arms about her.

The pain was great; he felt his skin pulling at the wound sites. He gave himself time to absorb the closeness before speaking. Finally, he broke the silence. "I realize I was shot, but I don't remember what happened."

Turning her head, she looked up at him. She realized he wasn't talking because he was trying to figure out what was going on, and he only trusted her. Otis popped in her head, and slowly, she turned in the water to face him. Reaching for her rose-scented soap, she fished the rag out of the water and began rubbing his chest, cleaning him. He leaned back, allowing her to take care of him.

She washed his face and kissed him before she asked, "What do ya member?"

"I remember chasing Will and then nothing," he answered.

"I ain't sure what happened. When I seen ya, I thought ya was dying. I has not asked questions. I will find out what you wants to know," she replied, leery that he would ask about Otis.

"Otis must be mad as hell at me. He hasn't been to see me," he said, but his tone was more a question.

It was subtle, but he saw it. She looked away, pretending to be focused on washing his shoulder.

"Tell me, Sunday … please."

She hated hurting him, but she gave him the truth. "I don't know what happened to Otis, other than he was shot to death. We buried him days ago."

He just stared at her. Black was sure he hadn't heard her right. He closed his eyes. When he opened them again, they were red, but he did not cry. He almost wanted to ask her if she was sure, but judging by her expression, he knew. Hanging his head, he tried to break eye contact. Sunday caressed his face, reassuring him that he was not alone and that he was loved.

"Tell me what you wants, and I will do it," she whispered.

"I need you to piece this story together. I am weak still. This bath has taken a lot out of me," he said, the disgust evident in his voice. He continued, "Elbert and the doctor …"

She cleared her throat and then answered, "I had the doctor stole from his home against his will."

He stared off toward the window, his thoughts taxing him. Otis, his brother and best friend, was cold in the ground, and Sunday was dealing with all of it in her condition. First he had to grow stronger; with Otis gone, that was not even an option. He needed to figure out what happened, and he needed to confirm Will Turner's death. Feeling his strength sapping, he decided on questioning Philip and Tim in a day or so. He would try to make it to his study … was Tim even here?

"I am ready to get out now," he said.

"I'll dress and get Paul," she said.

"No. You help me." Pushing himself up and grabbing the side of the tub, he managed to stand. His arms shook from fatigue, and sweat broke out on his head. Still, he made it, stepping over the side of the tub. Black held on to the poster of the bed while Sunday dried him and then herself. She helped him into the bed, propping him up, and he remained naked. The wounds looked better, yet he seemed to be favoring his left side. He had lost weight, but he still looked like her husband, especially since Paul had shaved him.

Moving around the room, she began to dress in fresh black trousers, a white shirt, and her gun. Black watched, and he was frustrated because he was getting tired. She cleaned the room and then brought the food to the bed to feed him. She spooned him some beef stew and made him finish the corn bread. She was about to open the door when he said, "Elbert and the doctor will not sleep in this room another night."

She turned at the door, trying to gauge him, but his expression was closed. He held eye contact and then added, "And you will sleep with me, not Elbert."

Putting the tray down beside the door, she walked back over to the bed. "What is happenin'?"

"What is happening is everyone is smitten with my damn wife."

He looked tired and hurt about Otis, and about putting her through this while she was pregnant. She would offer him the truth so they could move through it. "I been sleepin' on the floor next to the cot for days to be near ya. Elbert picked me up when I was sleepin' to put me in the bed, but I woke. I told him I cain't sleep in the bed witout ya. You don't has the energy to spend on somethin' that ain't happenin'."

Climbing back onto the bed, she straddled him. "I felt like if'n I slept in this bed witout ya, it would be declaring you were gone," she continued.

"Otis and I broke off from Elbert and James; we started working the Underground Railroad because of Mama and Mary. I am more like Elbert, and Otis was more like James. Grief and weakness draw the strangest behaviors from people. Elbert is a good man—until he is not. He is a stable man—until he is not. Men have changed for less."

She grabbed his hands, and placing them on her stomach, she said, "I has not changed. There is only you."

She saw him visibly relax. It was the middle of the day, and she had been about to take the tray to the kitchen. Instead, she undressed again, placing her clothes and gun on a nearby chair. Climbing under the covers, she curled up next to him, and just as they both were about to doze off, she said, "I thought ya said I could trust Elbert."

"My position as a man is different from yours with him. Men are always establishing and reestablishing their dominance. He is not looking to hurt you."

He left the thought there with the statement unfinished, and he was thankful that she did not push him or the issue. When she finally slept, he continued to fight sleep, trying to think. Otis gone … buried days ago, and he had slept right through it. He had not been able to pay his respects to a man who was always there for him. Everything seemed unreal, and try as he might, he could not reconcile reality, and he felt panicked. He understood what she told him, but he could not make the connection. For him, these events had not happened.

Looking down at Sunday, witnessing his child growing within her, he experienced feelings of defeat. He watched as the doctor spoke with her while looking over her shoulder to Elbert with fear in his eyes. Seeing Elbert ready to kill on her behalf as though she were his knocked him on the humble. As a man, he was shaken to watch his wife and child depend on a next man. He would right this situation by regaining his strength physically—and mentally he would respect defeat without embracing it. Examining the issues before him, he declared to himself that he was the best man to run Fort Independence, to be her husband, to be a father to their child. When he finally dozed off, it was because he was ready, not because he had no choice. The victory was small, but it was a win. He, Black, had been taken back to the basics.

The next morning she let the doctor in so that he could check Black. She realized that he needed time to deal with his feelings. They spent time together but did very little talking. He slept, and in her condition, so did she. Sunday had not realized how tired she really was until the day before. Paul brought dinner, and other than Mama coming for a few minutes, they were alone. He seemed different this morning, and she hoped the change was for the better.

Black sat on the edge of the bed, wearing black trousers, boots and no shirt while the doctor checked him and asked him questions.

"When I touch your shoulder, do you have pain or numbness?"

"Pain," Black responded.

"Ah. We need you to move the arm and not favor it. You need to rehabilitate. I cut the stitching, and the skin has knitted. Even though you feel better, you don't need to overdo it."

Off to the side, Black could see Sunday watching, an expression of concern on her face. She wore a peach-colored dress, and the color was good against her skin. He smiled at her, trying to reassure her. As for the doctor, he was done talking. He stepped back from Black, saying, "You are definitely on the mend. I could give you something for the pain; it will make you sleep, though."

"No."

Sunday stepped forward between his legs, kissing his face. "Ya looks so much better."

The doctor was packing up his belongings when he asked her, "Would you like for me to check you, Miss Sunday?"

"No, no. I's fine," she responded.

"Yes," Black answered, pushing her forward.

She turned and looked at him. His face was serious, but she knew his worry.

"All right, Doctor," she said.

Watching the exchange between the two, the doctor decided for this checkup he wouldn't touch her and would instead simply ask questions. "How do you feel?"

She answered truthfully, "I feels good."

"When was the last time you came around?"

She looked at Black, and he nodded. "July."

Dr. Shultz was thoughtful, and it gave her time to assess him. He looked as though he just shaved and bathed, courtesy of Iris, Paul, and Mama. It seemed like years had passed since that night, and though he seemed nervous, he was different. She was sure that without desperation at her back, everything looked changed.

"Looks like you'll have an April baby," he confirmed, smiling while pushing his glasses on his face.

Black's expression was closed, but he was paying attention. The doctor listened to her heart and her stomach and then talked with her about eating and resting. He backed away and smiled at her. "You are in good health."

Sunday smiled at the doctor and was about to thank him when he said, "If it is all the same to you, Miss Sunday, I would like to forget how we met."

Before she could respond, Black asked, "How did you meet?"

"She came to my home with four of the biggest ni—" he choked. "Ah, *men* you ever saw and threatened to kill me if I didn't help you," he finished, coughing and embarrassed.

"It's probably wisest to forget," Black said, trying not to laugh. "I will take care of paying you before you leave."

"Thank you," Dr. Shultz said, and he was completely red. "Miss Iris cooked. I'll be in the kitchen."

After the doctor left, Black chuckled, shaking his head. Sunday did not speak. She would do it again if necessary, and it was still too new to laugh about.

Black was up and dressed before the rest of the house. Sunday was still asleep when he strapped his gun on, and bracing himself, he opened the door. He fought the urge to climb back into bed; he was better, but he was weak. Stepping out into the hallway, he came face-to-face with Elbert, who was standing guard outside their room. Their eyes locked before Black moved past him on down the hall.

The sun was starting to rise when they stepped out on to the porch. Black leaned his good shoulder against the wall, and crossing his legs at the ankle, he watched daybreak. He left Elbert in his peripheral vision and watched the fort come alive. The quiet stretched out between them until Elbert broke the silence. "Did Sunday tell you … about Otis?" His voice was etched in pain.

Black could hear his hurt, and he could respect it. Otis was why he was standing out here, and his sorrow was acute. He had not even allowed himself to think about Mary. The thought of facing her and her anguish while he lived ... "Yes, she told me."

Out in front of him, he could see three men coming toward them from the direction of the barracks. It was a welcome distraction. He did not talk feelings with Otis, and he would not speak them with Elbert. Other than addressing the needs of Sunday and Mama, he and Otis had talked very little; they understood each other. As the men approached the bottom of the steps, he placed their faces; it was Philip, James, and—a sight for sore eyes—Tim. They all came up, shaking his hand and causing him to stand straight up. People began to mill about, and though they saw Black, they did not approach. The men standing around him appeared grave.

"Black," Tim said.

"Tim," Black responded, and he waited.

"I would like to move my wife and child here. I feel it will be safest," he said to Black.

"I agree," Black replied. "Did you see who shot Otis?"

"No. When Phil and I loaded you onto the wagon, that is when we noticed we hadn't seen him. We found him dead on the edge of the fields. He lit the fire, and the field was burning when we got there, but there was no one else," Tim said, his voice filled with regret.

Black listened as Tim relived that night, saying nothing. He just wanted to close the gaps.

Elbert chimed in, saying, "They sent for help, and we met them on the way here. We came to you and the men rather than come here."

Black just listened; the truth was he could add nothing because he had slept through the whole damned thing.

"Hunter shot you, and Tim killed him," Philip was saying.

"Will?" Black asked Tim.

"He got away. When we got you in the wagon, I tracked where he must have jumped from the window. I found blood—and in one place, a lot of blood. He was gone, like someone helped him," Tim was saying as he tried to think through it.

"You said that Wilson, Hunter, Matthews, and Robinson were present. I don't remember seeing them," Black said, trying to recall.

"Hunter shot you, but the other three hid behind the furniture. Once Hunter was dead, Philip made the decision to kill them all, so it couldn't have been them he got help from."

Black looked at Philip, a brown-skinned fellow with salt-and-pepper hair, who carried himself as if he were incapable of making such a decision. He was about fifty summers, with no wife and no children, doing his time in the barracks without complaint. Otis liked Philip, and Black left those decisions to Otis. Now he saw why. As for Tim, he was being gracious; what he had said without saying was Black had lost focus and gotten himself shot. *It's true*, he thought. He had pointed his revolver and taken the shot, and that was when he felt a burning sensation. The gun had kicked back slightly, and he realized he was shot when he attempted to aim again. He took the second shot, and then he was shot again. *Damn*, he thought.

"Has anyone heard news from the Turner plantation since we've been back?" Black asked, trying to determine the damage and track Will.

"Sunday ordered the fort locked down until you were back on your feet. When they went to get the doctor, I stayed here. Since I worked as an overseer, I don't think she trusted me."

Black nodded as he watched the fort's activity. Paul exercised the horses, the barracks was going through a shift change, the children rushed off to school, and the women opened their windows to begin cleaning. He listened to the men as they kicked around scenarios to explain Will's getaway. The most logical answer was that Will's wife had helped him. After all, Sunday had saved him. It was possible and plausible.

James gazed at him directly. "How do you feel, Black?"

"I'm here is all I can say for now," Black said, never really answering the question. James didn't push, and the conversation turned to Otis again. He listened and said nothing.

In their bedroom, Sunday rolled over to get closer to him, and when she reached for him, he wasn't there. Opening her eyes, she was disoriented, and sitting straight up, she called out for him. She hopped out of bed and frantically began dressing, her thoughts not processing.

After all she had been through, waking up and finding him gone … Otis. She flung the door open and began running down the hall. When she reached the kitchen, Mama was sitting to the table having a cup of coffee alone. Breathlessly, Sunday asked, "Has you seen Black?"

Mama was shaking her head, about to say she could hear the men on the porch when Sunday took off running past her. Watching Sunday, Mama felt sorry for all of them. Otis's death was hitting home. Sunday didn't want Black out of her sight. *Lord, I needs strength*, she thought.

The men could hear the frantic footsteps approaching the front door. They all stopped talking and stared at the door. Black was curious. He was about to step forward when Sunday appeared in the doorway, breathless, her huge eyes glassy and brimming with tears. Black watched as she looked between the men until she spotted him. Her relief was visible, and her tears spilled over. *Shit*, Black thought. *I should have told her I was stepping out of the room.*

He didn't speak. Instead, he reached his hand out to her, and she came to him, burying her face against him. She was shaking, and as he rubbed her back, the men moved off to the bottom of the steps so he could speak with her. Elbert stood unmoving, staring at her, and Black could read his thoughts. Finally, when Elbert looked up, his eyes collided with Black's, and Black's message was unmistakable. Elbert held his stare until James yelled, "Elbert, I need to speak with you!"

Looking back down at Sunday, Elbert moved on down the steps, conceding that Black was right and he was wrong. He was not aggressive toward Black, and he wouldn't be. He just wanted her to be happy.

At the bottom of the steps, James pulled him to the side, asking, "What the hell is wrong with you? You can't have the man's wife. After the loss of Otis, we needs to stick together."

"I would never … I was …"

"You need to get knee deep in some ass," James said, and Elbert did not comment. Looking over Elbert's shoulder, James saw Black's expression, and he nodded to indicate that he was addressing the issue. He yelled up to Black, "Are you lifting the ban? Because right now, no one is coming or going."

Black responded, his voice lazy, his eyes intense, "During the day, the lockdown is lifted from 7:00 a.m. to 7:00 p.m. After 7:00 p.m., I want the place shut down." He understood James's motive; he wanted to take Elbert into town so they could chase women. James was attempting to keep the peace, and Black appreciated it.

Philip chimed in, "I'll let the men know."

Black turned his attention back to his wife, saying, "I'm sorry. I obviously had not understood all you have been though." Taking her hand, he led her back down the hall to the study.

When he closed the door, she whispered, "I's sorry to embarrass you."

He sat on the sofa and pulled her onto his lap. "So you thought I ran off and left you." He was trying to be funny.

"My condition ain't helpin' me neither. I feels like cryin' for no good reason," she answered, ignoring his joke.

"Are you feeling all right?"

"I feels just fine. It's just seeing Mary. I …"

Black understood. He almost hated falling to sleep, because when he woke, he had to start over dealing with his feelings about Otis. Now that he had given it some thought, it must be the same for her even though he survived. He pulled her close, saying, "It is me who should be sorry for all that I put you through. I can't even face Mary." His voice was hoarse.

She hugged him, saying, "Don't."

But Black *did*. He blamed himself.

The furniture was gaudy, red velvet with matching curtains. The bed was round, and on top were lots of pillows. Several candles lit the chamber, giving just the right amount of lighting. The girl he picked had features like Sunday's, with huge brown eyes that took away from the illusion Elbert was trying to create. There was awareness in her eyes that told of all she had been through. Still, she was pretty.

She wore a black negligee that accentuated her slim figure, and though she was experienced, his dead eyes gave her pause. She approached him with caution, and to her surprise, when he spoke, his voice was gritty minus the aggression she knew he was capable of.

"Come, and don't be afraid. Hurting women does not thrill me," he said.

She assessed him, realizing he was brooding about a woman, and she understood. He wore a white shirt and brown trousers, and the material was of a higher quality than she was used to seeing. His skin was dark, and his hair was black and cut close.

When finally she stood before him, she asked, "What would you like?"

"Time away from reality," Elbert said, staring up at her.

"I can manage that," she said as she reached out her hand to him.

He stood, and she helped him undress, kissing his chest after his shirt was removed. When he was completely naked, she saw that he had scars and plenty of them. She was taken by surprise when he picked her up and carried her to the bed. Laying her down, he leaned up over her, giving her a moment. This was different, she thought, from all the crazy shit she usually got. He kissed her, and it reminded her of a time before she ended up here.

He was tired to his very soul; the loss of Otis and his confusion about Sunday had drained him. She caressed his face, and he felt comforted. He needed to feel connected. There was no foreplay, and for that, he was sorry. Pushing her legs apart with his knees, he entered her slowly until he was planted within her to the hilt. He didn't move right away. Instead, he leaned his forehead against hers, and closing his eyes, he whispered brokenly, "I just need time away from the bullshit."

She didn't speak. Instead, she kissed him, telling him physically that it was all right. Whatever she expected from him, it wasn't tenderness. He began to move, and it was actually pleasant, and she realized that— like him—she also needed time away from life.

He took her three times that night, and when they slept, his pain had eased just a bit.

Virginia

Will lay in the bed, his pain great. He could walk, but he would forever need the assistance of a cane. When he woke, Amber was by his side; she and Tilly were a constant. They were living in what was left of the house, and Tilly had gone for the doctor. He was shot twice—once in the shoulder and once in the hip. The shoulder wound went clean through, but the doctor could not get the ball out of his hip without causing major issues. He was crippled, and this would now be his life thanks to Black.

Will was dealing with the shame of running from Black, and he couldn't seem to move beyond that thought. Making matters worse, the law was crawling all over Virginia. Some lunatic attempted to take over the armory at Harpers Ferry, causing the cavalry to rain down on Virginia. The fact that his plantation was burned down and four of the major plantation holders from Virginia to South Carolina were found murdered in his home made everyone think this might have been the quiet before the storm. The situation was thought to be part of what had happened at Harpers Ferry with the infamous John Brown.

Several officers were sent to inspect his land and question him for information. He had taken the coward's way out and lied. "I recall screaming coming from outside the house, and I went to investigate. A slave began shooting at me. I attempted to get my gun, but it was too late. Hunter attempted to help me ..."

Officer Walcott questioned Will and knew he was lying about something, but he had so much work to do he just didn't have the time to chase a rabbit down a hole. "Just to recap, you're saying that you ran into the study, and Edward Hunter shot this slave, but we have no slaves who have been shot. How did you get away and they ended up shot to death?"

"I wish I knew. I blacked out," he said, appearing weak, causing Amber to step in on his behalf.

"My husband is tired, gentlemen; he is still recovering from this ordeal," Amber said with authority.

Officers Walcott and Dorsey turned to her. Walcott bowed to her before saying, "Thank you both for your time. Mr. Turner, we will be back to speak with you."

Amber saw them to the front door; it was Officer Dorsey, a plump, short man with black hair and glasses, who spoke. "Did you see anything, Mrs. Turner?"

"I was resting when I heard gunshots. I was afraid, so I hid in the closet," she answered, daring him to say otherwise. Both officers thanked her and left. It was clear they thought her words less than truthful, but they remained silent.

Back in Will's room, Tilly was serving lunch that consisted of tea and sliced ham sandwiches. They had about twelve hams; everyone that came brought a ham. Amber was tired of ham and just plain old tired of the South, but most importantly, she was tired of her damned secretive husband. She had heard the slaves giggling about her husband chasing a slave named Sunday. He had embarrassed her, and now she was biding her time until they left for Boston. When she got home, she wouldn't come back to this place. She was going to try to get away from him. She loved him, but he wasn't even showing up to the marriage to participate. She had a father that loved her; she needed that from her husband to continue on.

Will was laid up on the bed staring out the window; his hair had been cut by Tilly that morning. He looked better, but he had no drive, and Amber was angry, so she didn't feel motivating. She wouldn't tell him that she knew about him trying to get this slave back because he loved her; the embarrassment was too great. She was with child, and her goal now was to get back to Boston. The man she loved was so self-absorbed that he did not even realize she was pregnant.

"Dear, you promised to get out of bed and move around so you could gain strength for us to travel to Boston while this house is being rebuilt." It was the best she could do.

"I will try harder to get strong," he replied, gritting his teeth against the pain.

She watched as he reached for his cane and closed his eyes to brace for the pain. She noticed that he tried not to use the leg, anticipating the discomfort as he moved toward the door. On the way back to the bed, he broke out in a sweat, and Amber felt no empathy; she was tired of him and mad that she was in love with him. He would pay, and she would see to it.

When he sat down, he could see the disgust in her eyes. He was sure she knew what was going on, but she backed his lie as a wife should. She had lost weight, though she was still a little plump, yet every day she seemed more and more beautiful. He had not tried for sex. He couldn't. When he thought about anything bumping up against his hip, he couldn't get aroused. The anticipation of pain was a deterrent from the sex act.

He still wanted to hire the bounty hunters, but now he had the expense of replacing slaves. The house needed rebuilding, and the overseers were working longer hours trying to get the Turner plantation going again. As for Sunday, he couldn't see them moving forward now that he was crippled. Black, Will knew, wasn't dead; his gut told him so. He wanted to bring him down and erase the running scene from his brain. Will needed for his father not to be right about everything.

14

CHARLESTOWN, NOVEMBER 1859

John Brown stood confrontationally before the court as his sentence was handed down. His face registered no regret for his role in the uprising at Harpers Ferry in October 1859, where he and his men took over the armory. He had attempted to abolish slavery, and his stance was clear, and he offered no apology for his belief that every man should be free. Tim watched from the back row as John was found guilty of treason, conspiracy, and murder, and a cheer went up at the verdict. The Southern supporters were in full effect, and as John was escorted from the courtroom, his gaze caught and held Tim's. He nodded his appreciation that Tim had come all this way to pay his respects, and then he was gone.

Once on the courthouse stairs, he heard talk about the number of plantation owners that had been slain due to uprisings all over. Tim stepped forward into the conversation, offering nothing; the group of men gave an accounting of slave owners that had been killed in Kentucky, Missouri, and Virginia.

A tall, fat fellow with reddish-brown hair said, "Some say the Turner plantation was hit by John Brown and his group before they tried to take over the armory."

Another man, tall, thin, and angry, stepped forward. "I live close to the Turner plantation. They have never been able to control their niggers. My granddaddy talked about them, and the incident of '31."

"The Turner plantation was burned to the ground, and several owners were found dead inside. Turner himself is crippled now. It's for the best that John Brown will be hanged here to send a message," yet another man was saying.

Tim moved between the groups, and the consensus was the same in each. It appeared the cavalry would remain in Virginia well after John was hanged, and they would launch an investigation into who may have known and/or helped him in this crazy scheme. Tim would leave Virginia and move north tonight. With the state under siege by the government, he could find himself in jail. Charlestown was so crowded that he couldn't get a handle on who was there and who was not. He would not send a telegram; it was too dangerous. As he rode away from Virginia, he felt better.

He would get his wife and child and keep moving north.

In Boston, Rose and Anderson were fresh back from shopping when Alfred, their butler, stepped forward with a message. He handed it to Anderson and waited for instruction.

Anderson scanned the page and then looked up, saying, "That will be all, Alfred." When they were alone, he told Rose what happened. "It appears your brother has been shot, but he lives, and your childhood home has been burned down."

"Amber ..." Rose whispered.

"This message is from Amber. Apparently, she is fine, and they are here in Boston," Anderson said in an effort to stop her worry. It was not lost on him that she never asked after Will.

"I want to see Amber," Rose replied.

"I will take care of it," he said, unable to refuse her anything. He loved his wife, and he was thankful for her every day.

Later that evening, a carriage pulled in the front of the Wilkerson town house. The driver opened the door, and Amber stepped down. The street was upscale, and as she moved to the wrought iron gate, the front door opened. A serious-looking fellow stood in the doorway, prepared to take her coat. He was average height with black hair and blue eyes, and his nose was perfectly shaped, his lips thick. The butler was handsome and commanding in his post.

"Mrs. Turner?" he asked.

"Yes. I am here for Mrs. Wilkerson."

After hanging her coat, he said, "Please follow me."

Amber took in her surroundings. Off to the right was a staircase with a beautifully polished banister. Straight ahead was a long hall with blue-gray wallpaper. The floors were hardwood and shined to perfection. Where the hall ended was a thick brown carpet that led to the living room. Inside sat a large black piano, and over to the left of the room sat a large black chair. The sofa was burgundy with a matching loveseat, and the furniture was placed to accentuate the fireplace. On the sofa, Rose sat reading, and she looked up when Amber stepped into the room.

Amber was happy to see her. Rose had always been nice, and now they were family. Rose stood, coming forward to hug her. It was nice to have some sort of family around and a woman whom she could relate to, Amber thought. When Rose got closer, her excitement was evident at Amber's condition, and Amber turned red. She felt even more embarrassed by the situation with Will and this slave woman.

"Oh, look at you. When will I be an auntie?"

"The end of April, according to the doctor," Amber replied.

Upon seeing Rose and needing a friend, she began crying. Anderson, who was sitting in the black chair, stood, and when she started crying, he wanted to disappear, but there was only one way in and out of the room. The only other choices were the windows.

"Anderson, it's so good to see you. I am so sorry for my behavior," Amber said, her voice shaking.

"Please don't apologize. Come in and make yourself at home."

"Yes. Please come sit," Rose said.

Amber came and sat for a time and never really said much. Anderson, taking the hint, excused himself to give the women time to talk. When he was out of earshot, Rose came right with it.

"So you found out about Sunday?"

Amber looked shocked. "So you knew?"

"I had a feeling that's why my father and brother argued so. Since she was gone, I thought that was over until I heard that Will was tracking Black."

"Black," Amber repeated.

"Never mind that. It is of no consequence to you."

Amber's head was spinning; she didn't know what to ask. "He has embarrassed me with this ... a slave."

"No more than my father embarrassed my mother. I am so sorry you are going through this. Even if I would have told you, you still would have had to marry him."

Amber knew it was true. "Will has become mean and almost crazy. I want him gone from my life and my child's life."

Rose was truly sorry for all that Amber had been through. The Turner men had not been the kind of men who were considered strong, and she found herself reflecting on her father's choice in Anderson. Rose suspected it was his way to make amends. She loved Anderson. He was quietly strong, and his very presence made her feel safe.

"You can't upset yourself in your condition. I am here, and you still have your father."

"I know. I just need to relax," Amber whispered, but she couldn't. She wanted Will gone.

Will had been in Boston for weeks. They were staying with his father-in-law, and he felt like a child in Robert Myers's presence. Whenever he made a decision for himself and Amber, Robert overrode him, having the final say. Amber slighted him at every turn, and it chafed. He felt like a fool and disrespected by his wife. She was with child, and Robert spoke as if the child were his. He could not wait until his childhood home was restored and he could move his wife and child back to Virginia.

The town house they were staying in was a tight fit for the three of them and the staff. Amber had her belongings set in her childhood room by the butler. When the butler attempted to bring Will's belongings to her room, as well, she put a stop to it, saying, "I will need the same privacy you needed in Virginia. You, dear husband, are not welcome in my bed."

"Amber, I am your husband. You will do as I say, and you will not tell me where to sleep. My place is with you."

The butler stood stone-faced until Amber directed him to take her husband's things to the maid's room.

Her treatment of him stung. Will watched the butler do as Amber asked as though he hadn't spoken. The maids doubled up, and he was given one of their chambers. He was not treated as her husband, and though he was angry, he said nothing more on the issue. When they moved back to Virginia, she would see who was boss.

As the days passed, the pain was unbearable if he moved around, and it was worse when he was still. He was unfocused and sleep deprived, and the two made for a bad combination. There was no break with the pain, so he took up drinking. The drinking, he found, caused him to have to piss all the time, so he was up and down, overworking his bad hip. The aching in his hip was like bone scraping bone, and Will had not known that pain could be so intense. Between lack of sleep, lack of privacy, and his anger, he could not put a thought together.

One bitingly cold evening, he came downstairs and headed down the hall toward the family room. Listening as his booted feet hit the hardwood floor, he could hear the falter in his own steps. It was the small things a man noticed that made him fumble with his manhood. The sound of his lame steps made his temper rear its ugly head, and so he picked a fight that he could not win.

When he appeared in the doorway of the family room, Amber smiled, saying, "Good evening, my dear."

Seeing her sitting with her father made him angry, causing him to poke at her. "Good evening to you, my dear. I have great news. Looks like the house will be finished soon, and we can go home."

Amber didn't bite her tongue when she said, "Oh, good, then you can leave."

Will stared at her as she sat against the green sofa, smugly returning his gaze. "You are my wife. You will come with me."

After working through all that bothered her, she settled on saying, "I am not your mother, and I will not turn a blind eye. I cannot live with a man who does not love me. When will you be leaving?"

Will stepped forward as if to strike her, and Robert Myers quietly said, "Son, that is a bad move ... a very bad move. I'm going to have Francis pack your things, and Charles will see you to the train."

He assessed Robert and his bushy, unkempt hair, his wrinkly suit, his lackluster shoes, and his shiny revolver. Will knew it was time to leave.

"Robert, she is my wife, and therefore I am the law where she is concerned."

"Will, she is my child. I will have your things sent, as I cannot stand you in my home any longer."

Will was taken to the train that evening. It was for the better, he thought. Now he could deal with the real issue—Black. He would start anew when he got home, and though it would be a financial burden, he would see it through. There was no reason he couldn't hire bounty hunters that could execute the plan for him. He considered himself a roughened individual at this point, and he was man enough.

15

UPPER CANADA, NOVEMBER 1859

Black had begun working in his study again, but he still did not have the energy to paint. When he dressed in the mornings, he would stretch and work his fingers because he was experiencing a stiffness associated with the weather changing. Sunday was better about him leaving her in the morning as long as he kissed her before going. She slept longer in the mornings as her condition advanced.

Once in his study, starting from around 10:00 a.m., there was a steady stream of people that came to him with issues now that Otis was gone. They were lost, and to be honest, so was he. In order to make better use of his time, he worked from 5:00 a.m. to 10:00 a.m. on ordering supplies and other similar tasks. From 10:00 a.m. to 2:00 p.m., he listened to issues the people had and any concerns for the barracks. At 2:00 p.m., he attempted lunch, which never went uninterrupted because that was when people who did not have a formal complaint came to chat. Black limited chats to fifteen minutes once a week per person. Through it all he managed to stay sane, yet, to some degree, he needed the craziness to keep his mind off Otis.

There was a knock at the door, and he answered, "Enter."

It was Herschel, who had come to see how he was doing. He handed Black an envelope, and when Black opened it, he smiled.

"I thought you could use some good news," Herschel said, heading for the door.

Black looked up just as Herschel was about to leave and asked, "Mary ... how is she?"

"Pulling through, and she loves that Sunday comes every day. It helps. They discuss the baby, and it gives her something to look forward to. Congratulations to you, Black."

"Thank you, Herschel."

"I won't keep you; there is a line forming in the hall for you," he said, chuckling.

As he was leaving, Mama came in, and Black dreaded talking to her, and it was his own fault. He feared she would ask about Jacob Turner, and he did not want to face having lied by omission. Now that Otis was gone and Sunday was with child, he respected more her position about Turner. Sadly, the bell could not be unrung; he had been less than truthful, and he was paying.

"I ain't wanted to ask … given all the goin's on, but I needs to know. Jacob, is he all right?"

No sooner than he could think it, here it was without preamble. She was asking today, but she had anguished before coming to him. It appeared he could not get out of his own way.

"Mama, Jacob is dead." He did not beat around the bush. He addressed the truth, waiting for her next words.

Her voice caught when she asked, "When … how?"

"I do not know how, but he died before Sunday and I got married. I was trying to save you from the hurt, and I withheld the truth. I now see I was wrong. I am sorry, Mama."

He stood when she looked as though she would faint, hugging her as she wept. It was the worst for him seeing her break down like that, yet he was thankful that she took the comfort that he offered. When she stepped back from him, she looked wrung out, and her eyes were swollen. Her next word cut like a knife.

"I deserves the truth from ya always. I loved him, but I always put you first. I's hurt by yo jealousy, yo thoughtlessness, and yo dishonesty. Nat Hope Turner, how could ya treat yo mama so?"

Before he could answer, she walked away, closing the door quietly, and he stared after her. What the hell was he going to do? He had not heard that tone from her in years. Damn Jacob Turner to hell! The dead bastard was still getting him in trouble. He sighed as he went back to work. Now he had to deal with this issue. How does one apologize for insensitivity at this level? She loved him, of that he was sure. What could he do to show he cared?

Black took his dinner in his study; coward that he was, he couldn't face Mama. She had called him jealous and thoughtless, and to his shame, he found there to be some merit to her words. When he examined the truth, there was no escaping that Jacob Turner was weak, but Mama was not. It bothered him that she had grown to love Jacob, even though he was no match for her. Big Mama had accepted only strength from him, but from Jacob Turner, she had accepted weaknesses, setting aside freedom to remain his slave. It was not the first time she had called him on his feelings of jealousy, and it had angered him. Still, the very thought of her heart being broken because of him hurt. He would have to do something nice for her. *Damn Jacob Turner.*

It was late when he finally went to bed, and when he entered his bedroom, Sunday was drying off from her bath. Black undressed and stepped into water she had just exited. There was a fire burning, and he watched the flames as she moved around the room, readying for bed. She was showing, and seeing his child growing within her made him love her even more. He did not know he could love her any more than he already did.

Between being shot and her condition, he had not made love to her, and he wanted to. He was afraid to hurt her, and he knew it would be quick because he missed her so much. Shaking his head to clear his thoughts, he moved away from the road that led to frustration. He stood drying and then climbed into bed next to her. Sunday sat Indian style, and Black propped himself up, prepared to chat with his wife. She shocked him when she asked, "Does ya not feel well enough to make love?"

He smiled before answering, "Oh, I am well enough."

"Then why has you not touched me?" she asked, holding his gaze.

He became serious when he answered, "I am so afraid to hurt you."

"I asked Dr. Shultz, and he says long as we ain't rough, it would be fine."

Black hung his head and smiled. She had asked about it … he hated and loved that. The doctor was getting an earful. "I don't think I can be rough. I miss you so much, and it's liable to end before it gets started." He chuckled.

He could see her eyebrows knitting together before it dawned on her what he meant. "Oh," she said, laughing at him.

She wore a shift that clung to her, and her nipples were visible through the thin material. He was about to tell her how beautiful she looked when she whispered, "Why don't I takes the edge off it for ya?"

It was his turn to look confused when she pulled the covers back, exposing his raging erection. And with the firelight as a backdrop at the foot of the bed, she leaned over, taking him in her mouth. His hands fisted in the covers, and his hips rose slightly off the bed. Between the visual of her lips on him and the pleasure he felt from every stroke of her tongue, he was approaching that edge that she had spoken of. As she took him deeper into her mouth, she felt a powerful spurt at the back of her throat.

He pushed her back from him, and he was still hard. Before he could get himself under control, she hiked up her shift and climbed over him, sliding down his shaft.

"Shit, woman, do not move," he ground out.

But Sunday did move … she *rode* him. Black grabbed her bottom, squeezing her cheeks to help and restrain her as she threw her hips to a rhythm. She leaned over, kissing him, pushing her tongue into his mouth, and he could taste the salt from her tears. Sunday was emotional, and her pleasure was heightened, the combination of need along with promise of a life with him caused her to tremble. Up against his lips, she moaned, "Oh, Black … Black … I loves ya."

He rode the edge until he heard his name, and when she started trembling, he let go, groaning, "Ah, Sunday … baby … baby, ahhh."

When they stilled, she did not leave him. She kissed his chest, reveling in his smell, his touch, his taste, his masculinity. She listened to their rushed breathing as it calmed, never wanting this moment to end. Black rubbed her back to comfort her, as they drifted off to sleep.

Black was seated behind his desk the next morning, and he looked up at a knock on the door. He bade the person on the other side to enter, and in walked Dr. Shultz.

"You requested to see me?" he asked.

Black could see that he wasn't thrilled about being summoned. He put down the paperwork he was reading over and leaned back. "Good morning, Doctor."

"Black, how are you feeling?" Shultz asked.

He ignored the question, and getting down to business, he asked, "What do I owe you?"

Shultz had not seen a patient who could pay with anything other than a ham. "Fifty dollars is my fee."

"Fair enough. I see that you have not yet left. Maybe I didn't make it clear that you are free to go," Black said.

"I figured as much when Elbert stopped following me," he answered.

"I have been seeing some of the people and treating them for various ailments—the ones that will see me, anyway."

"Do I owe you more money?"

"No, but ..."

"Let's hear it," Black said, narrowing his eyes.

"Can you help me buy more supplies? I have run out, and I need to check some of the children."

"I will. Do you plan on coming back and forth?" Black asked.

"I had not planned on rushing off. I can move to the cabin I've been working in if you would prefer it."

"No, Doctor. I would rather you stay on the second floor as you have been. I like keeping an eye on you. I would also like to discuss with you delivering a baby."

The doctor stared at him before responding, "You plan to be in the room with her, don't you?"

"I do."

"It's not pretty."

Black smiled. "I am sure that it's not, but you will teach me. Correct?"

"When do we start?"

"Next week, every other day from 4:00 p.m. to 5:00 p.m. Is this all right with you?" Black asked.

"Of course. That is fine."

They shook hands, and Shultz went about his day. As he walked away, it was not lost on him that he had struck an agreement with a man that in the past he would have considered a savage. Life as he knew it was changing.

Over the next few weeks, Black saw that Sunday was slowing down, and though it took her longer to do things, she still stuck to her routines. She helped in the kitchen, walked down to Mary's house, and still assisted in the cleaning of the house. Shultz's presence helped as he explained to Black that a sedentary life was good for no one. Sunday was happy, and that was all that mattered to him. He had embraced the baby issue. Deep inside, he was excited to be a father, and he was proud to partner her.

Mama steered clear of him, avoiding him at all costs. He acted as though he hadn't noticed her anger, going about his day in the same manner. There was one small difference, though—every day for twenty minutes he made it a point to seek her out and ask her a question. Black asked about the weather, the baby, Sunday, her new dress … just whatever came to his mind. The most important part of this exchange was that she answered, because when the smoke cleared, she was *his* mama.

He finally found his way into the studio, but his motivation was nil. Black had to do the uninspiring; he had to paint with no feeling, going through the motions. Still, after the house quieted, he wandered to the studio to stand for hours. It was slow going, but he stuck with it, paying attention to detail. Often, when he painted and completed a work, it took no time, because he painted it in his mind repeatedly before he ever picked up a brush. It was not the case with this, and he struggled through every stroke, and the stiffness in his arm and shoulder did not help matters.

He was standing before the canvas when he heard a knock at the door, and he smiled, knowing it was her. The knob twisted, and in stepped Sunday dressed in his robe. There was a chill in the air, and he was worried that she would catch cold.

"No slippers? No good," he said.

Black stood barefoot at the canvas dressed in black pants and an unbuttoned white shirt. She was about to hug him when she stopped, staring at the painting. It was Jacob Turner in various degrees of his life—as a young, middle-aged, and elderly man. In one image he smiled; in another he looked serious; and in yet another he looked dignified. The detail was uncanny, and Sunday had to ask, "Why?"

"She is angry with me for not telling her he died."

"So this is yo peace offerin'?" Sunday asked, thinking he even got the clothing and the color right. She had seen Jacob Turner in those suits, but she wouldn't have remembered if she hadn't seen the painting. The eyes seemed to follow the observer. Sunday hated to admit it, but this was one of his best pieces.

"I hate being in trouble with her," he said, his face serious.

"I knows," Sunday whispered. "Betta you than me; I's so happy you's in trouble and not me I don't know what to do."

It took him a minute to think about what she was saying. Throwing back his head, he laughed, and it was a rare occasion. He pulled her close, wrapping his arms about her, whispering, "You are a bad woman."

It was Black's turn in the barracks. He had not served since he had recovered, since Otis died, and since Shultz moved in. At night, Paul and Iris went to their own cabin, leaving him with Sunday and Mama. He was in his study when Shultz came in, asking, "You sent for me, Black?"

"I did."

"How can I help you?"

"Starting tonight, I have to do my time in the barracks. You will do my time with me," Black said. The doctor understood that he was not being asked. *You will not stay in the house with my wife and mother without me,* Black was saying without saying.

He was going to be in the barracks with a gaggle of mean-ass colored men. Black, reading his mind, said, "Consider this a learning experience."

Later that evening Black and Shultz stepped into the barracks as the men were changing shifts. At the front of the hall, Black saw Philip and James speaking to the men as they came and went. Upon seeing Black, they waved him to the front of the line.

It was James that spoke. "Good to see you. I hadn't expected you this go 'round."

"No need to put it off. I am able bodied, and I need to get away from my study," Black responded.

"Doctor," James said by way of greeting.

Black smiled. Shultz was uncomfortable, but he was managing. "You and the good doctor can take any bed you like. Get some rest. At the shift change, you'll go out."

When they settled on two beds, the men came and spoke with them. As for Shultz, he spent his evening discussing the merits of cleanliness as a way to sustain health. Black wandered out the back doors, staring off into the night. Life had knocked him down a notch, and the reality of being here without Otis stung. He had loose ends to tie up, and he was floundering. The truth was that, with Otis gone, he no longer had the luxury of accepting death. Sunday, his child, Mama, and now Mary were his responsibility, and his goal now was to live. He figured he *would* die young, and when Sunday came into his life, Otis had reassured him that he would see to her when it happened. But now ...

What he regretted most was that he had to ride out, and Otis would not be at his back. Sunday would be his worst fight, and in her condition, the thought of leaving her upset troubled him.

While his mind raced, Tim stepped out into the darkness with him, saying, "Black."

"Tim, how was Virginia?"

"John will hang in about a week. They found him guilty, and interestingly, they think the commotion at the Turner plantation was John's doing. Virginia is crawling with the cavalry, and all eyes are on the John Brown case." Quietly, Tim added, "I saw John, and John saw me. He is not broken."

Black did not respond, and though he knew this would be John's fate, he was bothered by it.

Tim continued, "Virginia is volatile right now. Even the citizens are being scrutinized by the cavalry. What should we do with Will? I have moved my wife, Sarah, and my son, Daniel, here to keep them safe."

"I wanted to say thank you," Black answered.

Tim didn't know what to say. Black had saved him a time or two. He responded, "I am sorry about Otis." He didn't acknowledge the thank-you from Black; it wasn't necessary.

"I was reckless and could have gotten us both killed; I see my faults, and the situation with Otis is not your doing." Changing the subject, Black continued, "Why do you think Will would allow anyone to think what happened was John's doing?"

"The Turners are known for not controlling their slaves. Why would he say a slave that belonged to him caused this? He already has little to no respect from the other plantation owners. I saw that firsthand. Even your father was bought up."

"It also means Will is dealing in shame, and that could be a problem," Black said, and Tim agreed.

Tim was about to respond when James and Philip stepped out into the night. The conversation changed, and it was evident that they were happy to see Black among them. James talked about what he would do to serve his time, and Black took the orders like the rest. The doctor, they all agreed, was in his element, teaching and joking with the men. They were laughing when Elbert walked up and joined them.

The men moved along to their duties, leaving Elbert and Black standing at the back doors. The doors were slightly open, casting a small amount of light between the men. Black concentrated on the darkness, the noises from men inside the barracks, and the sounds of the night. He knew this meeting was coming, and he waited patiently.

Elbert was quiet for minutes before he began, "Black, I—"

Black cut him off. "You want my wife."

Elbert would not insult him by lying, and he responded, "I am attempting to right the situation."

"There are a couple of male dogs down at the stables. They get along and are always wrestling and running about together. It would seem they are companions, and from my study window, I have seen them chase a cat together. I have even seen them eat from the same bowl."

Elbert smiled as he stood staring off into the distance; he was being checked.

Black continued, "A female was added to the mix, and from the window, I could see them scrapping one afternoon. They changed toward each other, with the dominant male almost killing the other. It was apparent they could not share a bitch."

"Almost killing the other?" Elbert restated as if he were asking a question.

"Almost … but they were companions. Days later, I saw them from the window running about again, fur missing and limping. They managed to work through it," Black answered.

"Are you saying that we are like the dogs at the stables?" Elbert asked.

"The basics apply, yet as men, we are elevated. She is mine."

"I know," Elbert responded, and pushing off the wall, he turned to go back inside.

"I appreciate all you have done for her, my child, and me."

Elbert looked at him for a moment before speaking. "I would do it again. There was never another option."

"I know," Black said quietly.

Elbert reached out to shake Black's hand, and Black accepted. Before Black could think, Elbert pulled him close in a bear hug, clapping him on the back, saying, "I thought we would lose both—you and Otis. I am glad you are here."

Stepping back, Black nodded. "I think you are going soft."

Elbert laughed.

"Tell the men I am beginning my shift on foot," Black said, and he disappeared into the night.

He walked between the cabins off in the direction of the gate, and then it occurred to him that if the men saw him, they would want to talk. Changing directions, he continued to walk along the dirt paths. There was no moon, and he was thankful. The hour had grown late, and no one stirred. He moved off the path and into the shadows. Leaning back against a tree, he hung his head and cried. It was a private moment between him and his grief.

He howled his pain for the loss of Otis, for Sunday to survive childbirth, for hurting Mama, for Mary, for missing the shot, for getting shot, and, most importantly, for embracing death until he could not comprehend *life*.

Virginia

Now this is how one should live, Will thought as the doctor stuck the needle in his hip. *Pain-free.* He had discovered morphine, and the only drawback was that once it wore off, the pain was greater. Moving about without pain created the illusion that he was himself again, and he would overdo. He paid later, sending for the doctor in the wee hours. The cycle was becoming vicious, but he couldn't see it.

The pain was finally in the background, and he had become focused. He was replaying the scene in his mind, and for the first time, he could see Tim coming through the front door *with* Black. It was how Black stayed ahead of the game … spies. He went through all the paperwork, and he found nothing on Tim, and he was frustrated. Youngblood must not have known, or he wouldn't have been employed here.

He was broke, and, having to rebuild, his number of slaves had been reduced dramatically. The slaves that remained were elderly, ailing, and women; he had no workforce. He needed Amber back and the money that came with her. She was his wife; he would have to get her to see reason. It was clear that he needed to win her and get her back here before the child. It didn't help that he had been riddled with pain. As long as he could manage his comfort level, he could be a man to her. He would return to Boston and attempt to remove his wife from the clutches of her father.

Virginia had nothing to offer right now other than trouble. The cavalry was here investigating John Brown even though they had him in custody for some time. What Will had going on wasn't a crime. He just wasn't going to have anyone recording in government documents that he, Will Turner, was overtaken by the slave Black. Black had enough notoriety, and he would give nothing else. Boston was where he needed to be, and he could see that now. There he would find the bounty hunters, and it was closer to *him*. He would make amends with his wife and set right the injustices that were done to him.

The key to his success lay in his ability to manage his pain. If he couldn't stay in front of the pain, all else was lost. He had to learn to be flexible, prioritizing and reprioritizing based on events as they happened. Will understood now the value of problem solving, seeing more than one way to the result. The morphine that he managed to wrestle from the doctor was limited, but it would get him to Boston and see him settled. Once settled, he would have to search out a supply, and when the time came, bad hip and all, he would head to Canada. He would bring the bullshit to Black.

Will stepped down from the 5:45 train into the cold Boston evening, and catching a hansom cab, he appeared at his father-in-law's door. He gave two curt knocks before the door was opened by Myers himself. Robert stood in front of him wearing a wrinkled dark-blue suit with the jacket pushed back on the left side, revealing his weapon. His pain in the background, Will drew himself up, and staring his father-in-law in the eye, he said, "I love them, and I am willing to share them, but you cannot have my wife and child. I want to see my wife."

Robert was about to let his blood spill right there in the doorway when Amber stepped out from behind the door. Will had only been gone a couple of weeks, but she looked different, more beautiful. Amber's hair was pulled back from her face and hanging over her left shoulder. The dress she wore was gray, and it concealed her condition. He was taken aback at the rush of feelings seeing her evoked, and he didn't hide from it; he embraced it. While having her back would give him power, he realized that he loved and missed her.

"I need to speak with you privately … please," he begged.

"Step into the sitting room," she said, giving her father the eye.

Placing his hand on the black door, he pushed it back, and planting his cane firmly over the threshold, he stepped in, following her to the sitting room. Never did he look back at Robert Myers. He followed his wife, and watching her hips sway, he wanted her. He opened the sitting room door, letting her enter first. Closing the door behind him, he paused before speaking, attempting to get his emotions under control. His pain window was closing, so he had to get this right.

As she stood next to the window, holding the cream-colored drapes, she peered out, and he suspected it was to ignore him. He assessed the room, trying to determine where he could sit that would support his hip and back. Settling on one of the two burnt-orange chairs facing the brown sofa, he moved to the middle of the room, leaning heavily on his cane. Already feeling less of a man, he waited for her to sit; he would not sit first.

"I have shamed myself and you. Please tell me what to do," he said, causing her to look up.

He was handsome in his brown suit, but she could see he was far from fit. There were circles around his eyes, and he looked harder than when she had seen him last. She had been neglected by this man, yet the sight of him made her ache for what she could not have with him. The silence stretched out between them; she could not find the words. Emotions and her condition were more than she could handle, and she cried softly. She was defeated in her marriage by another woman, a slave. This other woman had nothing to offer him, she could not enhance him, and still he wanted this woman even at the expense of losing her.

He rushed forward, but she stepped back against the wall, and he stood in front of her. Looking down at her, he found he wanted her forgiveness. He had no one else—she was it. "I know you don't think so, but I love you and our child. I deserve to be shut out, but I am begging you not to."

Amber's voice was laced with emotion when finally she said, "Will, I cannot live with a man—"

He cut her off. "I understand, but I don't love her." The truth was he didn't love her anymore. Black was his real issue, and he wanted it resolved. The Turners had been living under the infamy of both him and his father for thirty years. And Jacob Turner placed the final nail in the coffin with that nigger Ellen.

She pushed past him, and he stumbled. When he righted himself, her back was to the wall. Will stood in front of her with one hand flat to the wall just over her head to steady himself. Leaning down, he kissed her, and while she didn't kiss him back, she didn't refuse him.

Against her lips, he whispered, "I love you, Amber. I am sorry it took me so long to figure that out."

Pushing his tongue into her mouth, he kissed her deeply, and she turned her face up to his. She was ashamed, but he never told her he loved her before, and she wanted to revel in his declaration for just a moment … she wanted to believe him. He was hard, and she could feel it against her. She reached for his pants, opening the buttons. Will helped her gather her skirts, and dropping the cane, he lifted her leg—and hip be damned, he entered her. Placing most of his weight on his good leg, he began to move. She was tight, and the friction was unbelievable. He felt his hip trying to come to, and he managed to ignore it. Sliding between pleasure and pain, he moaned, "Oh … oh … oh, don't leave me, Amber. Oh, ahh."

She missed his touch, and every stroke he dealt, though unsteady, was effective. He kissed her again, moaning against her lips, and she was so moved that she began to shudder. "Ahh … ahh. Uhh. Will."

Feeling her orgasm so intensely, he followed. And there against the wall on a bad hip, riding the edge of pain, he came … calling her name and pleading with her, "Please … Amber. Oh … be my wife … be my wife."

Their ragged breathing and moans filled the room as they tried to catch their breath. Will stepped back from her, righting his clothes. Helping her adjust her skirts, he kissed her again. He was shaken because he meant everything he said. She looked away, and lifting her chin with his finger, he gave her the truth, his voice rough from pain and emotion.

"I am less than the man you married. There will be days when the pain rides me so bad I am evil. Amber, there will be days I can't satisfy you. I am telling you the truth when I say I love you and only you."

In the hall, Robert Myers stood listening, and he knew the bastard was back.

16

DECEMBER 1859, BOSTON

Will took an independent hansom cab when he went to conduct business. He didn't need Robert Myers's driver leaking information about him. He went to a gentlemen's club called the Sire in a less-than-reputable part of town. It was three in the afternoon, overcast, and cold when the cab stopped in front of what appeared to be an uninhabitable building. The surrounding buildings were the same, factories that seemed abandoned. Stepping down from the cab and up on the curb, he eyed the door before him. Turning back to the cabbie, he yelled, "Wait!"

At the black metal door, he rapped twice with his cane, and out stepped the largest white man that Will had ever seen. Looking down at Will, he asked, "And you are?"

"I am here to see Max," Will replied.

The man was dressed in a blue suit of high quality with a red shirt and red handkerchief. His style of dress didn't match their surroundings. He had blue eyes and black hair combed back neatly, and his nose was slightly red.

"And you are?" the man asked again, dismissing his question the same as Will dismissed his.

"Turner," Will said, giving nothing else.

He eyed Will, and Will gave as good as he got. Turning, the man opened the door, saying, "Straight ahead."

The corridor was long and dark, and the smell of cigar smoke assailed him as he began his trek toward the light up ahead. The sound of his uneven steps coupled with the clipping noise from his cane rang

224

out as he walked in front of the nameless man. Reaching the light, he adjusted his eyes, and before him were billiard tables, chess matches, card games, and well-dressed men taking their leisure. The women were in various stages of undress and appeared to work there.

At the right of the room was a bar, and like the floor, it was polished to perfection. In the farthest corner of the room was a large sofa where men sat interacting with the almost-naked beauties. The inside was an oasis at total war with the outside of the building. A beautiful woman with blonde hair, deep-red lips, and breasts that were spilling out of a silver and very tight dress walked toward him.

"Can I help you?" she asked in a throaty voice.

Moving out from behind Will, the large man said, "He is here for Max."

Introducing herself, she turned to Will, saying, "I am Georgia. And you are?"

"Nice to meet you, Georgia. I am Will Turner," he answered.

"A Southerner," she said with a smile, commenting on his accent. "Follow me."

As he followed her across the room, he could feel his hip trying to wake up, but he was a man on a mission. He had made some inquiries, asking questions in the roughest parts of town, until finally he was directed here by a strange-looking fellow called Ape. Walking up the three steps to the large sofa brought him to stand in front of a brown-haired man with tiny brown eyes, full lips, and a large nose. He was a plain fellow who looked even plainer surrounded by the beautiful women vying for his attention.

When the man looked up at Will, the woman said, "This is Will Turner."

He assessed Will rudely before asking, "What exactly do you want with me, Mr. Turner?"

"I would like to make a purchase," Will answered as he stared Max in the eyes.

"What makes you think I have something to sell?"

Will looked at him, thinking, *I don't have the time or the patience for a witty war of words.* Turning, he retraced his steps, heading for the corridor and the hansom cab that waited. He heard Georgia calling after him. He stopped, and when they were face-to-face, she said, "He will see you in his office."

He stared at her and nodded, following her through a door just beyond the bar. Once inside, Max and the nameless man stood silent until the woman closed the door. Will was sweating, and the pain was trying to get in front of him.

Max broke the silence, asking, "Who sent you, and what is it you need?"

"A strange-looking fellow named Ape told me to seek you out. He said you could be trusted not to poison me. I would like to purchase morphine," Will said.

"That shit will kill you," Max responded, watching him sweat. This was interesting. He did not know a man named Ape.

"Yes or no?" Will asked, his voice tight.

Max produced four small blue bottles, and Will paid him. Their business was just about complete when Will asked, "Bounty hunters—can you help me with that?"

An addict asking for bounty hunters, Max thought. "I can."

"What do I have to do?" Will asked.

"Well, you sound Southern; will it matter if the men are black or white?" Max asked.

Will didn't give a shit about that now. It would probably be better if he could get a black tracker; he was more likely to be trusted. "It doesn't matter to me."

"How many will you need?" Max asked.

Will added and subtracted in his head before saying, "Five will be a good start." It wasn't the twenty he would have gotten before, but Hunter had a good point: he only wanted *Black*.

"I will see what I can do," Max replied. "This will be a costly endeavor."

Max was shorter than the man that showed him in and dressed just as elegantly in a cream shirt and black trousers. It would cost, Will thought, and he would have to pay the bounty hunters and this Max fellow to get the ball rolling. "I understand."

"Come back a week from today, and you will meet at least three of the five hunters, and it will be up to you if you hire them."

Max moved toward the door, and they stepped back into the gaming room, leaving the crude office with its desk and two mismatched chairs.

A woman with black hair and who was almost six feet tall approached him in a see-through dress. Her breasts were firm, and there wasn't an ounce of fat on her. She was sexuality at her best. "I would like to get to know you," she said to Will.

Will smiled, thinking about Amber and how much he enjoyed making love to her. They had adjusted their lovemaking to accommodate his hip, and even in pain, he loved it. At times, all he had to do was maintain an erection, and she took care of the rest. He would not chance catching something and giving it to her. He was gracious when he said, "I don't think I can handle you, love."

She pouted and moved on.

"I have not seen a man refuse Jessica," Max said.

Will did not comment about the woman. Instead, he said, "I will see you in five days. Thank you for your time." He turned and left.

Outside, the world looked brighter as he made his way to the horse and carriage that waited. Now he could see the end result.

The cab dropped him off at the corner from the town house he shared with his wife and cranky father-in-law. The December air was dry and chilled, and he could see his breath as he made his way back to the house. A boy selling newspapers yelled, "The infamous John Brown hanged! Read all about it!"

"I'll take one," Will said to the boy, flipping him a coin.

"Thank you, sir," the boy responded.

Reading the front page and a small part of the article, Will's anger grew. The story mapped out John's route across the South, adding the Turner plantation as his last stop before trying to overthrow the government. Leaving him nameless, it listed the plantation owners found dead in his home. Folding the paper, he placed it under his arm and began walking with purpose toward the town house.

Once in the foyer, he could hear familiar voices, and walking the long hall, he stepped into the family room to see his sister and her husband. Rose stood, coming to him and kissing him on the cheek. She looked good, and he was happy about that, but he was not happy to see her. He was agitated, and he wasn't feeling like company.

"Will, it's good to see you," she said.

He smiled at her, knowing full well that she could take him or leave him. She loved his wife, and that was why she was there. "It's good to see you too, Rose." Looking across the room where Anderson stood, he said, "Anderson."

"Will, how are you feeling?" Anderson asked after him.

"I am managing; some days are better than others," he said.

Amber stood, coming to him, and his mood lightened. She kissed him on the cheek.

"I missed you," she said.

Against her ear, Will whispered, "Tonight I want to see just how much you missed me."

Amber turned red, and Will smiled at her. Rose, watching the exchange, stared in disbelief. Robert Myers rolled his eyes to the ceiling, but secretly, he was pleased that the asshole Turner came to his senses. They all stepped into the kitchen for cold turkey sandwiches left over from a too-quiet Thanksgiving. Anderson and Myers talked about guns and the law while Will, Amber, and Rose talked about the baby. Will excused himself one time, giving himself a shot in the hip, pushing the pain all the way in the background.

And later, he showed Amber again that he was sure about loving her.

There was a knock at the door, and Will was annoyed because Amber and her father had gone out visiting for the afternoon. They had servants, although he couldn't understand why they never did the things servants should do. Robert answered the door when they had guests call, and still he paid the servants ... *to answer his own door.* Making his way to the front door, Will opened it, prepared to tell whoever it was that Robert Myers wasn't home, but one of the two men at the door spoke first.

"I am William Garrison, owner and writer for the *Liberator*. This is

Frederick Douglass; we were hoping to speak with Mr. Turner," Garrison said.

Behind Garrison stood a black man with a haughty air about himself. He did not speak, and Will could see the future in his eyes. He had salt-and-pepper hair that was combed back yet still bushy, and wearing a brown suit, he stood with his hands behind his back, eyeing Will while Garrison spoke.

"Is Mr. Turner available?"

"I am Mr. Turner, and I do not wish to be interviewed," Will ground out.

"Oh, I was hoping for your take on the matter," Garrison continued, drawing him in. He was good at being engaging even when the situation was hostile.

"Your paper is called the *Liberator*; I'm sure you will give a fair accounting," Will said dryly.

"It can't be any worse than what's being said," Garrison said. "The paper even makes mention of the revolt of '31. I was a young man then, but I remember."

Will was tight at the mention of Black's father, but even hopped up on morphine, he was closed mouthed. He stared at Garrison for a moment before saying politely, "I am busy, Mr. Garrison. Please excuse me."

"Of course, Mr. Turner. We are unannounced in the first place," Garrison replied before goading him. "You know my stance on slavery, and given the way your slaves have run wild, many think you're against it, as well."

The dam leaked. "Oh, I am for slavery," Will returned, holding the black man's gaze. "I am tracking all my runaways with bounty hunters; I am a responsible slave owner. Good day to you, Garrison. Please don't come back," he said, slamming the door.

Garrison and Douglass moved down the steps, and once back on the street, Garrison said, "I was hoping to get something about John that I could print. I hate that they are trying to make him look crazy, but I have the feeling that Black is behind the Turner plantation being razed. I'd rather not draw attention to that."

"I agree, and I'll notify Black," Douglass said as they began walking away from the house.

Canada
December 1859

Sunday placed a package on the desk, saying, "It's from Frederick."

"Thank you," Black said, smiling at her.

She walked over to the sofa and sat watching him work until he finally looked up, acknowledging her. She wore a blue dress with a white collar, and she was the very picture of health. Sunday's hair grew, and it was all combed together in a french braid with a white ribbon tied at the end.

Smiling, Black asked, "Is there something I can do for you?"

"I's waitin' for ya to open the package from Frederick Douglass," she said, and it was clear she thought he was hiding something.

"I have something for you," he said, and reaching into his desk drawer, he pulled out what looked like a book covered in a plain brown wrapper.

He stood, bringing it to her, and she attempted to guess what it was by the feel of it.

"Open it."

Tearing the paper off, she stared at the gift, and her eyebrows drew together. It was an official document, and he had framed it. Slowly, she read it and saw that it was their marriage license. Her eyes watered up. It was beautiful, and she couldn't help crying.

Black's eyes sparkled when he said, "Are you crying because it's official that you are stuck with me?"

She cried and laughed at once. "No, I's cryin' 'cause you's the one stuck wit' me."

He sat on the couch, leaning back next to her, and she cuddled up to him. Staring out the window, they could see a light snow was falling.

Hugging the marriage license to her, she laid her head on his chest, and hearing his strong heartbeat, she was content … for now. She had not missed that he refused to open the package from Frederick Douglass in front of her.

There was a knock at the door, and Black called, "Enter."

Mama walked in, asking him if he had seen Sunday. "I's here, Mama," she responded.

"Good. I wants to start on makin' baby clothes," she said, not looking Black's way again.

"You wants to go to town? We can go to Sally for material, and we can go to Virgil's to get the baby bed."

"Oh, that would be nice," Mama said.

Sunday, who took a little longer to get up, finally stood, and walking over to Mama, she handed her their marriage license. They both stared at it, and Mama said, "Let's go hang it in yo room."

Sunday doubled back and kissed Black, and then they were gone. Black stood, and before dealing with the package and all the issues that came with it, he walked down the hall to his studio. Removing the canvas of Jacob Turner, he headed back to Mama's room. In Mama's room he removed the picture of her and replaced it with the picture of Jacob. He brought the picture of her back to his study and hung it over the sofa.

He avoided the package as long as he could, and finally turning his attention to it, he opened it. Inside was the daily post with a headline that read THE INFAMOUS JOHN BROWN HANGED. Starting from the front cover of the newspaper until the last page, he read about John. The paper outlined his route through the South, causing mayhem for honest plantation owners and businessmen. There was great deal of talk about the Turner plantation being John's last stop, and Black almost missed it, but it was there in black and white. The paper discussed the slave revolt of '31 and the hanging of Nat Turner; it went on to say that many upstanding white citizens had died because of the Turners' inability to control their plantation. It was believed that John Brown symbolically chose the Turner plantation to finish his reign of terror.

Folding the paper and placing it back on the desk, he stood and walked over to the window. He noticed that the snow had stopped and the sun was out. After reading the paper, it became clear to him that Sunday was right; this wasn't about her. Slavery, he thought, was a sword with two edges. If he had been taught to believe he was inferior because he was a black male, then Will had been taught he was superior because he was a white male. The pill must have been hard for Will to swallow, realizing that he would have to be more than white to best him. Men are in constant search of their manhood and the place where they can be considered king. *What if the kingdom you are handed is an illusion,* Black thought, *with slavery only real as long as the slave believes it and not a minute longer?* He understood Will a little better, but he still had no empathy.

Jacob Turner loving Mama and not Will's mother must have embarrassed him. Watching his father make decisions based on his love of a black slave was what ignited the situation. Black shook his head. He himself hated that his mama loved Turner, but she had not embarrassed him. Mama had put him first, not as Turner had done Will. The peace really was fragile, and now he understood why. Seating himself back at his desk, he continued going through the package. There was a letter from Frederick.

> *My friend,*
>
> *I hope this letter finds you well, as I have heard you were under the weather. I am sure, if I know you, you are already back on your feet. I have enclosed a newspaper to keep you abreast of current events. I also wanted you to know that I have seen our good friend Will. He is here in Boston, as well. You will be happy to know he is still standing in light of all that has happened.*
>
> *I have also enclosed a list of bounty hunters that have been known to steal free black men and sell them back into slavery. I spend a lot of time avoiding these types, as they have been known to widen their traps to include Canada ... but I digress.*

Please accept my condolences in the death of your brother Otis.

Kind regards to you and your family,

FD

Patrick Smith, John Williamson, Ned Madison, Thomas Fields, and Shawn Green were the names on the list. Black had heard these names before, and the name Thomas Fields stuck out in the bunch because he was a colored man himself. He leaned back in his chair to think. Every time he got rid of an issue, he got two more. Bounty hunters coming for him, and his wife was pregnant. Black was tired. John, swinging from the gallows—a good man gone, and nothing had changed.

Later that evening when the house was quiet, he thought over his day. He met with the doctor for an hour, spoke with James about the barracks, ordered supplies, and chatted with several people about a host of issues they wanted his opinions on. He was overwhelmed with the issue of safety not just for his wife but for everyone, and as long as Will wouldn't let the matter drop, he couldn't either. Black sighed and stood. Though it was dark, he headed for the front door.

At the door, he removed his black leather coat filled with fur from the peg on the wall. For his bald head, he had a matching hat that was form fitting and also filled with fur. Opening the door, he could see the men making their rounds. Stepping from the porch, he stared at the tree where he had hung the noose back in the summer. It was still there, and the grave was still open. Looking in the direction of the gate, he could see the moon just above. The air was cold and thin, and he felt winded as he made his way toward the cemetery. He could see his breath as he walked, and he knew he was out of shape. The walk was long, yet he did it with purpose, and when he stood at Otis's grave, he did not linger. It was closure for him, having slept through the whole event. Turning, he walked back in the direction from which he had come. Grief had held him hostage long enough.

Black made one small detour on the way back. He didn't want to, but it was time. Stepping up to the door, he knocked, and when no one came, he banged. He could hear the sound of someone moving around inside, and under the door, he could see a faint light that became brighter as someone drew nearer. The curtain was pulled back, and he saw Mary's face. She opened the door to him.

There was a smile on her face when she said, "Black, come in."

He stepped into the cabin that Otis had shared with Mary. It was warm, and a fire burned. There was a large round table just before the fire. At the left of the room was a green sofa that sat on a large beige area rug with two black matching chairs facing it for the purpose of cozy conversation. Deeper into the room, he could see the kitchen and the potbellied stove. Their cabin was the largest, and over her shoulder, he could see Herschel on the steps leading to the second floor. He smiled at Black and went back upstairs to give them a moment. Black remembered asking Otis why he didn't build a larger home. Otis had replied that he didn't want to give Mary another room to sleep in when she was mad at him.

"Is everything all right?" she asked.

"Mary, I am sorry that I haven't come sooner. I was a coward, and I couldn't face you," he said, his voice filled with emotion.

She snorted before saying, "*You*, a coward? I don't think so. I love you, and we have done good work together. I am looking forward to being an aunt, and I am glad you are well."

He was about to speak, when she stepped up, hugging him, and he hugged her back. When she stepped back, she said, "Tell Sunday I will come there tomorrow so that she will not have to walk in the cold."

He swallowed hard and nodded. She had taken the conversation from him, letting him off the hook. She didn't blame him, and for him, it was the first step.

When he was back in the cold, he retraced his path back to the house, but instead of climbing the steps, he continued on to the barracks. Entering the barracks, he saw that some of the men were up, and others were sleep. He smelled cigar smoke and moved toward it straight to the back doors. Outside, he found Elbert standing alone, smoking, and he appeared deep in thought.

"What are you doing out and about at this hour?" Elbert asked.

Black stood next to him, and for a time, he didn't speak, gathering his thoughts. When his thoughts were organized, he said, "I received a package from Frederick Douglass."

"This package has you up at night?" Elbert inquired.

Black smiled. Elbert wore a black hat and a sweater, his conditioning for the weather apparent. He passed him a flask, and Black drank deeply, warming himself from the inside out with whiskey.

"The package and other matters have me out at night," Black said.

"How can I help?" Elbert asked, and Black could hear his unmasked excitement.

"Have you heard of these men Patrick Smith, John Williamson, Thomas Fields, Shawn Green, and Ned Madison?" Black asked.

"I have not heard of Ned Madison. These names are important to you. Why?"

"It would seem Will Turner only has eyes for me," Black said, chuckling. Becoming more serious, he added, "I need to ride out."

Leaning his head back, Elbert blew the cigar smoke into the air before saying, "I think you should let them come to you. I know that you wish to stop an attack on the women and children of the fort, but I would take my stand from here. You have power here, and you have me. I would not leave my wife and child chasing this."

"You have a plan, then?" Black asked, his brain starting to churn.

"It's winter. When they come to Canada, it will be colder. They will seek the warmth of a woman before they seek you. We men always do, and we will be waiting."

Black needed to give this some thought. He turned to leave when Elbert said, "You need to recondition yourself to the elements. Bullshit happens in all seasons. That damn study is going to kill you."

Black laughed. "I will meet you tomorrow night on the front porch. Bring shovels."

"Oh, I will be there," Elbert said, his anticipation evident.

When he stepped into his room, Sunday was sitting propped up with the pillows behind her. She looked annoyed, and he just couldn't handle a fight. He sat in the black chair and removed his boots before removing the rest of his clothing. There would be some discussion, he knew, but in her condition, he didn't want to upset her.

"I came lookin' for ya," she said.

Once he was naked, he didn't speak. He stood, moving in front of the fire to warm his skin. He found that he was tired and could not form the words he knew would stress her. When it became clear that he wasn't going to tell her anything, she climbed out of bed to stand next to him.

She touched his arm to get his attention, and when he looked down at her, he said, "Later ... let's talk later." His voice was gravelly.

Taking her by the hand, he led her back to the bed, and he allowed her to climb in first. Climbing in behind her, he spooned her, and placing his hand over her stomach, he went to sleep. Sunday stayed awake thinking about the package. She realized that he was hiding things from her to keep her from worrying. Finally, she closed her eyes and slept too. She would talk to him in the morning.

The sun was shining brightly through the window when Sunday realized he was not in bed with her, and she sat straight up. Looking frantically around the room, she found him sitting in the chair staring at her. Lying back on her side, she stared at him, and he was smiling. That was a good sign. She dozed back off, and minutes later when she opened her eyes, he was still there. It was her turn to smile this time. It felt like they had only slept for an hour before it was time to rise again.

Black watched her as she went in and out of sleep, and she was lovely. He had not gone to his study yet; he knew she wanted to talk. She had been gracious and allowed him space; he would not ignore her now.

"You's smilin'; it cain't be that bad."

"It's not good, and it is not me I'm worried about," he said.

"Let's have it then," she said, trying to appear brave.

"Bounty hunters have been hired by Will to track me down." He held her gaze when he spoke.

She tried to keep the panic from her voice when she asked, "Is you leavin' me, Black?"

He smiled, attempting to reassure her. "I am not leaving you. I will take my stand from here. I will be at the barracks a great deal. There will be nights you won't see me while I work through this. Can you handle that?"

"Do I has a choice?" she asked.

"No."

"Will you leave the fort?"

"If I have to leave the fort, it will be for a few hours. I will not leave you with the baby coming. If you need me, send Paul. You have Iris, Mama, and Mary to help. Mary will come here today for you; she said she doesn't want you walking in the cold."

"Ya seen Mary?" she asked, sounding surprised.

"I did." It was all he was willing to say.

She didn't push. Instead, she smiled, happy that he had been able to face Mary.

Black continued, "I need your help."

"Yes, of course."

"You will need to take over the study handling issues and defer only to me. If you have an issue, again, send Paul. The only appointment I will continue to keep will be with Dr. Shultz for one hour every other day."

"You ain't gon sleep wit' me?"

Black laughed out loud. "Did you hear anything I said?"

Sunday pouted. "I hears ya. It's just that when we's in this room, you gets to be Nat. Anywhere else in the house, you's Black and it's all bidness. I loves all of ya, but the time we spends in this room means everythang to me. In this room, I ain't got to share ya."

He sighed. "I will try coming to bed nightly, but it will be late. Sometimes I will be getting in the bed as you are getting out."

Sunday smiled at him, and Black turned serious, saying, "I want you to read more. It's important to me."

"I will. I promises," she whispered.

"Good. I will meet you in the study to let you know what I want handled in an hour. Is that all right with you?" he asked as he stood.

When he stepped out into the hall heading for the kitchen, he smiled. She was his world. He needed Will Turner to back the hell off so he could live. Black entered the kitchen on his way to his study; Mama was in the kitchen drinking coffee. She looked up when she saw him and smiled.

"Come sit," she said.

He did as she asked, and when he was seated, she continued, "Want something to eat?"

"Coffee for now," he responded.

She stood, pouring him some coffee, pushing the cream and sugar to him as she sat. "I seen the paintin' of Jacob."

Black had no response. Jacob Turner was the last person he wanted to talk about. She could see that he was tense, but she continued, "I knows ya hated paintin' him." She was smiling now.

Placing the cup on the table in front of him, he stared her in the eye. "I love you, Mama."

She nodded her acknowledgment. He wasn't going to discuss the painting, so she said, "I loves you, son."

"You and Sunday can't leave the fort for now," he said quietly.

"You want to talk 'bout it?" she asked, wanting to help.

He sighed, and then he stood. "No. I don't want to talk now. Later, Mama, I promise."

He left the kitchen, and she could see he was troubled. They could talk through things, but she guessed he needed time to figure things out, especially with Otis gone. She didn't press him; she made a plate for him and set it aside. She began cleaning. Iris would be there soon to discuss patterns for baby clothes. Mama decided she would be patient and wait on him to come to her.

He was seated behind his desk when Sunday came in. They went over the books and discussed supplies; he was patient when he explained what needed to be done. She repeated what he said back to him to make certain she understood, and he was pleased. Finally, she asked, "Why you meetin' wit' the doctor every other day. Is you not well?"

Black smiled. "I am fine. He is teaching me about childbirth. I want to be in the room with you. I don't trust anyone else. I know the basics from working with animals, but he's readying me for what to expect. We talk about all kinds of things concerning advancements of medicine. It's interesting, though I do not have the stomach to be a doctor."

Sunday was mortified at the thought of him in the room with her. It was unheard of. "Black, I don't thank I will live through you being in the room."

"Sunday, you will live," he said quietly.

"Po' choice of words. I means to say you seein' me like that." She was embarrassed already.

Black's hurt was apparent when he asked, "After seeing me at my weakest moment, you would be embarrassed for me to see you at yours?"

"If'n I say I don't want ya there, would you be there anyhow?" she asked.

"Would you abduct the doctor again?"

She stood and began pacing before saying, "I would."

"No. I would respect your wishes. I would wait in the hall and worry."

"It's messy," she said.

"I need to be there with you, messy or not," he said, his voice laced with emotion.

Coming around to the front of the desk, Black leaned on it, and catching her by the hand, he pulled her to him. "Sunday?" Her name was a question.

"I'll agree, but you has to promise me somethin'," she answered.

"Let's hear it," he said, prepared to negotiate.

"You has to agree to a second child." She smiled at his shock.

"Let's just get through this," he whispered, kissing her.

"Black, yes or no?" She had him, and she knew it. They would have other children, no doubt about it. She just wanted him to embrace the thought.

"Yes."

There was a knock at the door, and they both yelled for the person to enter. It was Mary, along with Mama and Iris. They came in talking about baby clothes and furniture, and to Black's surprise, Paul stepped in saying that he would like to make the cradle. Sunday was being ushered out of the room when she walked over to him, saying, "I can stay and work, if'n ya needs me to."

"No. Go with them and report here tomorrow at 9:00 a.m."

"You comin' to bed tonight?" she asked.

"Late … very late."

She nodded.

It was midnight when Black stepped out onto the porch, and Elbert—true to his word—was waiting with two shovels propped against the wall. A pale yellow moon hung low and large out in front of them. Thin white clouds danced in front of the moon, moving slowly on the wind. It was freezing, and both men were dressed in all black, thick sweaters, leather gloves, and hats laced with fur, gun at their sides. Elbert passed him the flask, and Black drank.

Passing the flask back, Black pulled on his gloves. "Ready?"

Elbert handed Black a shovel, and saying nothing, they moved down the steps into the night. They ran, and Black paced himself. Once deep into the woods and well beyond the cabins, they stopped and began to dig. The temperature dropped, but they continued working, conditioning themselves to the elements, breaking the frozen ground. They dug two large graves, and leaning the shovels against the trees, they walked back toward the house.

When they reached the house, they did not separate, continuing on to the stables. There they met with James, who turned the barracks over to Philip for the night. All three men mounted their horses and rode out toward town. As they passed through the gate, Tim was there on horseback, and he fell into step with them. Moving with purpose, they made their way to the pussy parlor on the edge of town. Outside, they tethered their horses, with James and Tim taking up post on the porch.

An older woman of mixed parenting, appearing to be both white and black, answered their knock at the door. Seeing Black and Elbert, she stepped aside to allow them in. When they stepped over the threshold, she eyed James and Tim on the front porch before closing the door.

"You boys aren't here for fun, I'm guessing," she said, staring at them.

Black took in the red velvet couch with the matching chairs. In the center of the room was a round sky-blue couch that sat six, and in the middle of the circle was a mirror. There were potted plants in the corners of the room to add to the decor. The staircase split the room, making it seem smaller, and at the top of the steps were doors lined up in either direction. On the first floor at the back of the room were three doors. One was open, and he could see it was a kitchen. The other two were closed, and he suspected they were bedrooms. There was a bar on the left side of the room just before the kitchen door. A blonde woman in a tight green dress was serving drinks to the one or two patrons they had. The walls were a peach color, the place gaudy but clean.

Elbert said, "Miss Cherry, we would like to have a word with you in private. Is that all right with you?"

Cherry had seen the man speaking before, but not the man with him. She didn't know either of their names, and she asked, "Who is *we*?"

"I am Elbert, and this is Black," Elbert said, and he waited.

She stared at Black, her eyes narrowing. "You are bigger than I thought you would be."

He smiled but said nothing.

"Right this way," she said, leading them to one of the two back rooms. Black turned, assessing the two men at the bar, and reading his mind, she said, "They are here to protect the women. No patrons tonight."

Following her through the middle door, they stepped into her office. It consisted of the basics—a brown desk with two brown chairs facing the desk and a large chair behind the desk. There was a window at the back of the office with the drapes drawn. She sat behind the desk. Elbert and Black stood.

She spoke first, saying, "What can I do for you gentlemen?"

"We would like to make a deal with you," Elbert said.

She stared at Elbert, and his eyes said, *This man is dangerous; one should not think to cross him.* The one called Black moved back and was leaning against the wall on his left shoulder, arms crossed and staring at her. He had not spoken. He was dangerous, and there was no mistaking it. And though they were asking, she didn't think she could refuse.

Elbert passed her a list, and she responded, saying, "I can't read. Say what you have to say. My memory is perfect."

He nodded and read off the names. "Have you heard of these men?"

"I have only heard of Thomas Fields," she said with disgust in her voice.

"We have reason to believe these men are heading to Canada. If they should stop here, we would like for you to get word to us, and we will handle the rest," Elbert said.

"How on earth would I get word to you? We don't have horses," she replied, annoyed. "When we have to travel, we rely on a hansom cab."

Black said, "We will send men to protect the girls nightly while they ... ah, work. And we will pay you for your trouble." He had her interest. "You can get rid of the two drunks out front."

"How much?" she asked, knowing she had to do it. At this point, she was gauging the value.

"I will pay you fifty dollars a week and protect the place," Black said, holding her gaze.

"Done," she said.

"During their shifts, my men will not drink or mingle with the girls," he said.

"Understood," she responded.

"I will send four—two outside, one inside, and one you will not see. We will take it from here. Should you have a problem, you will come to me or Elbert only."

Again she responded, "Understood."

"We will start tomorrow."

Cherry nodded as she watched Black and Elbert exit the office. They were heading for the front door when a young woman who resembled Sunday approached them. Elbert smiled down at her, and stepping off to the side, he spoke with her privately. She listened attentively to what he said and nodded. When he stepped back from her to head for the door, Black heard her say, "All right."

They stepped back into the cold, mounted their horses, and rode for the fort.

When he rode through the gates of the fort, Black was exhausted. They rode for the stable, and the stable boys took the horses, readying them for the stalls. The four of them walked back to the barracks, with Black and Tim continuing on toward their homes. They separated at the steps of Black's house, and they shook hands, with Tim continuing on. It was dark out as Black climbed the steps, but he knew there was only about an hour or two before daylight.

Once in the house, he headed to the kitchen and found it empty. Carrying the buckets of water from the kitchen, he headed for their room. When he began pouring the water in the tub, she woke. Lying on her side, she smiled as she watched him undress. He stoked the fire, and stepping into the tub, he leaned back, allowing the water to work his tired muscles.

"Can I come scrub yo back?" she asked.

"You can," he answered, smiling and closing his eyes.

Leaving the bed and kneeling beside the tub, she fished for the rag. Soaping it, she scrubbed his back, touching where he had been shot. When she rinsed the soap off, she handed him the rag and sat beside the tub watching him. He washed his face, and when he opened his eyes, she smiled, saying, "Ya looks tired."

He could see her nipples through her wet nightdress as she sat beside the tub. It was strange seeing the way he felt about her reflected in her eyes.

"Go change your nightdress; you will be sick," he said.

She stood and walked over to her chest, pulling out another nightdress. She turned as he stood to get out of the tub and watched the water cascade down his body. Sunday loved the sight of him engaged in whatever activity—thinking, working in his study, walking, and looking angry, which he did best. She smiled, asking, "Ya wants me to shave ya?"

The amusement evident in his eyes, he stared at her for a moment before saying, "Is your hand steady enough?"

She held her hand up, making it shake noticeably. He laughed, and sitting in the chair, he allowed her to shave him. Leaning over him with the straight razor, she removed any sign of hair with sure and steady strokes. This was one of her duties as a slave, and she had not known it could be intimate.

When she was finished and was wiping his face and head, she asked, "Why do you shave? You has beautiful hair, Nat."

Looking up at her, he said, "I look meaner. That is what I am going for—dangerous, not cute."

"I see," she said with laughter in her voice.

"I see I need to start showing you my dangerous side," he replied.

"I thank so, and will you show me now? Do you wants me naked

243

to show me yo mean and ornery side?" she asked with anticipation in her voice.

Black actually laughed as he stood, leading her to the bed. He helped her to remove her nightdress, allowing her to climb in first. He made love to her, paying homage to her first with his mouth, kissing her from her lips to her feet, lingering where his child flourished. And when he loved her with his body, wringing soft, seductive moans and cries from her, he was overwhelmed by his love for her.

Men, they feared him … but his woman, she did not.

17

BOSTON, JANUARY 1860

Will sat on the couch at the far end of the room waiting to be seen by Max. He had been waiting for an hour watching the activity in the gaming room, but he did not participate. Will understood the tactics being employed here; they thought he would become involved with one of the women, giving them control. Patiently he waited, declining drinks and offering the bare minimum in conversation as the naked women attempted to engage him.

When finally he was tired, he stood, placing his hat on his head. He moved toward the two steps to carry him from the platform that the couch rested on. He was making his way to the hall when Georgia came running after him, saying, "Mr. Turner, Max will see you now."

Turning to look at her, Will smiled. "I was about to leave; he must be pretty busy. I no longer wish to speak with him. Thank him for his time."

She looked puzzled as she watched him turn, walking away with his awkward gait and cane tapping. Just then, Max himself emerged from the office, calling, "Mr. Turner, you weren't going to leave without saying good-bye, were you?"

Will stopped and stared at him. He was dressed in a brown suit, and he wore no jacket. Wearing just the vest with the sleeves of his shirt rolled up, Max looked as if he had been hard at work.

Will did not bite, and he said, "I can see that you are busy. I was just telling Georgia to thank you for your time."

Max narrowed his eyes before saying, "What are you about, Turner?"

"I am about business, Max, and you clearly are not," Will said, holding his gaze. "I am attempting to pay you for services, and I am constantly met with disrespect. Is this the Northern way?"

"This is the way we handle dope fiends, Mr. Turner, and don't bother to say you are not. You are sweating as we speak."

Will held his gaze and smiled. He would not explain himself to the next man. He was attempting to get a service done, and he was willing to pay. If they didn't want to do business with him, why tell him to come back in five days?

"I am attempting to right some wrongs done to me. Either you can help me, or you can't," said Will.

Max was in need of cash to keep his ventures floating, and he didn't need to be dealing with anyone that couldn't pay. "Now tell me again—who sent you to me?"

"I told you this before—a strange-looking fellow named Ape," Will responded.

"That is the thing, Mr. Turner; I don't know a man named Ape."

"I have told you the truth, Max; the man sent me here for morphine. He also told me if I have other issues, you would be able to assist me," Will said, his voice tight.

"May I ask a favor of you, Mr. Turner?" Max asked calmly, though Will felt there was no refusing. He nodded and began to follow Max toward his office. When he reached the door, Ape sat in one of the chairs with blood on his face. He stared at Will, and he was afraid.

"Is this the man who referred you to me?"

"Yes, of course," Will confirmed, and his confusion was obvious. "I thought you said that you didn't know him."

"We don't. Did you pay him?" Max asked, his voice menacing as he stared at Ape.

"I gave him a few dollars for his trouble," Will answered, unsure what to say, so he settled on the truth.

"Take him out back," Max said.

Will never reacted, but inside he was scared; he knew it was all for the purpose of letting him know they wanted their money for services rendered. Ape, on the other hand, was being made an example; he was short and stout like an ape with brown hair that was greasy. The large man whom Will had met the first day dragged Ape through a door on the side of the office that Will hadn't noticed before. Once through the door, Ape began screaming, and then his screaming stopped abruptly.

"Do you still wish to work with us, Mr. Turner? Clearly we can track a man if needed," Max stated calmly.

Turning to the three men left in the small office, Will noticed for the first time that one of them was black. They did not offer names, and Max got down to business.

"We will offer a service, and we will expect half up front and the last part when we complete the business."

"I'm sorry. Before we move forward, what exactly did this fellow Ape do?"

"He directed people to me and collected money from them as if we were in business. He directed people to me," he said again, to make clear that he did not like underhandedness.

It was a sign of weakness to ask about Ape, but it was better they thought he was paying attention than not. Max stood between a colored man and another white fellow. The colored man had a scar that started in his hair, ran down his forehead, and skipped his left eye, picking back up again down his cheek. He was six foot four, and he wore brown trousers, a white shirt with his sleeves rolled up, and his gun at his hip. Upon closer inspection, Will could see that the gun handle had blood on it.

The white fellow to Max's left was about six feet tall, and he had black hair and gray eyes and shrewdness written all over his face. He wore the same brown trousers and a bloodstained white shirt. They all just stood assessing each other the way men do when trust is not a factor. Will, on the other hand, was hopeful for the first time in a year. They were just what he needed.

It was Max who stopped the staring contest by asking again, "Mr. Turner, would like to work with us?"

"Price?" Will inquired, and he held his breath.

"It's $2,000 up front and $2,000 after we complete the job," Max said, watching Will's reaction closely.

It would take some doing, but Will could make that happen. "We have a deal. When can you start?"

"What is the assignment?"

"I have been trying to track a slave for some time. I want him found," Will said, holding eye contact with Max.

"You are willing to pay $4,000 for the recapture of a slave? Look around you, Mr. Turner. The world is changing."

"He is not just any slave. There is a reward for him, and I am willing to pay and forgo the $2,000 reward. The slave is known as Black."

The white fellow whistled and shook his head before saying, "That is a pretty tall order."

"So you have heard of him?" Will replied.

"We will collect $3,000 from you and $3,000 upon delivery, because no one will care in the South. As I said, the world is changing. This is personal for you. Who would we collect the reward from?"

The families of the slain plantation owners, Will thought, but he didn't bother to go there. Instead, he said, "I will pay. I want his head. Bring me his head only."

"We will leave three days after you bring the money."

"I will bring it tomorrow."

"When we complete the job, we will send to the town house for you to collect the final payment," Max said, staring at him and making clear that they would track him too, if necessary.

"No need to threaten me, Max. I will pay, and while this will deplete me, I have one other request."

"And that is?"

"Black has a woman. Find her and kill her."

"How much is she worth to you, Mr. Turner?"

"I will pay $250 for her," Will replied, and he felt better just saying it. He wasn't having her killed because he hated her; he was having her killed because she chose wrong. "He is in Canada at a place called Fort Independence."

Canada 1860

The fort was on lockdown again, with an emphasis on the safety of the women and children. Black held a meeting with the men explaining his position. To a smaller group of sixteen men, he got down to business, explaining what he wanted done. They listened, and when he was finished, one of the men asked, "When do we start?"

"Tonight," Black said, pausing for a moment before he continued. "While you are at Miss Cherry's House of Comfort, you are to seek no comfort. No mingling with the women, and no drinking while on duty. Is there a man among you who does not understand the rule?"

No one spoke, so Black said, "Tonight will be the first night, and two of you will partner with me and Elbert. That is all for now."

When they left, Elbert said, "I will pick two and discuss the plan."

"Good. I have to tend some business at the house. I will meet you at the stables at nine," Black said as he headed for the door.

Stepping out into the sunshine, Black headed back toward the house. It was cold but not freezing, and he could live with that. Climbing the steps, he walked into the foyer just as the doctor was coming down the steps.

"Dr. Shultz," he said.

"Black," Shultz said.

"Can I see you in my office?" Black asked.

"Certainly. Lead the way," Dr. Shultz said.

Opening the office door, they found Sunday at the desk working. She looked up when they walked in, and putting her pen down, she leaned back in the chair, smiling. Black approached, kissing her on the lips.

"I forgot you were in here. The doctor and I can find somewhere else to talk," he said.

"No, you's fine. Come in, both of you. I can step out if'n ya needs privacy," Sunday said, standing slowly with Black's help.

"I was hoping to examine you tomorrow, Miss Sunday, if that is all right with you. I can come to your room around 10:00 a.m.," the doctor said.

"That will be fine, Dr. Shultz," she said, staring at him. Sunday could see he was still leery of her, but he wasn't afraid of Black, who would kill him just as soon as look at him. She almost laughed out loud with the thought.

"Doctor, I have business to tend in the evenings, and you are staying in the house with my wife and mother," Black said.

"Would you like me to move out to the cabin I see patients in?" the doctor asked.

"I had thought of that, but should my wife have an issue, I would like you available. There will be a guard in the foyer. He will be here when I am not. Do you understand, Doctor?"

"I do," the doctor responded, smiling. After what he had seen of Miss Sunday, he didn't understand why she needed a guard.

"Great," Black said. "That is all I need. Thank you, Doctor, for working with me."

"Surely, Black. I am headed to my office if you need me," he said, and then he was gone.

Black laughed when the doctor left. "I think I should be insulted that he fears you and not me."

"I sees that," Sunday said.

Black started walking to the door when Sunday asked, "Where ya going?"

"I am going to take a nap. I am up too early for what I have to do tonight," he said.

Sunday started walking to the door. "A nap is a fine idea."

Once in their bedroom, they undressed, and when they were totally naked, Black massaged her. He rubbed her whole body, lingering on her back and feet, and she moaned from the pleasure. When they snuggled against one another, Black reached under the pillow and pulled out a black velvet box. Handing it to her, he said, "I'm sorry I am so bad about these things. Open it."

Her voice was filled with wonderment when she asked, "What is it for?"

"Your birthday. I know it's late. I get so caught up in handling problems I forget the important things. Please open it," he said.

Inside the box was a ruby bracelet sparkling against the black velvet, and she was breathless at the sight of it.

He hugged her, whispering, "I love you, Sunday."

Black stepped into the stables at exactly nine, and there he found Elbert talking to the young men who brought the water and the wood. They looked eager to help, and Black stood back while Elbert handled them. They asked questions, and Elbert patiently answered, being clear about what he expected. The weather had taken mercy on them, because it was mild for a January night in Canada. When they rode out, all conversation stopped as they readied themselves for the night ahead.

At Cherry's, the four of them separated, with Black and the young man called Luke taking the front porch. The young man Anthony sat in the lounge speaking with no one, and Elbert disappeared into the night. The patrons came and went without incident until Black heard a commotion coming from inside. Elbert stepped out of the shadows and posted up on the porch with Luke. Black stepped inside and locked eyes with Anthony, who was standing next to a white woman spilling out of her dress.

The woman said, "He hasn't paid, trying to get something for nothing."

The man was white, tall, and thin. He stepped toward the woman saying, "I could get better. I ain't paying this bitch. You rushed me."

Cherry stepped from her office, and Black could see her from his side view, though he never took his focus from the man. Anthony said quietly, "You will pay one way or another."

The woman stepped behind Anthony, and the man, assessing his situation, reached into his pocket and handed her the money she requested. Anthony stepped forward, taking all the man's money and giving it to the woman, and the man nodded. Black opened the door, and the man left.

Anthony moved back into the corner, Black went back to the porch, and Elbert faded back into the night. The rest of the night was uneventful.

During the following days, the men worked in shifts at Cherry's, and excluding the one incident, it was dull. The patrons came and went, and seeing the presence of Black and the men, they understood they were there for business. While women reaped the benefit of their presence, Black worried, and he felt no closer to an answer. Time passed, and no one new got off the train or rode into town on horseback.

Virginia

Tom Fields and Max headed south, first starting from the beginning to trace what little information they could learn about Black. Once at the Turner plantation, Tom moved among the slaves asking questions, and he found that the few slaves who were left acted as though Black was just a fable. The overseers knew even less, other than—since that fateful day when Hunter, Matthews, and Wilson were shot—Black was real. The plantation was being rebuilt, and Max could see why Turner took the matter so personally.

What Tom did find out was that while the slaves wouldn't talk about Black, they would talk about a slave called Big Mama and another female slave called Sunday. While most of what they said was basic, Tom did glean one small helpful fact by just observing. Whatever went on here at this plantation was personal for the one called Black, as well. When they left Virginia, they traveled the back roads, attempting to retrace the Underground Railroad, and Tom had knowledge of this because he had not always been free.

As they headed back north, they found two empty safe houses that were fully stocked. Once they hit Boston again, they questioned Will, and while he was forthcoming, one could tell there were some things he didn't speak of, and Max determined that it was due to embarrassment. Continuing to roam slowly through the back roads, they came to a farm on the edge of Pennsylvania where a colored farmer lived with his wife, sister-in-law, and four children.

When they stepped into the clearing, they saw a house, a cabin, and stables. It was twilight, and the weather was bearable. On the porch of the house sat two rocking chairs, and down in front of the steps was a child's wagon. On the right of what appeared to be the main house sat a small cabin. The stables were farther to the right and modest and held few animals. As darkness enveloped the small property, Tom was sure the people here knew Black. It was the way the place was set up—if they had happened along here in complete darkness, they would have missed it. *Yes,* Tom thought, *the strategy was well thought out.*

As they rode up, Max said, "You will do all the talking."

Tom nodded. When they approached the house, a man stepped outside carrying a shotgun.

"Who is calling?" the man asked in his politest voice, still holding his gun.

"We are traveling and were hoping to stop here for rest," Tom said with his hands in the air.

Max hung back and didn't move.

Tom continued, "We mean you and your family no harm."

The man lowered his gun, and Tom swung down and approached. Stepping up the three stairs, he said, "I am Tom; my friend back there is Max. We can sleep with the horses if it's not an imposition."

"The stables are that way. I will have one of the women bring you some food," the man responded.

Turning to Max, he nodded in the direction of the stables. When the horses were fed and put up, the man appeared with a woman carrying two plates. He did not introduce her, and she came forward, handing them the food. They accepted, and when she turned to leave, Tom said, "May I know your name?"

The man became jittery, answering for her. "No, you may not."

Tom stood to his full height and glared down at him. In order to keep the peace, she stepped forward.

"Camille. My name is Camille," she said.

Turning his attention back to Camille, he said, "That is a nice name. I have given my word that I will be no trouble, but he is provoking me," Tom said, his voice deep and proper, yet there was no mistaking the situation was dangerous.

Max finally spoke. "Thank you for your hospitality," he said to the man, the statement dismissing and meant to warn.

The man nodded. "Will ya be gone first light?"

"Yes," Max said.

"Come, Camille," he said.

"She will be along shortly. Good night," Tom said.

Although it was cold and she wanted to go with her brother-in-law, she touched his arm. "I don't mind keeping his company, Frank."

Frank was about to resist when Tom said, "Frank, I said I will walk her back to the house shortly." Defeated, Frank handed her the lantern and headed back to the house.

He reluctantly left Camille standing in the stables with the two men, and though Camille was afraid, she smiled. When Frank was out of earshot, Tom turned his attention toward her. She was about five foot seven and slender, and her hair was in two plaits that were pinned neatly on the top of her head. She was dark skinned, and he gauged her to be about forty summers. There was definitely an appeal about her, and when he spoke, he could tell it threw her.

"Do you know Black?" he asked.

She judged his question and his tone. Still, she answered the way Black always told her to answer should she have trouble. "I do."

It was a gamble, but he felt she would know him. He did not expect her to be truthful. His eyes narrowed. "We have been through several states, and no one admitted to knowing him. But you did. Why?"

"I have found in my life when peoples ask certain questions, they already knows the answer," she responded, and he smiled.

She saw the other man had lain back in the hay after eating, pretending to pay them no mind. Tom stepped forward, and she had to actively fight not stepping back. He was taller than most, and his hair was cut close. He had small eyes that missed nothing; his nose was large, and his bottom lip had been busted in the past and had healed with a line of extra skin in the middle, creating a bubble on either side. Still, she could see that once one got past the scar that didn't take his eye, he was handsome in the extreme.

"What do you know about Black?" he asked.

"I knows that we opted not to live in Canada, so we stayed in Pennsylvania. I have not seen him in four years, but I do know that he is in Canada. I ain't heard different. Personally, I don't know more than he helped us from the Hunter plantation."

He stared at her, judging her honesty, and when he saw her shaking, he realized it was a combination of being cold and fear. Removing his coat, he placed it about her shoulders, and she whispered, "Thank you."

"Don't thank me yet. I am going to walk you to the house and ask the same questions of them. If they have a different answer, I will kill you for lying to me." His voice was deep and without emotion.

She nodded, and turning, she preceded him to the house.

Patty and Shawn rode straight for Upper Canada once the first payment was made, their progress deliberately slow to give Tom and Max the opportunity to catch up with them. Ned had gone farther back into the South to determine the money factor and the reward. They reached Upper Canada by horseback one clear evening, and it was so cold that they decided to seek shelter at the local inn. Shawn wanted to find some willing ladies, but Patty refused, saying, "We at least need to determine if Black is here."

While Shawn felt the Black situation would keep, he followed Patty's lead. And though it was dark, the hour was still early when they dropped their horses at the public stables and headed for O'Reilly's. It was a small hike even though one could see the inn from the stables. Stepping up on the wooden sidewalk, their booted feet marked determined strides as they took note of their surroundings.

The inn was a redbrick building on the end of the street, and it looked smaller from the outside than on the inside. The innkeeper saw them move past the storefront window before the door swung open. In stepped two characters that looked out of place for their small town. Two very tall white males moved toward the counter, one was very thin, the other muscular. They resembled each other, both having brown hair, brown eyes, and almost the same nose. They wore black leather coats lined in fur with tan saddlebags that hung over their shoulders. The innkeeper was sitting behind the desk when they walked into the lobby.

Shawn approached the counter. "Two rooms."

The innkeeper, who was seated, stood and moved to the counter. "We have two rooms on the second floor."

Patty said, "That will do."

"All right, that will be two dollars per night, or $8.75 a week. What names do you go by?"

Shawn stepped forward, paying him for the night and ignoring his question about the names. The innkeeper handed him two keys, saying,

"Ahead of you is the stairs; take them to the top. When you step onto the second floor, they are the first two doors on your left."

Taking the lead, Patty nodded and moved toward the steps, taking them two at a time. He assessed the place as Shawn spoke with the innkeeper. Coming through the front, he noticed the counter where the innkeeper sat was straight ahead. Off to the right was a small lounge where guests could eat, and small brown tables and chairs dotted the room. At the back of the lounge was a brown curtain that separated the dining area from where the food was prepared. Opposite the dining room was a long hall with doors on either side; next to the hall were the steps that led to the second floor. The walls were painted white with a floral-patterned carpet that was a riot of color.

As he reached the landing, Patty found he didn't like that the steps were carpeted, because he couldn't hear even his own booted steps. Looking down the long hall, he found another disturbing fact—there was only one way in and out.

Standing in front of the room, he thought a whorehouse might have been better. This was too quiet, and turning to Shawn, he said, "I think we need to sleep in shifts."

Shawn nodded, but he was annoyed. "You go first. I'll sit downstairs in the lounge."

Patty felt this setup was all wrong and decided that he would sit in the lounge with Shawn. Shawn finally asked when they made their way back downstairs, "So we both aren't going to get any sleep tonight?"

Patty ignored Shawn and the innkeeper, who look perplexed as to why they would pay for rooms and then sleep in the lounge.

Black stood in the barracks with Elbert, watching the men leave for Cherry's. He and Elbert were sitting it out tonight to get some rest; they had gone out almost every night, standing in the shadows and waiting.

Black voiced his anxiety. "We have been at this for at least two weeks—and nothing. I need this resolved before she goes into labor."

Elbert listened while drinking deeply and passing the flask. Taking the flask, Black drank, and finally Elbert said, "Why can't you just enjoy her and what you have built?"

"Her safety ... and the child ... at times, I think I should just go and kill Turner."

"The bounty hunters are in place; it won't stop them. Kill him last," Elbert said.

Black knew he was right. "Should anything change, come get me."

Sunday had slowed down even more, and he was afraid to leave her at night. He was damned if he did and damned if he didn't. They were resting tonight, and he was going to pay his wife some attention. She was changing into her nightclothes, and she was completely naked when he stepped into their chamber. Seeing her ripening with his seed only deepened his love for her. His wife's stomach was bigger, and a dark line appeared in the middle of it. Her breasts were larger and heavy with milk, announcing her advanced state of motherhood. Sunday was a sight to behold, and she was his world.

"Oh, Daddy, you home early," she breathed, happy to see him.

He smiled. She had started calling him Daddy, and he loved it. "I have come to sleep with you. I miss you."

Walking over to her, he helped her with her nightgown and then undressed himself. They climbed into the bed. He propped her up, and lying next to her, they talked about their baby.

"I wants to talk wit' you 'bout names," she said.

"Hmm."

"We has been so busy, I wanted to find the right time," she said. "You has a name ya favor?"

She sounded serious, and it caused him to lean up on one elbow and stare at her. "I had not given names any thought. Whatever you pick is fine with me."

She looked at him for a moment before saying, "I has two names, one for a girl and one for a boy."

She was about to spring something on him, and with all this shit going on, he really hadn't given this any thought. They were baby names. How bad could it be?

"Let's hear it." He smiled.

"Well, if'n it's a boy, I thought Nat Hope Turner II is what I would like, and if'n it's a girl, I would like Natalie Hope Turner. Is this all right wit' you?"

All his life, his name had been a burden, and she knew he felt this way; it was why she had hesitated. When he didn't speak, she rushed on, "I know how ya feels, but you's my hero. How can I name our first child anythang else?"

He pulled her close, spooning her, his large hand on her stomach, and he didn't dare speak. When she felt safe that she had his approval, she dozed off. Black lay awake for some time, thinking and feeling one with her as he held her. Finally, after a long day and feeling content next to her, he started dozing, and that's when it hit him: the faint smell of cigar smoke.

Easing back from her, he stood quickly, haphazardly dressing, and Sunday never woke. He wore black pants, black boots, and a white shirt. When he was strapping his gun at his side, he opened the door and stepped out into the hall. In the hallway stood Elbert, cigar between his teeth, along with James, Tim, Philip, and the doctor, who looked terrified. Elbert said, "Patrick Smith and Shawn Green are at the inn."

18

CANADA

Black's blood began to race through him as the anticipation of problem solving became real. He did not speak. Instead, he stepped back into his room where his wife slept, and reaching for the straight razor that sat on the vanity, he folded it and shoved it into his boots. The men fell in line behind him as he headed for the door. At the front door stood Paul with his shotgun, and when they stepped out onto the porch, he heard the door lock behind him.

They rode hard, and at the edge of town, Philip went to Cherry's, relieving two of the four men there. The two extra men rode and caught up with Black. Leaving the horses among the trees, they moved out on foot toward the inn. They passed the stables, and the boy running it stood in the doorway watching. The six of them separated with Black and Elbert heading straight for the front door. They approached from the side of the building that would not cause them to have to cross in front of the large window.

As they stepped into the lobby, Patty Smith stood cursing under his breath. Shawn stood, and together they drew their guns. A loud booming sound came from the back behind the curtain where the back door had been kicked off its hinges. In stepped James and Tim with two sawed-off shotguns pointed at them. The other two men filed in behind Black and Elbert, pistols drawn, and behind the counter, Virgil stood with the business end of his shotgun pointed at them for good measure.

Elbert and Black stood among the hardware, and Elbert broke the silence. "I am *elated* to see you again, Patty."

James stepped forward before it became a debate and slammed Patty in the back of the head with the butt of the shotgun. "Drop the damn guns!" he yelled.

Black didn't speak for a moment because he was busy up in his head. *Two down, three to go,* he thought.

Patty and Shawn dropped their guns on the floor and kicked them forward.

Black stepped forward, staring at both men before saying, "Tie them up."

Turning and heading for the front door, Black could see that the stable boy brought the carriage around, pulled by their horses. Loading Patty and Shawn into the carriage, Black climbed in behind them and shut the door to stop Elbert from getting in. He sat facing them, assessing them for weaknesses, and found that the one called Patty was the strength in this pair.

When the carriage began to roll, Black spoke, his voice cold and hard. "How far behind are your other men?"

They stared at him, unmoving and not speaking.

Black restated, "How far behind are your other men? And what else are you here for besides killing me?"

The one called Patty chuckled and looked to the window, ignoring him, and Black became unglued. Reaching down in his boot, he pulled out the straight razor, and in a swift movement, he brought the blade across, slashing into the darkness. The razor connected with Patty's throat, causing blood to spray all over the inside of the carriage. Patty bled out in seconds, making gurgling sounds as he took his last breath. Shawn was shaken as he stared into the shadows.

Black spoke. "Let's take it from the top."

As the carriage rolled through the gates, they moved toward the woods. When the door opened, Black stepped down from the carriage covered in blood, and Shawn was also dead. He kept his own counsel, but he was shaken too. Will had paid extra to have his wife killed. It was just as he had feared, and hearing the words spoken caused him to cut Shawn's tongue from his mouth.

They released the horses, and making the hole larger, they pushed the carriage into the grave, men and all, and set it on fire. The smell of burning wood and flesh saturated the air. When the men turned to leave, two stayed behind to control the blaze.

Day was breaking when Black and the other men headed back for the barracks, and all of them were exhausted. Black was about to break off from them and go home when Elbert said, "You can't go to her like this."

But it was too late. Sunday had awoken, and in his absence she had stayed up in the foyer waiting for him. Paul tried to deter her, but she wouldn't give. He was forced to wait with her, and when the sun began to rise, she could hear the men talking as they approached. She opened the door, looking out and feeling the cold against her skin. Off in the distance, she could see black smoke billowing into the air. Turning from Elbert, Black saw her, and he climbed the steps still covered in blood. Paul grabbed her to keep her on her feet.

Black said, "This is not my blood. Go to our room, and do not leave it. I will come to you when I have bathed." To Paul, he said, "Please have one of the boys bring water upstairs, and have these clothes burned."

She nodded and did as she was told. Once Paul got her to their room, he woke Ellen to come keep Sunday company. Mama knocked on the door and then entered. Sunday sat on the edge of the bed, staring at the door, dazed. Walking over to the bed, she sat down next to her.

Hugging Sunday, Mama said, "You's in a heap of trouble wit' him, ya know."

"I know," she whispered.

"I understands that since he was shot, you's 'fraid to lose him. But he is still a man, and he will do the thangs men do. You cain't stop it."

Sunday shook her head and could not answer. Mama continued, "When he comes, do not spar wit' him, 'cause he will be nasty. All he does is in defense of you ... us ... the fort. This situation will get worser 'fore it gets better. Yo' onlyist job is to survive birthing his child. That is all he cares 'bout."

Sunday shook her head, still unable to speak.

"I's gone back to my room. Come to me later so's we might talk 'bout the baby. This is all he wants ya to thank 'bout."

"Yes, Mama," Sunday whispered, and then Mama was gone.

The boys brought more water as Black stood naked in front of the fireplace thinking, ignoring the activity going on around him. This was his second bath, and still the water kept turning red. He did not want to go to her until the blood was gone. In truth, he was angry with her for searching him out. All he wanted her to do was survive having his child; he would take care of the rest. There was a small thought in the back of his mind that was trying to take root—seeing him covered in blood like that might make her afraid of him. He was out of it when Elbert told him to come to the barracks and clean up, but she had opened the damned door.

He was stepping from the tub a third time when Paul came with new clothes and boots. It was Paul who said, "Would you like a shave?"

"No," Black responded.

"You angry, and having a shave will relax you. I'm sorry that I ain't do a better job of keepin' her from the door this morning," Paul said. His voice was strong and laced with authority, causing Black to look up.

"I understand," Black said, and Paul had his full attention.

"When you taught her how to shoot, I was nervous till I saw you was right. You pushed her to be self-sufficient in yo absence. And when you were down, she stepped up, shuttin' down the fort and issuin' orders to save you. When the doctor refused to treat you, she dragged his ass here, telling him that if you took yo last breath, so would he. She deserves some scolding for disobeying you, but you are her world too. I saw that with mine own eyes, and never once did she notice or acknowledge Elbert or his feelings. You were her focus, and her goal was saving you. You have taught her well. I am impressed by you both."

Black nodded but did not speak, and Paul continued, "A woman who will shed blood to save you is a woman that ain't gon fear ya when ya have to shed blood to save her. Seein' you covered in blood, I promise all she was studyin' was that you are still standin'."

"I am ready for that shave," Black said.

When Black was seated in the chair and leaned back with cream on his face, Paul said, "I knew your father well ... he would be proud, damn proud."

They each sat submerged in their own thoughts. The only sound in the room was that of the razor as it scraped skin.

Sunday was seated on the side of the bed when he stepped into their chamber, her huge eyes watching him. He sat in the chair, holding her gaze, and she looked down at her hands, breaking eye contact. As he watched her, he thought about Will paying to have her killed. He could understand a man wanted him dead, but his sweet wife? He could not comprehend it.

Finally, he said, "I gave you direct orders that should you need me, send Paul."

"Yes, and I's sorry." Her voice shook, but she did not cry.

"Your job is to survive having our baby. That is it." His voice was tight.

She nodded.

"Come," he said to her, raising his hand and waving her to him. She slid off the bed, waddled over to him, and climbed into his lap. He held her, reassuring himself that she was safe. Sunday snuggled against his chest, and he found that he was still shaken.

He said, "I am damn angry with you."

"I loves you, Nat," she responded.

Holding her a little tighter, he realized that she had won the fight.

Black stood in the barracks among the men, watching as Elbert issued orders concerning covering all the roads leading into town. Leaving the men assigned to Cherry's in place, he added a new unit of ten men to cover the entrances into town. The small town itself was watched by the stable boys and by Virgil, who was posted up at the inn. Even though his bases were covered, Black still patrolled the back roads with the men and Elbert at his side. Elbert didn't like that he was exposed, but Black refused to sit idly by, and as a man, Elbert could understand that.

Elbert finally got up the courage as they patrolled one evening to ask, "What did they tell you that night in the carriage?"

Black stared at him as they stood listening in the bushes. Finally, he answered, "Will has paid extra to have my wife killed."

Elbert's heart stopped and then restarted as he heard the words. The conversation ended where it started with them continuing to watch the road. A light rain started, and still they stood unmoving, both of them thinking too much. They heard it at the same time: horses moving toward them … and behind the sound of hooves came the sound of wagon wheels. Elbert eyed Black, and the plan was hatched.

Elbert stepped out in front of the wagon, letting a shot off into the air, scaring the horses to a fitful stop. Black stepped out just as the wagon came to a stop. Two figures sat in the front seat, and at first sight, Black felt them no threat, but he still acted. Elbert had his gun aimed at the driver as Black reached up, grabbing the passenger by the collar snatching him from the wagon.

"Black, it's me, Camille," she said, winded from being yanked from the wagon.

Black's eyes narrowed. "Camille? What are you doing here, woman?"

She could hear the agitation in his voice, and she faltered when she answered him. "I came to warn you that two men came to the farm looking for you."

"Shit," he hissed, and looking up at the back of the wagon, he could see four children staring at him. Next to the children sat Camille's sister, Flossy.

"Frank, follow me," Black said before picking Camille up and setting her back in the wagon.

They headed back to the fort with Elbert taking the lead and Black bringing up the rear. The rain started and stopped several times before they rode through the gates. They continued on until the wagon pulled up in front of the house. While it was dark, it wasn't late, and he knew Paul would still be there. They all climbed from the wagon, and though the rain had stopped, they were all wet. Black took the lead now, and Elbert took the rear as they climbed the steps and entered the house. He could hear the women at the table talking, and he knew Paul would be nearby.

The hall by the door was cast in darkness, and hearing the commotion caused the women and Paul to head for the door. Paul lit the lamps, casting some light on the situation.

Black stood in the middle of the hall between both crowds and said, "Mama, Iris, I need your help with the children."

Mama and Iris came forward to lead the children upstairs when one of the children stepped forward, saying, "Sunday."

"Curtis, is that you?" Sunday said, and then it dawned on her.

He came forward, hugging her, and she hugged him back. "I missed you," he said.

"Oh, my little friend, I missed you," she whispered, and she smiled down at him even though she was dying inside. He had gotten taller, and his hair needed cutting, but his little face was sweet as ever. "Go with Mama and get dry. We don't want you to be sick."

Mama hustled him off with the other children. Over his shoulder, Curtis said, "I want to see you again before I go to bed."

Sunday nodded.

The children gone, Frank, Flossy, Camille, and Elbert stood at one end of the hall by the door, and Sunday and Paul stood at the other end by the kitchen. Black gazed at his wife before he spoke; his voice was laced with tension. "Frank, Flossy ... Camille, allow me to introduce my wife, Sunday."

Sunday knew who Camille was—she was the woman looking heartbrokenly at her husband. There was no mistaking she loved him; Sunday knew the look. The faceless Camille now had a face—and a beautiful one at that. Camille stood in a black overcoat, her hood pushed back exposing two long braids pinned on top of her head, her dark skin flawless, and her appeal evident. Sunday felt awkward and unattractive as she senselessly compared herself to the slender and tall Camille. Looking back to her husband, she realized they were all at a standstill until she gave her approval.

While it was painful to be mature, she said, "Won't y'all come in the kitchen and warm yoselves in front of the stove?" Turning, she led the way.

The three followed her, leaving Elbert and Black standing in the hall for a moment. They did not speak, and Black leaned against the wall looking down at his boots. She had come all this way to warn him, and if he had to be honest, he just wanted them to go away. He did not want to face Sunday after this, but it seemed he was facing shit from all angles. Being a man that was closed to others, he had not seen it before, but he saw it tonight; Camille loved him, and his wife ... well, she saw it too. He could see Camille's pain as she realized that Sunday was heavy with his child. There was no comfort that he could offer her; he had been truthful with her, but it had no value, because he continued to partake, minimizing the way he really felt. As he watched her with her sister and her sister's husband, he realized that she had not looked for love, because she was devoted to him, and he was now devoted to Sunday.

Elbert stirred in the corner, and Black looked over at him. "You back with me?"

"Yeah."

Pushing off the wall, Elbert preceded him into the kitchen. The women were seated, and the men stood, and Elbert got them back on track.

The men began speaking, and Frank explained, "They rode up, and when I tried to get them to move along, they decided to stay the night. The black bounty hunter called Tom questioned Camille in the stables, threatening to kill her if she lied."

Camille sat with her eyes lowered, staring at her hands. She was avoiding eye contact with the younger beautiful woman who sat across the table carrying *his* child. His distance made sense now. He had chosen a mate, and though she understood he did not love her, she had not expected this, and it was painful. Sunday had young, tight skin, and her cocoa-brown complexion made Camille feel old. Sunday's hair was neatly braided in little braids all over her head that hung just above her huge eyes. She wore a peach-colored dress that did not conceal her condition, making Camille feel inadequate as a female; she had never been able to produce—and for Black, she would have. Flossy sat beside her with her hand on her thigh under the table, trying to comfort her, and Camille was thankful.

Elbert directed a question at Camille, and she could barely think, the pain was so great. "Camille, do you remember the other man's name?"

Lifting her eyes finally to Elbert, she whispered, "It will come to me. I was afraid of the one called Tom, and I couldn't think."

Black asked, "Can you tell us what he looked like?"

Turning her gaze to him, she began describing him, and he could see the strain she was under. He felt about the same, and Flossy—sitting next to Camille, making her anger evident—didn't help. Elbert continued to ask questions, trying to get her to think, and Flossy, being unable to stand seeing Camille in pain, said, "We have ridden to give word 'cause she been loyal. She tired; we all is. Give her a moment, and she will remember. Yo pushin' won't help."

Elbert nodded, and Black took over. "Paul will show you all to a cabin, and we can pick this up in the morning."

Sunday, who had been quiet through the exchange, pushed back from the table, standing. Flossy, feeling Camille tremble, hissed, "I sees why you hasn't been to see my sister. Ya been busy. Happy to see that though you ain't been to warmin' yo feet wit' Camille, that you hasn't been cold, neither. And here I was worried that you might go witout, but I sees I was concerned witout reason."

Camille's eyes brimmed with tears, but they did not fall, and Black, being the man that he was, said, "Camille, I was hoping to have a moment to speak with you in private. Since your sister has made this already uncomfortable moment anything but private, I want to say that I realize you're hurt, and I respect it, and I respect you. Please understand I never meant to hurt you, and while I never meant to do so, I know that I have. I am hoping one day you will accept my apology and my friendship."

Camille nodded, looking up at him. She wished Flossy would stop; she just wanted to be away from here and him. Flossy, who was younger and protective of her older sister, became even angrier at his flowery excuse, saying, "How nice. Maybe yo sorry excuse will keep her warm nights."

Frank, knowing that his wife could be a handful, said, "Flossy, let's go so we can rest."

Flossy turned on him, her words biting. "What has I done wrong other than point out that the legendary Black ain't so damn great?"

When Black spoke, his voice was low and tight, his eyes on Frank.

"When a man steps out of line with me, I am sure on how to proceed. If a woman steps out of line … well, that has never happened. If she continues down this disrespectful road without regard for my wife or Camille, I am going to tune your ass up for not getting your damn wife under control."

Frank stared at Black. He was a well-built man of five foot ten, light skinned with brown eyes and crooked teeth. He had come all this way to warn Black because he had helped get his wife and his children free. Now here he stood, a spectacle, because Camille thought her old ass would marry him, and Flossy, after all these years, still couldn't stay quiet. He nodded at Black and then said, "Flossy, that is enough."

She was about to speak again when Camille whispered, "Flossy, please, no more. Black, I am truly sorry for this situation, and I would not disrespect you or your wife."

He could see that she was attempting to hold herself together and defuse the situation, and he gave in for Camille. "Paul will show where you will sleep, and Elbert will come and speak with you in the morning. Please try to remember the name of the other man."

"Yes, Black, as you wish. It was nice meetin' you, Miss Sunday, I hopes all goes well wit' you," she whispered before following Paul down the hall to the front door.

"Thank you, and nice to meet you," Sunday responded.

Sunday watched her go, and hearing the front door close behind them, she said to her husband, "I's gon to bed." She did not wait for a response; she just turned and left.

Black stared after her, and Elbert said, "You have to get this woman's business under control, or we will be blindsided. Send them away with men to look after them and keep tabs. The sister is a nasty bitch, and that needs managing. Who can you spare?"

"Pick anyone other than yourself, James, Tim, and Philip, and resettle them in New York for now. Have someone watch that cabin and them for the time they are here. Follow up with the men, both on patrol and at Cherry's. Come to me if there is an issue; I need to deal with my wife."

≈　　≈　　≈

Sunday was tired from the whole exchange and was dressing for bed when he came to their room. She did not want to talk about Camille or how much she loved him. He crossed the room to her, helping her with her nightgown, but it was Sunday who broke the silence.

"Can you do something for me?" she asked.

"Anything," he said, and he was desperate to please her.

"Tell me you loves me and only me."

She was asking the bare minimum at yet another embarrassing and weak moment for him. Since her condition had advanced, he had backed away from taking her. He only allowed himself the pleasure of holding her, but he needed her more than she needed him. Leaning down, he kissed her, and feeling safe with her even in this debacle, he whispered, "Sunday, Sunday, please can I make love to you?"

She pulled his face to hers. "Yes, Daddy."

Black took her slowly, tenderly, and unhurriedly. And as she requested, he told her over and over that there was no one for him but her. The encounter was sexual and so much more. He recognized this moment as the very moment when he realized his life was uncivilized and that she loved him, anyway. Sunday taught him that marriage was a civil agreement for uncivilized times.

The hour was early when Camille opened the door to the cabin. It was cold but not freezing as she sat on the top step looking out into the distance. The sun was promising to make an appearance after the rain the day before, and she could see day beginning to break. The travel had been grueling, and the exchange in the kitchen had overstimulated her. Flossy, though she meant well, had embarrassed her, and Black apologizing for having known her made her want to die. She understood what he was offering then, and foolishly, she allowed herself to think that the cause was why he hadn't committed. After looking at his beautiful wife, it was clear that he did not feel the same—period. Strangely, she was happy for him, but she did not want to see him again. She had warned him, so her work here was done.

Leaning her forehead against her knees, she began to weep, allowing herself some sorrow for what she could not have. When she heard someone clear his throat, she looked up, and it was Black.

"I came to make certain you were all right," he said.

Wiping her eyes with her sleeve, she stood, looking at him. "I'm fine, Black."

He did not feel sorry for her; she deserved better than that. "I came to ask if you wanted to resettle in New York, leaving the farm in Pennsylvania for now. I want you to be happy, and if you choose not to take Curtis, I'll find other arrangements for him."

"No. I love him. He is the brightness of my day," she whispered.

"Camille, I didn't understand love until now, and my ignorance has cost you greatly," he said, holding her gaze.

Sighing, she couldn't help giving him a hard time. He looked so pitiful that she said, "Black, I know you thinks you wonderful, but I will live just fine witout you."

His eyes narrowed as he stepped closer. She had a smirk on her face, and he couldn't help laughing.

"So what you're saying is you figured out that you can do better than me. It's only been a few hours, woman; I don't think my ego will survive this."

She giggled, and he was pleased. "I will go to New York and take Curtis, if that is all right wit' you. I cain't speak for my sister and her husband," she said.

He smiled down at her, thankful for her ability to lighten the mood. *I can speak for them*, he thought. *Frank owes me.* "Thank you for coming all this way to warn me. I can't send you back to the farm; it's too dangerous. After this is over, if you want to go back to the farm, you can. I will continue to look out for you and the boy; I promise."

She nodded, and as he was stepping past her to head back toward his house, she said, "Max—the man with Tom … his name is Max."

He nodded, and he was gone.

Tom and Max had reached Upper Canada, but they were unable to locate Patty and Shawn. The two roamed the outskirts of town, venturing into town only temporarily and then leaving again to wait on their backup. Tom contemplated what could have become of Shawn and Patty, and he only had one answer. Black must have killed them or taken them hostage. He had worked with Patty, Shawn, Max, John, and Ned for many years, and they never failed to be where they were supposed to be when they were supposed to be. Moving about in the shadows made it clear that the town was sewn up. Even the whores were in on the action; the men standing on the porch of the place looked too serious to be just bouncers for a whorehouse.

There were a couple of nights when the weather was mild, and they took advantage. They had no options, so they resorted to psychological warfare in an attempt to buy time while they waited on Ned. On the first night of mild weather, Tom walked into the stables unexpectedly; the man seated in the chair was nodding off. When he realized Tom was there, it was too late, he stood reaching for his gun, but Tom was too swift. He stepped to him, stabbing him repeatedly where he stood and watching him drop with a look of surprise on his face. Dropping the blade, he walked off, fading back into the night. This would get the fire started.

In the morning Black and Elbert stood in the barracks listening as the man that was to relieve Murray at the stables gave an account.

"He was stabbed and bled out right where he stood."

"The body?" Black asked.

"I went to Virgil, and he helped me get him in the wagon. I didn't have time to clean up. Virgil handled that part and followed me later. He is at the bathhouse and will be along soon," Chauncey answered.

When Chauncey stepped away from them, Elbert said, "The upside is he had no wife and children—if that could even be considered an upside."

Black nodded. "This was meant to beat us down mentally, to say they aren't going away."

Elbert nodded.

Over the next week, it was quiet, uneventful, and meant to give a man too much time to think. The men continued to patrol, keeping the town and Cherry's on lockdown. Sunday had advanced yet another month, and Black left her less and less often. At night when she was asleep, he walked the house inside and out, making sure it was safe. Outside, he circled the house several times a night, sometimes standing in the backyard under their window, listening to the night.

As he circled, he often met the men on patrol, and he spoke with them, giving directions or listening to accounts of their day. Most times he sent them to walk between the cabins, making certain that everyone was safe. One night just before daybreak, he stepped onto the porch, and the doctor stood, waiting for him. He stopped, staring at the doctor, his concern obvious.

"Sunday?" he asked.

Shultz smiled before saying, "She is fine. I checked her out today. All is well with your wife and child."

"Then why are you out here?"

"I thought you could use some company," he replied. He liked Black and hated seeing him troubled. "Is there anything I can do?"

"How long does labor last?" Black asked.

"It depends on the woman, but I would say on average it could take about a day," he answered.

"A day," Black responded, incredulous. "Can she survive that?"

"Yes, and again, the truth is I don't know. I have been in situations where they send for me, but when I get there, mother and baby are resting, and I missed the whole thing."

Black nodded.

The doctor continued, "I can shoot a gun if needed."

Black smiled as he stared off to the gate. He appreciated the doctor's offer. "Shultz, let's hope it doesn't come to that, but I respect that you will."

Shultz nodded. They stood there for a time in silence as the sun came up before entering the house.

When they reached the kitchen, they saw that Mama had started breakfast. She spoke to both of them before she waved the doctor over to sit. Black continued on to his room.

"I's baking those biscuits ya likes, Doctor," Mama said.

"Do we have syrup, Mama?" Shultz asked, and Black shook his head, smiling to himself.

"We do, sugar," she answered.

~ ~ ~

Boston
1860

"So, on top of being a jackass, you are a dope fiend, as well," Robert Myers said, staring at him. Will had just stepped into the living room, and he was drenched in perspiration. Robert noted that his white shirt was open at the throat, and his pallor was made even pastier in comparison to the shirt. He wore a blue overcoat and black trousers, and it appeared as though he was about to go out.

Will had just taken the edge off his pain, and when Myers spoke, he just stared at him. He really didn't give a damn what his father-in-law knew or thought he knew. "Robert, I am sure that you don't like me, and I don't like you, but we both love Amber. I can take my wife and child and go home, or I can stay here and allow you access to your daughter and grandchild. The choice is yours."

"I could blow your head off and think nothing of it," Myers said.

Will laughed out loud before saying, "The last two years have been a heap of regret for me. The saddest of it all was realizing too late that I actually love and adore my wife. I am twenty-nine summers and crippled for life at this point ... poor choices and all that. I spend my days managing pain and praying that I can satisfy my wife, who deserves better than me. Robert, my friend, you can't kill me; I am dead already. Please don't get me wrong—there will come a day when I will beg you to shoot me and put me out of my misery. And that day is coming sooner rather than later, and I am clear about one thing: you, Robert, are an old bastard, and you won't put me down because you will enjoy my pain way too much."

Will turned on his heels, heading for the door with Robert staring after him. Whatever he expected, it wasn't this, and he shook his head. Robert Myers hoped that Jacob Turner was burning in hell.

Making for the street, Will headed to the corner for the weekly standing appointment he had with a hansom cab. Amber was out with Rose, shopping for baby things, and he wanted to make it back before she did.

Stepping up on the curb in front of the club, he knocked, and the big fellow that he now knew to be Sam let him in. Once he made it down the hall, Will sat, and Sam explained that they had heard nothing yet.

"When can we expect to hear something?" Will asked.

"I'm not sure. They will come when the job is done," Sam said.

Will nodded. They didn't understand Black, but he did. "I hope they haven't underestimated him, because that could be a problem for all of us."

"Mr. Turner, go home. We will take care of it."

As he pulled away in the hansom cab, he thought of his wife. She was more beautiful each day, and being heavy with child made her glow. Robert confronting him didn't matter; Amber loved him, and he knew it. He was, however, blown away by his need for her—not sexual but as a companion. The morphine owned him, and he still managed to carve out a small piece of his former self for her. He just wanted Black brought down, and he wanted to know that he was man enough. When he thought about Sunday, he had to admit that he wanted her dead, because in her case, he could do nothing with her. He was barely servicing Amber. His hip couldn't take two women.

Will's mind turned to Black, and he thought about being tied up while he stole Sunday. He thought about the freedom Black was afforded by his father. As for his mother and her pain, he just stayed away from the thought, trying not to examine her embarrassment. He was also agitated about his sister and the shame she endured. If he had to face the truth, this wasn't a slave-and-owner issue or a black-and-white issue; it was a man-to-man issue. The idea that Black kept coming back after he had escaped as if he owned the place, reopening the same old wound ... Will wanted to know that his father wasn't right about everything, but it looked as though he had been.

It was twilight when he stepped down from the hansom cab on the corner. As he made his way to the town house, the weather was cool against his skin, and he needed that, because he was sweating profusely.

Up the street, he could see his wife stepping from their privately owned carriage, and he moved with purpose toward her. Seeing him, she smiled, saying, "Will, I missed you."

She hugged him, and he smiled. He helped her as best he could with her packages, and at the top of the stairs, Charles the butler appeared. Will hated him too; he had brown hair, small brown eyes, a big nose, and a mouth that was always set in a line of disgust. He was of a pale complexion and about thirty summers with a good hip and always smiling at Amber. Life was now forcing Will to notice his shortcomings in every man he encountered; his wife was the only person who saw him as the man he never really was. He only had brief glimpses of life, and those moments were meant to confirm what he could never have again.

"I missed you too, love. I want to see what you have purchased and hear all about your day," he said.

They climbed the stairs slowly at his pace, and when they reached the hall, Robert stood at the other end. He was dressed in the same gray wrinkled suit he had worn for the last two days, his unkempt appearance marked as he eyed Will, looking for nervousness—and Will showed none.

"I believe your father wishes to speak with you, darling," Will said, holding his gaze.

She turned, looking at her father, and Robert, seeing the glow in her, backed away, saying, "Amber, please don't buy a crib, because I wish to purchase it."

Will smirked at the old bastard. *Mine, Robert … not yours.* He wasn't finished, though, and still holding his father-in-law's gaze, he said, "Amber, my love, your father knows about the morphine."

She was looking at Will when he spoke, but her head whipped around to look at her father. Robert watched as she reached for Will's hand and interlocked her fingers with his. Will spoke again, his eyes still on Robert.

"Robert, I am sorry for all the trouble I have caused. I will remove myself and *my* family from your home while I work through my problem."

"Yes, Daddy, I am so sorry too," she whispered.

"Amber, I understand that you young people have problems that you are working on. I would like both of you to stay here, especially in your condition. I want to be around my grandchild," he said, staring at his daughter. He was desperate and didn't want her to leave.

She nodded but said, "Will and I will discuss it, and the final choice will be my husband's. Thank you, Daddy, for understanding."

"Yes, thank you, Robert. My wife and I will work through this and get back with you," Will said, and he could see that Robert was visibly shaken.

Will was a sore loser and a sore winner.

19

UPPER CANADA, MARCH 1860

Sunday was eight months along, and she was slow but still on the go. The women made clothes that were for a boy or a girl. Paul finished the cradle and brought it to their room one morning as the women stood taking inventory of what they had for the baby and what they thought they needed. Black stood in the doorway marveling at all the things a little person needs. He had adjusted the furniture so that the cradle would fit next to their bed. Mama, Iris, and Mary were so excited that they could barely contain themselves, and for Black, it was nice to see Mary happy.

Though Black was concerned about other issues, he had no choice but to move forward with embracing his family. The baby was arriving whether the Will issue was resolved or not; time stood still for no one. He still patrolled with the men inside the fort, staying close and not leaving to watch over his wife. Elbert, on the other hand, left the fort every night, and unless it was important, he didn't bother Black. The silence in regard to the bounty hunters was getting to him, but he covered it well to keep his wife from worrying. He worked hard at controlling his moods and his thoughts to keep her stress-free.

Later that night he sat on the side of the tub washing her back. While a fire flickered in the background, he watched her relax. Black took in the sight of her and smiled. Her skin was flawless, and her hair had grown. When he finished washing her back, she lay back in the tub, her round belly and full breasts visible. He couldn't take his eyes from her.

She smiled at him before asking, "Is you all right?"

"Am I all right? I think the question is, are *you* all right?" He chuckled.

"I feels fine; Dr. Shultz checked me again and said all is well. I don't wants ya to worry," she whispered, and she touched his arm, causing warm water to drip on him.

"It's getting close; I can't help but worry about you," he said, and his voice was tight with emotion.

"I know, my love, but if'n I ain't feel well, I promises I would tell ya."

He nodded, needing to hear her say that. "Come, let me help you get out and dry off. I am going to tell you a bedtime story once I get you in bed."

"A story? Really?" She giggled, stepping from the tub.

"Yes. I am practicing for our child," he said, trying not to laugh as he helped her dry off.

"What's yo story 'bout?" she asked, and he knew he had her interested.

He was helping her with her nightgown when he said, "You would like a story, then?"

She walked over to the bed. Black had three steps carved out of wood on her side to help her climb in. He undressed quickly, getting in with her, and when she was snuggled against him, he began to speak, letting his deep voice fill the chamber.

"Once upon a time, there lived a man whose heart was cold as a December night. This man worked hard and kept his own counsel. It was the way of things."

"This man ... was he bald and huge?" she asked, trying not to giggle.

"How did you know?" Black asked, and then theatrically, he continued, "The man was summoned by an old queen who knew the lawmaker. She told him that he needed to help this princess, but there was one rule—the princess needed to be taken to the land of the free."

"The princess ... was she beautiful?" Sunday asked, and she giggled again.

"She was so beautiful that instead of taking her to the land of the free, he stole her for himself. He couldn't bear to part with her, so she became his captive. The lawmaker found out, and the old queen summoned him, asking if he had taken the princess to the land of the free."

"Oh, Lawd, what did the lawmaker do?" she asked.

"Well, the man told the queen the truth, and she told him that he needed to do as he was told, because the lawmaker was coming. He told the queen that the princess was his and that he could not give her up."

"Did the princess love him back?" she asked, smiling.

"Of course she did, and he slew the lawmaker for her. He kept her safe, and she became his queen," he said, stressing the point that the princess loved the man.

She giggled and began yawning. "I loves ya … but ya ain't that great a storyteller."

"Really?" He chuckled.

They talked in low tones until she fell asleep, and then Black eased from her side and dressed again. Descending the front steps, he circled the outside of the house like a caged panther.

Ned Madison finally joined Tom and Max on the outskirts of town. In his travels, he had found nothing about the one called Black that he could use. He was agitated about Patty and Shawn. Like Tom, he felt they were dead. They stood in the darkness, the leafless trees their only shelter. Ned was smoking a cigarette that he had just rolled, and taking a drag, the light became brighter and then dulled as he blew out the smoke before speaking.

"We need to burn the gate so we can see their response time."

"It's risky, because I think they patrol the inside and the outside of the gate," Tom said.

"We could call it and leave, but I agree with Tom that they will hunt us," Max said.

"You think we should add more men?" Tom asked.

"We could, but we will end up paying them—bear that in mind," Ned said. "Let's burn the gate and determine their response time. Then we will see if we should leave and come back when his guard is down."

Tom nodded, but he did not say what he thought. He was sure that Black's guard was never down. Patty and Shawn having gone missing was not a good sign. They were good trackers; they knew the business and the pitfalls, and still they were missing. Tom had the good sense to be afraid, but he didn't say so. Some jobs, he found, weren't worth the trouble. When he killed the man in the public stables, he watched them afterward from a distance, and they seemed unfazed. The next night, a new man was posted up in his place, alone, with no fear in him. They had not scrambled to regroup; instead, they had gone about business as usual like nothing happened.

Max stepped in with the final say and agreed with Ned. They rode for the neighboring town of Chatham a day and a half away and picked up the necessary supplies. There they ate, rested, and bathed in preparation for the days ahead. They kept a low profile, getting rooms late at night and leaving well after dark to head back. At the general and all-purpose store, they purchased lamp oil and no lamps.

As they were touching the outskirts of the town that Black had sewn up, Tom said, "I think we need to head back to Boston and think this through."

"Are you willing to give Turner his money back?" Max asked.

"No," Tom answered.

"Then we move forward with Patty and Shawn's money getting broke down between us. It may seem cold, but this is what we all knew could happen. They would have done the same," Ned answered.

It was midnight, and there was no moon as they cautiously moved in on foot, dousing the fence, the grass, and the shrubs with lamp oil. Tom had been right; there was a patrol that rounded the fence every fifteen to twenty minutes. The fence went on for miles, and they picked a location that appeared unoccupied and isolated. The weather was mild as they stood giving the last patrol time to move on. They worked in a window of ten minutes, and finally Ned lit his cigarette, took a few drags, and then tossed it against the wall. The fire sparked as the cigarette bounced off the wall and rolled into the grass. A reddish-orange flame began climbing up the fence from the grass, causing the blaze to take control. Stepping back into the shadows, they waited.

Black was rounding the side of the house when Elbert walked up from the barracks. Stepping into the backyard, they both saw the flames off in the distance and the men rushing forward trying to contain it. Calmly they climbed the stairs to the back porch for a better view as they watched the events unfold. Black stood with his arms crossed and one hand on his chin as if he were deep in thought. The men of the fort moved quickly toward the flames, but Black remained silent.

Elbert said, "I was wrong. I thought we could get them at the whorehouse. Seeing the fire and the women standing in the pathways afraid ... I see why you didn't want the fight brought here."

The silence stretched out with Black saying nothing. The back door opened with Paul, Mama, Iris, and Sunday looking anxious. She stepped forward to him, and he put his arm around her, saying, "Go back to bed, queenie. You have nothing to fear." He had a smile in his voice.

Over her head, he stared at Mama and Paul before saying, "You all need to go to bed; this is handled. Iris and Paul, stay upstairs for now."

Dr. Shultz stood looking upset as well. To him, Black said, "Take my wife in and check her out and report back to me."

Sunday was about to protest when he whispered in her ear, "I'll be along shortly. I'm not going anywhere." She nodded, doing as he said.

Elbert stood watching the exchange between Sunday and Black, careful not to stare. He stepped up to the line but did not cross it, admiring the beauty of motherhood in her. Turning his attention to Mama, Elbert reached out his hand, and Mama stepped into his embrace. He squeezed her shoulder, whispering, "Black is right, you know. We won't let anything happen to you. Go to bed."

When they went back into the house, shutting the door, Black asked, "Have I ever told you how I met my wife?"

Elbert turned to him in the darkness, unsure of what to say. Sunday had been a sore subject between them, and like tonight, that had been his fault too. He was sure that Black had known her for a time; she was raised by Mama, but for conversational purposes, he said, "No."

"I was making a run into the South because Mama sent for me. She asked me to bring Sunday here because Jacob Turner wanted to sell her to the Hunter plantation. She was a child that I had never paid any attention except to understand that she was under my protection, along with Mama." He paused for a time, organizing his thoughts. "When I found her, she was naked, preparing herself to become Will's personal body slave ..."

Elbert said nothing; this was the most he ever heard Black speak.

Black continued, "As luck would have it, I got there first. One look, and she was *mine*." He chuckled before saying, "I took her, and it never even crossed my mind to kill him. All I wanted was her. All I could think about was her." He shook his head, smiling. Elbert smiled into the darkness. He could understand; he loved her too.

"The fault lies with me, and it has from day one. You were not wrong then, and you are not wrong now, my friend. I attempted to back away from love to regain my strength and judgment, and that cost me. There were no moments of clarity, and when I embraced love, fear set in, impairing my judgment further. I see that now," Black said more to himself than Elbert.

They stood watching the flames in the distance, Black with his arms crossed and feet apart. Elbert leaned against the wall, smoking a cigar. The fire was dimming, and they could hear yelling as the men organized the water, buckets, and the line of people attempting to out the fire. As Black looked on, he began to see the solution in pieces, and backing away from fear about his wife's safety, he could see the light at the end of the tunnel.

Anthony appeared. "The fire is under control and will be out soon."

Black said, "Good. Go around front and into the pathways, reassuring the women and children."

"James and Tim are handling that. Mary and Herschel have been checked on; they are well," Anthony reported.

Black nodded. "Pick four men you can trust and meet me in my study tomorrow at one."

Anthony responded, "Yes, sir, Black," and then he faded into the night.

When they were alone again, Black turned to Elbert, saying, "They are out there watching. This was meant to gauge our response."

"I agree," Elbert said.

"I am unable to leave her now; we are just weeks away from the baby coming."

"What do you need?"

"I want Will brought to me. Yank him from the streets of Boston and be discreet. The bounty hunters need to be caught tonight, or they will go underground. Our response has made them change plans, I'm sure. After tonight, dismantle the watch on the town and Cherry's. Bring those men in to watch over the women and children here. I want you to move out in two days."

"Consider it done," Elbert said as he descended the stairs, fading into the night.

Black stood by himself for a time, thinking, when he heard someone approach from behind. Turning, he said, "Doctor, my wife—is she well?"

"She is well, but anxious, and I can't remedy that. She wants you," Shultz said.

Black nodded. Turning, he headed for his bedroom. When he stepped into the chamber, she was seated in the chair in front of the window, watching the fire. Feeling his presence, she turned and said, "They burned the wall. Is you leaving me to handle this?"

Walking over to her, he helped her stand. "Take off your nightgown, and come to bed."

She lifted her arms, and he helped her undress. Then he undressed himself, and they climbed into bed. He propped her up on the pillows and smiled at her. He kissed her belly and felt his child move within her. They snuggled close, and when he felt her relax, he said, "I am not leaving you. We will see to the birth of our child together."

"I knows ya has pressin' matters ..."

"I do have pressing matters, and that is being with you when my child comes," he answered.

"Is you sure? Ya don't talk to me anymore," she said.

"Because nothing is more important than your health and that of my child, I have stepped down leaving Elbert in charge of the Will issue for now. I need this time with you. They will leave for a time to handle some things for me, and I will see to the fort and you."

Snuggling even closer, she fell asleep, and he lay awake thinking for a time. When sleep claimed him, it was deep and dreamless; he now had a handle on the situation.

Outside the wall, the three began moving back toward the outskirts of town. They didn't speak for safety reasons, but they all drew the same conclusion: they would leave. As for Turner, two of their men died, and there would be no refund based on the severity of the situation. When they began moving away, it was well before the fire was out; the cover of darkness was all they had, and they had to make the most of it. They all heard it at the same time—hooves pounding and dogs barking, heading straight for them.

The three separated, but the men on horseback were relentless in their search. They carried torches to light the way, and Ned had a moment of regret that he didn't listen to Tom. He ran into the bush for cover, the dogs followed, growling, fangs exposed. The larger of the dogs ran into the bush, pulling him out by the leg of his trousers, and Ned attempted to fight it off when he heard a deep voice yelling, "Down, boy!"

The dog whimpered but backed off, and then the voice spoke to Ned.

"Up on your feet." A man stood dressed in all black, with his shotgun pointed. "How many?"

Ned stood, and behind the man with the gun were three men on horseback. The dogs stood between the horses, and they were all focused on him. They weren't going to let him live—that he understood—so he stared forward and did not speak. Ned's thoughts wandered to Patty and Shawn, and he knew that Patty had remained silent when questioned. He could not say the same for Shawn.

James stepped toward him, and Ned did not flinch. To the men behind him, James said, "Tie him up." When Ned looked past James for who would tie him up, James slammed him in the face with the butt of the gun, dropping him where he stood. Looking to his men for answers, James asked, "How many do we have?"

Anthony responded, "The others got away; we don't have a count."

James nodded. "Let's head back. We have two days to fix the outer gate before we move to the next leg of the plan."

They stripped Ned of his gun before placing him in the back of the wagon driven by Philip. Before remounting his horse, James stared off in the distance. He knew they were out there. There was a time and place for everything; he would stay the course, working in the time allotted for each situation. Day was breaking, and they would go back to the fort.

Tom and Max met up at the horses. Dividing the supplies, they headed back the way they came. They rode at a neck-breaking speed, leaving Canada and slowing only to rest the horses.

It was Max who said what they were both thinking. "The one called Black knew we were coming. We have had harder jobs and been successful."

Tom nodded his agreement, and he thought, *Shawn gave us up.* Somewhere in the back of his mind, he gave thought to the fact that Black may have known from another source. He pushed the thought away because it gave Black too much power. Tom wanted to forget this whole matter and move on to the next job. He thought about Ned and backed away from that thought, as well. Once in Boston, he and Max would divide the money, and he would disappear to let the dust settle.

Black stood on the front porch; he was awakened by Elbert and Paul. After reassuring his wife, he stepped out into the early morning sun to see one of the men responsible for the burning of the gate. The air was thin and cool against his skin, and he smiled at the scene before him. The man stood surrounded by James, Tim, and Anthony, a purple bruise on his left cheek.

Elbert spoke in quiet tones for only Black to hear. "We caught only him, but rest assured, we will get the others. He's not talking, not even his name."

Black nodded, turning his attention back to the man. Descending the stairs Black approached, holding eye contact, his men backing away to give him room. The man had black hair and gray eyes that never left his. He wore blue trousers and a white shirt, his hands tied behind him. It was clear he understood his situation, and Black was sure he would give nothing. Still, Black leaned in and spoke for only the man to hear.

"We both know where this is going, and I know that you are prepared to tell me nothing."

The man held his gaze, quietly confirming what Black already knew. Black turned to Elbert, saying, "Have the doctor come out and bring his bag."

Elbert nodded and disappeared into the house. Turning back to the man, Black leaned in and continued, "This could go one of two ways. The doctor will help me remove your manhood—balls and all—right here, right now. Then we will keep you alive in pain for a time … or you can tell me what I want to know, and I will walk you into the woods and shoot you, ending it for both of us. Of course the choice is yours to make. I am easy and will go along with whatever you decide."

The man looked over Black's shoulder just as the doctor stepped out into the morning sun with his black bag in tow. Turning to Black, he said, "What do you want to know?"

Black smiled before saying, "It's the choice I would have made. Now, tell me everything, even if it seems unimportant."

The men stood back in wonderment as Black and the man spoke, with Black nodding and listening carefully. They could not be heard, and if not for the man's hands tied behind his back, they almost looked leisurely. Their conversation continued for a time in hushed tones, with Black chuckling at one point. The man remained leery as he spoke. The rest of the group stood out of earshot, watching and waiting for direction. Finally, when the man stopped talking, Black stepped back and just stared at him, weighing his words for the truth.

Turning to his men, Black finally offered, "Ned and I will go for a walk. I will be back."

The two turned and started walking into the trees away from the cabins. Along the way, the people of the fort stood out in the pathways watching. They felt reassured that the fire situation was being dealt with. Black nodded at some of the men as they moved along, and they nodded back. When they reached the graves that Black and Elbert had dug, they stopped.

Ned asked a question even though he knew the answer. One grave was open, and the other had fresh dirt. He asked, "Shawn and Patty?"

Black nodded. Ned stood at the open grave, and Black stepped up to him from behind. Placing the muzzle of the gun to his head, he pulled the trigger. Ned dropped where he stood, and Black pushed him into the grave with his booted foot. Turning, he walked back toward the house, wiping blood from the blowback from his face with his sleeve as he continued to weigh Ned's words.

Back at the house, the men dispersed, leaving Elbert, James, and Tim waiting for Black on the porch. The sun was shining, and the morning was warming up. He conveyed what Ned told him, the men paying close attention. Black concluded the discussion by saying, "Send someone to cover the body."

Sunday had already gone to the office to work on the books. Paul got a bath ready and burned yet another set of bloodstained clothes for Black.

When Black finished bathing, he stood naked in the window of his room watching as the men completed the gate off in the distance. He would sleep until it was time to meet with the young men he would use in the absence of Elbert, James, Tim, and Philip.

At midnight on the next night, the men stood at the gate, torches lit and horses dancing with anticipation as Black, Elbert, and James spoke privately. Black spoke his mind, saying, "Freedom is to be maintained at all times. I will understand if all doesn't go as planned."

Elbert threw his cigar on the ground, snuffing it out with his booted foot before shaking Black's hand.

James smiled before saying, "You take care of Sunday. Let us handle the rest."

Black nodded as he watched them climb into the carriage that waited. The men opened the gate, and two black carriages and six men on horseback rode out. He smiled as he watched them depart; he was no longer on the defense. Turning, he saw the young men waiting for him as he began walking back toward the barracks. They fell in step, and he gave direction on the shift change, patrolling, and the barracks. Separating from them, he headed to the house to be with his wife, and they kept on to the duties that waited.

Boston

Black's men made it to Boston in the quiet of the night. They set up post in the black part of town with former slaves putting them up and asking no questions. The first part of the mission was the gentlemen's club, the Sire. They simply watched the comings and goings to decide the best avenue to shut the joint down. The second leg of the mission was to follow Will and determine his schedule.

Elbert and James stood in the shadows watching the door to the gentlemen's club. It was being manned by a big fellow who scrutinized all the patrons. Around them, the men moved in and out of the surrounding buildings and determined that they were vacant. James said, "I say we snatch Will first and then burn this and the surrounding buildings."

"I agree," Elbert said.

"Between the two of us and Tim, Turner will recognize us. We have a small window to abduct him, and if we miss it, we will alert him," James said.

"He doesn't seem to come at night," Elbert replied. "We'll have to take him in broad daylight."

Fading back into the night, they hashed and rehashed the plan.

In the days that followed, they sent one of the younger men to follow Will. He had a schedule of taking a short stroll with his pregnant wife. His sister, Rose, had been spotted coming from the town house where

Will was staying, and once a week he went to the club and stayed about two hours in the afternoon.

"Have you heard anything?" Will asked Sam, the club doorman.

"I have not. When there is something to tell, I will let you know. These things take time," Sam responded, but he *had* heard something—Ned, Shawn, and Patty were dead. Max, who was back in Boston, came out only at night to avoid Turner until he could decide the best course of action. They even considered killing Turner to bring the whole matter to a close.

Will nodded; he was getting anxious. They didn't know Black … not like he did.

Black's men followed Will Turner for two weeks, and his schedule was the same. Elbert took in the variable of Turner's pregnant wife and decided on taking him sooner rather than later. Turner would be taken on the streets, and the club would be taken at night. On an occasion of watching the club, Elbert saw Tom Fields entering the club. He observed him speaking angrily with a shorter white man, and he knew he had them.

They started with Will first. They watched him as he stepped down from the hansom cab on the end of the corner from his home. It was four o'clock in the afternoon, and the weather was mild. Will was moving toward his home when he looked up to find Elbert standing in front of him. He remembered Elbert, and when Elbert had escaped the plantation. Will also remembered feeling relief because of Elbert's dead eyes, among other things. He reached for his gun, but Elbert grabbed his hand just as a black carriage pulled up, and two men stepped down, taking Will's gun and his cane.

"After you," Elbert bit out.

The two men on either side of Will each took an arm and tossed him into the carriage. Elbert climbed in after him, and James was already in the cab. The two other men disappeared into the following carriage. James and Elbert sat opposite Will, as James broke the silence.

"Who killed Otis?"

Will just stared at them, saying nothing. *Is this what it boils down to—being captured by my own slaves?* He shook his head and did not answer; he would not be bullied. Elbert reached over, grabbing him by his belt and yanking his hip forward. The morphine was wearing off, and to Will's shame, he screamed like a bitch, causing Elbert to smile.

"I don't know … I don't know," Will responded as he gulped for air. Grabbing him by the collar, Elbert punched him, outing his light.

The carriage rode for the edge of town where Philip and three younger men took over transporting Will Turner to the fort and his fate.

Later that night the men stood in the shadows, watching the door to the club. Elbert, James, and Tim stepped up to the door with Elbert knocking on it. The big fellow swung the door open, stepping out, and before he realized what was happening, he was surrounded. James stood holding the muzzle of his shotgun to the doorman's chin. The man put his hands in the air, and James nodded to the left, backing him from the door. Elbert and Tim stepped forward into the corridor with the men behind them, ready.

Elbert stepped off into the room first, letting off a shot into the air, getting everyone's attention. The men moved into the room, guns drawn, and Elbert said, "We are here for Tom and Max … and whoever stands in the way. All the women to the left side of the room, and move quickly. As for the men, I want you all to undress down to your underwear. My man is coming around for your guns."

Tim was standing behind Elbert when the bartender started reaching. Tim stepped forward, taking two shots, bringing the bartender down. Chauncey came forward, collecting the guns as Elbert scanned the room for Tom and Max. He settled his eyes on the black couch that sat on the platform, and moving forward, he came to stand before them. Elbert contemplated taking them as prisoners, though he had not remembered Tom being that big. He smiled, deciding to cut his losses. Pulling his gun, he shot Tom twice in the face right where he sat. Turning his gun on Max, he did the same.

Outside, Elbert heard James's gun go off, and he knew the doorman had been put down. They allowed the women to file out first, giving them directions to move on and to not look back. At the door, a tall black-haired woman smiled at Elbert, and he remembered Black's words. He smiled, shaking his head, and then he nodded for her to keep it moving. When the women were gone, he turned and assessed the men. He gazed around the club, giving them a moment to see that this could go either way. The place was well lit now, and on the black couch sat Max and Tom, dead, with half their faces blown off and blood spattered against the mirror. The men sat in their underwear as Black's men moved among them.

Finally Elbert said, "Are there any among you who can't move forward from this night forgetting it ever happened?" He didn't expect an answer, but he waited, giving them a moment, and then he continued, "Line up. My men will see you out to the street. Understand should you speak about this to anyone, we will come back, and we will kill you."

As the men filed out, Tim and Elbert went through the office, finding nothing. Behind the bar was a strongbox filled with cash. They took it, and as they backed out the club, they knocked over the oil lamps, setting the place on fire. In the surrounding buildings, bottles filled with kerosene and burning rags were tossed in, causing the flames to accelerate. When the club was engulfed in flames, they turned the horses for Canada and did not look back.

20

UPPER CANADA, APRIL 1860

Sunday was awakened by a sharp pain in her back. She attempted to get comfortable, but after a time, the pain hit again. She climbed out of bed and stood trying to stretch and move around. Black entered the room in the wee hours, and he saw her standing, holding on to the chair. The pain hit again, and she doubled over. He ran to her.

"Sunday, baby, are you all right?"

She shook her head, trying to ride the pain, and when it ebbed, she said to him, "I thank it's starting."

He was alarmed and felt helpless.

Calmly, she coached him, "Go get the doctor and Mama."

Turning on his heels, he did as she asked. At Mama's door, he knocked, and when she said, "Enter," he stepped in. "It's Sunday. I need you."

Mama could see his worry, and she attempted to calm him. "It'll be fine. Go on—get the doctor now."

He turned to go and do as she instructed, taking the steps two at a time. He banged on the doctor's door. The doctor answered, and he was dressed in his robe.

"My wife ..." Black's voice trailed off.

The doctor stepped from his room, knocking on the door next to his. Iris came to the door in her robe.

Dr. Shultz said, "Miss Sunday is starting."

"I'll get dressed now and meet you in the kitchen," Iris responded. She squeezed Black's hand, and then she was gone.

"Go to the kitchen. Remove that shirt, put on a clean one, and wash your hands all the way up to your elbows. I will be down shortly," the doctor said to him.

Black nodded and went to do as the doctor instructed.

The doctor, Iris, and Paul all met him in the kitchen. Black was at the sink washing his hands when Shultz stepped up to the sink and began washing his hands. He spoke calmly with Black, educating him on what to expect to start with, and then they headed for the room. Mama and Iris stripped the bed down, covering it with a rubber sheet. Paul and Black brought in the water, and the doctor began speaking with Sunday.

"I would like to check you out, if that's all right," the doctor was saying just as a pain hit.

She screamed, releasing the built-up energy, and then began panting. Black was frozen with fear as he stood in the corner watching. When she rode the pain out, she answered breathlessly, "All right."

Looking at her husband, Sunday felt as sorry for him as she did for herself. When Paul left the room, she said to her husband, a weak smile on her face, "Why don't ya go and look after Paul?"

"Naw, he wants to stay. He just don't know what to do," Mama said.

Black just nodded.

"Go help her on the bed so's the doctor can see 'bout her," Mama continued.

Sunday reached out her hand to him, and he rushed to her, thankful to be useful. As he was helping her, she asked, "Is ya all right?"

Finally, he found his voice, asking, "Are you all right? That is a question for you, not me."

"I's hurtin' like a summamabitch. I been betta," she answered, and he couldn't help smiling.

Black wasn't sure what he thought the doctor meant by checking her, but when she lay back on the bed, the doctor lifted her nightgown, sticking his finger between her legs.

Black was appalled, and Mama turned to him, saying, "You wanted to be here; ain't no gettin' 'round it."

He nodded again, feeling scolded.

The doctor ignored him and spoke to Sunday. "You are almost ready. How long had you been feeling pain?"

Another pain hit, and she began panting. "I started feelin' back pain the day 'fore yesterday, but I weren't sure; I thought I's just tired."

"Still 'bout ten minutes 'tween the pains," Mama commented.

Black found a rhythm as he held her hand and spoke with her, tuning out the rest of the room. When the pain hit, he became encouraging until the pain ebbed. She was beginning to look tired, and they continued like that with the pain hitting every ten minutes, until Black asked the doctor, "Can we give her something for the pain?"

"I could, but it drugs the child, as well. She is not in a bad place. If that happens, I promise I will," Shultz answered.

Black nodded, but he looked to Mama helplessly. "This is the way of thangs," Mama said.

The time pressed on, and Sunday could be heard screaming from the pain all the way down the hall to where Paul sat. Even he was a little shaken; he had buried Black's mother. He was trying to back away from the thought when in walked Elbert and James. Paul had never been so thankful to have a distraction. Sunday screamed again, and they all just looked down the hall.

When the screaming stopped, Paul asked, "Did all go well?"

"Yes," Elbert responded.

They were all shaken by the screaming.

"Where is Black?" James asked.

Paul nodded in the direction of the room, and Elbert whistled. They all left to stand on the porch, trying to turn their minds toward something else.

In the room, Black continued to encourage when Sunday began to bear down. The pain began coming in shorter spans of time. Iris and Mama lit several oil lamps, the doctor encouraged Black to help Sunday move down to the end of the bed between pains. She cursed them all, saying that she didn't want to be moved. Mama scolded her too, getting her back on track. Once at the bottom of the bed, she screamed and began bearing down again.

The doctor said, "Very good. We see the top of the head."

Black stepped forward, and Mama took his spot, holding Sunday's hand and encouraging her. He had never seen the likes. The baby's head slipped through, and then the shoulders, and his poor wife just yelled her head off. The doctor looked alarmed when he saw the cord wrapped about the baby's neck, and he was attempting to loosen it, but she began bearing down again. When the hips came forward, Black could see it was a boy. The doctor cut the cord quickly and began unraveling it from about his son's little neck. Then he attempted to get him to cry, slapping him on the bottom, and nothing …

The doctor called for Iris to tend to Sunday, and taking the baby over to the light, he attempted to get him breathing. He cleaned out his mouth and nose. Still nothing. It started to set in what was happening. His son wasn't breathing.

Just then, Sunday began breathlessly asking, "What's wrong? What's happenin'?"

The doctor met Black's eyes, and he shook his head. Black had been so concerned about his wife that it never occurred to him that his child wouldn't make it. He was in a fog when he heard the doctor say, "Go to your wife, and let me clean him up."

Black nodded, and when he went to Sunday, she was reaching for the baby, saying, "Why ain't the baby cryin'?"

Mama stepped back for him to sit with her, and she went to look at the baby.

"Nat, what is happenin'?" She started screaming at him, and he was helpless, unsure of what to say.

Iris was cleaning her up and trying to get her to calm down.

Finally, Black found the nerve to say, "He's not breathing."

Sunday broke down and cried, yelling, "No! No! I wants to see my baby! Please, Mama brang him to me!"

Black leaned in, speaking to her softly, trying to console himself and his wife. She stopped sobbing abruptly and began screaming and bearing down again. The doctor, seeing what was happening, wrapped the baby up and rushed over to Sunday. Black stayed at her side. He couldn't take anymore, and Mama helped the doctor. The head came forward, and then the shoulders and hips. It was a girl. The doctor never slapped her bottom; she was squalling loudly already. The doctor and Mama stared at each other, giving a prayer of thanks for this miracle.

Sunday was weak now, and some of the fight had gone out of her. The doctor took the baby over to the table, cleaning her mouth and nose and making her presentable to meet her parents. Iris and Mama dealt with the babies as Shultz helped Sunday push out the afterbirth. Black went to the babies while Iris helped clean Sunday up and get the bed ready for her.

As Black stood looking down at his children, his daughter was crying and moving around as Mama diapered her and wrapped her up. His son lay still, wrapped in a blanket, only his little face showing. Behind him, Black could hear his wife weeping.

The doctor said, "Take your daughter to her first. Still, she will want to see him and name him. You have to be strong and in control of the situation. We will give you time with the children, but you must push her to move forward. Your daughter needs you."

Black swallowed hard and nodded. After getting her settled, Mama, Iris, and the doctor left the room. Their daughter was in the cradle, and their son was on the table. Going to the cradle, he reached in, unsure of how to hold a baby. Picking her up, he looked down at the little face, and she looked back at him sleepily. She was gray with a head full of black curls, and his eyes watered up. Sitting down next to his wife, he handed her their baby girl, and she continued to weep.

"Our son," she wept.

Sitting on the edge of the bed, Black leaned down and kissed her forehead. "I know."

"I needs to see him." She was crying in earnest. He noticed that she couldn't get focused on their daughter. Taking the baby from his wife, he placed her back in the cradle and went to the table where their son lay.

Picking up his lifeless child, the pain was so great it almost brought him to his knees. Crossing the room to her, he handed her their son, and she held him to her breasts and sobbed. "Oh ... oh, Mama loves you."

Life constantly had him baffled; when he thought he had it figured out, he found that he didn't. He was about to go stare out the window and give her a moment when she said, "Come lay wit' us. They will take him away soon."

Those words made the difference for him. She wasn't shutting him out; she was sharing her grief with him. Even in this, she was a queen. He rounded the bed and lay next to her as she held their son. They cried and told him how much they loved him ... basking in each other's strength.

"Nat Hope Turner II," she called him.

About an hour passed, and the doctor came for him, and she didn't weep. Instead, she turned her attention to their daughter, saying to her husband, "Handle it."

He nodded, leaving her to go do as she asked. Stepping into the hall with his son, the family was there to see him. Black smiled at them, thankful for their support before saying, "Nat Hope Turner II."

Mama and Iris cried, and the men misted up too. Paul came forward with a small box that looked more like something for jewelry than a coffin, and Black thought it beautiful. He moved past them and went to his studio, shutting the door. Lighting the oil lamp, he stared down at his son, and taking his finger, he pushed open one of the baby's eyes to see the color ... gray.

Placing him in the box, he stepped from the studio, and with Elbert, Paul, and James in tow, he walked to the cemetery.

Three days had passed since the children were born, and one thing was clear: there was a new queen in town, and her name was Natalie Hope Turner—Born April 5, 1860, weighing five pounds. The doctor had put some rules in place—no visitors to keep down germs, and only necessary people around the baby for the first few weeks—and everyone complied. They were moving along nicely since the death of their son, and Sunday seemed to be focused on Black and their daughter.

When he came in at night, they marveled at her. He watched his daughter at his wife's breasts, and he did not know that life could be so wonderful and sad at the same time. She was filling out, and her complexion was darkening. Her hair was black and curly, and when she looked up at him he was lost. Natalie had gray eyes like her brother;

their color had not come in yet. Mom and Dad were in love, but there was still a sore spot that needed time.

While they lay in the bed admiring their daughter one evening, Sunday said, "I's thankful you was wit' me. I would have died witout you after our son …"

Black felt useless and helpless. Still, she had thanked him.

"I love you, Sunday." It was all he could say.

∾   ∾   ∾

Boston

Amber had gone into labor and delivered a healthy baby girl. Grace had the perfect little face with blue eyes and not very much hair. She was a beautiful baby, but Amber couldn't appreciate it. Will, her husband, had gone out for the afternoon and never returned. Amber had become despondent and unable to cope. She was beside herself, and she had her father bring in the police, but there were still no leads. Rose was coming by daily to help with her niece and to make certain that Robert was taking care of himself, because he was so worried about his daughter. She had to push Amber to deal with her daughter. She felt sorry for her, but life had to go on.

"He wouldn't have just walked off," Amber whispered.

Rose nodded because her sister-in-law was right. "Amber, Grace needs you. You must pull yourself together for her sake and your own."

Rose cared for the baby during the day, and Robert Myers cared for her at night. He was thankful for Rose's help. "I'm not sorry that bastard brother of yours is gone."

"I know, Robert, but try being patient. Will is her husband, and she misses him," Rose responded.

"You know what happened to him, don't you?" Robert asked.

"If I did, would you try to get him back for her?" Rose asked.

"No," he said quickly.

"I really do not know, Robert. What I do know is that Will had a tendency to act as though he was on top of things when really he wasn't. He was never humble, and as a result, he caused the people who loved him great angst. My father's relationship with our slave didn't help matters."

Robert knew about that. Jacob loved the woman, and there was no mistaking that. "Your brother had become addicted to morphine, and it showed. I don't think he was long for this world because of it."

She had not known what he was addicted to, but she had known it was something.

Francis appeared, saying, "It's time for the baby's feeding."

They both nodded and stood, prepared to go do battle with Amber to get her to feed the baby. Charles, the butler, was in her room speaking with her in low tones. He handed Grace to Amber, and Amber took her, putting the child to the breasts in front of him. Robert and Rose backed out of the room.

It might be all right, after all, Rose thought as she headed for home.

Watching the butler with Amber was a humbling experience. Robert knew Charles had feelings for his daughter, but he wanted better than a butler for her, and look where that had gotten him. When Charles appeared later, Robert said, "Thank you, Charles, for your help."

Charles stopped and glared at Robert. When he spoke, his tone was even and slow as he made his position clear. "Don't thank me, Robert, because, like your son-in-law, I don't like you. I care deeply for your daughter; that is why I have stayed. You are a damn snob … it is why you overlooked me."

Robert Myers was man enough; looking Charles in the eye, he admitted, "I am an old dog that can learn a new trick."

Charles stared at Robert before walking back down the hall to continue his duties.

Canada

It was noon, and the day was overcast as Black stepped onto the porch. A storm was coming, and he could smell the rain. He stood watching a dark cloud off in the distance. A breeze blew, and it was warm. The people of the fort stopped their chores upon seeing him and approached. Men, women, and children came to stand at the bottom of the steps, and he was unclear what was happening. He stood looking down at them, and a woman said, "Congratulations to you, Black, and Miss Sunday."

Black smiled down at them, understanding. "Thank you all for your support and your well-wishes."

Someone from the back of the crowd yelled, "We are both happy and sad for you!"

Black continued to smile. "It is a happy and sad occasion. When the doctor gives his approval, I will bring my daughter and wife out for you all to see. I will tell Sunday of your prayers. As for now, they are both well."

The crowd clapped, and he nodded as everyone began to disperse.

He stood thinking of the task at hand. He had not so much as inquired about Boston. There was no room for anything other than his wife, daughter, and son. Emotionally, he was saturated, and he just didn't want to deal with anything, but he was a man in charge. He did not have the luxury to forgo decision making. Dressed in all black, gun at his side, he moved toward the barracks to find Elbert, Tim, and James. It was time to look Will Turner in the eye. He knew they had him.

Stepping into the barracks, he could see Elbert standing at the back door with James. When they saw him, they moved toward him.

Black said, "Boston."

James responded, "Walk with us."

Black nodded as they walked and talked about Boston. They moved through the pathways to the edge of the cabins, just before the woods. There at the last cabin was a man guarding the front door. He nodded to Black before stepping aside. When Black entered the cabin, he was assailed by the smell of urine. It was midday, and though overcast, there was light. Still, Black's eyes had to adjust to that of the room. The basic one-room cabin was small and mostly used for storage. Just to the left of the door and on the floor was a blanket. Next to it was a bowl, and in the far corner, there was a bucket. There was one chair by the window facing the door. In it sat the master himself, shackled at the feet and cuffed at the hands. He was sweating profusely, his face dirty. His white shirt was stained at the armpits, and his hair was limp and stringy. There was something about this meeting that lacked the climax Black was looking for, and he couldn't put his finger on it.

When the door opened, Will had to adjust his eyes to the extra light, and he blinked, placing his hand over his eyes. He had been there for days with no sign of Black; he was beginning to think that Black was going to keep him a prisoner. Will was in and out of his right mind, and the pain owned him. As Black stepped through the door, Will could see he was dressed for his name, gun at his side. Black leaned back against the door frame, holding his stare, and Will was assailed by weakness and defeat.

Black broke the silence. "It would seem we have come full circle on so many levels."

Will had the shakes, and the withdrawal he was experiencing had him perspiring, though he was still cold. The pain was such that though he tried not to, he still moaned involuntarily. He couldn't walk, and at times, he couldn't tell what was real. When he could get mentally in front of the pain, it didn't last long, because he was tired. He didn't respond. Instead, he just stared, mostly because he couldn't even remember what Black had said.

Black's eyes narrowed as he watched Will, and stepping a little closer, he really observed him. Then, without another word, he stepped from the cabin where the guard, Elbert, and James stood. Heading back toward the house, he didn't speak. He needed time to contemplate the new twist on the situation.

When they arrived in front of the house, Black stood for a moment before saying, "It would appear Turner has a new master putting his ass to the whip."

James shook his head, saying, "I agree, and the new master has a name—morphine."

"What do you want done with him?" Elbert asked.

"I will get back with you. In the meantime, keep the guard on the door," Black said before taking the steps two at a time.

He did not go to his room or his study; he went to his studio to paint, for the first time since he painted that bastard Jacob Turner. Removing his gun, shirt, and boots, he stood at the canvas, and he was on fire. He began painting, and when the sun went down, he cracked the window and lit several oil lamps and continued working. Calling on his memory at times, he would walk to the window. He could hear the rain, and off in the distance, he could see lightning flashing. Black was filled with emotion about the last few days and now about Turner.

When his frenzy ended, he dimmed the lamps and stood staring out into the darkness. The warm rain blew into the studio, wetting the floor and his feet, and still he remained at the window. He thought of Will and how he couldn't even follow his conversation, and that galled him. After all that had happened, attempting to have his wife killed, Otis, getting shot ... Black wanted to see recognition in his eyes. After this long wait to get Turner where he wanted him, the situation had no value. He wanted Will to understand how they had arrived at this point.

As he was tossing ideas over in his head, there was a knock at the door.

"Enter," Black said.

Sunday stepped into the studio, shutting the door behind her. She wore a white day dress that was tighter around her fuller breasts. Her hair was pulled back in a french braid, and she was lovely. He stepped to her, asking, "Is everything all right?"

"Everythang is fine, my love," she whispered.

"The baby?" he said.

"She wit' Mama for a moment, and I came lookin' for ya," she said, smiling.

He dimmed the lamps even more because he didn't want to talk about the painting. Backing her against the wall, he kissed her. "Go back to our room. I am coming."

Closing and locking the window, outing the lamps, and picking up his gun, shirt, and boots, he headed to their chamber. Mama was gone from the room when he entered, and Sunday was seated in the chair breast-feeding their daughter. In the quiet of the room, he could hear the sucking sounds Natalie was making with only the back of her curly head visible. He bathed while she handled the baby, and when they climbed into the bed, they talked.

"I sees you has painted him," she commented.

"I did, and I wish to paint you while breast-feeding," he responded, changing the subject.

She smiled when she asked, "Why?"

"It's beautiful," he responded.

"You only gon be mad if'n someone sees it." She giggled.

"This is true … but I need to paint it," he said, laughing.

They had fallen asleep when the baby began to fuss. Sunday went to get her, and Black stayed her, going to get the baby himself. Picking her up, he smiled down at her.

"Daddy's got you, little miss," he said as he paced the room.

Sunday watched as he tended their child, and her love for him deepened.

Two days passed, and he had not addressed the man in the cabin. He worked in his study handling the books, supplies, and paying the men—everything except Will. It was getting on to late afternoon when he made his way to the cabin alone. At the front door stood Anthony, and he stepped aside when Black approached, nodding his greeting. When Black opened the door, his sense of smell was attacked. He entered, shutting the door behind him.

Will, seated in the same place from two days earlier, just stared at him. Wave after wave of pain hit him, and he moaned, cursing under his breath. He still had the shakes, and there was a throbbing that was happening behind the pain that would not let up. He had no mental function; his severe discomfort voided all thought. He noticed Black, but that was all.

Black couldn't even be sure Will recognized him. Again, he turned on his heels and left, frustration following him as he walked back to the house. Once in the study, he sent for the doctor. He was standing at the window when there was a knocking at the door.

"Enter," he said.

In stepped the doctor looking visibly nervous. "You wanted to see me?"

Hearing the emotion in the doctor's voice, Black turned, asking, "Is something wrong, Doctor?"

Clearing his throat, the doctor said, "I figured that you felt I failed in delivering your children."

Black turned and looked at him, crossing his arms in front of him. "I am insulted, Shultz."

The doctor turned red and began to perspire. "I have not meant to insult you."

"But you have. My son came from her still; I saw that. Why would I blame you?" Black asked.

"I thought ..." he whispered, and his voice faltered.

"We have forged an easy camaraderie. If I have an issue with you, I will tell you. I had not known you thought me unreasonable," Black said.

"Miss Sunday, she and I started off ..."

"I thought you and my wife had an issue because you didn't treat niggers. Are you mixing up the two, Doctor?" Black asked.

The doctor turned beet red at that point. He kept adjusting his glasses and pushing his hair off his face out of nervousness. "Point taken," Shultz answered.

"You know what I see?" Black asked.

"What?" Shultz sighed.

"You are unreasonable. You are grieving, and you are blaming me. Delivering a stillborn is sad for everyone," Black said, and he smiled reassuringly.

The doctor nodded because Black was right. He had never delivered a stillborn before, and he was troubled by it. The child being that of a friend hurt even more.

He was about to leave when Black said, "Where are you going? I wish to ask a favor."

"Certainly," the doctor said, glad for the change.

Black nodded before saying, "There is a man in one of the cabins that I *actually* have an issue with. He is a fiend, and when I attempted to speak with him, he is incoherent. He has been without for days; he moans and does not recognize me."

"You wish for me to help save him?" the doctor asked.

"Pay close attention, Doctor. I wish for you to make him aware of his surroundings and of me," Black said, and his voice was tight.

"I understand."

"Tomorrow," Black instructed, "find Elbert, and he will take you to him."

The doctor turned to leave, and thinking on it, he asked, "Miss Sunday ..."

"She is well. I hear you will check my daughter tomorrow," Black responded.

"Yes. I will see her first, and then I will handle the other matter for you," Shultz answered.

"I appreciate it, Doctor," Black said, and his brain was already onto the next issue.

The next morning Shultz did as planned, examining Natalie first. Sunday was happy to get a great report. The baby was gaining weight, soiling enough diapers, and actually growing in length. Black hung around their chamber and watched as Natalie was checked. She cried a bit, and when the doctor finished, Mama picked her up, consoling her. Turning toward Black, he nodded, and to Sunday and Mama, he said, "We can add one more guest to meet the little one, but that is it for now. Please make certain they wash up at the kitchen sink first."

"Yes, Doctor," Sunday said. "When will ya check on her 'gain?"

"In about two weeks, and I am around if you have an issue or question," the doctor responded.

He was about to walk out when Sunday said, "Thank ya, Doctor, for everythang, hear? Black says you blames yoself; please don't. I's glad you was here for us."

Shultz was packing his bag when she spoke, and his head popped up. He looked from Sunday to Black and then to Mama. The doctor nodded, his face turning red, and then he was gone.

When Shultz stepped from the house onto the porch, Elbert was waiting for him. He assessed the doctor in the morning sun, and he appeared emotional. Elbert said, "This way."

Not even having to deal with Elbert could change his mood. They walked for a time until they came to a storage cabin at the edge of the woods. There was a guard in front of the door, and when they approached, he greeted them and stepped aside. Elbert opened the door, and the smell almost turned the good doctor's stomach.

"Please send someone to help me clean this up," the doctor said.

Rolling up his sleeves, Elbert said, "I am all you got for help."

They stepped in, removing the bucket. There was a hole dug, and the waste was poured in and covered up. Next they opened both the windows, and the blanket was hung over the wood post to air out, but when the doctor got a better look at it, he ordered it burned. Lastly, Elbert unlocked the shackles and the cuffs and roughly undressed the man. When Will was naked, the doctor moved the chair outside and threw buckets of cold water on him, causing him to scream and then moan from the shock.

Shultz assessed the situation and didn't ask any questions. He just worked, never allowing his mind to wander. He examined Will and found him to have breathing problems, and his hip looked twisted. Shultz gave him a dose of morphine and stood back. They dressed him in black trousers and a coarse white shirt before shackling and cuffing him again. When they began moving him back to the cabin, he began to show signs of life. The man stared at him and then Elbert and smiled.

Elbert stared at Will. His dead eyes focused on him, and Will showed no fear, breaking the silence.

"So he wants me to recognize my fate," Will said, his voice hoarse from screaming from the pain. After making the statement, he fell asleep.

The doctor turned to Elbert, saying, "We both need a bath at the barracks, and I will report to Black."

Elbert nodded as they headed out.

It was just after noon when the doctor appeared in Black's study to give his report. Black put down his pen and leaned back in his chair, staring at the doctor. He had on all black, and his hair was wet, a sign that he had cleaned up to fight germs. Black spoke first.

"Well, Doctor?"

"The man is mentally worn out from pain and withdrawal. I gave him a dose of morphine, and he is resting. It will take a few days to get him where you want him, and I will have to give him more morphine," Shultz said.

"Two days … that is all." Black's response was tight and cold.

"I will keep you posted," Shultz said before leaving him.

The doctor had real food brought to the patient, and he gave him another dose of morphine to keep him on track. His breathing was labored, but Shultz suspected that it wasn't going to matter. Late in the evening, the doctor gave him enough medicine to get him through to morning. He would come back and check on his patient and give him another dose to keep him moving in the right direction.

Will was in and out of sleep, yet little by little he was becoming aware. Where the doctor came from he did not know, but he was sure that he wasn't thankful.

The next morning when the doctor appeared, Will was sitting in the chair glaring at the door. Shultz bought some food to try to get him to eat on his own. He looked weak as a kitten, but his anger was apparent.

The doctor approached and asked, "How are you feeling?"

Will did not respond. The bastard had brought him back from oblivion, and now all he could think about was Amber and their child. He was now aware of his surroundings, and he knew where this was going. In truth, it did not matter; it was better for all concerned. As for his father, he had been right, but that was spilled milk. The doctor continued trying to assess him, and Will remain closed.

"Sir, are you feeling any pain?" the doctor asked. "I need you to eat something."

Turning his head from the window where he stared in an effort to ignore the doctor, his eyes narrowed, but he did not speak. The message was clear that he wanted no part of the doctor, but Shultz had his orders.

"If you refuse me on eating the grits or taking the medicine, I'll have Elbert come and force-feed you. You and I both know he would love to choke you instead. It's up to you," said the doctor.

Will nodded, taking the bowl from him, and slowly he ate a couple of spoonfuls of grits. He drank a small amount of water, and he was tired by the time he was done. The doctor shot him up again and helped him relieve himself, and in no time, he was sleep. When the doctor stepped from the cabin, Elbert was there.

"I will be back later, and I will report to Black the progress of the matter," the doctor said.

Elbert nodded but didn't speak.

The doctor came back throughout the day, checking on Will and administering the medicine. Will never spoke, although Shultz could tell he understood what was happening. He ate very little, and the doctor could see that the breathing issues were getting worse.

The doctor attempted to engage him, asking, "Sir, are you comfortable?"

Will continued to stare out the window while lying on the floor, even though it was dark out. He closed the doctor out as he thought of his wife and the child that he knew was here by now. Feeling the way his body continued to decline, he knew this was best for her. He lay now just thinking, plagued by regret and sadness. Lastly, his mind turned to Sunday, and he wondered had they at least killed her. He wanted that bastard to hurt like he did. And when the doctor left, he engaged in sorrow by crying softly for his wife and the child that would never know how much he loved him or her. He cried for himself for allowing pride to be his companion instead of his family. Sleep claimed him in the throes of his sorrow, and he was thankful.

When he woke, the doctor was there offering food that he refused and medicine that he took. He helped Will relieve himself and sat him in the chair to watch the sun come up. The doctor did not try to engage him again, and he continued as though the doctor wasn't there as best he could. Will noticed that the doctor had not stayed long before he heard the cabin door close.

Shultz wandered slowly back up to the house, and though it was still early, he went to Black's study and knocked on the door. He found Black reading the newspaper seated at his desk. Black spoke first.

"Good morning, Shultz."

"Black," Shultz replied.

"How is the assignment going?" Black asked.

"As well as could be expected. I came to say he is ready."

Black nodded. He noted that Shultz looked tired. "I will take it from here and get back with you should I still need you on this issue."

"You can find me at the cabin where I see patients if you need me," he responded, and then he was gone.

When the study door closed, Black turned his mind back to the *Boston Post* that Frederick Douglass had sent him. On the front page, the headlines read Boston Fire Rages on for Days in the Old Factory

DISTRICT. People had been questioned, and no one seemed to know how the fire was started. As he read on, he found on page 4 that a prominent landowner from the South had mysteriously gone missing from the streets of Boston. Reading the paper cover to cover, he shook his head, and then finally he stood and headed for the cabin.

As Black approached, the guard nodded and stepped aside. When Black opened the cabin door, there was no smell to assault him, and the cabin was clean. In the chair at the window sat Will, and when he turned toward the door, his eyes widened slightly, and Black knew he was with him. Will adjusted himself in the chair, and the shackles made a clanking sound as he did so. They eyed each other for a time with Black assessing him. He still looked weak, but mentally he was able, and Will broke the silence.

"Hope, I see you came to visit."

Black smiled and remained quiet. *Yes*, he thought. This is what he wanted—a glimpse of the bastard that would dare order his wife murdered.

Will continued, "You can't understand how sad this makes me that you are not dead. Do you plan on keeping me as your slave? If so, the joke is on you. I can't even walk."

Black leaned against the door frame just watching Will. It had come down to this moment, and there was disappointment that this situation wasn't more of a challenge—that all this time he, Black, had been shadowboxing with himself because Will was never able. He could see that now, and he openly smiled. Love had actually turned him upside down. Sunday was both his weakness and his strength.

"You have gone through the trouble of making me comfortable. I wonder why," Will said, his voice rusty and his frustration at Black's silence mounting.

Black wasn't the only one experiencing displeasure. Will was inundated by it. As he looked at Black, he realized he always hated him. This meeting lacked the luster he needed, as well, and in an effort to wrestle a response, he went where he knew it would hurt.

"Sunday must be dead," Will said. "You know I never even struggled with it. I made the decision and felt better immediately."

Black did not respond. It took some doing, but Black made certain that not even an eyebrow twitched when Will made his statement. He wanted to pull Will from the chair and strangle him, but something held him in check. And he allowed himself to be engaged much to Will's surprise.

"No, my wife, Sunday, is not dead." His voice was deep and nonchalant.

"Now that is a damn shame. Are you saying the bitch still lives?" Will goaded.

Black smiled. "She does."

"Good help is hard to find," Will continued, more to himself than to Black. "Then why all this? What's the point?" he said when he focused on Black again.

Silence.

"Ah, you needed to see me to understand my wanting to kill her. Are you disappointed? Because I am." Will chuckled. He was done playing this game, and he turned his attention to the window, dismissing Black.

Black turned to open the door, when Will said, "You know what's bothering you? When you shot me that night, you killed me. I'm dead on my feet, so to speak, and you don't know what to do about that. You can't kill me, because I am already dead, and you're furious because you can only kill me once."

Stopping to stare at him, Black decided he was right. Getting his rolling emotions under control, he said, "I was just about to call Elbert in. I wanted him to confirm your wife's death. He strangled her while she was still with child ... she never delivered. I was too busy to kill her, and he enjoyed the task."

"You lie ... damn you. You are lying." Will had become panicked. He began yelling his wife's name.

Black stood emotionless as Will yelled his wife's name repeatedly until he was hoarse. He felt the first stabs of satisfaction as he watched Will attempt to get up from the chair and fall. Turning the chair over, he ended up on the floor, and when he began to quiet, Black added for good measure, "I pulled you from oblivion so that you might know what became of your wife and child. You will remain coherent so that you might think on it long and hard. I did not struggle with it. I made the decision and felt better immediately."

Black stepped from the cabin with a smile on his face as he listened to Will yelling after him.

"Amber! Amber! Hope, nigger, come back here. My wife! My wife!" he moaned and sobbed.

Sending for the doctor and Paul, Black saw them separately, giving them both assignments.

At home later that evening, Black was in a better mood. Mama took the baby in the room with her to give Black and Sunday a moment to sit out on the porch. The moon was out, and Sunday sat feeling the breeze as it blew intermittently. She noticed his demeanor, and she was happy that he seemed at ease. Black stood behind her, always on guard, making her feel safe.

"The night air feels good," she said.

"It does. Are you feeling rested?" he asked, interested in her well-being.

"I's fine," she said as she noticed Elbert approaching.

Black noticed Elbert and Paul approaching, and Sunday stood to go in the house so that they might talk. He reached out for her and drew her near, saying, "You are fine. Do not rush off."

They climbed the stairs, and Elbert spoke to her first. "Good evening, Sunday. Good to see you are well."

"Thank you," she answered.

The oil lamp on the table just inside the front door was casting enough light that Elbert could see her beauty. There was a maturity about her that was not there before, and he had to focus. He nodded, turning his attention to Black and Paul.

Paul said, "Thangs is ready for ya, Black."

Black nodded, saying nothing.

They would have spoken more, but not in front of Sunday. When they turned to leave, Sunday took them all by surprise. "Elbert, the doctor says we can has another person come and see the baby. I thought you might come in the morning to see Natalie for the first time. I thanks ya for everythang you has done to help me."

He had not expected that, and he looked to Black, who just shrugged. "Yes, I will come in the morning."

Elbert was about to walk away when she stepped to him, hugging him tightly. Then she stepped back and leaned into Black. "See ya in the mornin' then."

He nodded, and then he was gone. Paul followed suit, going to his cabin to be with his wife. When they were alone, Sunday said, "I has a surprise for ya."

"Do you now," Black's deep voice responded.

"Too soon for anythang else, but the doctor says I can bathe wit' ya," she whispered.

Black pushed off the wall, saying, "After you."

Once in the house, he filled the tub. Sunday went to Mama's room and fed the baby. When she finished, she came to their room, and Black was dumping the last bucket of water in the tub. She was about to undress when he said, "Wait."

He undressed first and climbed in, and then he said, "I am ready. Now you undress."

She giggled, and then she unbuttoned her white shirt and removed her yellow skirt and her underclothes. Black's eyes never left her. She was stunning. Since the baby, her breasts were fuller and her hips rounder, and sexuality dripped from her. She tried to hide her stomach. It was darker, but still it was flat.

"Don't hide from me," he said.

She moved her hands and then stepped into the water, settling between his legs.

"You feel so damn good," he groaned.

She leaned back, experiencing their familiar intimacy as he wrapped his arms about her.

They sat for a time quietly when Black said to her, "Elbert is in love with you."

She smiled, saying, "Yes, I knows, but I thank it's clear that he loves you mo'. He ain't never uttered one disrespectful word, and when ya was down, his goal was the same as mine ... never did he falter."

He reined in his jealousy at her words.

In the morning Elbert came to the house, and he was all cleaned up to meet his niece. He had just bathed, and even his fingernails were clean. Black came to the kitchen and led him into their bedroom, and Sunday was sitting in the chair holding the baby. When he came into the room, she stood, directing him to sit, and then she gently placed the baby in his hands. He was moved, and looking down into her little caramel face, he felt it hard to swallow. The baby had a head full of curly black hair, and she was sleeping while sucking her fist.

"Black, she is beautiful," he said, and the emotion was evident in his voice.

"Yes, she is, and thank God she looks like Sunday," Black answered, and they all laughed.

It was the first time that Sunday had known Elbert's eyes to be so warm.

≈   ≈   ≈

The sun was high in the sky as Black made his way back to the cabin. Just before he stepped through the door, he saw that Elbert and Paul had him set up. Upon entering, he found Will seated in the chair where he left him the day before, and seeing Black, he began yelling, "You killed my wife and child!"

"I did, but that is not why I am here today," Black said, his voice relaxed.

Will was growling and straining against the chains with what little strength he had.

Black continued, "You were right, and I had not realized what the problem was until you explained it. I actually feel better now that I know how to proceed."

Black had his attention. Will spat, "I hope you burn in hell."

"Oh I will, just not before you." Black smiled.

Will moaned and turned his attention back to the window, his pain over his wife and child acute. Black watched, understanding Will's feelings. He was troubled by the thought of someone wanting to hurt Sunday.

Will dismissed him, and Black smiled when he said, "You were correct in explaining that I wanted to kill you, and still I was at a loss."

Black saw that Will disengaged from him and his surroundings. He was still coherent, but he was refusing Black any further satisfaction. Yet Black was not dissuaded.

"I have decided how to carry on, and I think you will find it interesting," Black said.

Black stepped from the cabin, and Will heard a loud thumping sound and then something slamming onto the porch. When Black reappeared, he had a crazed look about him, and it caused Will to pay attention. He was now getting a glimpse of the Black he knew. Will held himself in check. Just behind Black stood Elbert and James. Will knew the time had come. Seeing Elbert made his blood boil, but he was helpless, and he turned back to the window, offering what little disrespect he could by ignoring them.

Black said, "I have decided not to exert myself where you are concerned."

Will never looked back from the window, so he didn't see Black step to him. Grabbing him by the shirt and trousers, Black yanked him from the chair. When Black stepped from the cabin onto the porch, Will saw a large pine box with its lid leaned against the wall. He looked at Black, understanding and fear dawning. Black tossed him unceremoniously into the coffin, and Will tried to struggle to no avail. There he lay as Black, Elbert, and James stared down at him.

"I think this is fitting since you are already dead. No need to dirty my hands any further on this shit," Black said.

Will was about to speak, but Black had had enough, and he leaned down, shoving a handkerchief into Will's mouth. Lifting the lid to the coffin, Black dropped it on top, and Elbert and James nailed it shut. The three of them picked up the coffin and carried it to the grave that was dug behind the cabin. Dropping the box into the ground, they could hear Will's muffled screaming and moaning.

Will could still see the sunlight through the cracks of the coffin. He could hear and feel the dirt being thrown on top of him. Eventually, there was no sun, no noise. It all just faded to black.

COMING SOON
SNEAK PREVIEW

ELBERT: THE UNCAGED MIND

PROLOGUE

Beacon Hill, Massachusetts
May 1860

Elbert stood on Beacon Hill watching a house in the afternoon sun, waiting for her to go about her daily chores. Miss Anna had not spoken to him, but she had not failed to make eye contact, either. She was a fine-looking woman with light-brown skin and arresting chestnut-brown eyes. Elbert wanted to keep company with her. He waited, and with his booted foot against the fence, he took a slow draw on his cigar. As he leaned his head back to release the smoke, he heard the door to the little house. Dropping his cigar, he snuffed it out and stood to his full height of six feet.

He saw that her stride faltered upon seeing him, but she still stepped down the two steps leading from the front of the house. And he was not deterred.

"Good afternoon, Miss Anna."

Again she did not respond, but that was fine. He assessed her; she wore a gray short-sleeved dress with a white collar and black shoes that peeked out ever so slightly from beneath her hem as she walked. Holding the gate open, he waited until she passed through, and once she was on the street with him, he fell into step behind her. Smiling to himself, he knew she was unnerved, but she managed to hide it.

"You mind if I come along?" he asked, even though he was already following her.

They walked for a time in silence, with him behind her instead of next to her. She stopped, looking back at him before smiling and continuing on. It was a small victory for him, her smile; he had been following her for almost two weeks. During the two weeks, she offered nothing at all. She was not what he had chased in women in the past, and he was sure he was going about it all wrong.

He strolled a few paces behind her until they reached the dry-goods and laundry storefront. She wandered in without looking back, and he waited just off to the side of the door. When she was out of sight, he began to assess his surroundings. There were people milling about from store to store. Traffic was a steady flow of horses, wagons, and buggies coming and going. He noticed two colored men standing on the opposite side of the road, and they appeared to be talking.

The bell to the dry-goods store chimed, signifying the door had opened, and he turned just as Anna stepped from the door frame. Elbert was about to move in to help her with her basket when up on the curb stepped a tall white man. Moving with purpose, the man stepped off into her path and grabbed her arm, yanking her. She attempted to pull away, but he punched her on the side of the head, dazing her. Springing into action, Elbert grabbed him from behind, locking his arm about the man's throat.

When the man became weak, Elbert wrestled him to the ground and commenced to beating him. So focused was he on breaking the man down that he did not see two more white men step onto the curb. They tackled him from behind, and he could see Anna swinging her purse in an attempt to help him. She was screaming, "Let him go! Let him go!"

The tables had turned, and he was lying on his stomach in the dirt and manure of the roadway. Elbert could feel the knee of one of his captors in the middle of his back. They grabbed his neck roughly, placing the metal collar on him. A crowd had gathered, and he could see the two colored men backing the crowd off so his captors could work at getting him collared, cuffed, and shackled. Lying on his side, he could also see a large fat man slap Anna before cuffing her. The fat man walked her toward a wagon with a cage on the back of it and pulled her onto the bed. The man chained her to the outside of the cage before ripping her dress down about her waist, exposing her breasts.

Elbert watched as she attempted to cover herself, when the man slapped her again. He closed his eyes against the scene and his failure.

When she was subdued, the three of them began struggling with him to get him into the cage. They had Anna, so he gave in so that she wouldn't be alone, and when they closed the cage on him, he looked about for help, and the crowd had dispersed. This was a common occurrence.

The wagon reached the outskirts of town, slowed, and then stopped. Elbert finally looked her in the eyes, but he said nothing. She was afraid, and he reached his hand through the cage and squeezed hers. He saw that her eyes watered, but she did not cry. Although he appeared not to be paying attention, he was. He listened as the men argued about what to do with him.

The taller man that had initiated the snatching of Anna said, "We need to kill him. The nigger can't be broken. It's in his eyes."

There were now four men instead of the three, and the newly arrived man disagreed. "There ain't a nigger alive that can't be broke. I say we sell him. We'll get top dollar."

Elbert listened as the debate raged on; he would go with death, though he hated to leave her like this. Shit, he welcomed death, but when the debate came to a close, it was three against one in favor of selling him. Anna looked relieved, as she leaned her forehead against the bars of the cage.

The men stood in a circle, and the taller man who wanted him dead had the last word. "We should kill him, cut our losses, and sell the female. Mark my words, this is the wrong nigger."

1

MISSISSIPPI, JUNE 1860

He stood weighted down by the shackles at his hands and feet; the large collar at his neck was strung to a beam in the ceiling, allowing the smallest amount of slack. In the stall next to him, a horse snored while he continued to struggle in his discomfort. They had broken his leg, of that he was sure, but he was managing. He wasn't sure of the time, but the hour was late, and the plantation had settled for the night. It was June, and the heat was stifling, the air thick and still. He was unclear of how long he stood in the same space, relief unattainable.

There was no going back to life as a slave now that he had tasted and lived freedom. They were attempting to break him, and in truth, they had; his silence gave the illusion that he was stronger than he really was. He stood because he had no choice; to sit was to welcome death. They had strung him up cleverly, leaving enough slack to rest on a small stool, if it could be called rest. Fatigue had set in, and now it was just a matter of time. His mind turned to his brothers and the women in his life, and he smiled.

He had wandered off alone, telling no one where he went, going down into the black sector of Boston. A woman piqued his interest, and he had gone back to get a closer look at her. She was a free woman, and her entire existence had been on Beacon Hill with her mama. Finally, after weeks of following her and speaking to her, she had given him a smile, nothing more. Now here he stood in this stifling actuality, the smell of horse sweat, molded hay, and his own urine assailing him. He was making peace because he would sit, thereby hanging himself.

Sifting through his life, this was a better death than he thought he would get. When he stood, the familiar sound of the chains clanking made him smile again, and leaning back against the wall, he started his slow descend toward the dirt floor. Yes, he was accepting death over bondage.

He was just about to lean forward and asphyxiate when the barn door opened, and in stepped two figures. They moved toward him, and he was disappointed, because at this late hour, whatever they were about would not bode well for him. He had procrastinated, now his death would be on their terms rather than his own. He was twilighting, but still he was too alert. As he began fading, a third man stepped forward, and when Elbert looked up, he could see Tim standing in the back with a torch as Black and James moved forward, standing him up.

Into the silence, Black said, "I thought we agreed freedom before everything."

"No agreement has been broken; I was just about to set myself free," Elbert said, his voice weak.

They set about cutting him down, and still leaving him chained, they headed for the door. Tim smothered the torch in a nearby bucket of water as they stepped out into the night. They began moving toward the trees when Elbert said, "I want her."

Black smiled before asking, "Where is she?"

"Anna is in the main house," he responded as he leaned heavily on Black.

James responded, "I'll go. You two keep moving."

Tim stepped in, helping Elbert. Anthony and Luke followed James, fading into the night. Moving down through the slave quarters, all was still.

Once in the trees, Black began issuing orders, and he asked, "Can you stand?"

"I think my leg is broken," Elbert said.

Black nodded, dragging him deeper into the woods. Tim separated from them for a moment, and then he was back. "The carriage is down yonder. I will drive. Give him a gun, and the rest of you stick to the shadows."

Silently they moved toward the carriage and attempted to help him in. *Shit*, Elbert thought. *I am going to pass out.* And he did.

Black smiled and whispered to Tim, "I don't think he'll need a gun."

~   ~   ~

As Elbert began regaining consciousness, though disoriented, he realized he was in a carriage and moving. How long he was out was unclear. Finally, he opened his eyes. She sat staring at him; they had been riding long enough for the first rays of sun to begin shining through the window curtain. The carriage, cast more in darkness than light, rocked slowly, and she said, "Are you all right?"

He was not all right. He was angry, and his leg hurt like a son of a bitch. She sat staring at him, and he considered her. Anna had light-brown skin, brown eyes, a medium nose, and very, very full lips. Her hair was shoulder length and pinned in the back. She was afraid of him … most people were. He liked it that way; it meant less bullshit.

Finally, he said, "So you can talk?"

"I don't talk to men I don't know," she whispered.

She looked away, breaking eye contact, and he asked the important question. "Were you abused while we were there?"

Bringing her eyes back to his, she held his gaze for a moment, and he thought she would speak, but she did not. He wanted her to answer, but when she didn't … it was still an answer. As she stared out the window, he decided to let that go for now. He would get a name, and he would deal with it. The carriage continued to rock, and he closed his eyes. She had dismissed him, and he would allow it for now. Eventually she would learn that he wouldn't be ignored.

When the carriage stopped, she looked at him, and her voice was small when she finally asked the question weighing heavily on her mind. "Are you taking me back home to Beacon Hill?"

"No," he responded, and the word had bite … finality.

"Oh."

He stared at her, waiting for her to say more on the matter, but she didn't. The carriage door swung open, and James stood, staring at them. He looked from one to the other, and then to Anna, he said, "We at a safe house in Illinois. Come, let me show you where you can clean up."

James reached out his hand, and she hesitated, looking back at

Elbert. Inside, Elbert was pleased by the way she looked to him, and he said, "Go. They have to remove the chains."

Turning to James, she placed her hand in his, and he helped her from the carriage. When they were gone, Black and Tim appeared with tools to remove the collar, cuffs, and shackles. The process was painful, but Elbert made not a sound. As the last chains fell from his person, Tim was about to toss them when Elbert said, "I want the chains. Leave them in the carriage."

Black said, "You and the woman are free. I want you to forget this."

"I will forget this … until my leg heals," Elbert returned.

Black shook his head, and Elbert continued, "I smell foul. I need a bath."

"We brought supplies. Luke and Anthony will help you. The leg needs to be stabilized until we can get back. If we keep moving, we will be back at the fort in no time," Black said.

Anthony and Luke stepped forward to help him into the cabin. She was seated in a chair by the window, her eyes huge with fear and uncertainty. He looked away and assessed the small cabin. Out in front of him was a small fireplace that was not lit, and to the left was a small wooden table. There was a window on the side of the door, and with the curtain pulled back, he could see her sitting at the table watching him as they approached. He now understood Black not wanting to be seen as weak in front of Sunday. On the right in the small cabin was a black screen that divided the room giving the illusion of privacy. Behind the screen sat a tub and a bed—the basics … nothing more.

They helped him to a chair at the table, and she turned looking at him as they went to fetch water. She looked tired, and he was unsure what to say. It occurred to him that she might want the water first, and so he asked, "Would you like to bathe first?"

Anna shook her head, and reading her mind, he stated, "I will stay out here. Black keeps the place stocked for women and children; you will find clothes in the chest at the foot of the bed. I will use the water after you."

Anthony and Luke reappeared with buckets and began filling the tub. When they finished, they disappeared, leaving them alone. Elbert told them he could manage, dismissing them. She stared at him and then moved toward the screen that divided the room. Once behind the screen, she turned to see if she could see him, and she couldn't. Spying the chest, she looked through it and found a brown dress and some underclothing. The bed was large and neatly made with a colorful quilt. Laying her newfound clothing on the bed, she began to strip from the clothing given to her at the plantation.

She wanted to cry from being overwhelmed, but he was just beyond the screen, and she didn't want him to hear. The trackers had taken them to the Bridges plantation, and she did not think she would have survived. They had separated her from Elbert, and she thought they killed him. Truthfully, she was afraid of him, but she could not dispute that he had tried to help save her, getting his own self sold off in the process. While she feared him and those lifeless, threatening eyes, safety lay with him, and she was sure of that. All she wanted to do was go home as though all this never transpired, and she knew that could never happen. Life had changed for her. Fear had set in, and now that she had glimpsed the brutality of slavery, she didn't know if she would ever feel safe again.

When she stepped from behind the screen, she looked at him, and he was sweating. He was also shaking as if he were cold, and she knew fever was setting in. There was no question that he was sick, but his voice was calm when he instructed her, "Go get Black and James."

She moved quickly to the door, and she saw them off in the distance dealing with the horses. Hurriedly she approached James, and when he noticed her, he began stepping toward her. Black moved in behind him, and she couldn't help it; her voice broke when she said, "He has a fever, and he doesn't look good. Please help me."

They dropped what they were doing and headed toward the cabin, with Black issuing orders. "Set up watch. We will get the leg stable so we can move out."

The tall white man responded while handing Black a bottle of whiskey. "I got it out here. Let's get him right so we can move."

Elbert looked up when Black and James appeared in the doorway. They moved to stand on either side of him, and as they separated, she stood just behind them, her anxiety visible. Elbert directed his words to her when he said, "I will be all right. Go get some fresh air. Black will come get you when I'm settled."

She looked as though she was about to argue, but she didn't. Instead, she nodded. Turning for the door, she stepped out of it, closing it quietly behind her. Black and James set to work getting him in the tub and finding him some clothes and boots. He didn't want to put the boots on, but Black told him it was to help keep the leg straight. Getting the boot on the injured leg was hard on him, and he felt dazed, but they got it on. James left and came back with a branch that he cut down the center, and placing Elbert's leg in the middle, they began stabilizing the leg. He grunted and cussed, but he did not cry out when they tied cloth strips as tightly as he could take it, all the way down the leg. When they finally finished, his leg was throbbing, and Black handed him the whiskey.

"We can stay here longer if you need it," Black said, staring at him.

Looking up at Black and James, he replied, "We move at nightfall."

Black nodded, and turning for the door, he said, "I'll get the girl."

Elbert watched as they headed to the door. It was quiet until she appeared. He lay on the bed propped up, staring at her. Her expression was filled with pain. She held his gaze, and her eyes were glassy, but she didn't look away. He reached out a hand to her, and she hesitated, causing him to smile. His voice was deep and etched in pain when he said, "You can't do both."

"I don't understand," Anna whispered.

"You can't be afraid of me and want to be around me. Come lay next to me," he said, holding out his hand.

She stepped forward to the side of the bed, and he grabbed her hand lightly. He could feel her shaking, so he offered her the bottle of whiskey, saying, "Take a swig ... liquid nerve."

He thought she would refuse, but she reached out, taking the bottle turning it up to those beautiful lips. She coughed, slapping her chest, and yet she took a second sip before handing it back to him. He just stared at her, impressed. "Come lay with me."

Gathering her dress, she climbed in the bed between the wall and him and lay down. When she was settled lying flat on her back, she asked, "Does it hurt?"

"The pain is better. Go to sleep. We leave when it gets dark," he answered.

She shocked him by snuggling close and laying her head on his chest. And when he wrapped his arm around her, she wept softly, and wrapping her arm about him, she snuggled yet closer. When she was done crying, she dozed, and he continued to just hold her, saying nothing. When he felt her relax, he turned his mind to his anger. It was the safest. The pain rode him, but he wouldn't give into the throbbing that was happening just beyond the whiskey. Anger was the best place to start.

As she lay next to him, he thought of her trying to help him as two more trackers stepped in to help the first. There were two colored men standing in the crowd on the edge of the struggle—sizable men, and they did nothing to help. It was clear they worked for the trackers, and it was as if they were standing guard against the crowd. He, Elbert, lost the brawl, and they were both treated like animals while colored people stood in strong numbers and watched. He could not understand, and his blood boiled from the concept. Yet he was forced to do nothing; the leg had him helpless and weak. He had been about to kill himself, now here he sat stewing in his own juices, revenge on his mind.

There was no question they would be sorry that they took him, and they would pray for death for having taken her.